THE
HEALING SLAVE

ELIN PEER

ISBN-10: 1523384166
ISBN-13: 978-1523384167
The Healing Slave
First Edition
Graphic Design: Jaclyn Hicken
Editing: Martin O'Hearn

Books in the Slave series

The Slave series consists of separate, but intertwined, stories. For the best reading experience, this is the recommended order to read them in.

Book 1:
The Accidental Slave (Aya's story)

Book2:
The Healing Slave (Sybina's story)

Book 3:
Never a Slave (Sofia's story)

Book 4:
The Feisty Slave (Uma's story)

Book 5:
King of Slaves (Jenna's story)

PLEASE NOTICE

This book contains Sybina's full story.
It's intended for mature readers only as it contains
graphical language and sexual scenes.
All characters are fictional and any likeness to a living
person or organization is coincidental.
Consider yourself warned!

Before you start searching Google Maps to locate
Spirima, don't! The country is fictional and used to
represents religious fanaticism across our world and
throughout human history.

DEDICATION

The Healing Slave is for my dad.
Thank you for always believing in me - for the night time stories and all the kisses you gave me as a child.

I'll see you on the other side, soldier.

Elin

CHAPTER 1
The Foreign Prisoner

Sybina jumped up from her desk when the door slammed open and two Masi warriors entered her infirmary dragging an unconscious man between them.

"This one's for you, witch," the tallest of the warriors growled. He was barely more than twenty but already a hardened soldier.

"Put him on the bed," Sybina instructed and moved closer. "Be careful with his head."

Harshly they threw him down on the bed she had pointed to.

"I said careful."

The two warriors' scowls told her they couldn't care less about the man's head.

"What happened to him?" Sybina asked in a calm voice and moved to the side of the bed.

The smallest of the warriors, an aggressive guy called Mika whom she had saved from a gunshot only six months ago, answered nonchalantly: "Nothing bad, just some kicking and beating." Sybina arched an eyebrow. The longer this damned civil war lasted, the more the soldiers worried her. Their tolerance for violence grew, they numbed themselves with drugs and alcohol, and they beat up prisoners and started brawls among themselves in desperate attempts to pass on the fear and vile hatred they felt inside. Their raw attitudes didn't fool Sybina; she had the warriors alone when she treated their injuries and she knew of their nightmares and fears, and she saw the desperation and regret in their eyes when death came to claim them.

"I'll see what I can do," she sighed and stopped when she noticed the blood on Mika's uniform. "Your blood or his blood?" she asked and nodded toward the spot on his shoulder.

Mika shook his head. "Could be mine, I think I was shot."

"You think?" Sybina said and leaned over the unconscious man. She was relieved to find that the man's pulse was normal, and she let her expert hands search his skull to feel potential fractures or bumps.

"How can you not know if you were shot or not?" She regretted her question, as she already knew the answer. It wasn't hard to see that Mika was high on drugs, with his dilated pupils, crazy eyes, and tense jaw.

"If you want me to take a look at it, you'll have to take off your shirt," she instructed without looking at him. Sybina's eyes were on the man in the bed. Her fingers stopped when she felt a big bump on the back of his head. Quickly she proceeded to check his pupils by lifting his eyelids. They were unequal in size and only reacted slowly to the light. She couldn't yet tell what degree of head trauma he had but she made sure that nothing was blocking his airways and that his neck had support. Then she ran a quick search over his body for any dislocated or swollen body parts and noted that he had a lot of cuts and bruises. She assumed he had been dragged along a dirt road; but for now her biggest concern was his head injury, and it would be easier to determine the extent of it if she could wake him up.

"I don't have all day here," Mika said impatiently, and Sybina looked up to see he had removed his shirt. She wasn't comfortable leaving the unconscious man but she had been working for the Masi warriors long enough to know that a soldier came before a prisoner, and so she went to assess Mika's injury.

"Yes, you've been shot."

"Is the bullet still in there?" Mika asked.

"No, it only grazed you and the wound looks superficial, but I'll still need to clean it."

"A little blood never killed anyone... I'm fine," Mika claimed with a rough laugh to his younger colleague.

Sybina was tempted to roll her eyes, but smart enough to not undermine Mika in front of someone he evidently wanted to impress.

"Even though no vital structures are hit and there is minimal blood loss, there is still a very high risk of wound infection from the bacteria contained in the fibers of your clothing or growing on your skin. I would strongly suggest that you let me clean your wound."

Mika growled annoyed. "How long will that take?"

"Not long if you sit still." She pulled him over to a bed and gently pushed him to sit down. Mika had an eerie energy about him that made her cautious. His skin was hot and sweaty, and all her instincts told her he was unpredictable and dangerous like most drug addicts.

Sybina didn't talk while she swiftly and effectively cleaned his wound, and she was relieved when the two warriors left her infirmary and she could finally return to her unconscious patient.

Gently she shook the man and called for him to open his eyes. While she waited she took in his features. He was clearly foreign with his dark blond hair, and she had seen blue eyes under his eyelids. From his uniform, military haircut, and muscled body he looked like a soldier, but the logo on his shirt said Spread Life, and as far as she knew that was a humanitarian organization.

"Come on... time to wake up." She shook him again.

His eyelids flickered open and before she knew it, he had his hands around her neck, squeezing his thumbs against her throat with wild eyes.

Sybina struggled to get out of his strong grip, her eyes trying to communicate to him that she wasn't his enemy.

He released her as suddenly as he had attacked her and pushed her away.

Sybina stumbled back, coughing hard with her hand on her throat, trying to regain normal breathing before she turned to look at him. His eyes were full of confusion and then he started to ramble in a different language, one she guessed to be English.

"I don't understand," Sybina told him and it made him switch into Spiri.

"There was a woman. A blonde woman... Aya, her name is Aya... have you seen her? Where is the woman?"

Sybina shook her head. "I don't know, I haven't seen her." She didn't know if the man had heard her, because he was now leaning over the bed and throwing up. Sybina sighed and found the means to clean it up.

"Who are you?" he asked quietly as she was cleaning the floor next to him. He spoke Spiri well.

"I'm the healer," Sybina answered calmly.

He closed his eyes and she could see how pale he looked. He was not feeling well. Sybina got him a glass of water and put it on the side of his bed.

"Where does it hurt the most?" she asked softly.

He pressed his lips together. *At least he's not a whiner like so many of my other patients*, she thought.

"Can you point to where it hurts the most?" she asked again.

He pointed to his head and she let her hand feel the bump again, her eyes asking him if that was the place it hurt. He nodded and she signaled for him to lie down again.

"What's your name?"

4

"Aston Tailor."

She smiled in a friendly fashion. "Hello, Aston, my name is Sybina."

"Are you a doctor?"

She shrugged. "I'm a healer."

Just as she said it Aston's face turned white and Sybina could see he was going to be sick again, but this time she was ready and held out a bucket for him to throw up in.

While he was emptying his stomach, the door opened and a young girl with large green eyes walked in. Sybina looked back at her.

"Hi, Uma."

The pretty girl pointed to Aston. "What happened to him?"

Sybina smiled wearily. "The soldiers kicked him in the head. I think he's got a concussion."

"Can I help?" the girl offered before looking down at her hands, both wrapped in bandages. Uma was Sybina's last patient. She had been in the infirmary for more than a month with a fractured skull, two broken hands, four broken ribs, and bruises that covered most of her tiny thirteen-year-old body. Sybina had come to care very much for the girl, who had courageously taken on two grown men when they tried to rape her. One came out of the incident with a broken nose and the other with deep scars from her scratching and biting. Sybina felt no pity for the two men, but her heart went out to Uma, who was the only child in this hellhole.

Unlike Sybina, Uma was born a slave and had never known a life outside the walls of the mansion where her owner, the general, and his thousands of warriors fought for the right to keep slaves and perform human sacrifices in the name of their Masi religion. Uma had only been eight when the Masi religion had been officially banned, and now five years later she was still stuck in this isolated place. Despite Uma's harsh destiny she was the most resilient and feisty person Sybina had ever met. Her real name was Umbra, meaning shadow, but Sybina always found that name ominous and gloomy so she lovingly called the child Uma instead.

Sybina smiled at Uma. "No, my dear. Leave the patient to me. You just stay under the radar and be careful, alright?"

Uma nodded and closed the door behind her.

Aston was done barfing and looked up at Sybina apologetically. "I'm sorry."

"Don't be. You hit your head... throwing up is to be expected."

"I'm sorry about before too." He was referring to his strangling her but Sybina didn't blame him. She understood that the last thing he had seen before passing out was someone attacking him, and his first instinct when he woke up was to protect himself.

She put a cold wrap on his forehead and looked into his apologetic blue eyes. "It's okay. Don't worry about it."

Aston swallowed hard.

"How do you feel?" she asked

"Not good."

"I can see that, and you need to rest, but first I have to rinse your wounds." Aston was covered in dirt and blood, and Sybina wanted to cut off his clothes but she had nothing else for him to wear. "Okay, we are going to get this shirt off you. Just follow my lead." With as little movement of his head as possible Sybina removed his green shirt slowly.

The skin on his chest was lighter than his tanned arms. He had toned muscles and a bit of golden chest hair that Sybina was curious to touch, but didn't. She had only ever treated men with dark or olive skin, and they all had black or dark brown hair. Aston's light skin and golden hair were fascinating to her.

"Okay, I'm going to remove your pants now." She kept a professional tone and started to unbuckle his belt and open the buttons in his pants.

"Just don't take advantage of me in my weak position," he said and winked at her.

Sybina opened her mouth to speak but no words came. *Is he flirting with me?* She quickly dismissed the idea and gently pulled down his pants until she had them low enough that she could pull them off him.

"It's going to hurt a little," she warned him before she started washing the blood and dirt off his legs with long strokes. She continued to his arms and shoulders, which had the most cuts, and moved her hands over his chest and neck. Sybina could feel him looking at her intensely and it made her nervous. She was used to soldiers jumping at her every touch because rumors had it that she was a witch doctor with powers to curse a man and make him impotent. Sybina had done nothing to correct their superstitious nonsense, as it worked in her favor. In a place where women were raped daily, the warriors' ridiculous fear of witch powers served her as a protective shield.

"How long have you been a healer?" Aston asked between small sounds of suppressed discomfort. Getting all the tiny pieces of dirt out of his wounds took time.

"I've been a healer for many years now."

"And you work for the Masi warriors?" He said the last two words with resentment.

"We all have a role to serve. Mine is to heal… although I would rather be in a village instead of this place."

"So why do you stay?" He asked.

She smiled at him, like he was a sweet child missing the obvious. "I'm a slave, Aston."

His facial expression changed immediately. "Ohh," he said quietly. "I didn't know."

Sybina shrugged and pulled the fabric of her dress over her shoulder, revealing that she carried the mark of Masi, a symbol branded into the skin of all the general's slaves.

"How long have you been a slave?" he asked her more softly.

"Since I was eleven."

"How old are you now?"

"Twenty-seven."

"What happened to you? How did you become a… slave?"

Sybina helped him move to his side so she could work on his back. For a long time she didn't answer him. It wasn't something she liked to talk about or cared to remember. There were too many painful memories. She focused on her task and was happy when she finally removed the last piece of dirt and could start applying her healing balm. She could feel him looking at her, still waiting for her answer.

"It's a long story… but basically my father owed some people money and when he couldn't pay they took me instead."

"Where did they take you?"

She smiled at him, surprised by his interest in her. "I'll tell you some other time; maybe tomorrow, when you feel better." He accepted with a nod and she made sure he was as comfortable on the bed as possible.

"Rest now, Aston," she instructed. "I'll see if I can get some of the dirt and blood off your clothes, and I'll be right here to wake you and check your pulse so we're sure the concussion isn't anything more than that.

"Thank you. You are very kind," he said gratefully.

"Now try to sleep," she ordered in a friendly manner.

Aston closed his eyes, and soon after she heard his breathing deepen and slow. Her patient was sleeping for now and she could return to her daily routines.

After soaking his clothes in the sink, she quietly collected some of the many flowers and herbs hanging to dry from the ceiling. Not only did they provide the room with a sweet fragrance, they were also needed ingredients for her homemade homeopathic medicine. Sybina had an impressive collection of drops, powders, and teas. Most ingredients were supplied by her herb garden outside, with additions from the villages. Sybina was well organized, and whenever she ran low on something she made sure to stock up again. She didn't have access to modern medicine but it didn't matter. She was trained in traditional healing and it worked just as well. With calm movements she ground up the chosen plants and divided them into small bags.

When that was done she cleaned Aston's clothes with baking soda and vinegar to get the stains out. She managed to get all the dirt off but the bloodstains were still slightly visible. *It'll have to do*, she thought and hung his clothes to dry in the vegetable garden. The sun was burning hot, and they would be dry in less than an hour at this time a day. She went back to the infirmary and started her daily cleaning of the place. Hygiene was a vital part of disease control, and the infirmary was not only where her patients slept and recovered, it was her home. She slept on a bed in the corner and had tried to make the room as warm and welcoming as possible. Through her five years in this place she had built a collection of books on herbs and medicine. They were stacked on a shelf above her bed and provided some color against the white walls. The infirmary was conveniently located in the cool basement and the only window was high up, offering a limited view of the outside world. To compensate, Sybina had painted a decoration under the window that took up most of the wall. It was a picture of a family picnic that she remembered from her childhood. The happiest day of her life: her parents sitting on a blanket looking at their three children playing. Sybina could still remember that day like it was yesterday. Her sister Millie had been five and chasing butterflies, while her brother Ollito had been eight and determined to find a four-leaf clover. Sybina herself had been eleven, and it was the last memory she had of a happy family time. She pushed the memories away... they always came with a burden of sorrow and longing, and she was in no mood for a pity party. She went back to check on Aston's clothes and, as expected, they were dry. She was on her way back to the infirmary when she heard an explosion followed by shouting and shooting and soldiers running. Sybina ran as quickly as she could down to her infirmary. She hurried to check on her patient and found Aston lying very still with open eyes, woken by the loud explosions.

"Here, I brought you your clothes," she said and pulled his blanket away, signaling that she wanted to help him dress again. He was wearing only boxers and was clearly tense because of the bombing and shooting outside, but with her help he got dressed quickly. She tugged the blanket around him again and sat down next to him. Without thinking she took his hand as a simple act of kindness.

"Don't be afraid," he said and she realized he thought she took his hand for comfort, when it was really the other way around.

"I'm not," she said bravely but still didn't let go. *We are just two people, caught in a war zone and trying to get through.*

Sybina knew it wouldn't be long before she would be busy again. Explosions and gunshots always meant injured soldiers, and she would likely be operating soon. With a last squeeze to Aston's hand she got up and checked that everything was ready in the adjacent operation room. It was quickly done and then she returned to Aston's side.

10

"It's close by," Aston said, referring to the shooting.

"Yes, it is," Sybina answered and said a silent prayer inside. *Please let us be safe and let us be free.* She always prayed for the same two things.

That afternoon Sybina was busy. First she patched up several warriors with minor injuries; then a soldier was brought in with a bullet that needed to be removed from his right leg. The general's nephew Kato came storming in, asking for supplies to stitch up his brother Jonul, who had been badly injured and was bleeding substantially.

"Why don't you just bring him here?" Sybina asked, confused.

"He doesn't want to go… I'll just have to help him as much as I can."

"Do you know how to sew a flesh wound?" she asked skeptically.

"No, but his new slave does, she'll help me."

Sybina didn't have time for more questions; she had her other patients she needed to get back to and dead corpses she needed to register.

Quickly she gathered the needed equipment and handed it to Kato.

"Good luck," she said but internally she hoped that it wouldn't be enough to keep Jonul alive. The man was abusive and evil, and last year he had killed his personal slave with his bare hands. She hoped for his new slave that she wouldn't meet the same destiny.

Later that day Sybina went to the morgue and registered the dead, and when she returned she had a full house. The soldier with the bullet wound was sleeping due to the amount of poppy-seed oil she had given him as a painkiller. She had left him to sleep on the operating table with a pillow and a blanket, since both her patient beds were already full with Aston in one and a warrior with a broken rib in the other. On the floor a soldier sat with an icepack on his swollen ankle and a sprained arm resting in a sling. She had treated many other minor injuries, but had sent them all back to their quarters to heal.

"I want a bed," the soldier on the floor demanded in an unfriendly tone.

Sybina had already told him he could go back to the soldiers' quarters. "I don't have any free beds. I'm sure you'll be fine in your own bed," she answered patiently.

"Ha," he snorted. "Hardly, witch. I can't move around, I'll need help with everything, and that's your job."

"You could ask your friends for a bit of help. I'm sure they would do it for you," Sybina suggested, with an impassive expression put on to hide her irritation with this soldier whom she recognized. His name was Lukas and he was not only a loud whiner but a very ungrateful and unpleasant patient. Last time he had been down here had been with a broken wrist, and he had bossed her around and shown no intention of ever leaving the infirmary. He saw it as a small vacation from his life as a Masi warrior.

"The prisoner can sleep on the floor; he doesn't get a bed when a warrior needs it," Lukas argued and shot hateful glances toward Aston.

Sybina tried to dismiss Lukas. "The prisoner needs the bed more than you do."

With a threatening hand on his gun Lukas laughed. "He won't need the bed if he's dead." By now he was pointing his gun at Aston, who scowled at Lukas with clenched fists like an alpha male ready to stand his territory. The room was dripping with heavy testosterone and she had to move fast; without hesitation Sybina stepped in front of Aston, shielding him from danger. "That won't be necessary." Her tone was arctic. There were many things she wanted to call Lukas, but she knew that if the general got involved he would most likely side with Lukas and probably just shoot Aston himself.

"Lean on me," she said and helped Aston up. He was more than a head taller than her and walked slowly, with a hand to his head and a face tight with pain. Sybina led him to her own bed in the corner and tucked him in.

"Stop pampering the prisoner. Come back here and help me into bed," Lukas growled.

Sybina made sure Lukas couldn't see her face when she rolled her eyes and shot Aston a grimace, silently communicating that she found Lukas insufferable and rude. Aston smiled conspiratorially back at her before Sybina turned to Lukas and asked him in a matter-of-fact tone, "Would you like fresh sheets on the bed or does your body hurt too much for you to wait that long?"

He almost spit out his response: "Of course I want new sheets. I wouldn't want to get whatever that cockroach has." His eyes radiated disgust in Aston's direction.

Sybina silently changed the sheets and then she helped Lukas to the bed. He shouted at her for walking too fast, then too slow, then for not supporting him enough, and for the bed being too hard and the pillow too soft.

"I'll be happy to have some of your colleagues come help you back to your own bed, if you'd prefer," Sybina suggested but only received a snort in return. "How about some more pain medicine?" she asked Lukas.

"Yes, give me some more. I'm in great pain, you know."

"I know." Sybina offered him a drink and he swallowed it quickly.

"I hope you'll sleep well," she said and suppressed a smile, knowing she had just given him sleeping medicine that would make him quiet for the next twelve hours or more.

Ten minutes later the room was silent, with only snoring from Lukas and the other soldier. It was late; Sybina was tired to her bones. She needed to rest and pulled over a chair to sit next to Aston, who smiled at her.

"How are you feeling?" she asked him and put a hand on his forehead.

"I'm feeling a lot better now, thank you."

"I'm glad," she sighed and rolled her shoulders back.

"You look tired, Sybina, why don't you go to bed?"

She smiled at him. "I gave it to you."

Aston got up on his elbows. "I'm in your bed?"

She nodded and signaled for him to lie back down.

"I can sleep on the floor—I really don't want you sleeping on a chair." He sounded genuinely concerned.

"I'm the healer here and you need to get well, not catch pneumonia from lying on a cold floor. Don't worry about me. I'll be fine. Just close your eyes and get some sleep. I'll be right here if you need me."

Aston seemed to be considering his options, and then he moved towards the wall and lifted the blanket. "We can share the bed."

Sybina was touched by his kindness but the bed wasn't big enough for two people to sleep side by side. She shook her head. "The bed is too small," she said. "I want your sleep to be restful so your head can heal. Now be a good patient and go to sleep." With her hands she tugged the blanket back around him and gestured for him to go to sleep, and he finally gave in.

CHAPTER 2
The Lazy Ones

Sybina was up several times during the night checking on her patients. She dozed off a few times on the chair, but never for long before her uncomfortable position made her wake up again. She was completely exhausted from sleep deprivation. Her last months had been full of intense work and short nights. As the disciplined healer she was, she did a last round at five in the morning and then she sat down on the chair again and rested her arms and head on the wooden foot-end of the bed frame.

She hadn't been sleeping long when a sound woke her up. It was birds chirping outside, announcing that morning had arrived. For Sybina that meant a long day of serving Lukas and the other soldiers... and Aston of course, but somehow that felt less like a chore. Wearily she opened her eyes and found that Aston was quietly watching her from his pillow.

For what seemed like minutes they just looked at each other without speaking. Sybina couldn't break the connection and felt drawn to the many expressions in Aston's blue eyes. She saw concern, care, and admiration, and it made her warm inside. Looking into Aston's eyes brought back memories of a boy that Sybina remembered from her childhood. She didn't know the boy's name and she never actually spoke with him, but the day she was sold on the slave market the boy had been in the crowd of people watching and she had seen him begging his father to help her. His brown eyes had expressed concern and care for her and he had cried when his father told him they couldn't afford to help her. They barely had enough to help

15

themselves. The boy had been her age and he had sobbed when Sybina was sold to the village witch. The witch was the nightmare of all children in the area and Sybina herself had been so terrified that she wet herself, even though she was eleven and no longer a baby.

The scary stories of the witch turned out to be exaggerated, and when Sybina understood that the old woman wasn't going to turn her into a toad, nor eat her for dinner, she had found herself accepting her new life as the healer's apprentice. But for sixteen years she had kept the memory of the caring boy in her heart.

A slamming door upstairs broke the silent connection between Sybina and Aston, and with rosy cheeks Sybina got up.

The day moved along slowly. The soldiers kept her busy with demands for food, medicine, and support to get to and from the toilet.

She never heard Aston ask for anything but she made sure his needs were covered anyway. Having him around was a breath of fresh air. He treated her so differently than the others did, and thanked her again and again.

In the early afternoon the general's nephew Kato came back.

"How did it go with Jonul? Did you manage to stop the bleeding?" Sybina asked him.

"Yes, he's doing better but he's still very weak."

Sybina tried to hide her disappointment that Jonul was still alive, and focused on Kato instead. He was an odd soldier who seemed out of place as a Masi warrior. Sybina was a skilled judge of character, something that came with her job and her extensive experience with humans under stress, but Kato was one of the few she hadn't made her mind up about. So far he was completely different from his brother Jonul and his uncle the general, who were both sadistic and violent; but then again Kato had only arrived last year and would probably catch up to them in time.

16

Kato looked around the infirmary and pointed to the wounded soldiers. "The general wants to know how they're doing."

Sybina tilted her head slightly; it was unusual for the general to care about two or three soldiers when he had thousands to keep track off.

"They'll all survive and be fine again soon," she said and looked into Kato's eyes, trying to read him. There was sadness and worry in his amber brown eyes, two emotions she saw in most eyes around here. Her intense glance made him break their eye contact and furrow his brows. Maybe he was superstitious too and afraid she would emasculate him... but no, he didn't act like she frightened him. In fact he walked close by her towards Aston, and his closeness made her notice how appealing his symmetrical features were and how light-skinned he was compared to most other locals.

"How is the hostage doing?" he asked to Sybina's surprise.

"He's alive and he'll heal, but it will take time."

They both looked down at Aston, who was sleeping.

Lukas interrupted their conversation. "Who cares if the infidel lives or dies? I'm starving over here. Get me some food, witch."

Kato raised his eyebrows, clearly annoyed by the interruption, but otherwise ignored Lukas. "I can see that you are very busy, I will leave you to it." He nodded a goodbye to Sybina and left. Out of the corner of her eye she saw him leave a note on her table and she was curious to see what it said, but Lukas insisted on her attention, so the note had to wait.

An hour later the general came storming in, flaring his ice-cold gray eyes around the room. He was in a foul mood and growled loudly at the soldiers. "What are you all doing here... we need you back on your posts." Sybina couldn't

17

help wondering whether Kato's visit had something to do with this surprise visit from the general.

"I sprained my arm and twisted my foot," Lukas defended himself.

"Ha," the general snorted and it made his small beer belly jump. Sybina didn't like to look directly at him, because despite the fact that he wasn't big or muscled, he frightened her as much as he frightened his soldiers. The man was a dangerous sociopath; she had a theory that he had personally fueled this war because it gave him an excuse to murder and torture people. Right now Lukas had the general's attention. "What do you think this is… a spa? Get your lazy ass back to your quarters… You can walk on the foot that works and you can shoot with the one hand that can still hold a gun. This is a war, god damn it, not a summer camp."

Lukas pressed his lips into a fine line but did as ordered and got up from the bed.

"And what about this one?" He pointed to the soldier with the broken rib.

"He's got a broken rib that needs to heal," Sybina explained.

"Do his feet work? Can he walk?" The general oozed with irritation.

"Yes, but it will be painful for him."

"Then give him some pain medicine and send him back to his own bed for the night…" The general pointed a finger in the soldier's face. "I want you back on your post tomorrow morning, is that understood?"

"Yes sir," the soldier replied.

"Any other of my men lying around here doing nothing?" the general asked in a loud voice.

"I have one other patient in here," Sybina stepped into the operating room. "He had a bullet in his leg that I removed yesterday."

"Shallow or deep wound?" The general asked.

18

"Relatively shallow; it won't cause any problems for him, if it heals well."

"Good, then patch him up and stick him in a uniform... we are under pressure and I need every man I can get." The general turned to leave. "I'm sure we can find a job that doesn't require him to walk or run. I don't want the infirmary to be an escape for the lazy ones."

Sybina nodded. "I understand, sir."

"And the prisoner, how is he doing?" The general send a glance in the direction of Aston, who pretended to be sleeping.

"He's in bad shape. Head trauma. It might take a while."

"Can he walk?"

"No, sir."

"Can he talk?"

"Not yet, sir," Sybina lied.

"Hmm." He grunted, displeased. "Do what you can to speed up his recovery. We need him for promotional purposes."

Sybina suppressed a gasp. Promotional purposes meant a sacrifice to Masi, filmed and broadcast to the world. Aston would be killed, and it wouldn't be a painless death.

The general stepped close to Sybina. "Just do your job... witch." His voice was threatening.

It took Sybina less than an hour to change the bandages on the soldiers, pump them up with pain medicine, and get them back to their quarters.

When she returned to the infirmary Aston told her a woman had come by with clean sheets and linen.

"Good," Sybina said and started changing the bed sheets and preparing the beds for new patients. When she was done she helped Aston into a clean bed and changed her own sheets too.

"You're very efficient," Aston commented as she continued to clean the infirmary like she did every day.

She gave him a small smile in response.

"The woman who came by before... is she a slave too?" Aston asked casually.

"All women here are slaves, no exception."

"But I saw a child yesterday. Hopefully she's not a slave... is she?"

"Yes, she is," Sybina said with a knot in her throat. "The girl you saw was Uma. Her mother is one of the general's sex slaves, and I'm very worried about her."

"Who? The girl or the mother?"

Sybina stopped in her tracks. "Both, I suppose, but I was talking about Uma."

Aston didn't answer but his eyes asked her to elaborate.

"When the men here try to take her, she fights back."

"Good for her," Aston said impressed.

Sybina frowned. "There are only so many times I can heal her injuries, and I'm afraid one day the general will get so mad that he kills her. He's done it before to others."

"What?" Aston looked doubtful. "Surely he wouldn't kill an innocent child, would he?"

Sybina looked away. "You obviously don't know the general, and you forget that in this country a thirteen-year-old is not a child. If he's willing to go to war against his king to have his way then what makes you think he would blink before killing a slave that rejected him?"

Aston narrowed his eyes. "He can't hurt her if I get to him first."

Sybina gave a wistful sigh. "I know, but I'm afraid it's not that easy. There are guards outside this door and the general is always armed."

Aston looked around. "Do you have any weapons in here?"

"Only my scalpels and the knife that I use to cut herbs and flowers with."

Aston smiled grimly. "They will do just fine."

His heroic expression made Sybina laugh and shake her head. "Don't be stupid. You can't take on the entire Masi army, with their guns and grenades, with only a scalpel and an herb knife. You must have hit your head harder than I thought."

"I don't need to take out the entire army... I'm going to take out the general."

"And then what? Do you think the others are gonna run home because their leader dies?"

Aston was about to answer but Sybina didn't give him a chance. "One thing is for sure, your head needs more time to recover... otherwise you'll pass out before you even get out of this bed."

They both knew she was right, and he sank back in the bed looking frustrated.

"Get some sleep, Aston." Her words were firm but gentle, and when she reached his bed and started tugging the blanket around him she felt him observe her closely. She didn't speak but moved to stand by his head and brushed her hands over his eyes, closing his eyelids and healing his head.

"What are you doing?" he whispered

"Tapping into your energy field and clearing the flow to your head."

Aston opened his eyes. "I don't believe in that sort of energy stuff."

"Your energetic flow doesn't care if you believe or not. Now go to sleep and let me do my work." Once again Sybina brushed her hands over his face and closed his eyes, and with her strong fingers she found the points on the side of his neck and the base of his skull that would make him go to sleep quickly.

"That feels nice," he said drowsily, and with a contented smile she applied just the right amount of pressure to send him to dreamland.

CHAPTER 3
The Letter

Aston

Aston woke up and instantly noticed that his headache was less significant. Sybina was at her desk, and he took a minute to look at her sitting in her own bubble. He felt grateful for all the care she had given him and the kindness she had shown him. Sybina was unlike any slave he had ever met before. She had an authority that was uncommon, and he reckoned it was connected to her position as a healer.

She wasn't submissive in the way she walked or talked, and unlike other slaves she dared look into his eyes and hold her head high. That was why it had surprised him when she had first told him she was a slave.

Sybina looked up, sensing he was awake and it made him smile. *How does she do that?*

Yesterday she had kept sensing his needs before he expressed them, and he was curious to know how she knew when he was thirsty, hungry, had to pee, or couldn't stand the pain anymore, all without ever asking him.

He returned her smile and noticed how naturally pretty she was. Even with her hair tied up, no make-up, and that dull green dress, she was attractive, with her appealing warm smile and eyes that radiated kindness whenever she looked at him.

"Good morning," she said

"Good morning."

Sybina got up and moved to the side of his bed. "I think this is for you." She held out a folded piece of paper.

23

"What is it?" Aston asked and sat up in the bed.

"A note that was left on my desk yesterday. It's not in Spiri and I can't read it, so I think it's a message for you," she said. "I'm sorry that I didn't give it to you yesterday, but I got distracted and forgot about it until this morning."

Aston eagerly reached for the note. His eyes quickly skimmed over the single line and then he translated the English message into Spiri. "It says A is alive and well. He closed his eyes with relief. "A must be Aya."

"Is Aya the blond woman you spoke about when you first arrived?" Sybina asked.

Aston nodded. "Yes, she's my colleague and she was my responsibility but I failed her." The sound of Aya's soul-breaking last scream made him close his eyes. It had been a scream of pure horror, and he remembered the burn mark on her shoulder. The bastards had branded Aya as a Masi slave and it had been days now... she would have been sold and raped like all the other slaves. He bit his inner lip trying to suppress the anger and guilt that filled him. Beautiful, innocent Aya had put her life in his hands, and he hadn't been able to protect her from the worst possible destiny.

"I'm sure it wasn't your fault," Sybina said

Aston shook his head. There was nothing Sybina could say that would take away his guilt.

"Who gave you the note?" he wanted to know.

"A soldier named Kato. He came by yesterday when you were sleeping."

"Do you know him?"

"I know who he is."

"But he must have Aya then." Aston stopped talking when he saw Sybina suddenly go pale. "What is it?"

"I'm not sure... just something Kato said the day you were brought to me."

"What? Tell me!"

24

Sybina tilted her head and squinted her eyes as if she was mentally weighing evidence. "Does Aya know how to sew a flesh wound?" she asked slowly.

Aston nodded eagerly. "Yes. She's a nurse."

Sybina took a long deep sigh. "Then I think I might know who has her."

"And it's not Kato?"

"No! It's his brother Jonul."

"Are you sure?"

"No, I can't be sure. Kato just mentioned that his brother had a new slave and that she knew how to sew."

"Do you know where I can find them?"

Sybina looked down. "I'm sorry, Aston, they don't live here and I don't have access to the outside world, so I don't know."

"What *do* you know?" he asked pleadingly. He didn't have to be a mind reader to see from her body language that this Jonul was bad news.

"Kato told me his brother Jonul was weak and wounded."

"That's good!" Aston said, mostly to himself. "What else do you know?"

"That's all he said."

"Alright. I'm going to get out of here and find Aya, so I need to know as much as you can tell about what happens to the female hostages and what happens to Aya in case Jonul dies?"

Sybina hesitated but he pressured her. "Tell me... please."

Sybina exhaled deeply, showing Aston that he wouldn't like what she was about to say. "I don't know what's going to happen to Aya, but in general, female prisoners are either sold to brothels or used as personal sex slaves. And a few, like me, work here at the headquarters cooking, cleaning, washing and..." she paused.

25

"And what?" Aston asked and put his hand on her shoulder.

"And servicing the soldiers' sexual needs." Sybina said it quickly and looked down.

Aston felt anger overwhelm him. No one deserved to be treated as a slave, and the thought of amazing women like Sybina and Aya in the hands of these sorry excuses for the male gender made him furious.

"I have to find Aya and get her out," he exclaimed with determination.

Sybina got up from the bed with a long deep sigh. "Let's just hope you heal faster than Jonul does," she said and returned to her desk.

CHAPTER 4
Cold Showers

Sybina

Aston and Sybina didn't speak for a while. They were both consumed with heavy thoughts after their conversation about Aya. Sybina tried to distract herself by keeping busy with chores and duties. It was her usual coping strategy, but she didn't find it very effective today. Aston's presence brought up so many unwanted emotions in her. The dominant one... hope. Hope that Aston could change her situation. Hope that he could help her break free. But allowing thoughts like that was dangerous when there was only a slim to nonexistent chance of her hopes coming true.

She also felt a deep envy for this Aya, who had only been a slave for two days but had Aston, who would do anything in his power to save her. Sybina had been a slave for sixteen years and no one had ever tried to help her, except the little boy with the brown eyes.

That's not true, her inner voice spoke. *Your dad tried to protect you from slavery.*

She snorted internally: *Yeah, by killing me. How loving is that?*

After two long hours a soldier broke the silence by knocking on the door and asking Sybina to come to the morgue, where a body had been brought in.

Sybina picked up her notebook and went with the soldier. Inspecting the dead was a routine job for her but she never got used to seeing so many young men torn to pieces by bullets, bombs, and grenades; it always saddened her when a life was lost due to this senseless civil war. The morgue was really just a big room in the farthest part of the basement and it didn't take long to get there.

As they entered the room Sybina noticed the soldier wrinkling up his nose and making a disgusted grimace. She didn't blame him for finding the smell in the morgue pungent. It had taken time for her to get used to it too, and she had noticed that when the soldiers died after drinking brawls and their bodies were full of alcohol they stank more.

"It's okay, you can wait outside," she muttered and walked into the cool room where three bodies were lying on stretchers. Two of them she dismissed, knowing that she had already filled out the paperwork on them. The cause of death had been easily established, as the general had personally decapitated them both for being deserters. He had done it in front of a huge crowd of soldiers and called it a sacrifice to Masi, but Sybina believed it more of a warning to his audience that leaving his army was not an option.

Sybina moved closer to the third body and narrowed her eyes. The man was big and part of his face was missing. She went around the stretcher to get a better look and then she froze. *Unbelievable.*

If it weren't for the scarring on his face she wouldn't have recognized him. The upper half of his head was blown apart and she knew without looking further that he had been shot through his palate with a big firearm of some kind. This was the body of Jonul, the general's nephew. The scars on what was left of his face made her

28

sure, as she had treated his wounds only a month ago herself.

Sybina closed her eyes in a moment of relief. She had treated too many of Jonul's victims to feel sorry for him.

Quickly she filled out her report and went upstairs to deliver it to the general, who already knew about the death of Jonul and told her it had been suicide.

"Kato told me," he muttered and took a sip of his whiskey.

"Anything else you need, sir?" Sybina asked and started to back out of the room.

"No, just leave me, witch." He waved her away and emptied his glass with a moan.

Sybina hurried back to the infirmary and found Aston sleeping.

"Wake up." She shook him slightly and kept her distance, just to be safe.

Aston opened his eyes, and there was a small smile on his face when he saw her.

"Good news." It was hard for Sybina to hide her excitement.

"What is it?" Aston pushed himself up a bit.

"Jonul is dead. I just inspected his body and he shot himself."

"Really?" Aston eyes grew big. "Then there's no time to waste. I need to find Aya before they sell her to a brothel... help me up, will you?"

Sybina shook her head. "I'm sorry, Aston, but you are still in no condition to go anywhere." She leaned down and let her hands move over his skull, inspecting the bump on the back of his head. It was smaller than when he had arrived but he was still pale and weak, and she knew his head needed rest.

"Look at me," she said and gazed into his eyes to check his pupils. The proximity to patients wasn't something that usually affected her, but looking so closely into his blue eyes was strangely exciting. She used her flashlight, and it made him close his eyes to avoid the sharp light.

"Aston." Her voice was soft and she gently stroked his face. It was like her hand moved on its own, and it made her flush and pull it away. There was a line between being kind and affectionate that she had just crossed without wanting to.

Aston opened his eyes and she saw a hint of a smile on his face as he allowed her to shine the light into them.

Still feeling flustered from this new and very warm feeling in her body, Sybina pulled back as soon as she could but Aston grabbed her hand and made her look at him.

"What's the verdict?" he asked, and his question made her shake her head.

"I don't know for sure, but you need at least a day or two."

"Argghhh," he mumbled, frustrated.

Sybina ignored him and moved to her desk and started mixing some herbs to distract herself from the odd sensations Aston brought out in her.

She could feel him observe her and found it distracting.

Aston broke the silence between them with a question: "Do all the slaves dress like you and that woman who brought clean sheets?"

Sybina looked down at her long simple dress, soft and practical with long sleeves and a round neck cut.

"Yes, all the slaves wear dresses like these. I always wear dark green, but others wear blue, gray, and purple too."

"And your hair. Does it have to be braided?"

Sybina smiled and realized that she hadn't had time to do anything about her hair; it was still in a loose braid from yesterday morning.

"No, our hair we can wear as we please unless we are told otherwise. Personally I prefer to have my hair restrained so it doesn't fall into my patient's blood or puke."

"Good point," he said. "Where do you shower?"

Sybina smiled again and could see that he had spent his time in the infirmary wondering about her life as a slave.

"There are showers for the women on the third floor but I typically shower under the hose in the operating room when there are no patients. The water is cold, but it's practical."

"I could use a shower," Aston said

"I'll be happy to help you," Sybina offered and was happy they had moved on from their talk about escape.

He looked at her with that expression she couldn't quite read. It was like a private joke that she was missing. "Are you sure about that?" he asked.

"Of course," she insisted and helped him out of the bed, noticing that his strength was slowly returning. It made her bite her lip, thinking that she wouldn't be able to keep Aston in the safe infirmary much longer before the general found out. *A severe headache won't be enough to keep him here.*

Sybina let him through the door to the adjacent operating room, where a simple hose served as her preferred shower.

"This way," she said and led him to the operating table. "Sit down."

He did as told and when she started to pull his t-shirt up that strange expression on his face returned.

"Do you want me to stop?" she asked, confused.

His smile widened. "Not at all. I was quite enjoying your hands on me."

Sybina felt a warm sensation in her belly and the thought hit her again. *He's flirting with me?* She had no personal experience with flirting, but had seen it in the village where she grew up and lived before she came to work for the Masi movement.

It made her nervous and she could feel her hands slightly shake when she stepped between his legs and gently pulled his t-shirt off. She tried not to stare at the golden chest hair that she found so inviting, and took on a professional tone.

"Lean back a little," she said and Aston complied, still observing her closely.

She hoped he didn't see how her hands were shaking when she unbuckled his pants.

"Try to stand up," she said. "And place your hands on my shoulders for support."

He got to his feet and then she started to remove his pants. All the time she was expecting him to pull back from her, but he didn't. Aston wasn't afraid of her; she needed to remind herself that he didn't know the superstitious rumors that she could destroy a man's manhood just by touching it. She wondered if he would believe the rumors, if someone told him.

Aston was completely calm searching her face for something; she didn't know what it was. After she removed both his t-shirt and long pants he was standing in his boxers only.

"Are you sure you want to do this?" he asked her with a sly smile.

He's just another patient, she told herself and gave him a raised eyebrow before she bowed down to pull down his boxers. It almost made her gasp when his erection popped free and stared her straight in her face.

No frightened Masi warrior had ever felt aroused around her, and with tomato-red cheeks she forced herself not to stare at his erection but to stay professional and pretend that it was a perfectly normal sight for her.

"Sit down again," she instructed and then she handed him the hose and turned on the water. He started washing himself while she stepped back to avoid getting wet and tried hard to look anywhere but at his crotch. Sybina's heart was racing, and when she saw him close his eyes and wash his face she couldn't help a few secret glances at his naked body, wondering: what had caused this arousal in Aston? She had never seen anything like it, except on paintings in the general's bedroom. Obviously she had seen penises before but always when they were relaxed and wrinkly little things on her patients.

"Do you need help washing your hair?" she said to her own surprise, and he nodded.

Sybina couldn't bring herself to stand between his legs when he was naked, and she couldn't get to his hair from behind him without crawling up on the wet table.

"How do you want to do this?" Aston asked and for a moment she sensed that he was a little amused by her uncertainty.

"Would you mind kneeling down?" she asked

"I'm not that kind of man," Aston responded and winked at her. Sybina was puzzled.

"Is kneeling down wrong where you come from?"

"Sorry, Sybina, it's just that in England men kneel down when they propose to a woman..."

"Why?"

He thought about it. "Hmm, I actually have no idea. Tradition I suppose."

"Well, I'm just the healer trying to wash your hair, so would you mind kneeling down anyway?" she said patiently, trying to decide what to make of this confusing man.

"No, I don't mind." Slowly Aston got down from the table and with a firm grip on the edge he lowered himself down to a kneeling position.

Sybina stepped to his side and quickly shampooed his hair and rinsed it. He didn't complain about the cold water as so many of her other patients did, but she noticed that his erection was now less significant.

"Wait here for a second," she said when she was done and then she turned off the water and found a towel to help dry him carefully. All Aston's cuts and bruises were still healing and even though he didn't express it verbally, she saw flashes of pain in his face when she touched him.

"How do you feel?" she asked, concerned.

"It's much better now. It only hurts when you touch the wounds, and the worst part is my headache." He smiled at her. "Don't frown, Sybina, you did a great job patching me up... I'll survive."

She forced a smile, thinking, *not if the general finds out you can walk and talk. You could be dead in an hour.* It left her cold and sad to think about it.

"Come on, I'll help you back to bed... you need to sleep."

He didn't object when she took him to his bed and tugged a blanket over him. "I feel much better now," he said comfortably.

"Good." And just like she had done every night, she took time to heal his head with her hands. This time he didn't object, he just closed his eyes and relaxed.

"Sybina."

"Yes."

"You said you would tell me your story," he said, sounding almost drowsy.

"Alright..." She was trying to figure out how much to tell him.

And as if he could read her thoughts he said, "I want to hear it all."

She sighed and then she began. "I can remember being very happy and carefree one day and terrified and trapped the next day."

He didn't talk but just gave her time to summon her thoughts.

"It was a normal day, except I can remember thinking that my dad was uncommonly generous with his homemade apple cider at dinner that night; every time my brother and sister asked for more cider he would let them have it. I didn't ask for more because I didn't like it, but I didn't want to hurt my father's feelings so I pretended to like it and discreetly spit it out in the plant. If I had known what he was trying to do I might have swallowed the whole jug, but I didn't understand until I woke up that night and realized our cottage was on fire. I tried to wake up my brother and sister but they were completely drugged and wouldn't wake up." Sybina wiped away a silent tear and felt grateful Aston had his eyes closed. She didn't need his pity.

She kept working with her hands to put pressure on the points she knew would relieve his headache while she continued to talk.

"I ran to my parents' bedroom to get help and found my father with my mother in his arms. He had a bullet hole in his head so I knew he was dead, but I tried to shake my mother awake and called for her again and again. She must have been drugged as well, and if I hadn't run out of the house just before it collapsed, I would have died with them. Instead I watched the cottage burn down to the ground, unable to save my family."

Aston opened his eyes and looked at her. "I'm so sorry, Sybina."

She quickly sniffled and dried away her unwanted tears before she composed herself and with a matter-of-fact tone said: "Yeah, well, in the end I was the only asset left to pay my father's dept to his creditors, and the next day I was sold in the marketplace to the highest bidder."

CHAPTER 5
Prisoner of War

Aston

Aston was deeply impacted by Sybina's story, and it surprised him. He had heard plenty of heartbreaking stories during his many years in war zones, and over time he had learned to keep an emotional distance to protect himself. As a soldier he needed to focus on doing what part he could to improve the situation, and an emotional breakdown over the abysmal horror around him was not helpful to anyone.

Sybina's destiny was without doubt traumatic; he couldn't even begin to relate to being only eleven years old and not only losing one family member but seeing your entire family go up in flames, not to mention being sold as a slave. But Sybina wasn't the first person to impress him with incredible personal strength and resilience. Aston had concluded that the hardships of this country separated people into two categories: the ones that got bitter because of the situation and the ones that got better and stronger. It hadn't taken him long to see that Sybina belonged to the latter group.

He admired Sybina and felt attracted to her soft and kind personality that could easily fool a man into believing she was fragile and needed protection, something that always played to his masculine calling. After all, he had become a soldier to protect and serve.

Rationally he understood that Sybina was strong and competent and used to taking care of herself, but there was something about her that intrigued him and made him wonder how much of that strength was her core and how much was a façade. Everyone had fears and weaknesses, and he sensed that underneath the surface she was worried and frightened. Her compulsive cleaning and busyness told him she had a big need to control her surroundings, and he suspected it was a way to compensate for lack of control in other areas—or maybe just a distraction to keep her mind off something unpleasant.

Sybina had told him about her life as a slave here at the Masi headquarters and only briefly touched upon the fact that all female slaves were servicing the Masi warriors sexually. It made him sick to think about, and he was grateful that so far no one had come to sexually abuse her while he had been here. He wondered if the warriors called her away or came here when they preyed upon her. Unaware, he formed a fist at the thought of Sybina being raped right in front of him. He wouldn't be able to look the other way. His eyes scanned the room looking for weapons he could use if it came to that. The flowers hanging to dry in the ceiling all had string tied around them, and he could use that to strangle whoever tried to rape Sybina or just use his bare hands.

It was something of a paradox that he wanted to protect her from any man that would hurt her and yet he couldn't help flirting with her at any opportunity. It was stupid and irresponsible, as he knew there were several ways of hurting a woman and he was playing with her heart by being flirtatious.

He didn't do it on purpose; it was just part of his nature, and Sybina intrigued him. With her long brown hair, big brown eyes, and quiet personality she was very different from the type of woman Aston was usually drawn to. He always went for blue or green eyes, big breasts, and a dirty mind. He chose women he could have fun with before he moved on, and as a result the longest relationship he had ever had with a woman was four months—and even that had been a long string of breakups and getting back together. Aston was used to women accusing him of being heartless and a womanizer. He couldn't help it. He loved the chase and the sex and felt compelled to flirt whenever he saw a beautiful woman, and Sybina was definitely beautiful. Admittedly, she wouldn't have gotten his attention in a nightclub back in London, where he would have thought her dull and plain compared to all the stylish beauties of his home country. But now that he was close to her, he found her very attractive.

Sybina had most likely never worn make-up in her entire life or used any sort of beauty product and her hair was always tied up in a practical braid, almost like she was trying to hide her natural beauty. *Does she even know how pretty she is?* he wondered, and noticed that he couldn't see a mirror anywhere. Clearly Sybina didn't have time or need for vanity, and he couldn't blame her for trying to downplay her beauty if it meant attracting less attention from the Masi warriors.

But Aston was a man and he knew that not even her boring braid could hide the glow of her hair or her plump lips that looked so inviting, and there was no way any heterosexual man wouldn't find her big brown eyes with the long eyelashes or the perfect-sized nose appealing. He let his eyes slide down her body and decided that even if she'd had none of those features a man would still be turned on by her well-proportioned body that was lean but offered both breast and ass to grab. *Stop looking at her!* he scolded himself and closed his eyes. *And stop flirting with her.*

CHAPTER 6
The General

Sybina

Sybina started her morning with a cold shower. She had woken sweaty and with shameful thoughts of Aston's naked body, and the only remedy she had available to clear her mind was the hose. A cold shower wasn't about enjoyment, it was about getting clean. She washed her hair and body and put on a clean green dress. She dried her hair in the towel and let it hang loose before she walked back into the infirmary.

"You look nice," Aston said and paused when he saw her expression. "Did I say something wrong?"

Sybina shook her head. "No," she finally muttered, looking away. She didn't want to tell him that she had never been complimented by a man before.

"So he speaks now." Both Sybina and Aston froze on the spot as the cold voice cut through the room. The general had entered silently, and from his statement he had been eavesdropping outside.

Sybina looked down, trying to hide the panic she felt inside. Aston stared at the general, who moved into the room with two armed soldiers behind him.

"Excellent work, witch. We'll take him from here." The general nodded for the soldiers to take Aston with them.

"But his head is not yet healed," Sybina objected and stepped forward.

The general's voice turned into a low hiss. "Step back, witch. The hostage will serve his purpose just fine."

Powerless, Sybina watched Aston being dragged out of bed and half carried, half pulled out her door. She saw him resist and heard him groan when the general kicked him in his back to make him move quicker through the door. The hard kick made Aston fall forward, and Sybina couldn't help a small cry of fear even though she was trying hard to hide her feelings from the Masi warriors. The last thing she saw was the soldiers pulling Aston back on his feet, and then the general closed the door with a sadistic grin on his face. "Don't worry. You will soon have new patients. I promise."

The door closed and Sybina stood, unable to move. Time stopped around her. Aston was gone. The only man who had shown her any kindness in sixteen years. The thought of his chopped-off head with dead eyes made her stomach convulse, and she ran to the toilet to empty her stomach. She would never see Aston's handsome face again. She would never answer his questions that made her feel like she was a real person and not just a slave. She would never hear him compliment her again. She was devastated and desperate and covered her mouth as she fell to her knees crying. *Why does my life have to be so miserable? Why can't I be allowed to have a little piece of happiness and keep it; why does everyone I care about have to suffer and die? It's not fair... it's not fair... take me instead and let Aston live. He's got a life to go home to, family and friends... I have nothing...no one will miss me.*

Sybina didn't know how long she had been crying when a soft voice brought her back to the present.

"What's wrong, Sybina?"

Sybina looked up and found Uma looking at her. Sybina had never seen Uma's beautiful green eyes so full of concern. Normally they had a bright flame of resilience and feistiness to them.

She forced a smile for the girl. "Don't worry. I'm just sad because I couldn't save one of my patients," Sybina said and dried away her tears.

Uma helped Sybina to her feet and hugged her to offer her comfort. The girl was thin but almost taller than Sybina. "I understand," she said.

Sybina knew that if anyone understood what it felt like to feel powerless and unable to protect the one you cared for it was Uma. They hugged for a long time.

"Was there something you wanted, Uma?" Sybina asked softly

"My mom hasn't been back to the dorm since yesterday. I'm worried that something bad has happened to her. I think the general is keeping her in his room and I'm going to sneak in to see for myself. Will you go with me?"

Sybina frowned. "And if your mom is there, Uma? What will you do then? Free her? You know there is nowhere to run. The general is just going to drag her back and then your mother, you, and I will be in trouble."

Uma looked down. "I just need to know that my mom is safe... that she is still... alive." The word "safe" was so misplaced in the Masi headquarters, but Sybina couldn't blame Uma for wanting certainty that her mother was still alive.

"Okay, I'll go, but you'll stay here and wait for me," Sybina instructed.

Uma nodded.

Sybina grabbed a bag of powder; it would be her excuse to visit the general's room. If anyone stopped her, she would tell them she was bringing by more of his heart medicine. Quickly she walked out of the infirmary, moving quietly up to the second floor, down the hallways where soldiers on guard mostly ignored her. The female slaves were free to walk around the mansion and work in the vegetable and herb garden outside, but anything else was off limits; the soldiers all knew that.

When Sybina arrived at the general's bedroom she put her head to the door and listened. It was quiet. She

42

knocked a few times but heard no answer and then she opened the door. It wasn't locked.

The room was dark and she stood still for a second letting her eyes adjust, and then she saw a figure on the bed.

"Nilla, is that you?" Sybina whispered and fumbled to turn on a floor lamp next to the door. The light finally flickered on and allowed Sybina to see more clearly. For a second she slammed her eyes closed again, trying to escape the sight that was in front of her. Uma's mother Hunilla was lying on the general's bed strapped down to all four posts. She had an odd leather thing tied around her face with a black ball in her mouth, and her body was covered with whip marks. Sybina held a hand up to her mouth trying to swallow the nausea she felt from seeing her beautiful friend so abused. Hunilla's eyes were closed like she was either sleeping or knocked out. Sybina looked in horror at the clamps on her nipples. It had to be painful, and her fundamental nature of easing people's suffering won over her fear of being caught by the general. She removed the clamps and started removing the object from Hunilla's mouth while calling for her to wake up. Hunilla's eyes opened slowly, like she didn't want to return.

"It's me, Sybina. Wake up, Nilla."

"What are you doing here?" Hunilla whispered.

Sybina grabbed a glass of water from the nightstand and lifted Hunilla's head up. "Uma was worried, she made me come and look for you," Sybina answered and made Hunilla take a sip of the water.

Slowly Sybina lowered Hunilla's head to the mattress again and a weary smile brushed across Nilla's face. "My Uma," she said drowsily, and a tear escaped her eye and fell down onto the mattress. Sybina couldn't help see how starved and beaten Hunilla looked. She was being severely punished for the incident with Uma a month ago.

"How long is he going to punish you?" Sybina whispered, knowing that the general blamed Hunilla for not having trained her daughter to be more submissive to him.

Hunilla was too weak to answer. She just made a slight movement with her eyebrows.

"Is it because Uma broke his nose?" Sybina asked and caressed her friend's beautiful long black hair. The sound of footsteps outside the door made her stop and look up.

Hunilla was too tired for any strong reactions; she just sighed. "He's coming back."

"The general?" Sybina whispered and saw Hunilla nod with her eyes closed.

"What do you want me to do?" Sybina asked and thought of killing the general herself. Hunilla opened her eyes again and with a pleading look at Sybina she whispered, "Promise that you'll take care of Uma. Keep her safe."

Sybina nodded. "But what about you?" Sybina felt tears pressing. This conversation somehow felt so final.

"All I want is for Uma to be safe." Hunilla closed her teary eyes and whispered, "Hide" as a last warning, and then the door opened.

Sybina slid down under the bed, waiting. She saw the general's feet. First he stood still, and she could imagine him taking in the differences in the room since he had left it. Then he closed the door behind him and locked the door.

"My, my, my... looks like you had a visitor." His voice was threatening and Sybina felt terrified.

"Who helped you?" he hissed.

Hunilla didn't answer.

"Don't you turn your head! *Who helped you?*" He was shouting.

Hunilla still didn't answer.

44

In three long paces the general was by his selection of whips, where he picked up a long black one and returned to Hunilla.

"Tell me who was in here and I'll go easy on you. If you don't speak I will be furious and you'll feel it."

Sybina could hear Hunilla cry softly and then he hit her. The cracking sound of the whip smacking down on Hunilla's frail and already wounded body filled the room again and again, and Sybina had to cover her mouth not to scream out loud. Every whiplash ripped Sybina's heart apart, and her hate for the general was so strong that she wanted to kill him in pure hatred. Only her promise to Hunilla kept her from jumping up and attacking him. She needed to be strategic and honor the sacrifice that Hunilla was making for her daughter.

"You might as well tell me right now... *who removed the clamps*? You know I won't stop until you give me a name." Sybina waited under the bed and heard the general untie Hunilla. From what she could hear he positioned her differently.

"I thought you said you couldn't take more fucking. So why are you begging me for more?" he asked in a cold voice.

It was almost inaudible but Sybina heard Hunilla mutter. "I'm not."

"Then why do you defy me, you little slut... it must be because you love to be punished for it."

A loud smack was followed by a sneering command: "Open your mouth, slave. Don't resist me or it will just get worse."

Sybina squeezed her eyes shut and tried to tune out the images in her mind of what was happening to her friend less than an arm's length away from her. *He's choking her.*

"Uhhm," the general moaned "Deeper, that's right... take it all the way in."

45

Sybina heard muffled choking sounds and then weak slapping on the mattress.

A shift of weight in the mattress above her and abrupt gasping sounds from Hunilla told Sybina that the general was letting her get air.

"Now do you want to tell me or do you prefer me to fuck your mouth some more."

Hunilla didn't speak.

"Was it one of the soldiers? Was it one of the slaves? Was it Uma?" For every question he received only silence.

And then the scenario kept repeating itself over and over again with the general getting rougher and angrier. After what seemed like ten minutes at least he changed tactics.

"Maybe I've been fucking the wrong hole... maybe it's easier for you to talk to me when I'm abusing your tight little ass instead."

Sybina heard pained groans from Hunilla and started crying silently under the bed when the general took her friend hard and mercilessly while calling her vile names.

"You're nothing buy a filthy little cunt and you don't get to defy me. I own you, and you'll tell me who came in here right now."

Loud smacking sounds made Sybina cover her ears but it still didn't block out the moans from the general, who was clearly finding Hunilla's pain and suffering as arousing as Sybina found it horrible.

What worried Sybina the most was that she no longer heard any sounds from Hunilla... no begging to make him stop, no discomfort, no groans of pain. Nothing. *He killed her.*

"Look at me, slave," she heard the general order. "Open your eyes and look at me... that's right, I knew you could hear me. Now listen... there is no refusing me. Either you tell me who was in here or I will give you to the soldiers for the next week. No restrictions."

Sybina bit her lip, swallowing her need to scream on Hunilla's behalf. She had treated female slaves after they'd received that sort of punishment. A week in the soldier's dorm would mean repeatedly being raped, degraded, and beaten. As loving as these men could be to their wives and daughters at home, just as primitive and animalistic they became when they were all together and felt challenged to show off their masculine power.

There were a limited number of female slaves at the headquarters and visits to the brothel weren't a weekly thing, which left most soldiers sexually starved. With the lack of privacy it was completely normal to participate with comments and masturbation when someone was taking a slave. Sybina had seen groups of men surrounding and cheering on their friends raping, and she had begged the general to spare the women when they were torn and ripped. So far he had never listened.

All the slaves at the mansion belonged to the general but they were replaceable, and he needed his soldiers to stay happy and not think of deserting.

"What do you say to a dorm with fifty soldiers all sharing you? He sounded so full of hatred.

"*Answer me, slave!*"

The fury in his voice made Sybina curl up; this man was the devil incarnate.

"Don't think I won't do it," he hissed and then he left the bed. Sybina could see his feet move to his desk and she held her breath, afraid he was going to see her under the bed.

"This is Mantonis speaking." He was talking on the phone.

"I have a disobedient slave here. Maybe some time with you and your boys would teach her to respect my commands. I'll give you a week to bring her around... Yes, now.... You will have to come and get her... she's a little

47

tired after my encounter with her." Sybina could picture his grin. An evil grin. And then he returned to the bed.

"I will see you in a week, slave, and then you better remember to obey my every word." There was still no reaction from Hunilla, and the healer in Sybina was convinced the general had either already killed her or signed her death sentence by sending her to the soldiers. In her weak condition she needed tender love and care, not more violence and raping.

Maybe the general realized that too because something changed, and Sybina heard him crawl onto the bed and kiss Hunilla. "See what you made me do, Nilla." He suddenly sounded so different, almost apologetic. "I'm not a cruel man... you know that. Why are you making me do this to you? It's your fault, you know... you could just tell me... Do you think I like sharing my favorite slave with the soldiers?"

There was no reaction from Hunilla, not even sobs or crying.

And then his pleading voice turned into a roar of anger. "Have it your way, slave." The general walked out the door, slamming it hard behind him.

Sybina instantly crawled back up and looked at Hunilla. The woman was lying on her side bleeding from flesh wounds where the whip had hit her the hardest.

"Nilla... can you hear me?" Sybina checked her pulse and it was weak but still there.

Quickly she ran to the general's desk and got a bowl of sugar next to his coffee cup. She hurried back to the bed and poured sugar into the water on the nightstand. She lifted Hunilla's head up and made her drink the water.

Slowly Hunilla started regaining a little bit of color in her cheeks, and she returned Sybina's glance with the most extraordinary brave look.

"Promise you'll keep Uma safe," she said with an exhausted but defiant smile.

"I promise!" Sybina said and heard Hunilla sigh.

"Now go before they come for me. Go to Uma and tell her that I'm... okay."

Sybina dried away the tears she couldn't hold back. "I can't leave you like this... give me a second." She went back to the general's desk and went through his drawers. The general often had severe migraines and she supplied him with strong pain medicine. She found the bag of red vein kratom she had been looking for and took what she needed.

"Swallow this," she said and returned to Hunilla. "It will numb your pain and make you feel indifferent for the next twenty-four hours."

"Thank you." Hunilla said and managed a small exhausted smile. "You are so kind. Now go."

It was hard for Sybina to leave Hunilla but she forced herself to do as Hunilla asked her to, and returned to the infirmary pale as a sheet. Before she entered the room she pulled herself together and prepared to meet Uma's questions.

Uma sat in the corner, out of sight, but as soon as she saw Sybina enter, she jumped up. "Did you find my mom?" she asked.

"I did."

"Did you talk to her?"

"I did."

"What did she say?" The girl's large green eyes shone with worry.

"She asked me to tell you that she is okay."

Uma gave a big sigh of relief. "Oh, thank you, Sybina. I'm so happy. Will she be back tonight?"

"Not tonight. The general wasn't done with her, but she asked me to take care of you, so why don't you stay here for the night?" Sybina put her arm around the girl.

"Thank you. I feel lonely without my mom."

Sybina hugged her tight. "I know, darling, but you can stay with me. I promise to take care of you."

That night Sybina slept with Uma in her bed. The girl clung to her, and Sybina felt a strong feeling of protectiveness grow inside her. It was hard to sleep with this unfamiliar feeling of closeness to another person; instead Sybina lay still, contemplating plans on how to kill the general. She was a healer, not a killer, but the general had taken Aston away and there was no way she would ever let him to do to Uma what he had just done to her mother. She decided on poison.

CHAPTER 7
Concerned

Sybina

From the time Sybina got up in the morning until she went to bed in the evening, every footstep outside her door made her jump with fear that Aston or Hunilla was dead and it was time for her to fill out her morgue reports.

But no one came to fetch her and she filled her day with cleaning as usual, teaching Uma how to read, and contemplating how to murder the general. There were many considerations when it came to poison, and she had to weigh her wish for him to die fast with her need to make it look like a natural death.

The easiest thing would be to slowly poison him by adding a few ingredients to the medicine he was already taking. He would gradually get sick without anyone suspecting her, but it would take time—and who knew what he would do to the people she cared about in the meanwhile?

Sybina was concerned and worried about Hunilla being abused in the soldiers' dorm for the next week and about Aston, who would be sacrificed to Masi any minute now. She tried to hide her fear from Uma but she knew she couldn't shield the girl, and that the general would soon order her to his bedroom, now that he wasn't occupied with her mother anymore.

In the evening she tried to go to Nilla but was denied by a sergeant who didn't want her in the soldiers' dorm. "We don't want you to make us all impotent, witch…"

51

I would, if I could, she thought before insisting that she had come to check on the soldiers she had sent back to heal. The sergeant had finally allowed her in to see them. It had been impossible to get close to Nilla, and she had left even more frustrated. It was like her head was exploding with worst-case scenarios; Sybina even worried about Aston's friend Aya, who she didn't know at all. She felt sorry for the girl, to have been Jonul's slave, and pitied her for what was ahead of her as a sex slave in a brothel. *Poor girl.*

Having Uma around forced Sybina to stay strong and keep up an appearance of being composed and calm, and only when they were lying closely together in bed again and Sybina was absolutely sure the girl was sleeping did she allow herself to cry silently.

"Wake up."

Sybina felt tired to her core after several nights of poor sleep but Uma insistently kept shaking her shoulder.

"What is it?" Sybina yawned.

"It's today… you said I could get my bandages off today." There was excitement in her voice.

Sybina mustered a smile. "Are you ready to see if your hands work again?"

Uma held out both her hands and smiled expectantly.

"Alright, then let's do it," Sybina said and sat up.

Uma was humming and smiling while Sybina unwrapped the bandages on her hands. Sybina didn't like to remember the mental images of Uma's young body beaten to unconsciousness by the general and his nephew. Instead she focused on guiding Uma in forming a fist and stretching out her hands, one by one.

"They work again," Uma exclaimed excitedly.

52

"Yes, but I still want you to take it easy, Uma. Your hands will feel a little weak and funny for a while."

"Alright, but I'm going to show the others right now," Uma said smilingly and pushed herself up from the chair.

Sybina smiled. "I'll come with you," By the others, Uma was referring to the other female slaves, and at this time of day the best place to go was the kitchen, where they could get breakfast and meet most of the women.

"Let's go." Sybina led the way out the door but only made it a few steps before she saw a dark figure walking toward them. She instinctively pulled Uma behind her, stepped to the side, and looked down to avoid any confrontations.

"Hello, Sybina."

It shook her to hear the person use her name and not call her a witch like all the other soldiers, and she glanced up to see Kato standing in front of her.

"Hello," she said, intrigued by the look in his eyes. *He's different!* There was a new glow and light in Kato's eyes that hadn't been there before, but when he spoke he sounded earnest.

"How is the prisoner?"

Sybina put on her professional mask. "The general took him the day before yesterday."

Kato wrinkled his forehead. "But I asked about him yesterday and I was told he was still in the infirmary."

"No. I'm sorry!" Sybina wondered why Aston was of such interest to Kato, and she wanted to ask him about Aya.

"Promotional purposes," Sybina added and looked down to hide her emotions.

Kato frowned. "Ohh... I see!" He turned to walk away but then he stopped and looked back. "Was he fully healed?"

Sybina shook her head. "No, of course not, but the general didn't care."

"Right," Kato scoffed and left them.

Uma and Sybina continued to the kitchen, where a lovely smell of freshly baked bread met them.

"Uma, my dear, come get your morning hug," one of the females exclaimed and opened her arms to Uma, who soon was being hugged and pecked on her cheeks by all the women there, who shared in the joy of her healed hands.

"You got to stop growing, child, you're taller than most of us by now," someone commented, and they all wanted to measure their height against hers. Uma willingly stood back to back and shone with pride every time she was measured to be the tallest.

There were currently eighteen female slaves at the headquarters; most were in their twenties or early thirties and had been there for years. The oldest was Liva, who was also the formal leader of the slaves. The general relied on her to run the household, and she distributed the tasks to the others.

"Have you seen Nilla?" Sybina discreetly whispered to Liva while Uma was occupied with the others.

Liva shook her head with concern. "She hasn't been back at the dorm for several nights. I thought she was with the general, but he called for Aisha last night and she didn't see Nilla in his room."

Sybina moved closer. "He gave Nilla to the soldiers... for a week."

"No." Liva's eyes shot open in horror and she covered her mouth to dampen her gasp of despair.

"Shhh..." Sybina urged Liva and gave a fake smile to Uma, who looked over to see what was going on. "Get your breakfast, sweetie."

As soon as Uma moved away to fill a plate, Sybina returned her attention to Liva. "Someone needs to go up to the soldiers' dorm and get Nilla food and water. She was very weak and starved when I saw her yesterday."

"You know we are not allowed up there and it's dangerous," Liva whispered.

"I tried getting up there yesterday, but I couldn't get close to her. There's got to be something you can do."

Liva was thinking. "After they killed Hannah the general is having the soldiers clean their own dorms. The only thing we do is provide clean sheets and pick up the dirty ones...."

"Then today is laundry day," Sybina said. We need to get to Nilla and fast. Here." She pressed a little bag into Liva's hands. "Make her chew that. It will numb her."

Liva nodded. "I'll go myself."

"Be careful, Liva."

In the afternoon that same day Sybina was helping Uma with her reading when a loud knock on the door made them both turn around. A soldier stamped in.

"We have a prisoner for you," he called and a second later Aston was pushed into the room by another soldier behind him. Sybina felt her toes and hands tingle with the sight of Aston pale and dirty but in good health. Another push brought him farther into the room and almost made him fall over because of the chains on his feet and hands.

Sybina got no explanation as to the sudden change of heart from the soldiers, and she didn't want to ask any questions out of fear that they might take Aston away again. She wondered if Kato had something to do with this and decided he was her favorite Masi warrior, if he was behind this.

"We'll be outside in case you need us," one of the soldiers told her before they closed the door behind them.

As soon as they were alone, Aston broke into a smile and Sybina couldn't help giving him a big hug.

"I'm so happy to see you alive," she muttered low so the guards outside wouldn't hear her.

"I don't plan on dying anytime soon," Aston grinned back, probably unaware of the general's plans for him or how close he had come to dying, and then he looked at Uma.

"Hi there," he said in a friendly way.

Uma nodded at him but didn't smile.

"What's your name?" he asked.

She didn't answer but hid behind Sybina, who had a million questions herself.

"Aston, what happened, where did they take you?"

Aston walked away from the door and signaled for Sybina to follow him. He was moving slowly because of the chains but pointed to the bed farthest from the door.

"Let's talk over here," he said in a low voice and took a seat.

Sybina went to sit next to him.

"They took me to a prison cell further down the basement. There were eight other guys in the cell. All government soldiers and all ready to fight. Three of them are weak, though. They've been here for months, and apparently the Masi warriors are planning to use them in a prisoner exchange."

Sybina felt Uma tugging at her dress. "What is it, Uma?" she asked gently.

"Why does he talk so funny?" the girl asked, and it made Aston smile.

"Uma, this is Aston. He was born far away in a country called England where they speak a different language."

Uma seemed surprised that not everyone spoke Spiri, but then again she had never seen the outside world, let alone another country.

"Show me what knives you have," Aston said in a whisper.

56

Sybina glanced at the door, afraid of someone eavesdropping, and then she gathered what she had and brought it to him.

"How is your head?" she asked.

"I have a nasty headache, but nothing worse than from a massive hangover."

"I'll give you something for the pain." She got up and headed for her medicine cabinet.

"Don't worry about it. I'm the master of hangovers. It's my specialty." There was sarcasm in his tone.

"Alright, but at least let me take the worst of it," she said, concerned, and returned to sit next to him, taking his hand and putting pressure on the points that would lift his headache.

For the next hour Sybina and Aston sat closely together whispering about possible plans of escape while Uma sat quietly in the corner reading in one of Sybina's books.

It was afternoon when they heard shouting outside the window. It sounded like a brawl between at least two soldiers, which wasn't too uncommon. What was uncommon was the sound of a woman. Sybina didn't recognize the voice but she knew that any female slave found outside would be severely punished, and a new thought made her uncomfortable. Aston had asked her to escape with him and she wanted to, but she couldn't go without Uma, and it would be challenging enough for Aston to kill the general and find Aya without having Sybina and Uma to worry about as well. But one thing was suddenly clear to her: Whether they succeeded or got killed in the attempt to escape, the result would be that there would be no healer left to help the slaves.

What would happen to this woman outside? Who would heal her when she had taken her punishment and was left physically broken? What would happen to Hunilla? Who would heal her if not Sybina? She felt selfish for letting the innocent slaves down, but she wanted badly to be free again and she wanted even more to take Uma away from this dangerous place before she could be raped like her mother.

The plan Sybina and Aston had come up with was dangerous. Sybina was to lure one of the guards into the infirmary, then knock him out, take his weapon, and use his key to unlock Aston's chains. Once free, Aston would free the other prisoners and together they would storm the general and his men.

It was an ambitious plan, as the Masi headquarters had more than two hundred soldiers living there and thousands living close by.

"If we could only get hold of a telephone and communicate with the outside world, then we would have a much better chance," Aston thought out loud.

"Who would you call?" Sybina asked, confused.

"The prisoners are all government soldiers, remember; they could call for backup. We need as many hands as we can get."

"I can get a phone," Uma said eagerly.

Sybina swallowed hard. "No, Uma. It's too dangerous." But the girl was already out the door. Sybina wanted to bring her back but Aston stopped her with a hand on her arm. "Give her a chance to help."

"But if something happens to her…" Sybina's heart was beating fast because of her protectiveness towards Uma.

"She knows this place, right?"

Sybina narrowed her eyes. "Of course she knows this place, she grew up here. It's all she knows."

"Then trust her. To me she sounded very confident, and I believe she can do it. Have some faith," he pleaded.

To Sybina every minute was painfully long until voices outside the door made her stand up, full of nervous energy. The guards were talking with a man, and she prayed that it wasn't the general who had come for Aston or Uma. Aston grabbed her hand and pulled her down when they heard motion.

"Get down on the floor," he whispered but there was no time before the door swung open and a woman came rushing in with Kato right behind her.

Sybina pulled back when she saw the tall, blond woman fix upon Aston and throw herself around his neck. She was hugging and kissing Aston with immense relief and joy. It wasn't hard to figure out that this had to be Aya.

Aston tried to hug her back but the chains made it difficult.

Aya asked him questions with the speed of a machine gun and Sybina heard him answer. From what she could guess, Aya wanted to know if he was all right, and he confirmed that. His apologetic tone told Sybina he had apologized about failing to protect Aya.

Kato stepped closer and Aston shot him an unfriendly glance before he returned his attention to Aya, shaking his head, and then he pulled her closer and whispered something with another glance at Kato. Sybina looked at Kato and her instinct told her that Kato understood English, because he scowled and tensed his jaw like he didn't like what Aston was saying. It wasn't hard to see that both men were protective of Aya, and it made Sybina study the woman closer. Whoever could make a Masi warrior knock down his colleagues and look this protective of her had to be special! Aya was taller than Sybina and like something out of a story from strange countries where the people were all tall, blond, and blue-eyed. Sybina looked at Aya's exotic beauty and saw her look frustrated as her hands grabbed Aston's chains.

Immediately Kato stepped closer and silently unlocked the chains and pulled Aston up. Sybina saw Aya look Aston over and then pull at him.

59

Sybina didn't know what to think, it was all happening so fast. She and Aston had spent the last hours planning to escape, and it had made her hope for more than a life as a slave—and now Aston was being freed. She felt a knot in her throat, realizing that she wouldn't blame him for taking the chance and leaving her behind.

Aston didn't look at Sybina. He was intensely focused on Aya.

"Wait, Aya." He was speaking Spiri and shaking his head. "I'm not leaving without Sybina."

Sybina swallowed air when she heard him say it and then she felt Aston look at her. "Sybina saved my life. I'm not leaving her behind, and there are other slaves as well, even a child." Aston pushed his chest forward. He was not to be argued with.

Sybina only had time to send Aston a small smile of gratitude before Kato stepped forward and handed the gun and the keys to Aston. "You can free Sybina and the others if you like. The general is dead, soon chaos will break loose upstairs. I have to get Aya to safety; this is the best I can do for you."

Aston nodded and shook Kato's hand. "Thank you," he said. Sybina heard Aya object but Kato pulled her with him.

Aston called reassuringly after Aya in a hushed voice, and then he jumped up and instructed Sybina, "I'll free the other prisoners and you'll find Uma."

Sybina followed him outside the infirmary and saw a soldier lying lifeless on the floor. *The work of Kato,* she figured and kneeled down to feel the man's pulse. In the distance she could hear locks opening and chains rattling as Aston opened the prison cells. Sybina didn't know how many cells there were. Prisoners were always brought to her for treatment; she had never been in that dark part of the basement where she could now hear excited voices coming from.

Then from out of the shadows Uma appeared. "Here," she said triumphantly and held up a phone. "I stole it from a soldier."

"Excellent." Sybina took the phone and with a strong grip on Uma's hand they ran to Aston.

CHAPTER 8
Breaking Free

Aston

Sybina came running with Uma behind her. "Uma found a phone," she half whispered, half shouted.

Aston put a finger to his lips and signaled for her to be quiet and then he took the phone with a nod to Uma. "Well done!"

The girl didn't smile but just frowned and looked around at all the large men staring at her. He didn't blame her; they were a frightening sight.

"Give it to me." A lean guy with glasses said and stepped forward. "I know who to call."

"Good, then take it." Aston handed him the phone and watched the man open the phone.

"Shit!" the man complained. "I need a code to open the phone."

"Don't be stupid, just call the emergency number and have them transfer you to General Kahlon, they can do that," someone said.

"Alright, I'm trying but there's no reception down here, I need to get upstairs." The man looked at Sybina and Uma. "Can you show me the way?"

"No," Aston stepped forward. "Sybina and Uma are staying with me. I don't want to put them in danger."

"I don't mind," Uma said heroically. "I'm not scared."

Sybina pushed Uma behind her and looked at the man with the phone. "If you go straight ahead you'll get to the infirmary. Two soldiers are lying on the floor; you could take one of their uniforms if you want to blend in upstairs.

The man with the glasses spat on the floor. "I'll rather die than wear a Masi uniform."

While they were talking, more prison cells were found and more men released. Aston looked around and counted thirty-three men, some weak, but all highly motivated to fight the Masi warriors. One of the new men stepped forward and spoke quietly but in a very deep and authoritarian tone, and from his uniform Aston could see he was a captain.

"I know some of you probably want to make a run for it and try to get home, but I say we take down the Masi headquarters from the inside."

"Hear, hear," the men muttered around him.

"We need weapons and we need to call in reinforcement."

Aston spoke up. "We know the general is lying dead upstairs and most likely hasn't been found yet."

"Excellent," the captain muttered and then he looked at Sybina and Uma.

"You know this place?"

They both nodded.

"Then give us a quick briefing on the house. Where will the soldiers be?"

Uma scowled while Sybina quickly explained where the soldiers had their quarters. The slaves. The kitchen, the assembly room. The armory. Where staircases would lead them to, and where back and front exits were located.

"And where will we find guards?"

"I just ran through the house, I can tell you," Uma said in a low voice, making the captain and all the men lean closer to her. She spoke calmly and only mentioned the most relevant information, and Aston couldn't help being impressed with her. This girl was not an average thirteen-year-old; she was acting exceptionally brave and fearless, and the way she stood with her legs slightly spread and her shoulders squared reminded him of a she-wolf talking

63

to her pack. She was the youngest and smallest in a group of dirty, desperate grown men and yet she looked at them as if they were inferior to her.

"Good!" the captain said and then he turned to the men. "Any snipers here?"

A few men raised their hands.

"Any alphas?"

Aston knew the alpha soldiers were the elite of Spirima, and he was surprised but happy to see three men raise their hands, knowing that three alphas were better than thirty normal soldiers.

"Our primary mission is to neutralize all Masi warriors, our secondary mission is to get all slaves out alive, and I want to see as many of you survive this as possible so don't hold back, shoot to kill."

All the men nodded.

"Alright." The captain pointed to the alpha soldiers. "You three and the snipers take over the armory and make sure everyone here gets a weapon, and then you take over upstairs.

"You," he pointed to the man with the glasses holding the phone. "You and I are going to find a signal and you..." he turned to look at Aston, who wondered why this man thought he had any authority over him.

"Will you take care of those two?" He looked at Sybina and Uma.

"I will," Aston agreed, since that was his plan exactly.

"Good luck to you all," the captain said and took off to find a signal.

Aston turned to Uma and Sybina. "Stay behind me. I'm gonna get you out of here before the shooting breaks out," he instructed.

"We need to find my mom," Uma whispered.

Aston nodded. "Where is she?"

Sybina looked at him and sighed. "The soldiers' quarters."

"Shit." Aston gave a grimace. "Listen, there's no way I'm taking you two to the soldiers' quarters. I'm getting you out of here and then I'll go back and find her."

Uma started to complain, and it made Aston bend down and tell her in a firm tone, "I'll find your mom, Uma. I promise! But first I'm getting you and Sybina out of here."

Sybina took Uma's hand. "Come on, Uma."

"Is there any direct way out from this basement?" Aston asked.

"No."

"Maybe you should wait here until it's safe?" he suggested.

"And what if you get killed?" Sybina argued. "No, we are getting out with or without your help."

Aston pressed his lips into a hard line and then he nodded. A second later they were all moving up the stairs. Uma's and Sybina's knowledge of the house came in handy; they moved in the shadows and had almost reached the door to the back garden when they heard shooting, and shouting, and people running. The attack had begun.

"This way," Sybina cried out and ran for the door leading to the back garden.

Aston only just reached her in time to grab her harshly. "Get back here," he hissed and received a confused stare from Sybina. He didn't have time to explain himself to her, and as a civilian she might not understand anyway, but it was his job to keep her alive—and storming out in unknown territory that was under attack wasn't a good survival strategy.

"Stay behind me if you want to live," he said and forced her behind him as he opened the door and assured himself that no enemy was waiting on the other side. He moved outside, signaling for Uma and Sybina to follow, and then he pointed to a shed and told them to run to it while he

65

covered their backs. Sybina held Uma's hand and they both ducked their heads and ran as fast as they could.

As soon as they were shielded by the shed, Aston took a look around and listened to get an idea of where the shooting was coming from. It sounded like most of the shooting was coming from inside the mansion, and then some doors flew open and a large group of women came running out of what he assumed was the kitchen. The women didn't scream but looked terrified, and behind them were two of the alpha soldiers with machine guns. *What's their plan?* Aston wondered and narrowed his eyes to see the direction the women were running in. *Trucks, they are running for the trucks*, he concluded and decided to take Uma and Sybina there too.

Silently Aston moved to Sybina and Uma and pointed. "Run for the truck over there." Uma and Sybina sprinted ahead without any questions. They had only been running a short distance when Uma stumbled and fell. Aston quickly helped her back up, but because he had his eyes on her he didn't see the Masi warrior coming from the side before it was too late. The guy had crazy eyes and a machine gun in his hands, and only the swift movement from Sybina who pushed Aston out of the way saved his life as bullets flew where his head had been a split second before.

Aston felt his gun fall out of his hands as he landed on the ground, and he heard Sybina scream out loud when new bullets were shot in his direction. Aston only saw a flash of the warrior's disturbing grin before he rolled out of the way, but he knew that it would be only seconds before the bullets would hit him, and he needed to get to his gun. Just as he grabbed his gun and turned to shoot he saw the warrior fall to the ground with a howl, shooting his own foot on the way down.

Uma stood behind him, and from the way the warrior was rolling around and holding his crotch, Aston knew

Uma had kicked him hard in his balls. But there was no time to give her praise; he waved his gun and shouted for them to keep running before he took the warrior's machine gun and shot him. This was not the first man Aston had killed and he felt no sympathy, knowing the man had been more than happy to kill him a few seconds ago. He turned to find Sybina and Uma, and instant fear filled him. Sybina and Uma had stopped running and in front of them stood Lukas, the warrior who had threatened to kill him in the infirmary to get his bed. Pure hatred radiated from Lukas as Aston ran towards them.

"Where do you think you are going, witch?" he heard Lukas shout while waving his gun around like it was a toy. Aston saw Sybina push Uma away from her, signaling for her to keep running, and Aston could see why. Lukas was completely focused on Sybina and oozing with disgust. His smug smile told how he would take pleasure in killing her as if she were a maggot to be crushed.

"Why don't you stick around and enjoy the party for a bit?" Lukas laughed loudly and then his expression changed back into loathing. "Or maybe not." With a finger on the trigger he pointed the gun straight at Sybina.

Aston had moved into position and pulled his trigger without hesitation. The bullet hit right between Lukas' eyes and took him out instantly. Sybina looked shocked but Aston didn't blink at all. "I never liked that guy... let's go," he said and pushed her forward toward the truck.

People were screaming everywhere, dying around them, and Sybina stopped running. Aston turned to look at her and could see the frustration in her eyes. Sybina was a healer and he imaged that every cell in her body was screaming for her to run to the wounded and help out.

"We have to get Uma to safety," he reminded her, and it made her nod and keep going.

When they were very close to the trucks, a loud sound made them all turned to look up, Uma screamed in panic. "My mom."

The south wing of the mansion was in flames.

"The soldiers' quarters," Sybina cried and started running toward the entrance. Aston ran after her and forced her back. "Stop, Sybina. There's nothing you can do if she's up there."

"But..." The horrible sound of the windows exploding and the roof collapsing drowned out Sybina's words and Aston protectively pulled her close to him. "We have to get out of here. We need to keep Uma safe."

Sybina nodded with tears running down her cheeks and a strong grip on Uma, who was crying hysterically.

The truck was leaving, and in a fast movement Aston pulled Uma up on his shoulder and ran the short distance to the truck. A few of the soldiers pulled her in and then he and Sybina jumped on board just before the truck sped up.

"My mom," Uma shouted at Aston. "You promised you would find my mom." Aston returned her glance with silent pity and then he looked around at the nine other female slaves in the truck, silently asking them if Uma's mother was on board. Sybina shook her head to give him his answer.

"Help me keep an eye out," one of the alpha soldiers shouted over the noise from the truck. Aston nodded and joined him. In a state of constant alertness he sat on the rear end of the truck as they drove away from the Masi headquarters, scouting for Masi warriors and snipers while Sybina sat with Uma under her arm and dried away her tears.

CHAPTER 9
Refugee Camp

Sybina

"The war is over, the war is over!"

The shouting woke up Sybina, who looked down at Uma; the girl was clinging to her in the narrow bed.

"Did you hear that?" Sybina asked and Uma opened her eyes, looking confused and disoriented.

"It's alright, we're at the refugee camp. We are safe... remember?"

Uma rubbed her eyes and blinked a few times when more shouting came from outside.

Inside the large tent, women and children were waking up and getting out of bed, trying to understand what was happening outside.

"Come on," Sybina said smilingly and pulled Uma with her outside the tent. The stream of people made it impossible to go anywhere but in the direction of the flow, leading them to an open field where a man on a tall platform was standing with a megaphone in his hand, patiently waiting for the crowd to quiet down.

The level of white noise was deafening with thousands of people asking questions and looking for more information, but finally a collective silence fell upon the crowd and everyone turned to face the man.

"The king has just declared that the war is finally over and you can all go home now," the man announced, and immediately euphoria broke out. Sybina and Uma hugged and kissed and raised their hands with loud cheering, but after her initial focus on Uma, Sybina looked up to see that while most people around her reacted with joy and cheering, others fell to the ground crying with tears of relief. It was an extremely emotional experience and soon Sybina was crying as well.

"What's wrong?" Uma shouted to break through the noise level.

Even with her shouting Sybina still couldn't hear Uma over the white noise of happiness, and she shook her head and smiled to signal that she wasn't sad, but happy.

This was the beginning of a new life and it filled her with hope and relief. She gave Uma another hug and shouted: "From now on everything will be fine!"

It took them more than an hour to find Aston in the crowd of people, but as soon as he saw them he spontaneously picked up Sybina in a big bear hug and kissed her on her cheek.

"Victory!" He grinned.

"It's the best day ever," Sybina said and returned his grin.

It was easy to see that Aston was high on euphoria like everyone else, and when he turned his attention to Uma to hug her too, Sybina noticed how the girl's smile faded and she pulled away. It would be a long journey for the girl to learn how to trust any man.

That night Sybina couldn't sleep. She was beyond exhausted but her mind kept racing, trying to catch up to what had happened. She could remember looking into Lukas' gun and thinking her time to die had come, but after that it was all a bit blurred.

Think Sybina, think! she forced herself.

And slowly glimpses came back to her of escaping on the truck and seeing the headquarters in flames behind them. She remembered vaguely being held up by government soldiers and loud voices shouting at them to stop, and hearing their driver frantically explaining that he was a sergeant himself and not a Masi warrior.

Sybina tugged the blanket around Uma and admired the beauty of the sleeping girl. Her long hair was falling around her shoulders and her full lips were slightly spread apart. It was hard to imagine Uma growing up to be anything than a stunning beauty. Sybina sighed and wondered if Uma would ever learn to trust a man, or whether the damage from the general and the other Masi warriors was too deeply rooted in her.

Sybina kissed Uma's forehead and remembered that she had done exactly that on the truck when they were let through to safety and she had felt secure.

They had been taken to a military base for questioning. Sybina remembered only a few of the questions, but she knew it had taken all night before they were driven to the refugee camp and finally given a bed to sleep in.

The calm breathing from Uma, who was lying on her side with her arms over Sybina's stomach, made Sybina yawn. She put her hand on the girl's arm, hoping it would reach Uma in her dreams and assure her that she wasn't going to leave her.

We are free! was Sybina's last thought before she closed her eyes and surrendered to the night.

Sybina's initial feeling that everything was going to be alright only lasted a few days. Soon the ecstasy subsided and Sybina began to understand that the nightmare really wasn't over. It had just changed into a different type of horror.

Hunilla's body hadn't been found and she was still officially missing, and that meant that Uma was Sybina's responsibility. Even though Sybina and Uma had a bed to share in the refugee camp, the place was unsanitary and unsafe, and she worried for Uma's future.

After the king's peace declaration, people started leaving the camp but Sybina had nowhere to go. She didn't want to go to the village where she had once been a slave. She had no family and friends there. The waiting time to talk to a caseworker was more than a week, and Aston, who had been an enormous support, would soon be leaving to fly back home to England.

In two days Sybina would be on her own, and she needed to find a way to support herself and Uma. Sybina had no formal education but she did have a profession, and she could try to find a village somewhere that would take her and Uma in. She could work for shelter and food. At least now she had her freedom and would be free to leave if the circumstances became unbearable.

Sybina could feel Aston's frustration with the situation. He wanted to do more for her and Uma, but according to standard protocols he had to fly back home for restitution and debriefing. It was mandatory after a hostage situation and involved a leave of absence with full pay; his departure was already overdue.

The only really good news they had received was that Aya had escaped back to her homeland, Norway, and she was safe. Aston was very relieved, and even though Sybina didn't know Aya, she was happy for her and glad that Aston had something to smile about in this otherwise depressing situation.

Because of his status as a security officer Aston managed to help Sybina and Uma skip the wait to the caseworker by arranging a private meeting in his tent. The caseworker was an older, tired-looking man. He presented himself as Jon and glanced over Sybina and Uma with only slight interest. "Look, I only have a few minutes." It was clear he wanted to get this conversation over with quickly.

Aston started by asking the first question. "What's going to happen to Sybina and Uma now that the war is over?"

Jon crossed his arms and leaned back. "Well, they are free to leave the camp and start a new life."

Aston didn't look satisfied with that answer. "And what if they have nowhere to go?"

The man sighed. "It's all so new, but my guess is that the government will eventually organize some sort of housing for the former slaves, probably in the city somewhere, but it's going to take time, so for now they can stay here with the other homeless people."

"What about food and work and what about school for Uma?" Aston asked while crossing his arms and wrinkling his forehead.

"How old are you?" Jon asked Uma.

"Thirteen," Uma answered and fidgeted with her sleeve.

Jon looked down at his watch and sighed. "Okay, well, the camp offers school a few hours a week. I think that's the best I can do."

"But..." Sybina objected but Jon held up his hand and shook his head at Sybina. "Listen, I wish I had better news but there are tens of thousands of people looking for jobs and places to live right now... Everything is chaotic, but in a few months I'm sure things will settle down and we can get you into a housing project in the city, maybe with a factory job so you can provide for yourself and your daughter."

"My mother is still missing," Uma corrected him.

"Oh, alright." Jon took off his glasses and rubbed his tired eyes before looking at Sybina. "So you are not the mother, but are you related to her?"

Sybina pulled Uma closer. "No, I'm not. But I promised her mother to keep her safe."

"And where is the mother?" Jon asked Aston.

"Still missing," Aston answered shortly.

The caseworker frowned. "Yes, well, I'm afraid that changes things a little. If the mother is still alive, the girl cannot be adopted and she will have to be placed with her closest relative."

Aston raised his voice. "Uma was born a slave. She doesn't have any family beside her mom."

"In that case she will be put on a waiting list for a foster family, although I have to warn you that there are so many children and so few families that's it's unlikely she will ever get one."

"But I want to take care of Uma," Sybina insisted.

"That's nice of you." Jon gave Sybina a polite smile. "But since you are homeless and unemployed with no family bonds to the girl you won't be permitted to do that. No... she will need to go to an orphanage somewhere, as soon as a spot opens up."

Sybina and Uma gasped, horrified, and Aston threw his hands in the air.

"So basically what you are saying is that your government doesn't know what to do with them and they will be left here for months until you split them up?"

"Yes, I'm sorry, but that's how it is." Jon nodded a goodbye and walked out of the tent. Sybina sat down on Aston's bed and pulled Uma into her arms.

Aston

Aston went after the caseworker, unsatisfied with what Jon had told them.

"There's got to be something you can do for them?"

Jon turned around. "I'm sorry, Aston, I wish there was. But look around you and see what I'm dealing with. There are thousands like them... houses and jobs don't just happen by magic, it's going to take time to rebuild this country."

"You can't just leave them to rot here," Aston exclaimed.

"I don't have much choice," Jon sighed and started walking again.

Aston felt frustrated beyond anything. Sybina had saved his life, and leaving her behind in this nightmarish place would be a cowardly thing to do. There had to be a way.

He ran to catch up to Jon again.

"Jon, I'm begging you, if there's any loophole or anything you can do... I'll pay you to do it."

Jon stopped and looked at him. "You have to believe me, Aston. I would help if I could, but I don't have anything to offer them."

"Then I'll just have to find them a place to live and pay for the rent!" Aston said with determination.

Jon looked away as if to gather his patience before he pinned Aston with an earnest glance. "You are not listening to me, Aston! There are no houses, apartment, sheds, or barns left to rent. There are at least twenty camps like this one in the country and we all have between six to ten thousand people who are now looking for a place to live. Not to mention all the people who are already living with their relatives because their houses were bombed. Some of the slaves are forced to seek out their parents asking for a place to stay, even though it was their parents who sold them into slavery to begin with... can you imagine how desperate you would have to be to go back to the person you hate the most?"

Aston's head fell forward and his hands grabbed the back of his head. With a sigh of defeat he said: "I understand."

Jon nodded. "Good." And then he turned to leave. He had only made it a few steps when he stopped and turned again. "Wait... Aston, there might be..."

"A place?" Aston said hopeful.

"No, I was going to say: a way."

"How?"

"You are English, right?" Jon asked.

Aston looked confused "Yes... and?"

"You could take them with you, back to England."

Aston shook his head. "England won't accept refugees from Spirima anymore. The country is no longer at war."

"True." There was a bit of silence and then Jon spoke: "But England would accept Sybina if she was your wife, wouldn't they?"

Aston narrowed his eyes and lowered his voice. "Marriage is not my thing," he said firmly.

The answer from Jon came quickly. "In that case you don't have much choice than to leave them to... rot here... do you?"

Jon's words hit Aston hard. The thought of marrying anyone was alien to him. He wouldn't be a good husband and he had no desire to take part in the concept of matrimony. Eleven years as a soldier had left their mark on his psyche and made him a cynic. Marriage and kids were for romantics and not for people who had seen the ugly face of human nature like he had. Sybina deserved better than a messed-up person like him, and he was sure she would have no interest in marrying him anyway. He thought of Uma and how many times he had been called out to violent incidents in this camp, when men had raped women and children. Uma was feisty but too pretty for her own good, and he knew that this camp wouldn't be any safer for her than the Masi headquarters had been. Without protection, Sybina and Uma would be easy prey for perverts.

"Argh." With an aggressive kick to the ground Aston left Jon and walked back to the tent. He was on pins and needles and wished he could hide his frustration better

"I hate this," Aston growled and paced the tent like a trapped animal.

"I know," Sybina said and got up. "I'm taking Uma out in the sun for a while."

Aston saw them leave the tent and felt restless and angry with the impossible situation where he was given the worst solution to a problem he couldn't turn his back on. There had to be another way, but after another hour pacing the floor he gave up and went to sit on his bed and pulled out his computer to do some research.

Slowly a plan started taking form and he drew up a draft for a contract.

Sybina

Sybina sat with Uma in the sun, thinking about her options. After the conversation with Jon everything seemed gloomy and depressing. She would happily take any job she could find but Jon was right; jobs and housing didn't just happen magically, and it would take time. Unfortunately time was a luxury that she couldn't afford, as she needed a steady income and a place to live to prove that she could take care of Uma, who was the closest thing to a family member Sybina had left in the world. She cared for Uma like a daughter and would do whatever it took to keep her safe.

Sybina could see how much Aston hated leaving them behind and she didn't want to burden him with her fears. It would only make the situation worse. She tried to tell herself that at least she didn't have to worry about him. He had a place to go home to where he would be happy. All she wanted for him was to be happy. *Right?* Doubt crept in with flashes of Aston over the last days. *NO!* She blocked all such thoughts. *I don't need anything from him and if I miss him, that's my problem, not his.* The worst part would be the waiting... the countdown to the moment of the goodbye. Sybina's new world was very limited and Aston was a huge part of it. She had leaned on him for emotional and practical support ever since her escape, but now she would have to bottle up her worries and fears, and send him off with a smile. *I can do that... I have to. For him.*

Sybina tried to cheer up Uma. "At least we can be outside as much as we want."

"Yeah, and at least we're not slaves anymore," Uma chipped in.

Sybina forced a smile and kissed Uma on the top of her hair. "I promise that I'll do anything in my power to get a job and a place to live, and then you can live with me and we'll be fine... somehow."

Uma leaned against Sybina. "You promise?"

"I promise."

A few hours went by with them sitting and soaking up the sun and thinking heavy thoughts, and then Aston's voice broke the bubble they were in.

"Sybina."

She looked up and blocked the sun with her hand to see Aston. *Yep, he's still in a foul mood.*

"I need to talk to you. Alone."

Sybina nodded and moved away from Uma. "I'll be back in a minute. Just wait here, please." And then she followed Aston back to his tent. He looked flustered when he sat down on the bed and gestured for her to do the same.

"Listen. I don't want to leave you and Uma here," he started.

Sybina watched him closely.

"I want to offer you a deal," he said.

The fact that he couldn't look her in the eyes made her nervous.

"A deal?" she said slowly and folded her hands in her lap.

"Yes," Aston took a deep breath. "I could take you out of this camp and back to my home in England."

Sybina was waiting for him to look at her. "Go on," she said.

He looked only briefly into her eyes before his eyes drifted around the room again.

"We have to stay married for two years until you have all the legal papers to stay in England on your own."

"I... I..." Sybina couldn't speak. She could see how uncomfortable he was about this offer.

"I know... if there was another way, I wouldn't suggest this. But think about it. What it would mean to Uma."

Sybina sat up straight with hope. "Uma would come too?"

Aston shook his head. "Not right away. You heard Jon, we can't take her out of the country until the papers are in order; and since her mother is missing we can't adopt her yet, but she could go to a nice boarding school here in Spirima while my lawyers work on getting the visa she needs to at least visit us.

"Where would we get the money for that?" Sybina asked.

Aston shook his head dismissively. "Listen, money is not the biggest problem here. I'll take care of the expenses, don't worry about it."

Sybina frowned. "I couldn't ask that of you. Why would you do that for me?"

Aston pushed his jaw forward. "Because I owe it to you."

"No, you don't," Sybina exclaimed forcefully.

"You saved my life... twice," he insisted.

Sybina wouldn't hear of it. "You saved my life too."

Impatient, Aston got up from the bed. "That's different, Sybina, it's what I'm trained to do."

Sybina followed his example and stood up beside him. "Same with me. I'm a trained healer." Their eyes met in challenge.

"I know," he said slowly, like he was determined to get his way. "But I'm not referring to you healing me. I'm talking about you stepping in front of a gun to save me when that soldier wanted my bed... and pushing me out of the line of fire on the run."

"You are making it sound like more than it was. I couldn't let Lukas kill one of my patients. I would have done it for any of my patients. *Are you sure about that?* and when I pushed you out of the way, it was a mere reflex," she argued. But in her heart she knew Aston was special.

Aston frowned. "Listen. I don't care if you understand or not, but I feel obligated to pay you back, and getting you to a safe and civilized country is a good place to start, even if it means that I have to marry you."

You sure know how to propose to a girl, Sybina thought, hurt, but quickly pushed aside her pride. Aston was right, this offer was not about love or romance; it was about survival.

She was trying to do the puzzle in her head. "How come you have so much money?"

He shook his head dismissively. "My family is wealthy and I've made good investments," he said.

Sybina didn't speak. She just sat there thinking about what he was saying.

"This marriage," she started and paused. She needed a few things clarified.

"Yes?"

"What about children?" Her limited knowledge of marriage all contained pregnancies and children, and ever since she was a young girl she had dreamt of becoming a mother one day.

"No, no, don't worry. There won't be any of that," Aston tried to assure her and completely missed the confusion and disappointment she couldn't hide.

"Then what about sex?" she asked.

He shook his head again. "I don't want to have sex with you. It's not about that, Sybina... It's about getting you to a safe place."

For a while she sat quietly in her own thoughts and then Aston grabbed her hand.

"Look, Sybina, I know it's a lot to take in, but you know it's the only thing to do. What other options do you have?" he had a genuine expression of concern on his face.

Sybina bit her lip. "Not a lot," she admitted.

"Good, so you accept then?"

"Accept?" Sybina said, lost in her tsunami of thoughts.

"Accept my proposal," Aston repeated.

She fought back her need to tell him that his presentation of the idea of marriage didn't qualify as a proposal, but she thought that would be both insensitive and irrelevant so instead she answered: "Yes, I accept your offer."

He jumped up like a man on a mission. "Good. I have to organize Uma's school and get your papers sorted. We will leave in four days and marry within a month." And then he pinned her with narrowed eyes. "It will have to look real, so you will be staying in my apartment and we will be playing the role of husband and wife in public. If the officials think that we have a fraudulent marriage you will be deported right away and I'll be in legal trouble, do you understand?"

Sybina nodded and then he left, leaving her to think about what had just happened. For someone who was clearly repulsed by the idea of marriage his offer was very generous. Aston was not only handsome and kind, he was also offering to take her away from poverty and danger to a life of safety and comfort. Sybina was grateful but deeply unhappy about the whole thing. She didn't want to be his obligation. His burden. His bad conscience. She hated herself for putting him in a situation like this. Mostly, she was afraid he would soon regret his offer and start to resent her for holding him back. What if he fell in love with someone he actually *wanted* to marry and then he couldn't, because of her?

Sybina went back to Uma, who waited for her where she had left her.

"Uma, how would you like to go to school?" Sybina asked and caressed her hair.

Uma looked up with eager eyes. "I would love to go to school."

"Aston has asked me to marry him and move with him to England. I want you to come "

"But I need to be here when my mom comes for me," Uma said frantically.

"I know, sweetie, so while I go with Aston and prepare the papers, you can stay here in Spirima at a school and learn as much as you want to. When your mom comes to ask for you here, they will know how to contact us and tell her how to find you."

"Okay," Uma agreed.

"So you would be okay with living at a school?"

Uma blinked, unsure, and Sybina regretted the question. Uma had no idea what a school would be like. She had only ever known the Masi headquarters. "I think so," Uma said bravely.

Sybina took a deep breath and kissed Uma's forehead. "Everything is going to be fine."

CHAPTER 10
A Different World

Aston

Four days later Aston and Sybina flew to London. It wasn't hard to tell that Sybina was a little overwhelmed by everything and he kept asking her if she was alright. As always, Sybina didn't complain or whine; she was a trooper and gave him a brave smile every time he asked.

"Listen, Sybina, there's something I need to prepare you for." Aston took her hand just after landing. "There's a chance that there will be photographers when we get off the plane.

"What do you mean?" Sybina asked.

"The media here have been writing about my kidnapping, and Spread Life told me to expect a bit of interest when I return." He looked almost apologetic.

"Okay." Sybina said it slowly, and he knew she probably had no concept of what he was trying to tell her. Media and press was not something she was familiar with.

"Just let me do the talking and stay close to me when we get out, alright?"

She nodded, and her trust in him made him feel protective of her. He had no idea what was ahead of them, but Spread Life had told him they would send someone to guide him and Sybina quickly through the airport.

They hardly made it out of the plane before a photographer spotted them and shouted out, "Welcome back, Mr. Tailor. How does it feel to be back in England?"

Aston gave a small wave. "It's great, thanks." And then he moved forward with his bag in his right hand and Sybina close by his side.

"Aston Tailor." A man wearing a suit stepped forward and waived them to him. "This way, please."

Aston walked over to the man, who introduced himself as the press executive from Spread Life.

"My name is Alan MacGregor, and I've made arrangements for a car to take you to your house. Now we just have to get through the media," he said and took Aston's bag.

Aston looked up to see the photographer standing in the background.

"Can I have a picture, please?" the man asked politely and Aston looked into the camera for a second.

"Thank you… and welcome back," the photographer said and smiled.

Aston looked at Alan with a smile. "That wasn't so bad."

Alan raised an eyebrow and nodded towards the friendly photographer. "That man is the in-house photographer from the airport. The others are not allowed in here but you'll meet them after customs."

Alan started walking, and Aston followed him with Sybina by his side. He could see the other passengers curiously looking at him, some taking pictures with their phones.

"Was that it?" Sybina asked.

Aston gave her a small smile that didn't reach his eyes. "No, I'm afraid not."

He was right. The moment they stepped out from customs a small horde of photographers descended in a blitz, shouting at Aston while others were pointing video cameras and microphones in his direction. Alan MacGregor held out his hands, shouting loudly: "You'll have to wait for the press conference. Right now Aston deserves to get home and have some peace."

Aston was paralyzed by all the questions raining down on him, and he turned his head to see how Sybina was dealing with this media monster when he realized she wasn't there. He was surrounded by press and Sybina was gone.

Without hesitation he turned back and pushed people out of the way to get through to Sybina, who was standing frozen to the ground with her eyes wide open. Aston had hoped to protect her from the public and he could see she was frightened. He pulled an arm around her to shield her.

"Stay close to me," he instructed and made his way through the crowd of press and regular passengers.

"What's the first thing you'll do when you get home?"

"Did you talk to Aya Johansen after her escape?"

"Is it true you killed the Masi general?"

"How does it feel to have brought down a terror organization?"

"Will you go back to Spirima?"

"Were you tortured by the Masi warriors?"

"Who is the woman on your arm?"

The questions came from all directions, and microphones were pointed at Sybina too, asking for her name and her role in Aston's life. Obviously Sybina didn't understand a word of what they were asking, and he wished they would just leave her alone. It made Aston look even sterner and hurry more. He would rather do an army crawl in mud and under barbed wire than to go through this media craziness, and the minutes it took to get to the car and finally take off felt like hours to him.

Once in the car, Aston took a long breath and turned to Sybina. "Are you okay?"

She nodded and brushed her hair away. "I'm okay."

"I'm sorry about that circus," he said, and when she smiled politely he wondered if she even knew what a circus was.

85

Sybina

To Sybina London was like a different universe, with tall buildings and people dressed in all colors of the rainbow. As they drove from the airport to Aston's apartment she saw cars that looked like something from a strange dream and a variety of domesticated dogs she didn't even know existed. To make it even more surreal, some of the dogs had clothes on, which made absolutely no sense to her.

"It's fun to see your reaction," Aston said and smiled at her as she was taking in everything from the car.

"People dress funny here," she said and pointed to a young goth woman on the street who was wearing a long black jacket and big leather boots. The woman had bright orange hair in a peculiar spike and when they passed her Sybina looked back and gaped, stunned that the woman had a black leather band around her neck like dogs in Spirima and her face was so pale with black lipstick.

"Look at her hair!" Sybina gasped.

Aston laughed. "It's called a Mohawk and don't worry, you only have to dress like that on Wednesdays."

Sybina tilted her head suspiciously, hoping he was joking.

"Do all women here wear trousers?" She asked.

Aston shook his head. "No, not at all. Women can wear whatever they want to, and some prefer dresses too," he explained.

Sybina felt overwhelmed with the adventures ahead of her. After having been cooped up for the last five years this was an overload of colors, sounds, and impressions.

The flight alone had been extraordinary; never had Sybina expected to see a cloud from above. To her the thought of flying had seemed as impossible as becoming an astronaut.

The closer they got to Aston's apartment the narrower the streets got and the older the houses looked in a charming way. He lived across from a theater in the west end of London, and promised her that he would take her to see a show as soon as she knew enough English to understand.

Sybina was curious when he opened the door to his apartment.

"Alright then... welcome to my humble bachelor's place."

Sybina could tell that Aston was slightly nervous.

"Feel free to take a look around." He nodded for her to go ahead.

The place was nice, and Sybina walked along the long corridor with an empty room to the left followed by a bathroom that looked unused. She turned her head to the right and entered the door to what turned out to be his bedroom. The room was completely white and sparsely furnished, and had an adjacent bathroom with both a bathtub and a shower.

Aston was leaning against the doorframe to the bedroom. Sybina passed him with a smile when she walked back into the corridor and headed to the end, where a door on her right let her into a combined kitchen and living room. The room was lovely although a bit void of color, but she liked the crown moldings and high paneling that made the flat look elegant.

"Do you like it?" Aston asked behind her.

She nodded and opened the last door to what was a combination of a dining room and office.

"It's very nice," she said truthfully and looked at the large flat screen on the living room wall. She knew what it was. She had seen a TV in the general's office, but it was still a curiosity to her.

"Are you tired?" Aston asked and Sybina shook her head. She *was* tired but this was all too exciting and kept her going.

"Give me a minute, I want to show you something," Aston said and headed towards the hallway. "Grab something to drink if you want, there should be sodas in the fridge," he called over his shoulder and pointed to the fridge.

Sybina looked to the fridge; the door was cracked open and it was turned off. It made sense if Aston hadn't been home for months. The fridge was completely empty except for beers and sodas on the top shelf. She picked out a red one, opened the can, took a sip, and made a grimace. It was room temperature and far too sweet for her taste. She took another sip but it was like drinking syrup and she put it away. There was a bottle of water in the fridge and she grabbed that instead.

After five minutes Aston came back and found her standing by the window looking out on the street below her. For the next two years this would be her new home, and she couldn't wait to get Uma up here as well.

"Come with me," Aston said smilingly and she willingly followed him to the master bathroom.

The lightning was soft in there with candles glowing in the darkness and someone was singing. Sybina looked around and realized he was filling the bathtub with bubbles and that soft music was playing all around.

"Wow... this is lovely," she said, impressed.

"No more cold showers," Aston said with a kind smile. "Oh and feel free to use my razor if you want to. I'll go shopping while you take a bath."

Sybina tilted her head when he left and wondered what he meant by *use my razors if you want to.* She didn't have a beard and couldn't imagine what he wanted her to do with his razor until an unwelcome thought hit her. The general always made his personal sex slaves shave their legs, armpits, and genitals. Sybina had noticed it on several of the women when she first arrived at the headquarters and had asked about it. Hunilla had shared with her that according to the general, men preferred women without hair but Sybina knew that was a lie! She had never seen a shaved woman in the village when she helped deliver their babies, and from the rate at which the women got pregnant she knew their men lusted for them despite their hair. Sybina had given the matter a lot of thought back when she had first seen the general's odd fascination with hairless women. She had come to the conclusion that it was not a common thing like the general wanted his slaves to believe, but instead it was connected to the general's disturbing lust for adolescent girls and it was a way for him to make Hunilla and the others look innocent and young. Was Aston as disturbed as the general? And how could she even think of bringing young Uma up here if he too lusted for young, innocent girls?

Sybina shook her head. She refused to think so little of Aston, and when he left the room, she pushed the thought away and stepped out of her clothes and into the bathtub. The feeling of sinking her body into the warm water felt heavenly, and when she leaned her head back and sighed with joy it was a feeling of wonder. How had she gone from being Sybina, the witch, living in a primitive basement in Spirima to being Sybina, the fiancée of Aston, living in luxury in London? It was surreal, and tears flowed down her cheeks partially because she was so grateful and partially because she was terrified that Aston would change his mind and send her back to Spirima.

Images and faces were flashing in front of her eyes as she was trying to digest the last few days. She thought about the flight and the stewardesses and their gentle smiles. An image suddenly popped up. She could remember watching them pass back and forward in their beautiful high heels, and although she hadn't given it much thought then, their legs had definitely been shaved... Hmm.... Maybe the general had been right after all.

Time disappeared in Sybina's bubble, and she made a startled jump when Aston came knocking on the door, worried she had drowned.

"I'm okay... I'll be right out," she called and decided to shave her legs and armpits in case Aston belonged to the group of men who preferred women without hair. *Why else would he mention it?* she thought.

When she was done she looked at her pubic hair. For hygienic and practical purposes she always kept it trimmed and short, but to shave it off completely was just too big a step for her. Instead she got out of the bathtub to find that the huge towel was another new luxury, with its incredible softness and the sweet perfumed fragrance.

While drying herself Sybina looked up and saw her reflection in a large mirror, and it made her stop and stare. She had never seen herself in full size and stepped closer, taking a few minutes to take in what she was seeing. The woman staring back at her looked like her mother in shape and size and it made her turn and twist in front of the mirror. Her mother had been only fourteen when she married and she had been only twenty-six when she died in the fire. It hadn't occurred to Sybina before now that she was already a year older than her mother had been when she died. In her short life Sybina's mother had carried five children, lost two, and become the mother of Sybina, Ollito, and Millie.

Sybina's destiny had turned out so different from her mother's and without the joy of children or love. She looked at herself in profile and dilated her stomach, wondering how she would look with a pregnant stomach. *It's not going to happen*, she reminded herself and blew out the air, making her belly flat again.

She used the towel to dry her hair; it looked much longer when it was wet and flat. Right now it went all the way down to her behind, but she knew that as soon as it

90

dried her curls would make sure it only reached her mid-back.

It was a relaxed and tired Sybina who finally joined Aston in the living room with red cheeks and a big smile, in a t-shirt he had given her since she had no other clothes than the dress she escaped in from the Masi headquarters. She had never owned a bra and luckily her firm breasts didn't need support yet, but she had been wearing the same panties since they escaped and after the cleansing bath she hadn't been able to bring herself to put the panties back on. His T-shirt went down to her mid thighs and showed nothing. *Aston will never know I'm naked underneath and he wouldn't care anyway*, she convinced herself.

"Tomorrow we'll go shopping for clothes," Aston said and gave her a cup of tea and asked her to sit down.

Sybina smiled and sat down on the white leather couch next to him.

The TV was running and she looked up with fascination.

"Listen, about bedrooms," Aston said hesitantly.

"What?" Sybina asked distractedly, looking around and trying to understand how the TV could make it sound like a car was driving behind her.

"Well, I understand if you prefer your own bedroom, but we should expect surprise visits from the immigration services."

"Uh-Huh," Sybina couldn't focus on his words; she was looking everywhere but at him.

"What's wrong, Sybina? Are you even listening to me?"

"I'm confused about the sound. It's like it's all around me when I can see with my own eyes that it's right in front of me." She pointed to the screen.

Aston smiled at her. "It's called surround sound and it's playing over the loudspeakers." He nodded towards the loudspeakers placed behind them, turned the surround system off, and turned up the TV volume. "Hear the difference?"

Sybina narrowed her eyes. "Yes, now it's coming from the TV only; right."

"Right, but listen, about the bedroom situation, I really think we have to sleep in the same room because they'll check our story and look for clues that this is a sham. Sleeping in separate bedrooms will be a sure sign that this is not real."

"Ohh." Sybina looked down, again reminded how desperate her situation really was.

Aston used a finger to raise her chin. "Don't be scared... I promise I won't touch you or anything."

"Okay," Sybina nodded and suddenly felt shy. She had never slept in the same bed as a man.

"Good!" Aston said with a smile. "Also I need to ask you a personal question."

"What?"

"Where are you in your cycles?"

Sybina didn't understand his question. "My cycles?"

"Yes. I need to know when you are menstruating since they might ask me about it when they come to interview us."

Sybina wrinkled her brows. "Why?"

"Because if we had a normal sex life I would know about that."

"Right," Sybina said slowly. "Well, I finished three days ago so it will be another twenty days or so."

Aston looked like he was taking mental notes. "I'll remember that and let you get some sleep then. You're really okay about sleeping with me, right?"

Sybina felt a swarm of butterflies when he said it and couldn't help blushing a bit. She wasn't sure Aston was aware that his use of words had a double meaning in Spiri. It could mean both sleeping beside and having sex with.

"Sure," she said as casually as possible.

92

"Good, then I guess my bedroom will be *our* bedroom from now on."

Our bedroom. Sybina thought about the big room with the adjoining bathroom she had been bathing in. The room was really much too white for her taste. White walls, white ceilings, white bed linen, and white shades on the night lamps. Even the curtains were white. The only thing with color was the wooden floor. Maybe Aston would allow her to add a little warmth and color to the large and almost empty room.

Aston yawned and stretched. "By the way, are you hungry? I bought food."

"No thanks." Sybina shook her head.

"Okay, I spoke to my mother while you were in the bath."

"Really?"

"Yeah, I figured I might as well take the scolding for not telling her I was returning today. If she had known she would have been in the airport with 'welcome home' banners."

"So why didn't you tell her?" Sybina asked, confused.

Aston arched a brow. "I just told you, she would have brought banners and shit."

Sybina didn't understand his perspective. There was nothing in the world she wouldn't do to see her mother again, and Aston was being ungrateful.

"But she's been worried about you. Shouldn't you be nice to her?"

Aston snorted. "I *am* nice to her. I called her the minute I got back to the refugee camp and I've been talking with her every day since then. Trust me, my mom has heard more from me this past week than she has heard from me in the past year... and besides, I invited my parents and my sister over on Tuesday. They all wanted to come right now, but I convinced them that I'm perfectly fine and just need to rest."

93

"What day is it today?" Sybina asked, confused. Days didn't normally hold much meaning for her, as every day in the headquarters had been a workday.

"It's Sunday, so you'll meet them in a few days."

For a while they didn't speak until Sybina set down her teacup and asked: "Did you tell your mom about me?"

Her question made Aston look away. "No, I told her I would call her tomorrow. I'll tell her then."

Sybina wanted to ask him why he hadn't told his mom but she concluded that it was for the best. There was only so much news a person could take at a time, and the fact that Aston was back in London was enough for one day.

"Okay," Sybina yawned and got up. "I'm going to bed."

There was a glimpse of something on Aston's face that she couldn't decipher; was it hope or excitement? Before Sybina had time to reflect upon the expression it was gone and replaced by a small smile instead. "Good night... sleep well."

Sybina went to the white room and crawled into bed. The sheets smelled nice and the mattress was very comfortable. This was so different from what she had ever experienced, and she wanted to fall asleep, but the thought of Aston soon lying beside her made her heart race and her mouth dry. He said he wouldn't touch her, but what if she touched him? The image of his golden chest hair popped into her mind. She had felt so curious to reach out and touch it.

After half an hour Aston came in. He moved around quietly. *Probably one of his elite soldier tricks*, she thought and then he finally got into bed. She could hear his breathing and it made every nerve ending alert in her body. She could hardly breathe, knowing that he was right there beside her. If she reached out she would feel him. But she was afraid to.

"Are you sleeping?" Aston whispered.

"No," she whispered back.

"Are you okay?"

"Yes."

"You are not regretting your decision?"

"No... are you?" Her heart almost stopped waiting for his answer.

"No."

"Good," she said and smiled in the darkness.

"Yeah." She couldn't see his face but she imagined him smiling back at her.

They didn't speak any more but she still couldn't sleep. Every sound and smell in the apartment was new. She listened to Aston's breathing and when he finally fell asleep she just followed his breathing to calm herself down. The covers and Aston's thick cotton t-shirt made her too hot and she longed to take it off. From the sound of Aston's heavy breathing, he was out cold. It was too tempting, and quietly she took off the t-shirt and placed it right next to her pillow; she would put it on again in a few hours when the night temperature had cooled the room. Comfortable and naked, she snuggled up in the soft covers and tried to fall asleep. But thoughts of Uma, alone in Spirima, kept her awake. *Everything is going to be alright*, she chanted internally for hours, and in the early morning she finally fell asleep for a few hours until her bladder forced her out of bed. Half asleep she walked to the bathroom and closed the door. Feeling drowsy, she peed with her eyes still closed and her chin resting in her hands, and her head still full of her confusing dreams. After flushing and washing her hands she saw her nakedness in the mirror and hurried back to get the t-shirt on and get under the covers before Aston woke up. She only made it halfway to the bed before he lifted his head and looked at her. It made her stop for a second; there was nothing she could do to cover herself up. Aston was staring at her and rubbed his eyes.

95

"I'm sorry, did I wake you?" she asked and got back under the covers.

He looked a little beside himself. "What happened to the t-shirt?" he asked.

"It was too warm," she replied apologetically.

Aston didn't say anything; he just had a bit more color in his cheeks than usual.

"So, do you want to get up and go shopping?" she asked him and put on his t-shirt under the cover.

"I'm gonna need a few minutes," was his only reply and then he rolled onto his side, turning his back on her.

CHAPTER 11
In Love

Aston

Aston was trying to push the sight of Sybina's body out of his mind, but his major erection and the fact that she was lying so close that he could reach out and touch her made it almost impossible for him to think of anything else than how much he wanted to play with her gorgeous body.

He had promised her that he wouldn't touch her but right now he wondered how the hell he was going to get through two years of sleeping next to such a beautiful woman without making a pass at her. This would take all the discipline and restraint he could muster. *This boner isn't going away unless you do something about it.* He sighed and got out of bed hoping Sybina didn't notice it.

He got in the shower and masturbated to mental images of Sybina's naked body. *Sybina might be done with cold showers but I'm going to need a lot of them to survive this arrangement*, he concluded and washed himself. *I need to bang someone and take the pressure off.* Mentally he went over women he could call but he couldn't risk anyone finding out, as it would undermine his new status as happily engaged and could potentially sabotage what he was trying to do for Sybina. God, if only she had been ugly and unattractive. He shook the water out of his hair and got a towel. Part of him wanted to book a call girl and fuck her senseless pretending it was Sybina, but another part of him rejected the idea and tried to focus on one step at a time. For now, he had to help Sybina find some clothes and settle into her new life.

Aston took Sybina shopping and felt amused by the way everything was so new and fascinating to her. He took her to a popular store and could see how she was quickly overwhelmed with the huge selection of women's clothes. She took forever browsing around, and he was beginning to get restless finding it hard to keep his dirty mind from constantly going in the wrong direction and noticing places he could have sex with her in the store. He imagined pulling her into a dressing room and taking her against the wall. Details played out in his mind; he could see himself bending her over and taking her from behind. Aston bit his lip trying to push away the image of spreading her cute cheeks and watching his cock slide in and out of her. He wondered how heavy she would be if he lifted her and if he would be able to carry her while he took her. She looked petite, so he figured he would be strong enough. The thought of removing her hairband and letting her hair fall down while having Sybina bouncing on his hips and moaning into his ear made him adjust himself and seriously consider picking up some men's clothes, just so he could use a dressing room and take care of the growing boner in his pants.

He was constantly battling his primitive, physical need and reminding himself why he was doing this, and that Sybina was a woman who had been sexually abused by men for years and deserved respect and friendship, not another horny man wanting to have sex with her. To his relief the thought of everything Sybina had gone through quickly made his erection go away, and he decided that it was time for him to attack this shopping situation like a true soldier.

"You know what?" he said, and it made Sybina stop and look at him with her beautiful large brown eyes. Once again Aston's mind played tricks on him, and flashes of Sybina in a kneeling position looking up at him with those large eyes while sucking him and licking her lips made him close his eyes and form his hands into fists.

"What?" she asked with her sweet voice.

Aston shook his head and composed himself. "Why don't you focus on finding pants and a summer jacket, then I'll take care of the essentials."

"Okay," Sybina said with a grateful smile.

Aston called on a store clerk and involved her. Together they picked out a fair supply of panties, socks, tops, hairbands, t-shirts, button-down shirts, cardigans, and a blazer. He also got her five different pair of shoes and sandals.

In the meantime Sybina picked out a pair of jeans, some shorts, and two summer dresses with flower prints that she said were the most beautiful dresses she had ever seen.

She didn't want any bras but agreed to his suggestion of a summer jacket.

Finally they were ready to leave the store and Sybina kept thanking Aston.

"Do you mind if I get the receipt? I would really like to repay you as soon as I have a job," she said and it made him smile. He had gifted women in the past and never had anyone been so grateful for so little.

Money had never played a big part in Aston's life, where values like honor, respect, integrity, and personal strength had a much higher importance than monetary funds. In a war zone no one cared how much money you had back home. They only cared if you could be trusted and if you could keep your head cool under an attack.

When Aston turned eighteen a large amount of money had been invested in his name as a gift from his parents. While he had spent time in war zones making money that he had used to pay off his apartment in only ten years, his investment had done extremely well and he was now both debt-free and very rich.

Having someone to share his wealth with was half the fun, and for that someone to be Sybina, who had never had anything, just made it more satisfying.

"Don't worry about paying me back, it's my pleasure."

He carried all the bags to his car and invited her to lunch. Sybina followed him to a restaurant where a host showed them to a window seat.

"What would you like to eat?" Aston asked and picked up the menu card knowing Sybina couldn't read it yet.

"I don't know. Can you help me order something?" she asked, and he could tell she was feeling more helpless than she was comfortable with.

"Sure, do you prefer fish, bird, cow, or veggies?"

Sybina shook her head. "Is that the only description they have?"

He smiled and started translating the menu when she interrupted him.

"I think I'll just have what you're having."

"Excellent, I have great taste in food," he claimed and closed the menu, signaling to the waiter that he was ready to order.

The waiter took his order and brought them drinks.

"What is this?" Sybina asked and took a sip.

"White wine. Do you like it?"

Sybina took another sip. "I'm not sure. It's very different but much better than the can in your fridge."

"Oh, you mean the Coke," Aston said and remembered finding a full Coca-Cola on the counter when she was bathing.

Sybina shook her head, showing her disgust. "It's too sweet."

"I know, but it's good when you mix it with alcohol."

She shrugged. "I wouldn't know."

"You never had alcohol?" Aston wondered if that was possible.

She smiled. "Aston, I was eleven when I became a slave, and slaves are not permitted to drink alcohol or do drugs."

"Right."

She fidgeted with her napkin and looked down. "I once ate some mushrooms that gave me a buzz, though."

He leaned closer. "You little rebel," he teased. "What happened?"

Sybina grinned. "I was always picking herbs and mushrooms in the forest, and I knew perfectly well which ones were poisonous and which ones were edible. But there was one mushroom that the old healer called the magic one, and she told me to stay away from it because it made people do crazy things."

"So you had to try it, didn't you?" Aston laughed. "How old were you?"

"I was young... maybe fourteen or fifteen... and I waited until she was sleeping and then I ate it some of it."

"How was it?"

Sybina sat quietly for a while. "Hmm. I've never tried to put it into words because I never told anyone about it... but I remember it very clearly."

Aston gave her time to collect her thoughts.

"First, all my fears came up and I saw my family die again, I was sold again, I was lonely again... I basically went through all my worst nightmares again, and I was crying uncontrollably for what seemed like hours."

"Didn't that wake up the old healer?"

Sybina scratched her arm, eyes gazing into the past. "It must have, but Aston, you have to understand that for the first year I cried every night and she just ignored me. Another night of me crying probably didn't worry her much.

"Anyway, after hours of the psychedelic horror show everything changed and I felt like I was connecting to this immense force of goodness, of connectedness and love. I had a clear understanding of all living beings as a connected consciousness and I felt permeated by abundance and kindness."

Aston made a small whistle. "That sounds amazing."

"It was, and somehow my description is so inadequate compared to the experience."

"Did you do it again?" Aston asked.

"No, never, because a few months after my experiment some teenagers died in our village after jumping from high cliffs thinking they could fly, and the witch revealed to me that she was scared someone would find out that she had sold them magic mushrooms."

Aston narrowed his eyes. "So she was the local drug dealer too?"

"I guess so."

The waiter brought their food and Aston saw Sybina dive into the salmon with pasta and a creamy dill sauce.

"What do you think?" he asked

She took another bite and smiled. "I like it but it's very mild."

He grinned. "I know, maybe tomorrow I can introduce you to the Indian cuisine, it's spicy and I think you'll like it."

"Sure, but just so you know it, I'm happy to cook for you, Aston."

"You can cook?" he asked, surprised.

"Of course. I cooked with my mother as long as I can remember and the healer taught me a lot too. Sometimes, if I didn't have patients at the headquarters, I would help out in the kitchen instead. I like to cook."

"Alright, then I'll take you grocery shopping and you can cook for me. I don't think I've ever cooked anything but microwave dishes in my kitchen, so it's past time that someone made a proper dish in there."

"Micro what?" Sybina asked and he smiled.

"Nothing... listen, tomorrow we need to look for a wedding dress for you."

"But I just bought two beautiful dresses," Sybina pointed out.

Aston couldn't stop smiling at her sweetness. "I know, but I want to invite my family for the wedding to make it look more real, and they will expect you to wear a white dress."

"Why?" Sybina asked and put down her fork and knife. "I don't like white. I like green better."

"Well, it's kind of a tradition to wear white when you get married here," Aston explained.

"That's silly. Why don't you just tell them that I'm not from here?" she suggested practically.

"You don't want to wear a white dress?" he asked to clarify.

"I just think it's silly since I'll only wear it that one time. I told you, I don't like white that much."

"Most women only wear their wedding dress that one time anyway," Aston said.

"I would like to wear one of my new dresses, if that's alright with you."

"Alright," he smiled.

"So when exactly are we getting married?" she asked.

"Tomorrow I'm introducing you to my family and then we'll marry in two weeks. That will give them time to..." He didn't finish his sentence.

"To what?" Sybina asked.

"To get used to the idea."

"You're afraid they won't like me?" she asked quietly.

"No, Sybina, I'm sure they'll like you, it's just going to surprise them... a lot."

Sybina didn't ask more questions but he felt a sadness from her, and he wondered how she really felt about this arrangement. He had tried to flirt with her a few times but she never flirted back, and although she was extremely kind to him he didn't for one second doubt that this was difficult for her.

"Would you mind not telling them I was a slave?" Sybina asked.

"Alright. What should I tell them instead?"

Sybina had thought about this. She didn't want her new life infected by her old. This was a new beginning for her and she would prefer to leave her past in Spirima. "Tell them that I worked as a healer but never sympathized with the Masi movement. If they question why I would work for them, explain that Spirima is a poor country and I needed the money."

Aston nodded. "Okay, I will.

"Sybina, can I ask you a personal question?" He pushed his plate away.

"Sure," she said and tilted her head.

He watched her closely when he asked his question. "Were you ever in love?"

Her face flushed red and he could see her squirm in her seat. *Yes, she's been in love.*

"Yes, I think so," she said slowly and he added to her scoreboard that she was honest even when it was uncomfortable for her. *I like that.*

"With a Masi warrior?" he asked.

Her head snapped up and she snorted. "Don't be stupid."

"With a guy from the village then?" he asked curiously.

"It doesn't matter. He didn't return my interest," she said dryly and looked away.

"Hmm. His loss," Aston said with a smile and received a puzzled expression in return.

"And you?" Sybina asked and blinked as if she was uncomfortable about the question.

"No, I've never been in love with a village boy," he said and winked at her.

Sybina raised her eyebrow. "You know what I meant. Have you ever been in love?"

Aston took another sip of his wine. "Infatuated is probably a better word for what I've experienced."

"What does that mean?"

"What... infatuation?"

"Yes, I'm not sure what you mean by that."

Aston wrinkled his nose. "Well, it's something that blinds you temporarily but it's short-lived."

"How does it feel?" Sybina wanted to know.

"Hmm, to me it's always been about the passion... you know, meeting someone that you can't refuse and who makes you crave... their company." He couldn't very well tell her that he had felt temporarily insane and insatiable with sexual appetite for different women.

Sybina smiled. "You were going to say sex."

Aston grinned. "You know me too well, already."

"So what you're saying is that infatuation to you means passionate desire?"

"You can say that."

"And you've experienced that several times."

"Uh-Huh." Aston bowed his head, looking at his hand, circling his wine slowly. He had experienced passion several times, but it was shallow and like a drug that left you thirsty for more instead of sated. He always wondered what it would feel like to have that spiritual connection that others talked about when they described a soulmate. He suspected that what he had experienced was a vague imitation of that. He was thirty years old and a practical man who had long ago come to terms with the fact that soulmates were for romantics and not cynics like him. He was content with the physical part of a relationship and didn't believe in true love anyway.

"When was the last time?"

"About a month ago," Aston frowned by the thought of Tara, his longest relationship; it had lasted four months but been an exhausting experience.

"Who was she?"

Aston grinned. "How can you be sure it was a she?"

Sybina blinked confused. "What, is it a man?"

"No, I'm just messing with you," Sybina was such a fascinating mix of mature wisdom and youthful innocence, it was hard not to tease her about it.

"She was a nurse at the refugee camp and it ended when she went home to England."

"How long did it last?"

"About four months, I think."

Sybina looked down. "Do you miss her?"

"Who, Tara?" Aston snorted. "She was crazy."

"Then why were you with her?"

Aston squirmed in his seat. He didn't want to give Sybina a bad impression and he didn't want to expose too much.

"Let's just say that Tara was very passionate and I liked that part about her."

"But it wasn't love?" Sybina asked in a low voice.

Aston looked up. "No, I never loved Tara or anyone else and I never pretended I did," he said with conviction.

"What's that supposed to mean?"

"Just that I never lied and told them I loved them."

"So you've never told a woman that you love her?"

Aston was trying to lift the mood and grinned.

"I might have told my mom when I was a boy, but other than that, no..." Aston could see that Sybina wasn't finding this funny and he sighed.

"I'm not that kind of man, Sybina."

Sybina was holding her glass tight in her hands. "Then what kind of man are you?"

Aston's heart was starting to race; maybe it was better to be honest and let her know what she was getting herself into. "Are you sure you want to know?" he said slowly, looking straight at her.

She hesitated a second before she spoke: "Yes."

"I'm a man who drinks, gambles, and whores," he said and observed her closely.

"Like the Masi warriors," Sybina spoke quickly with narrowed eyes.

"*No!*" Aston grabbed the table. "Not like the Masi warriors." He could feel a knot in his stomach. This conversation was taking a wrong turn and he regretted his honesty. "I spend most of my time defending the innocent abroad and when I come home I spend time with my friends who, like me, like to play cards and go to night clubs to pick up women."

"What kind of women?" Sybina asked quietly.

Aston frowned. "What do you mean?"

"I mean, what's your type of woman?"

"I don't know. Beautiful, funny, kinky... I guess."

Sybina tilted her head. "Kinky how?"

Aston looked down in his glass. "I don't think we need to talk about this."

"Alright, but at least tell me how the women you pick up look like. What's your taste?"

Aston crossed his arms. "Why, Sybina?"

"Why not? I'm trying to get to know you."

"Okay," Aston exhaled with force. "The girls I pick up are mostly blondes, with a good body and green or blue eyes."

Aston was observing Sybina closely to see her reaction but she just nodded and showed him nothing.

"I think you are pretty too, Sybina," he added.

She tilted her head and with a calm voice she said: "Pretty, but just not your type."

"Not my usual type, no," he said honestly, hoping she wouldn't take offense.

107

Sybina

The waiter came to clear the table, and while Aston paid the bill Sybina was trying to quiet her thoughts and hide her feelings. Aston had just told her he was into drinking, gambling, and whoring and that she was not his type, but somehow the worst part of this conversation was his definite *no* to her question about whether or not he had been in love. His answer had extinguished all hope that her feelings for him were mutual.

When he had asked her if she had ever been in love herself, Sybina had been honest and said yes, but from his teasing comments about it being a Masi warrior or a boy from the village she understood that he clearly didn't suspect that she was talking about him.

He had spoken of infatuations and passionate sex, and she knew that he had to be an experienced lover with needs that she couldn't fulfill.

Just let it go! she told herself and moved on to think about his comment that his family would be very surprised. She concluded that Aston didn't expect his family to understand why he would ever want to marry someone like her, and in all honesty she couldn't blame them. Since she had arrived in this country she had seen nothing but beautiful women. While shopping today Sybina had seen several women sending long glances at Aston. She wasn't the only one who thought him handsome and attractive. His family would know that he could have anyone, and they would wonder why he would choose a poor foreigner without education and family, who didn't even speak their language and had been part of a horrible war and possibly been damaged by it.

"Are you okay, Sybina? You are very quiet," Aston said with concern when they walked to the car.

Sybina nodded quietly.

"Listen." He stopped her. "How about this; for the two years we're married I'll do my best to stay away from drinking, gambling, and... women."

A thousand thoughts were running through Sybina's mind, and she felt guilty for intruding into Aston's life and making him change his ways. She couldn't ask him to live two years in celibacy and give up drinking and playing cards with his friends. The entire topic was making her head hurt so she decided to change the subject.

"I would like to learn how to read and write in English, and speak it too of course."

"And you shall." Aston smiled and then he shifted into English: "Be patient, darling."

Sybina tilted her head. "What does that mean?"

He translated and she felt a surge of warmth run down her spine. *He called me darling.*

Back in the apartment Sybina unpacked all the shopping bags and folded them neatly before she organized her closet. She heard Aston on the phone and saw him walk in. He was looking amused, and mimed that he was talking to his mom. The conversation sounded light and happy and when he hung up he laughed.

"My sister and mother are over their initial shock and dying to meet you tomorrow."

"Why were they in shock?" His comment hurt her a bit.

"Because they had given up on me ever settling down and now they are just very happy that I've finally found that special someone."

"But you didn't." Sybina turned and said the words slowly.

"They think I did," he answered. His laugh was gone and he got up and left the room. Sybina looked down. This was harder than she thought. Then her thoughts went to Uma, who would be trying to settle into her new life at the school right now.

Aston had spent quite a lot of money making the headmaster of a boarding school for privileged kids see the gain in taking in a former slave with no schooling. Sybina was very grateful that Aston was so persuasive but feared that Uma would be lonely in a place like that. She had no social skills and academically she would be hopelessly behind.

CHAPTER 12
Umbra

Uma

"Welcome, Umbra, to our proud school. My name is Mr. Tollon and I'll be your counselor. It's our pleasure to have you here." The man smiled and held out his hand to Uma, who had just walked into the school. She looked at his hand and back to his face, not moving a muscle.

Mr. Tollon lowered his hand and wrinkled his forehead. "Alright. I see. Well, follow me child." And then he led her up the staircases to the third floor. "Girls are in the right wing and boys in the left." He pointed and waved for Uma to follow him down a long corridor.

"How did you like the trip here?" he asked her.

Uma gave him a short "Fine" but otherwise followed him in silence.

"You will be right in here." He pointed to a door and she hesitated, unsure what he wanted her to do. "Go ahead, Umbra, it's your new home that you'll be sharing with seven other girls from eleven to eighteen. It's our philosophy that the older students help the younger students."

Uma stepped forward and opened the door. On the other side there was a square room with four bunk beds and four desks. "The other girls are in class right now but you'll meet them this afternoon."

Uma looked around and saw colorful posters on the walls with different beautiful people.

"You can just put down your things by your bed over there and then I'll take you to your first class."

Uma did as told and followed Mr. Tollon down again to the first floor while listening to him talk about the daily schedule of the students.

"From seven to seven-thirty there is running. If you want to run more than that, you are free to get up earlier. Breakfast is from seven-thirty to eight o'clock and that gives you an hour to shower, do a bit of homework, and get ready for class at nine."

Uma nodded.

"Lunch is at twelve and the school day ends at four, when there is sports, chess, and other activities. We eat dinner at six and from six-thirty to eight there is quiet time for homework followed by personal time until ten o'clock, when all lights are out."

Uma was taking mental notes while following the man.

"There is no eating or running in the hallways, no girls in the boy's wing and no boys in the girl's wing, and you'll address all teachers by their last name."

"Okay," Uma said and hoped she would be able to remember it all. She wanted to learn and was eager to meet other girls her own age. Until she came to the refugee camp she had never met another child and now she would be blessed with seven new friends in one day.

Mr. Tollon stopped in front of a door with a sign saying Room 22 Miss Bondun.

"Here we are, I'll introduce you to the class and Miss Bondun, who will be teaching you in Spiri and English." He put his hand on the doorknob. "Oh, and Umbra… Please know that my door is always open and you are more than welcome to come talk to me. We'll meet once a week for a session but if you have any questions, don't hesitate to come ask for help."

That's not likely, Uma thought but she forced a small smile.

"Excuse me, class," Mr. Tollon said as he entered the room.

Uma stood in the doorway and felt all the children's eyes turn to her. It made her cheeks burn and she didn't know if she was to smile at the girls or growl at the boys. Her expression remained stiff.

"Come in please." The teacher, who was incredibly tall and slender and so unlike typical Spiri women with her short hair and glasses, waved her closer.

"My name is Miss Bondun and you are Umbra Tailor, I understand."

Uma nodded. The Tailor part was new. She didn't have a last name, but Aston had told her to use his.

"I would like for you to introduce yourself to the class," the teacher said smilingly.

Uma pressed her lips into hard lines and looked down. She couldn't tell these kids about her background; it was a secret.

"Ehh, allow me," said Mr. Tollon and stepped in front of the class.

"Class... I know it's very unusual to receive a new student less than a month before the summer break but I would like to introduce you all to Umbra Tailor, who is thirteen years old and has been living abroad for most of her life. Her mother is from Spirima and that's why Umbra has joined us to learn how to read and write our language. She speaks it well though, so you won't have any problems talking with her." Mr. Tollon looked back at Uma, who tried to hide the fact that her heart was pounding and her palms were sweaty.

"Umbra's parents recently moved to England and that's where Umbra will go back to once she has perfected her Spiri."

Uma frowned a bit. She understood Mr. Tollon was using the cover story that had been agreed upon with Aston but it hurt to hear her mother completely ignored, as if she didn't exist. Uma knew her mother would find her any day now, so it really didn't matter what story was told about her. She knew the truth.

"Anything you want to add?" Mr. Tollon asked.

Uma bit her lip; it was hard to face twenty-two children all staring at her.

"Well, actually…" she started. "No one calls me Umbra, it's just Uma."

Miss Bondun took a step closer and put her hand on Uma's shoulder. "But that's a shame, Umbra is so beautiful… it's Latin and means… no, wait." Miss Bondun turned to the class and asked: "Does anyone know what Umbra means?"

No one raised a hand, and in the end she pointed to a boy in the back.

"Simon, do you have a guess?"

He looked uncomfortable being in the spotlight, and Uma wished the teacher wouldn't put him there because of her stupid name.

"Ehh… I'm not sure, but I think it means darkness or something."

"Close, Simon." Miss Bondun gave a little nervous laugh and shot a side glance at Mr. Tollon. "It means shadow."

"Just call me Uma, please," Uma said in a low-pitched tone and avoided eye contact with the other children.

"Alright then, you can take a seat next to Alec." The teacher pointed to a free seat in the middle of the classroom, and Uma made her way there and sat down as Mr. Tollon left the room.

"Hi, I'm Alec," the boy said with a small grin and leaned close to Uma when she sat down. "Good to meet you, Shadow."

Uma shot him a hateful glance. She had no tolerance for men, and boys were no exception. "My name is *not* Shadow, it's Uma—but don't bother to memorize it, I would prefer you never speak to me again," she hissed in a whisper.

"What's your problem?" he snarled back and received a "Shhh" from the teacher.

All through class Uma felt the other students stare at her and she didn't like it. She had spent her life avoiding attention and here she was suddenly, exposed to the interest of a whole classroom as the new "shiny object."

After class several people came over to introduce themselves. Unfortunately it was all boys and just the thought of being close to them made Uma angry inside. They were trying to be nice but she knew better and didn't trust any of them.

"Hi, my name is Werner." A boy, shorter than her, said with what was probably meant to be a charming smile. "Can I just say that your green eyes are amazing?"

Uma found it almost amusing how he took a step back when her "amazing" green eyes shot lightning. *Stay away from me*, she thought and hoped her cold front wouldn't have to last long. *Just until the boys leave me alone for good.*

Werner's friends were laughing at his humiliation. "Finally a girl who can resist your charm."

Werner looked only mildly disturbed and shook his head. "I was just paying you a compliment."

Uma rolled her eyes and headed for the exit when she heard Werner's comment to his friends. "Don't worry, she'll be a fan of mine in no time."

His comment made Uma stop and turn around. She didn't know what fan meant but she got the idea, and walked slowly back to the group and up close to Werner, who stood still waiting with big round eyes. For a second Uma didn't speak; she just stood there, looking down at him and letting an invisible cloud of loathing and hostility fill the space between them.

Werner shifted his weight from one foot to the other and made a nervous and very high-pitched laugh.

Uma didn't laugh; she stared him down and with a single raised eyebrow and bared teeth she sneered, "I will *never* be your anything and if you come close to me again I will hurt you."

"Whoaaa..." The boys grinned and pounded Werner on the shoulder, but he was out of words and just gaped at Uma leaving the room.

"She crushed you, man." Someone was teasing him and in a burst of bravery she heard him shout after her, "I'm not afraid of you."

Uma turned and saw Werner stand with his chest puffed up and his friends behind him. She could feel a cold anger in her stomach and gave him a sardonic smile that she had learned from the general. "You should be... all of you!"

"Is everything alright over here?" The teacher stepped closer after having been occupied by another student.

"Everything is just fine," Uma said politely and left the room. Once outside she found a restroom and locked herself in to regain control of her body and mind by taking deep breaths and trying to calm her heart rate. She kept touching her wrists that had recently both been broken, and memories of being brutally beaten by the general and his men came rushing back and made her nose tingle and her throat tighten. *I will not cry... I gotta stay strong and never show them my fear.* She took another deep breath and raised her arms in the air like her mother had showed her whenever she was upset. After a few minutes she felt calmer, and with a last deep breath she pushed her jaw forward, lowered her head, and put the cool façade back on before she walked out. *No guy is ever going to hurt me again. I would rather die.*

After three more classes Mr. Tollon came back to take Uma to her after-school activity.

"The chess team has an open spot if you want to try that." He pointed through the door to a classroom where around twenty boys were setting up boards and pieces to play. Uma couldn't see a single girl.

"If chess is not for you, then there is always dance."

"I think I would prefer dance," Uma said softly and followed Mr. Tollon to another part of the school, where he introduced her to the dance teacher, an attractive young woman in her early twenties with her hair tied up in a conservative bun.

"Welcome, my name is Miss Cornelius but you can just call me Miss C."

Uma smiled at her and instantly liked her. Pronouncing her name sounded like Missy and at least that would be easy to remember.

"Right now we are practicing the waltz. You can partner with Nico over there." The teacher was pointing to a tall, overweight boy who was standing next to a girl with bad skin and called him over. The boy came rushing to them, looking excited to have a new dance partner.

It wasn't hard to see that the girl he had been dancing with looked disappointed when she was asked to dance with another girl.

"Nico, will you lead Uma in the waltz, please?" Miss C asked, and the boy nodded eagerly and moved to the center of the room and waved Uma closer. With everyone looking at her, Uma walked to him, trying to fight the resistance she felt inside her and remind herself that it was only a dance... something she had seen the women she grew up with do on a few occasions.

117

Music started playing and the other eight couples started to dance around the room. Nico stepped closer and took Uma's hand while putting his other hand on her back. Uma didn't care that her face most surely looked like she had just swallowed a lemon and that her body was rigid and refusing to follow him in the dance.

"Just relax and let me lead," Nico said and pulled Uma closer to him while tightening his grip on her hand.

She reacted without thinking and pushed away from him, shaking with a galloping heart.

Miss C came rushing over. "What's wrong?" she asked and Nico shook his head, confused.

"I was trying to lead her but she pushed me away."

"Oh." Miss C frowned. "Well, try again and this time, Uma, remember that it's the gentleman's role to lead and it's yours to follow."

Uma swallowed hard and moved back into a dancing position, letting Nico lead. The others were twirling around them while Nico and Uma looked like bumper cars, with her trying to create as much distance as their joint hands could possibly allow and him trying to pull her closer. Soon Nico was sweating fiercely and the frustration on his face became more and more evident as they kept bumping into other couples.

The music was stopped by Miss C, who was biting the inside of her lips and looking at Nico and Uma. "Hmm, let's try something else."

"Tristan, why don't you come here for a moment, while Nico dances with Simone?"

Uma saw Nico change position with a tall, broad-shouldered, older-looking guy who looked anything but excited about the change.

Miss C started the music again and signaled for the others to dance. Tristan took a firm grip on Uma and prepared to dance, and all her defense systems were ready to beat him up for holding her so tight against his body. She was biting her tongue hard to avoid hissing at him to take his hands off her.

"Alright," Miss C said smilingly. "Uma, this is Tristan; he's a junior and the best dancer in my class. If anyone can lead you, it's him."

The arrogant smirk on Tristan's face made Uma dislike him more. If he was a junior he would be seventeen, and that explained why he looked like a grown man to her. Even though Uma was tall for a thirteen-year-old she was almost a head and a half shorter than him and felt his closeness as a mountain looming over her.

"Go ahead, Tristan," Miss C said and her words made Tristan move his feet.

Several times Uma stepped on his toes as he tried to explain the steps to her. His patience was running thin and he kept sending glances to Simone, the girl he had been dancing with until Uma came along and ruined it all.

"You have to count and pay attention," he sneered after another step on his toes.

"I am counting," Uma said angrily, but no matter how much she tried to focus, her head was clouded with the feeling of being in danger and having to create distance from him.

It was impossible to think of counting steps when it took all her discipline and will power to stay in his arms and not push him away.

"Stop pulling away from me," Tristan hissed and forcefully pulled Uma in with his hand behind her back, forcing her close to him.

The sound of him falling to his knees was drowned by the music but the reaction from Simone, who instantly ran to his side, made everyone turn and look at Tristan's pained expression and his hands holding his crotch.

Uma stood still with a pouting mouth and a racing heart.

"Uma, the headmaster and myself are the only ones who know of your past and I want you to know that we are sympathetic to everything you've been through, but there is no way we can allow you to assault other students... if Tristan reports this it will be on your records and we'll be forced to give you an official warning. Do you understand?" Mr. Tollon asked with a creased forehead.

"Yes." Uma nodded.

"I talked to Miss Cornelius, who agrees that dancing with boys is maybe not a good idea, so next time you'll be dancing with a girl."

"Okay," Uma said quietly.

"Alright, I hope there won't be more of these episodes, Umbra, I really do because boys will be all around you at this school; for every girl here, there's three boys."

"Why is that?" Uma asked

Mr. Tollon leaned back. "Because even though we encourage parents to give their girls the benefit of a full education, this is still Spirima and old traditions still rule. Arranged marriages and child brides are the custom. The girls here are all from privileged families and therefore older when they marry, but as you probably know most girls in this country are married by fifteen. You don't have to worry about that sort of thing as I understand customs are different in England; you might even get to pick your own husband one day," Mr. Tollon said with raised brows, indicating what a privilege that would be.

Uma scoffed discreetly. *I'll never marry. Not in a thousand years!*

Uma returned to her dorm, hoping that at least the day would end well with new friends. Unfortunately for her, three of the seven girls had been at dance class and Simone was one of them. She was absolutely furious with Uma for kneeing her boyfriend in the balls and refused to talk directly to her, but was more than happy to share her opinion about Uma with the others loud enough that Uma didn't miss a thing. Another girl had heard about her episode with Werner and was the only one asking Uma questions, although it was only to help Simone build a case that Uma was in fact a raging, violent lunatic.

Simone was not only the oldest of the girls but also the leader of the group, and the others all followed her example and ignored Uma.

Lying in bed that night, Uma listened to the girls talking about boys and sharing their summer plans. Uma would be staying at the school hoping for a visit from Sybina or a possible visa to go visit her and Aston in London. Now that the day was over, she found it ironic how she had been worried about what to answer to questions about her past when in the end no one had been the slightest bit interested in knowing anything about her. It was hard to fall asleep in her new bed. For thirteen years she had slept with her mother, Sybina, or one of the other female slaves. It felt empty and scary to be all alone and she wiped a silent tear away. At least tomorrow she would be talking to Sybina and hearing a friendly voice.

CHAPTER 13
New Family

Sybina

Aston's family came over, and although Sybina didn't understand what they were saying she found them all to be nice; like her they did their best to communicate with hands and gestures. She saw them sit quietly for a long time while Aston explained how he and Sybina had met. He left out the part of the arranged marriage and explained that they had fallen in love while fighting for their lives in captivity.

Finally his sister Nina, who was a few years younger than him and around Sybina's age, turned and looked at Sybina with tears in her eyes. "I love you already," she said and Aston translated.

Her words made Sybina smile shyly.

"No, I think we all do... for saving Aston and loving him like we do," his mother said and asked him to translate to Sybina. Aston looked down as he translated, and Sybina wondered what part of his mother's words made him uncomfortable.

Both his sister, his mother, and his father hugged Sybina tight and thanked her, so clearly he had explained how she had healed him and pushed him out of the way when he was shot at. That was a good start.

They stayed a few hours and talked about the wedding, and Aston translated here and there. Aston's sister and mother looked as if Christmas had come early when Aston agreed to let them plan a wedding reception.

"But we need more time, Aston, eleven days is nothing," his mother complained.

Aston merely shook his head. "Sybina and I both want it to be a small and simple ceremony and I already booked us in for that Saturday.

"Oohh… can we take Sybina dress shopping?" Nina asked excitedly and clapped her hands.

"She doesn't like white. It's not the tradition in Spirima. I want her to wear whatever she likes and she already bought a summer dress that she wants to wear," Aston emphasized and translated to Sybina so she understood what they were saying.

Sybina smiled and gestured for Nina to come see the dress and Nina happily followed her to the bedroom. Despite today's shopping the big closet looked almost empty. Sybina found the summer dress that she was planning to wear and held it up for Nina to admire.

Nina couldn't hide that she wasn't impressed. Clearly this was not a wedding dress in her eyes. "You don't like it," Sybina said and tried to show in sign language what she meant. Nina made an apologetic expression as if to say, *not really, sorry.* The two women returned to Aston in need of an interpreter.

"Can you tell her that her dress is pretty, but not really a wedding dress? Besides, the dress has to be a surprise to you, so if you've seen it, it's no good."

In the end they agreed that Nina would take Sybina on a dress hunt for the right dress the next day and Aston would support with translation per phone if needed.

They called him more than twenty times, and each time it was small sentences and he patiently translated. Sybina found a simple dress that she liked even though it was white, and Nina agreed it complimented her figure beautifully. They picked out white high-heeled shoes and a little white purse too.

Everything went fine until Sybina saw the prices on the items they had picked out. She felt horrible for spending so much money on things she really didn't need or want, and if it hadn't been for Nina she would have never gone ahead and bought it with Aston's credit card.

Nina took Sybina home and hung the dress in the guest room and made Aston swear he wouldn't take a peek at it. Aston translated so Sybina understood.

"I swear, I won't go near the dress," he said and held up both hands to emphasize how serious he was. It made Nina laugh.

"Trust me when I say you'll have a beautiful bride."

"I know," he answered and smiled, and again Nina forced him to translate his compliment.

Sybina thanked him and said goodbye to Nina, who was leaving.

Aston followed his sister to the door and when he returned he cheerfully asked:

"Are you ready for some adventurous grocery shopping?"

"I am," she said and couldn't help feel excited.

"Do you want to make a list of things that you need?" he asked and she shook her head.

"I have the list in my head."

"Alright, then let's go," Aston waved a hand towards the door and she walked in that direction, noticing that he always waited for her to go first; she wondered if that was a cultural thing.

When they arrived at the supermarket Sybina couldn't grasp the size of it. She had never in her life seen anything like it. The place had everything from clothes and furniture to music, TVs, toys, and food.

She had less than ten things she needed to buy for the dish she wanted to make, which was a simple one with rice and shrimp, but she couldn't help stop and look at all the marvelous things in the store; for half an hour Aston patiently followed her before he gave up.

"Sorry, Sybina, but if I don't take over here, we are still going to be here in four hours."

"I'm sorry," she said and looked up from a pair a baby shoes that she was completely entranced by.

"Don't be, I completely understand; but from now on I'm leading and you are following." He held out his hand to her and with a small smile she took it.

"Tell me your list," he told her and she listed the ten things.

"This way," he said and in his usual man-of-the-world style he led her to the food department.

Sybina found it strangely exciting to walk around the store with Aston holding her hand, and when he smiled at her and whispered: "We look like a real couple now, don't we?" she smiled back at him and felt a little flustered.

Aston was wearing a cap and sunglasses, afraid that he would be recognized from the papers but everyone seemed too busy to notice them at all, and in no time he helped her find garlic, shrimp, rice, spices, cream, parsley, flower, yeast, and lemon, and as always he paid for it all.

"I feel so bad about you paying for everything," she said when they left the store.

"Are you kidding me? I'm happy to pay if you do the cooking, but if you really want to do something then you could give me a hug."

"A hug." Sybina lowered her head and looked around. "Right here?"

He leaned in and whispered in her ears. "I told you, Sybina, we need to look like a real couple in public and we need to show affection."

Public displays of emotion were not very common in Spirima, and she looked around to see how others were behaving around them. Most people looked busy and not at all interested in her and Aston.

"Don't you think we should at least wait until we're married?" she asked cautiously.

Aston laughed and leaned close enough to whisper in her ear. "You are not in Spirima anymore. Here, couples kiss on the streets and no one cares." To her astonishment his mouth brushing her ear lobe send sweet chills down her spine.

"Alright, I'll hug you then." Sybina lifted her arms and wanted to give Aston a quick hug, but he pulled her close and buried his face in her hair, not letting go. Sybina closed her eyes and took in the feeling of her first hug with a man since her father died. There was a comfort that was greater than the physical closeness; it was almost like a silent promise of protection and it brought up hidden emotions in Sybina, who had been alone and strong for so long. She had loved and trusted her father but he had failed her, and now Aston was asking her to put her trust in him. It was tempting to lean on him but dangerous as well. *The greater the expectations, the more chance of disappointment*, she reminded herself.

"Was that bad?" Aston asked when he finally released her.

Sybina looked deep into his eyes. "No."

He kept looking at her and the long glance between them made her heart race, forcing her to break the eye contact and take a step back.

"We should get home so I can start dinner."

"Wow, you sound like a wife already," Aston said with a grin and started walking toward the car.

That night Sybina served Aston a traditional dish from her village, and even though it was spicy he didn't complain. After years in Spirima he was used to it; he praised her cooking and baking. Besides the rice dish, she had baked homemade bread and little cinnamon buns with a trace of cardamom and with lemon icing on top.

"You have something to live up to now," Aston said and grabbed another one of the small cakes.

"What do you mean?"

"Nothing... it's just that you're setting the bar high with all this delicious food."

Sybina was flattered that he thought so. Personally she didn't consider this food something special, and if it took this little to impress him, her job as his housewife would be easy.

"Would you have told me if you didn't like it?" she asked, curious.

"Hmm... " He looked thoughtful. "Would you want me to?"

"Of course."

"I'll remember that."

"Good."

Aston got up and started clearing away the plates. Sybina was fascinated that he didn't automatically expect her to do it. Her father had never lifted a finger in the kitchen and she suspected her mother would have preferred him not to.

A sound from Aston's phone made him pick it up and with a smile he exclaimed. "Excellent!"

"What is it?" Sybina asked.

"I arranged a tutor for you and he just confirmed that he can start tomorrow."

"A tutor?"

"Yes, his name is Jacob and he'll be coming here five days a week to teach you English. The only problem is that the press conference starts at noon, so I can't stay the whole time he's here. I'll have to leave you alone with him. Will that be alright?" Aston asked and again Sybina felt her heart melt by his concern for her.

"Yes, of course, Aston, don't worry about it." Sybina got up from the table full of excitement. "I'm just so excited that I'll be learning English. Thank you so much, Aston." Spontaneously she gave him a small hug.

"What's this? Did I somehow set off a hugging machine?" he said playfully.

Sybina released him and gave him a beaming smile. "Just be happy I'm not kissing you."

Aston gave her a sly smile and opened his mouth to speak but then he closed it again and bit his lip like he was censoring himself.

"What is it?" Sybina asked in a happy voice.

Aston shook his head and picked up a few more things from the table, avoiding eye contact with her. "It's nothing, Sybina, really."

She knew he was holding back on something and she had a feeling he had wanted to tease her about her kissing comment, but ever since he had seen her naked something had changed between them and she didn't know what to make of it. She had been as kind and loving to him as she could without throwing herself at him. But her hopes that Aston found her attractive too were fading with every day they slept together without him touching her. Tonight would be their fourth night sleeping in the same bed and he always came to bed late, making me think that he was hoping she was already sleeping.

She was grateful for everything he did for her and felt shameful about hoping for more. Aston had been honest from the beginning and told her there would be no sex and no children; it wasn't a real relationship and she needed to remember that.

CHAPTER 14
Tara

Aston

Aston sat on the couch watching an action movie that bored him. As a soldier he had to roll his eyes at the action scenes where someone got shot endless times and kept on fighting while throwing around one-liners. Right now the heroine in the movie, who had no military training, was in a gunfight against twenty or more men with machine guns and for some reason none of them could hit her, whereas she with her single gun could blow up things and take them all down. Ridiculous!

Aston yawned and looked at the time. It was past midnight and he should go to bed, but sleeping was the hardest part of the arrangement he had made with Sybina. He had tried to think of her as a sister, but that just made him feel even more disgusted with himself for having so many sexual fantasies about her.

Sexual abstinence wasn't new to him. Aston had gone without female companionship for up to six months when he was deployed in war zones, but that was different—because it didn't involve sleeping next to a beautiful woman every night and hanging out with her during the day.

His employer, Spread Life, had given him a paid leave; except for the mandatory debriefing at the headquarters, a press conference to satisfy the media, and a forced conversation with a psychologist to determine the level of pain and torture he had been through, he had all the time in the world.

It wasn't that he didn't appreciate Sybina's amazing home-cooked meals and seeing his apartment transformed from a colorless bachelor's flat to a lovely home full of warm colors and style; it was just that he felt like a constantly aroused schoolboy and it forced him to release the pressure several times a day to avoid getting painful blue balls.

Go to bed, Aston, this is getting ridiculous, he reminded himself and yawned again. This time he turned off the TV and headed to the bedroom, where Sybina was already sleeping. He went to her side and lifted the book she had been reading in. It was an English dictionary and it made him smile at her eagerness to learn. He closed the book and put it on the nightstand before he removed a lock of her hair from her face.

"Jacob," she muttered in her sleep and it made Aston frown.

Sybina was studying with Jacob, her new tutor, every day and Aston had to give her credit for her enthusiasm. Jacob didn't speak Spiri so he used pictures to build her vocabulary, and often they walked around the apartment or outside where she pointed to something and he told her the name of it. It was wonderful to hear Sybina starting to use English words and Aston admired how good a memory she had.

What he didn't like was the way Jacob looked at Sybina. Jacob was young and would soon graduate as a linguistic specialist from the university. It was Aston's mom who had arranged the whole thing, since she knew Jacob's mother.

Jacob had arrived five days ago as agreed, and at first glance he was a nerdy, hipster type with glasses and a backpack that made him look harmless. But with every day he came over Aston disliked him more, as it became increasingly evident that the guy was smitten with Sybina. Even though Sybina didn't seem to mind, it bothered

Aston to see how physical Jacob was with her when he turned her head to get her to look at something or took her hand to lead her somewhere. Aston had also seen them sit opposite each other with Jacob leading Sybina's hand over his face and body, teaching her the names for nose, ears, belly, thigh, and so on. After that episode Aston had pulled Jacob aside and told him to keep the touching to a minimum. He didn't care if Jacob thought of him as a jealous husband-to-be. He knew things about Sybina that he couldn't and wouldn't share with Jacob, and although he didn't know the extent of the sexual abuse Sybina had been subjected to as a slave, he would make sure no man ever touched her again on his watch.

Aston had considered speaking to Sybina about Jacob. But he had observed them together and she really wasn't flirting or leading Jacob on, so he felt sure she wouldn't see the problem, and he couldn't possibly ask her to be less sweet and likeable.

Aston had come to the conclusion that Sybina was oblivious to her appeal to men. Not once had he seen her return any of the long glances she received from men when they were out. But Aston saw it, and several times he had found himself scowling protectively behind her back.

Aston watched her sleep and without thinking he let his finger trace down her jaw. She was dreaming of Jacob, and he felt a prick of jealousy.

He couldn't help it but bowed down to kiss her slightly spread lips. It was a soft kiss to avoid waking her up but it made her turn her head away.

"No, Jacob," she said almost inaudibly and it made Aston close his eyes with relief. Even in her dreams she rejected Jacob's kisses. It was irrational and stupid but he kissed her again and this time he whispered. "It's me— Aston."

131

Her only reaction was a tiny curve on her lips that he took for a smile and it encouraged him to kiss her again. It felt so wrong to kiss her without her consent but her sweet little moan was like an aphrodisiac to him. He couldn't help spreading little kisses from her earlobe along her jaw and down to the base of her neck, and the sight of her leaning her head back in pleasure made his whole body ache for her. He felt his mind split, with his rational part observing in horror how his uncontrolled, primal brain took over and caressed Sybina's arm and let his fingers slide down on the top of her blanket over her breast and tummy and down to her inner thigh. He could see her breathing change and her legs very slightly spreading.

STOP IT!! the better part of him shouted in his mind, and he pulled away ashamed with himself.

For a minute he stood still and watched Sybina sleep. She was dreaming and he could sense her eyes moving under her eyelids. He wished she had been talking in her sleep to give him a clue of what she was dreaming about but he found comfort in the fact that she looked relaxed and unafraid. His kissing and touching hadn't brought out painful memories in her.

Aston gently tugged the blanket around Sybina. In four days she would become his wife. With her stubbornness and intelligence, he was sure she would soon be speaking English; and with Sybina's determination to build up a life to support Uma and herself, Aston had no doubt she would get a job and find independence.

That's what I want for her, he concluded with a feeling of doubt so small that he didn't stop to notice it.

When Aston woke up, Sybina was still sleeping but she had moved to his side of the bed and was leaning her head against his arm. His morning erection reacted like a forked stick to water and he turned to her, taking in her scent, and letting his hungry eyes move over her body that was so beautifully defined under the thin cover. She was on her tummy with her legs slightly spread, and the curve of her behind made his cock twitch and his heart pump faster. He couldn't stop looking at her and stroking his pounding shaft while his mind played images of how it would be to kiss her plump lips and bury his hands in her long curly hair. He would like nothing better than to wake her up while sliding into her from behind, kissing and biting her neck and earlobe and starting her morning with waves of orgasms. He was a skilled lover and knew he could deliver; the thought of Sybina crying out her ecstasy with him on top of her made him almost spill over.

He suppressed all sound from his now ragged breathing and let his hand move faster. She was so tempting—he had to use all his will power to not reach out and touch her. A guttural growl from the back of his throat escaped him and made Sybina move in her sleep. She turned and rolled onto her side with her back to him. She was right there, and every cell in his body wanted to pull her closer and take her, hard and punishing, for making him suffer like this. The thought of pounding into her made guilt wash over him, and with a deep sigh he moved away from her and went to the bathroom. He needed to clear his head before he did something stupid like touch her in her sleep again or try to seduce her. He was not a barbarian and had promised himself, and Sybina, that sex wasn't part of their agreement. Sybina had suffered enough and the last thing she needed was another male coming on to her.

Still, he wondered how fiercely she would resist if he tried to seduce her and if she had ever experienced sexual pleasure with any of the Masi warriors. The thought alone upset him and with a displeased growl he got under the shower, pushing images of Sybina away and settling for random images of sexual situations to make him come. He couldn't very well walk around with a boner all day; he was a man, after all, and he would have to be dead not to react to Sybina's sweet femininity. When he walked back into the bedroom he stopped. Sybina was still sleeping. She was gorgeous as she lay on her side with her mouth slightly open and a few tendrils of hair down her face, gently caressing her lush black eyelashes and her fine nose that looked so cute whenever she wrinkled it. He wanted to look away but the cover had slid down and revealed the top of her breasts pressed together, making them bulge generously.

Aston stood still for a few seconds; he closed his eyes and called upon all his self-control before deciding on a morning run in the park, hoping to burn off his sexual energy.

He was gone for almost two hours and when he returned he found a note from Sybina that she was with Jacob. Aston ignored the annoyance over Sybina and Jacob spending so much time together. After a large glass of water he headed for the shower again and had just gotten wet when he heard the doorbell ring. He waited for a second to be sure but it rang again, and he reckoned Sybina had forgotten her keys.

Swiftly pulling a towel around his waist and shaking his wet hair, he went to open the door.

"Hello, darling," Tara, his ex-girlfriend, said with a beaming smile and let her eyes fall over his naked torso. "Were you expecting me?"

Aston frowned in surprise. "What are you doing here?" He and Tara had broken up over a month ago and everything with her was always dramatic. He didn't want her back in his life.

Tara laughed and threw a hand up in the air. "What am I doing? I'm dehydrating... I think. It's crazy warm outside and a glass of water would be nice."

Aston didn't move and put on his most dismissive face while trying to find an excuse to not let her in, but Tara was never intimidated by his big strong demeanor and she simply stepped forward, placing both her hands on Aston's abs and making him pull back from her, thereby allowing her space to enter his apartment. Tara proceeded down his hallway, happily chatting like this was the most normal situation in the world.

"I can't tell you how worried I've been with you kidnapped and all. I even gave interviews... did you see them? I mean the pictures weren't all that good, but it was on page seven so that was pretty decent, don't you think?"

Aston shook his head and closed the door, then followed her. "Why did you give interviews?"

"Because I'm your girlfriend, silly..." she said and sent him a head shake over her shoulder.

Aston took a deep long sigh and entered the kitchen behind Tara, who now turned to him. "Did you have that glass of water or should I search for a glass myself?"

Aston got her a glass and scowled at her as she drank a tiny sip. "Listen, Tara, I don't know why you're apparently confused, but whatever we had ended in Spirima and we are no longer a couple."

Tara smiled and lifted herself up on the kitchen counter, signaling that she wasn't going anywhere. "I don't see it like that," she said firmly and spread her legs invitingly.

Aston rubbed a hand through his wet hair. "I honestly don't care how you see it, Tara... the fact is that you're not my girlfriend and I want you to leave my apartment."

Tara pouted and then she slid down from the counter and stepped close to Aston. "Don't be mean, A, we both know that there are certain things you adore about me."

She licked her lips sensually, placed her hand on his towel, and pulled if off him. "Look at my Mr. Happy down there, he looks so sad and not at all playful—that's a first."

Aston raised his brows and reached for his towel. "Give it to me," he said, annoyed, but Tara giggled and held it away from him.

"Why don't you let me remind Mr. Happy why I'm his favorite girl?"

Tara bent down to touch Aston but he moved back and held up his palm. "Don't."

"Alright, then why don't you come to me instead?" she said and started to undress in front of him.

"Tara... *stop*!" Aston demanded but she just laughed and continued to strip off her clothes.

Picking up his towel, Aston moved closer and grabbed her arm to stop her from opening her bra. Tara was quick to take advantage of his closeness and pressed herself against his groin and kissed his neck.

"Stop it, Tara... I don't want this," Aston said and felt her reach for his groin. Again he jumped back and shot her an angry look. "Get your things and leave me the fuck alone."

"Why?" Tara pouted with her hands on her hips.

"Just do it."

"Not until you tell me what the problem is... we couldn't be together because you wanted to stay in Spirima and I wanted to go back to London... well, problem solved, we are both here now."

"Look, it's not going to work, Tara, there's nothing you can do, so just leave."

Tara's eyes swelled up with tears. Aston had seen this dozens of times and it didn't affect him anymore. Tara was a drama queen and she would use any trick to get her way.

"What's wrong with me, why don't you want me?" she said with a tiny voice.

"Tara, I just don't, so please leave."

"Is it that woman you brought home?"

Aston paled at the thought of Tara harassing Sybina. Sybina, who was so kind and gentle, would be bulldozed by Tara's wrecking-ball personality.

"You are gonna leave both me and her alone, do you understand?" Aston took a step forward with a finger pointed at Tara's face.

"So *it is* her then... I saw you two on the news when you came home. Who is she?"

"She's my fiancée." Aston wanted to bite off his tongue, but his need to make Tara understand that she had no chance in hell of getting him back had gotten the better of him.

He half expected Tara to turn into a crazy siren shouting and yelling, but she calmly crossed her arms. "I don't believe you!" she said.

"Well, believe it. We are getting married on Saturday and I love her." Aston said it with conviction, wanting to scare Tara off.

Tara only snorted at him. "You told me you would never marry and now you want me to believe you're marrying an old woman from Spirima?"

"An old woman? What the hell are you talking about? She's twenty-seven."

"Well, that's four years older than me, and she looked really old on the news."

"You know what, Tara... you might only be four years younger than Sybina, but she is at least thirty years wiser than you and she is twice the woman you'll ever be." *Okay... that was unnecessary... no need to poke the dragon*, Aston thought and took a step back, wondering how the hell Tara always managed to provoke him to say stupid things.

"Oh, yeah? Well, maybe her old wrinkled face is the reason you can't get it up anymore," Tara shouted back and pointed to his crotch, covered by the towel again.

"Get the fuck out of my apartment," Aston roared, and this time he didn't wait for her to comply but grabbed her and pushed her down the hallway to the door.

"Aston, don't be like this… you know I love you and I've been so worried about you," Tara pleaded but Aston was furious and threw her cardigan at her and slammed the door in her face.

Afterwards he stood for a second with hands shaking and his heart trembling.

Good thing Sybina wasn't home, he thought and went back to the shower.

Sybina

As Jacob and Sybina went back to the apartment Jacob was pointing out everything on their way. Jacob was sweet and friendly, and even though Sybina knew he was being paid to tutor her, she felt that she had gained a new friend. She appreciated the way he made her laugh and feel relaxed in his company. She had sensed tension between Aston and Jacob and wasn't sure what the problem was, but she had an idea it was money-related and that Aston just wanted to make sure he was getting full value for his money. Sybina did everything she could on her part to study hard in the hope that Aston soon wouldn't have to pay for tutoring anymore.

"Door," Sybina said, and Jacob smiled and opened the door to the building for her.

"Starr," she said and took the first step up the staircase.

"No, Sybina, look at me," Jacob said and took her hand. Sybina turned and saw him pronounce "stair" with exaggeration. He made her repeat it until she had it right.

"Me go up stair." Sybina smiled and continued up to the third floor where she was surprised to find a woman sitting against Aston's door, crying.

Sybina looked at Jacob, who shrugged as if to say, "I don't know her."

"Hello," Sybina said and squatted down in front of the woman. "You okay?"

The woman was pretty, with big green eyes and light brown hair, but her make-up was running. Sybina empathetically took her hand.

"Are you Sybina?" the woman asked and looked up.

"Yes. I'm Sybina," Sybina smiled at her and felt the woman grab her hands.

"I'm Tara, and I'm Aston's girlfriend," she said.

Sybina shook her head and looked at Jacob to signal that she didn't understand. All she got was that the girl's name was Tara.

"I'm Aston's girlfriend," the girl said in Spiri, making Sybina's eyes grow big.

"I worked in Spirima for a year," the girl said to explain why she spoke Spiri.

"You are Aston's girlfriend?" Sybina said, surprised.

"Didn't he tell you about me?" Tara asked and sniffled.

Sybina shook her head. "No," she said.

"I've been so worried about him and now that he's back, he's being mean to me."

Sybina frowned. "What do you mean?"

Tara dried her eyes and looked into Sybina's eyes. "I mean that he loves me, but he's going to marry you and I've got no idea why."

Sybina took in a sharp intake of air. "Did Aston tell you he loved you?"

Tara's Spiri was broken, and although Sybina got the meaning Tara's accent was thick and her structure awkward, making Sybina hope she had somehow misunderstood her.

139

"Sure, Aston can't get enough of me—we have sex like rabbits… he's crazy about me." Tara started crying again. "It just doesn't make sense that he would marry *you*." The way Tara looked at Sybina would have insulted most people but Sybina hardly noticed it. She didn't need Tara to tell her she wasn't Aston's type; he had already told her that himself.

"I'm going to talk with Aston," Sybina said and stood back up, determined to confront him with why he had lied to her.

Tara looked slightly guilty. "You might want to wait… he's putting clothes on."

Sybina opened her mouth but nothing came out, so Tara continued.

"You know Aston, he can't get enough of sex, but I guess that's what makes him so irresistible, isn't it?"

Sybina looked at Jacob for help, and was grateful when he, not having understood the conversation in Spiri, stepped forward.

"Hi, I'm Jacob."

Tara gave him a weak smile. "Hello."

"You look upset, would you like a cup of tea?" Jacob asked in a friendly way and shot Sybina a reassuring smile. His question made Tara light up a bit and get up from the floor with a nod.

Sybina gave Jacob a small appreciative wave when he descended the stairs with Tara, and then she turned to put the key in the lock with a head full of questions and tension in her body.

The sound of water made her head for the bedroom, where she sat down on the bed waiting for Aston to come out from the bathroom. She could hear him in there and when he finally opened the door and saw her, he jumped back.

"Christ, I didn't know you were home already," he said and walked to his closet naked. Sybina tried to look the other way but she had already seen his magnificent body in Spirima and it was imprinted on her mind; covering it up would have made no difference.

"Are you okay?" Sybina asked and Aston turned to look at her.

"Yeah, yeah, why do you ask?" he said and put boxers and a T-shirt on.

Sybina tilted her head and creased her brows. "There was a woman outside who was very upset with you."

Aston rolled his eyes and blew out air. "Is she still there?"

"No" Sybina shook her head. "Jacob took her out for tea."

Aston, who was looking through his closet, turned with a pair of jeans in his hands and pinned Sybina with narrowed eyes. "Is that a joke?"

"No."

"Why the hell did Jacob ask her out for tea?"

"Maybe to calm her down or be friendly." Sybina shrugged. "Tara was crying and saying that you are mean to her."

"Great!" Aston rolled his eyes again. "You know her name... so I guess that means she talked to you?"

"Uh-Huh."

Aston put his jeans on and waited for Sybina to continue; when she didn't, he folded his arms and leaned against the closet. "What did she say?"

Sybina held her glance steady, relying on sixteen years of intensive training on how to hide her emotions and not show Aston how she was hurting inside. In a calm and matter-of-fact tone she said: "Tara told me she's your girlfriend and that you two have sex like rabbits."

Aston's face tightened. "Listen, Sybina... Tara's my ex and she came by to get back together with me, but I wouldn't have it and she got upset. That's really all that happened."

141

"Well, maybe she got confused when you told her you love her."

Aston unfolded his arms and threw them in the air. "She's lying!"

"Was she lying about you being naked as well?" Sybina asked coolly.

"She pulled off my towel... no, don't walk away from me." Aston stopped Sybina, who was trying to leave. "She interrupted my shower... I thought it was you at the door and I only had a towel on when I opened the door... but nothing happened."

Sybina shook free from his grasp and moved out of the room. "You don't have to explain, Aston. I understand," she said and went to the living room, where she got a book and buried her head in it. She desperately wanted a place to be alone and allow the emotional tumult she felt inside to settle down. Sybina wasn't a vain person but it was a blow to her self-esteem that Aston showed no sexual interest in her and yet apparently couldn't get enough of Tara and other women. *Sex like rabbits, ha!* Why was she so repulsive to him?

Sybina thought about bleaching her hair to make her more attractive to him, but she would never be like the girls Aston fancied with their blond or light brown hair and their fair skin and blue or green eyes. Even though she was light for a Spirimian woman she was still not a blonde and never would be. There was nothing she could do to fix that.

"Sybina." Aston was standing in front of her willing her to look up at him. "Listen, I need you to understand that nothing happened between me and Tara today and nothing will ever happen between us again."

"Okay," Sybina said, pretending to be uninterested.

"Good!" Aston nodded and sat down beside her. "How did it go with Jacob?"

Sybina felt a flame in her stomach, and although it was beneath her she couldn't help herself. "I like Jacob a lot, he makes me laugh."

She could see Aston's jaw tense. He clearly didn't like Jacob much but right now Sybina didn't care about his feelings. Aston had told her about his previous relationships and it had pained her to learn of his lust for other women, but meeting one of the women face to face made it a thousand times worse. The thought that Tara had experienced a side of Aston that was closed off to Sybina was causing a horrible ache in her belly.

Aston leaned back on the couch and placed his arm behind her; it made her scooch a bit forward to create distance. "I don't pay him to make you laugh, I pay him to teach you English," Aston said grumpily.

Sybina lost her cool and raised her voice. "Don't worry, as soon as I can, I'll pay you back."

"It's not about the bloody money," Aston yelled back and his face turned red.

"Really? Then what is it about? Why are you being mean to Jacob when he's my friend?"

Aston leaned closer. "What is that supposed to mean? Exactly how friendly is he to you?"

"Very friendly," Sybina said and crossed her arms, thinking about how Jacob would buy her ice cream and encourage her when she was having a hard time understanding him.

Aston lowered his head and narrowed his eyes. "Did he kiss you?"

Sybina got up from the couch and stood with her back to Aston. Jacob always hugged her when he came or left, and a few times he had kissed her cheek, but Aston did the same to his sister and mother and Sybina figured it was a customary greeting in England. She couldn't see that Jacob had done anything wrong, and turned around to meet Aston's inquiring look.

143

"Yes, he kissed me," Sybina said with her head held high, "and I liked it."

Aston's nostrils started flaring and he growled and got up from the couch too. "I'm going to kill that little twit."

Sybina stopped Aston with a hand on his shoulder when he moved past her. "Stop," she said with the same authoritative voice she had used with her difficult patients in Spirima. "I don't understand what the problem is. Explain it to me."

Aston stopped and looked down at her. His face was very close to hers. "As far as Jacob goes, all he knows is that *you are mine* and I'm not paying him to kiss my fiancée."

Sybina felt a strong pull in her stomach when Aston said "you are mine." She wanted to be his, but she knew that wasn't what he meant.

"So your male pride is hurt because he kissed me on the cheek?" Sybina said with brows raised.

Aston frowned. "What do you mean...? Show me how he kissed you."

Sybina stood still for a second. The tension between them was draining and even though she was extremely attracted to Aston she was also enormously frustrated with him. Only the fear of Aston firing Jacob made her comply, and with irritation she rose on her toes and gave Aston a hug and a peck on the cheek.

Aston gave her a suspicious glance. "Is that how Jacob kissed you?"

Sybina nodded.

"Alright then... just don't let him kiss you on your mouth," Aston ordered.

Sybina felt provoked by Aston's demands when she knew he had just screwed Tara.

"And where is Tara allowed to kiss you?" she hissed at him and scolded herself internally for showing her emotions.

"Nowhere," he said shortly. "I told you, I asked Tara to leave me alone."

"Right… and was that before or after you had sex with her?" Sybina said with a trembling voice.

"I don't need this shit," Aston shouted and turned his back on her, leaving Sybina alone, confused, and feeling miserable.

Aston

Aston was walking the streets of London full of anger. Everything had been going according to plan before Tara turned up and threw a fucking napalm bomb like she always did. Tara and women like her were unstable and crazy, and he blamed himself for having been with her in the first place. Aston had spent four months with Tara; she was like a bad acid trip that kept taking him high only to bring him lower than ever. Everything was drama with her, and even though he couldn't deny that she was a freaking magician in bed Aston was grateful she was out of his life—most of all because he didn't like the man she brought out in him. His time with Tara had primarily been occupied with three things. Him trying to break up with her. Her trying to convince him to stay. And them having make-up sex, morning sex, evening sex, kinky sex, sex in forbidden places, and always with Tara whispering dirty talk in his ears, something he had a hard time resisting.

Aston kicked an empty soda can on the street and stopped for a red light. He didn't know where he was going, he just wanted distance.

Fifteen minutes later he found himself on a park bench looking at people. Some were busy, others strolling along. Some were looking down at their phones and others engaged in conversation. He saw families with strollers and old people with canes. It felt good to not think about his own shit but just watch others walk by.

I wasn't even tempted! The thought stood out in his mind and was a powerful realization. *I'm sexually starved, practically naked, and alone with a woman who is willing and hot, and I'm not even tempted...* Aston leaned back and looked up in the blue sky. *What the hell is happening to me?*

This was so unlike him, but he had felt only frustration and anger with Tara; no part of him had wanted to kiss, touch, or fuck her.

If it had been anyone but Tara, he told himself and took a minute to look for beautiful girls that he would have sex with, given the chance.

Three girls were lying on the grass not far from him. They had books in front of them and he figured they were part of some study program. One of them was pretty with long blond hair, but then she laughed and she sounded like a pig, turning him off. His eyes moved to the next girl, who looked pretty too, but on a closer look she had bad skin; and the last girl was too masculine for his taste.

Annoyed, he got up from the bench, to seek out a cute girl to prove to himself that he was still the same, and Tara had been wrong when she told him he couldn't get it up anymore. It was ridiculous... he masturbated several times a day and had no physical problems, so it was only a matter of finding the right girl to get his attention. Aston pulled out his phone and scrolled over his contact list full of women he could call for a booty call.

These were all good-looking women but he kept wrinkling his nose, finding something wrong with every single one of them. After going through all of the women he headed home concluding that his deviant puritan behavior was temporary and only due to the wedding. Even though it was a sham wedding, it was still the only wedding he would ever have, and he had ethics and morals that were messing with his sexual drive for

146

beautiful women. It would pass once things settled down, and then he could find a discreet solution to his starvation. The thought of two years of celibacy seemed like torture to him.

Sybina

Sybina heard Aston come in and looked up to see him enter the kitchen where she was cooking.

From the way he moved she could tell he wasn't angry anymore.

Sybina turned the filet of chicken she was frying and returned to chop the rest of the salad.

"Is it safe for me to come near you with that big knife?" Aston jested and moved closer.

Sybina shot him a small smile. She'd had time to cool off too and she was embarrassed with her behavior. Aston was going far and beyond what she could have expected; she had no right to blame him for sleeping with an old girlfriend. He had promised her a sham marriage, but never his heart.

"Listen, Sybina, I hope you believe me when I tell you that nothing happened between me and Tara, and believe it or not, I wasn't even tempted." Aston leaned against the kitchen counter.

Sybina smiled and shrugged.

"I know I suck at this whole relationship thing, but I won't lie to you, Sybina. I hope you know that."

"It doesn't matter, Aston, you are free to do as you please. I don't want to stand in your way."

Aston looked surprised and puzzled. "It matters to me. If we are to live with each other for two years, we need to be able to trust each other, and you should start by trusting that I'm telling you the truth."

Sybina gave him a sugar-coated smile. "Where I come from, trust is earned."

He scoffed. "Where I come from, people know that I can be insensitive and a bloody idiot, but I'm not a liar."

"I'm making a chicken salad, so I hope you're hungry," Sybina said to change the subject, and maintained her friendly smile. She was done arguing with him; it was senseless and a waste of her energy.

Aston looked at her with an expression she couldn't read. "Yes, I'm absolutely starving," he said and looked away.

CHAPTER 15
The Run

Umbra

"How are you feeling?" Uma asked and squeezed the phone in her hand. Talking to Sybina was a highlight in her life.

"Nervous," Sybina admitted

"I wish I could be there to hug you and tell you that you are beautiful."

Sybina gave a small chuckle. "You are so sweet, Uma. I truly wish you could be here too."

"Is he a good man?" The question came out slowly. It was something Uma had worried about a lot. She didn't trust men and she didn't understand why Sybina would marry someone she hardly knew. She could understand a certain amount of gratitude to Aston for having saved them, but marriage seemed stupid.

"Yes, Aston is a good man," Sybina said and Uma could imagine her smiling into the phone.

"Does he hit you?" Uma asked cautiously.

"No, sweetie, he doesn't."

"Right," Uma said suspiciously. She wasn't sure Sybina would tell her if he did, but in her experience men mostly hit when they didn't get their way. Maybe Sybina was just good at giving Aston what he needed.

"To be honest, I think Aston would be very upset if anyone tried to harm me."

"Me too," Uma said and narrowed her eyes.

"I'll make sure to send you a picture from the wedding."

Uma had never seen a wedding and she didn't know any women who had been married, so it was all a bit mysterious to her. With her lack of freedom she had depended on the female slaves to tell of the outside world. Only a few had been born into slavery like she had, and even they had seen more than the inside of the Masi headquarters. Being the only child among eighteen women had meant being showered with affection; they had all done everything they could to make her feel good. One of her favorite things had been to listen to their stories about their families and siblings, running barefoot in grass and going to school. It was like fairytales to Uma.

"Yes, send me a picture, I would like that," Uma said.

"How is school?" Sybina asked.

Uma closed her eyes and kept her voice steady. "Good," she lied. She didn't want to trouble Sybina on her wedding day. Or ever. Her problems at school weren't something Sybina could fix anyway, so there was no point in spending the short time she had with her on the phone to talk about it.

"Is your favorite subject still math?"

"Hmm... No, I think it's English because it reminds me that I will soon be with you again.

"And the other kids?"

"What about them?" Uma said shortly.

"Any new friends yet?"

Uma suppressed a snort. "No, I've been too busy studying."

There were noises in the background and Sybina suddenly sounded distracted. "Oh, I think I hear Nina. She's Aston's sister, remember... she's doing my hair and make-up."

"Okay." Uma felt left out and wished that she too could be there to see Sybina and take part in the excitement.

Sybina sounded apologetic. "I'll call you in a few days, alright?"

"Alright. Have fun!" Uma said, mustering a happy voice before she hung up.

It was hard for her to imagine Sybina's life even though Sybina had tried to explain and had sent pictures too.

Uma's own life was also very different now. The school was in the northern part of Spirima, with a radically different nature than the south where she was from. Not that she had ever been much outside, but on the drive here they had moved from sand, rock, and dust to this lush and green part of the country which Uma found very beautiful.

Instead of sleeping in a dorm with grown female slaves that loathed the men who abused them, she was stuck with seven girls who couldn't stop talking about the boys at school. It made Uma physically ill to see how much the girls would crave these pimpled boys' attention and whisper about secret kisses and holding hands. The girls were so naïve and thought that these boys actually cared for them when Uma knew better. Boys became men and men were sexual predators. Uma didn't want to share with the girls that she had been almost killed only two months ago when she refused to let two men rape her, but she did try to warn the girls that they were playing with fire. Her warning only made them laugh at her and call her crazy.

After her first day where she assaulted her dance partner, rumors about her had spread like wildfire, and to the dislike of both her and the other girls it had only made her more interesting to the boys; she had heard of bets to pick her up. That would explain why several of the boys had approached her since then, pretending to be nice. Uma didn't fall for their trickery but scowled at them to let them know she could see right through them. *Men will try to lure you with honey on their thorn bushes; don't fall for it, my child,* her mother had told her, and she intended to keep her distance.

151

It would have been easier if the boys didn't constantly seek her out. One of them had even given her a letter with poetry talking about her beautiful green eyes. It was obnoxious and she made sure to tear it apart in front of him.

A teacher approached Uma and she hid her cell phone behind her back. There were so many rules at this school and she was still trying to figure them out. Even though she was pretty sure she wasn't doing anything wrong she preferred to keep her distance from the teachers to avoid being scolded and punished.

The youngest kids here were eleven and the oldest eighteen. With her thirteen years she was still among the young students, with limited freedom to leave the school. This was definitely a step up from being a slave but far from complete freedom.

She wanted to go out and explore nature but she was limited to the school grounds for safety reasons.

Every morning all students had to run, separated into groups according to speed and length of the route. The fastest group, called the fast trackers, only had strong and athletic young men in it; Uma envied them that they were allowed to leave the school grounds to run in the forest. She and all the other students ran on the tracks, and even though Uma was used to running up and down the staircases and always being on the move at the Masi headquarters this was much better; she got to stretch her legs and run full speed with nothing holding her back. It was exhilarating and gave her an amazing buzz that made her push herself to run faster and longer. Two weeks ago when she first started running her body had still been impacted by her long stay in the infirmary, but she was getting stronger every day and with her lean body, long legs, and more importantly her ability to ignore pain, running was something she was naturally gifted at.

The other kids were whiney and refused to run when it hurt, and it almost made Uma laugh. Pain didn't scare her, and she would take physical pain over gnawing fear any day. She knew both conditions better than any of the children here and if running was the worst that had ever happened to them, they were living in a dream world.

Today was Saturday, and on the weekends many of the kids went home to their families or took a day off to do as little as possible. Uma was planning to study all day. It was necessary if she wanted to catch up to the others and she had nothing better to do anyway. But before she went to the library she would indulge herself in a run. She ran downstairs and out the front door, where she saw a few other kids on the tracks. She started running towards them when her brain registered that the gates were wide open.

Maybe it was her lifelong dream of escape or a simple lust for adventure that made her run off school property without looking back. Uma had no idea where she was going but found a comfortable pace and took in the sights of nature around her. She could see mountains in the distance and a forest ahead, but for now she was running along fields of wet marshland. The sound of gravel under her shoes, birds chirping, and the fragrance of grass and summer were all new signs of freedom and she couldn't help smiling. She had only been running for five minutes when a sound behind her caught her attention. She looked over her shoulder and saw five runners far behind her. It had to be some of the fast trackers from the group of young men that were allowed outside the school property. *Shit!* Tristan was in that group, and although he hadn't physically tried to hurt her after the incident at dance class where she kneed him in the balls, his eyes were shining with a lust for revenge every time he looked at her. She needed to find a place to hide, and she remembered the headmaster's warning about the marshland. It was dangerous and had deep and treacherously hidden water holes. The forest was her only chance of escaping them.

Uma accelerated and sprinted toward the forest in the distance. It was a long stretch but it was either that or being alone with Tristan and four other predators, so she gave it all she had and kept pushing herself to run faster, ignoring the pain in her chest from her lungs begging her to stop. *Pain isn't dangerous, only unpleasant,* she reminded herself and kept going. She could hear them getting closer and knew they were bigger, stronger, and had longer legs than she did. Giving up didn't even cross her mind; instead she found a gear she didn't know she had and accelerated further. It was a marvelous thing to experience the strength of her body and the clarity of her mind showing her an opening in the forest in front of her where she could escape the young men. The pain was less now, almost like her body had accepted that she wasn't going to stop and it wasn't trying to make her anymore.

She ran to the opening in the forest and left the gravel road, knowing that she only had a few minutes before the boys would be here. She stopped for a split second and looked around. It was either climb a tree or hide in the bushes, and because she could hear them approach she decided on the latter and threw herself down on the ground. The thirty seconds it took for the guys to catch up gave her time to steady her breathing a bit.

"Where did she go?" The five boys had stopped on the road and she could see several of them bending and gasping for air.

Tristan was staring and pointing in her direction. "She went into the forest." Uma held her breath when she saw him walk in her direction. She could see his face was tomato red and he was dripping with sweat.

"She can't be far," he said and looked around.

"What was she doing, running away from school?" another guy asked and walked into the woods too. He stopped only ten steps from Uma, who mentally prepared herself to fight him.

"How should I know?" Tristan answered, annoyed, and walked further in.

"Are you even sure it was a girl? I mean honestly... can girls even run that fast?"

Tristan shook his head. "It was a girl for sure... I saw her long ponytail and I think I know who it was."

A guy who was still on the road gasping for air yelled to Tristan and his friend. "Can we go now?" He held his arms in the air and looked pained.

Tristan and the other guy were still walking around in the forest scouting. Tristan, who seemed most eager to find her, commented to the guy closest to him, "They want to leave a girl in a forest with wild bears, wolves, and snakes... she could get killed."

Uma's eyes widened in fear. *Is that true?* She couldn't see their faces and she wondered if Tristan was trying to trick her to come out from hiding.

"At least we should go back and alert the headmaster," his friend said.

"You're right, better that she gets expelled than eaten alive," Tristan agreed.

Uma bit her lip. She should have never left the school. It was stupid and reckless, and the thought of the headmaster calling Aston to tell him she had been expelled made her stomach churn. It would ruin Sybina's wedding day, not to mention Uma's own chance of an education. Where would she go?

Her heart was still racing but more because of their talk about bears, wolves, snakes, and being expelled than from the running. She didn't want them to report her and she certainly didn't want them to start a search party.

Uma thought of getting up and telling them to just leave her alone, but she would be in a forest with five very large young men and even though she had fought off men before, she knew this was more than she could handle.

She made a quick assessment and watched the two boys move further into the forest. Tristan was calling out for her. "Hello, girl... If you are here... say something."

They were walking away from her and she sneaked towards the gravel road, taking another opening that gave her a bit of distance from the three boys still standing on the road. There was no doubt they would see her if she made a run for it, and this time she wouldn't have as big a head start as before.

You can do this! she told herself before taking a deep breath, ducking her head, and running quietly back to the gravel road.

Luckily for her the three boys on the road were looking in the direction of their friends, and didn't notice her before the sound of the gravel under her feet made them turn their heads.

"There she is."

"Hey, stop!!" she heard them shout behind her.

Uma didn't stop; she sprinted back towards the school and didn't turn to look back.

"Catch her."

She could hear running behind her but she didn't know if one or all five were chasing her. It was a race she wasn't willing to lose, and again she ignored all pain and ran for her life until she entered an emotional state of clarity making her rise above fear and pain.

She almost made it to the school when she heard not only loud running footsteps but also breathing behind her. She tried to run faster but a hand on her shoulder slowed her down. "Stop!"

Uma tried to shake off the hand but the guy only pulled harder, making her lose her balance and take a fall.

It hurt! Even in her heightened state she could feel that her skin had been scratched badly and her elbow had

156

taken a blow, but she didn't have time to think about it and got up again to continue her escape from her attackers.

"Don't even think about running," a loud voice shouted at her and she looked up to face five red-faced, out-of-breath young men glaring at her with hostility.

"So we meet again, dance partner," Tristan gasped slowly with a hostile tone. "What are you doing outside of school?"

Uma felt a slight satisfaction that she was much less impacted from the running than they all seemed to be. She inhaled through her nose, puffed her chest and raised her chin. She wasn't going down without a fight.

Another of the guys stepped forward and she narrowed her eyes in a warning that he ignored. "He asked you a question... what are you doing outside of school?"

"Beating you up if you step closer," Uma hissed.

At first the guys exchanged looks of astonishment and then it changed into amusement.

"What did you say?" Tristan chuckled smugly and took one more step forward.

"Stay back," Uma warned again but it only seemed to entice him more.

He reached out to touch her. "Do you expect us to be afraid of a little girl?"

She took a step back and held up her hands with her palms towards the guys. "Don't touch me!" The words were low and growling.

She heard snorting dismissive laughter from the other guys and then Tristan stepped forward again. "You don't get to tell me what to do." He reached for her shoulder, and it made Uma pull back further and hiss at him with her head lowered: "Unless you enjoy pain, I suggest you leave me the fuck alone!"

"*Oohhh!!!*" The guys in the background were laughing now. "She's a feisty little thing, isn't she?" one of them shouted. "Is she the one that beat you up in dance class as well?"

Tristan wasn't laughing. She sensed his uncertainty about the situation; he looked back to see his friends waiting for his next move.

"You are coming with us," he said and sounded authoritative when he once again moved forward to grab her shoulders with both his hands.

It all happened extremely fast when Uma used his oncoming momentum to grab his elbows and shift his balance while she leaned back and bent her knees, taking him with her. In a fluid movement she lay down gently on the road and placed a foot on Tristan's stomach, making him flip over and lie flat on his back. Uma had spent hours watching Masi warriors train in fighting techniques in the courtyard, and she was going to use every trick she had learned before she would let anyone hurt her. She was back on her feet before they really understood what had just happened.

"What the fuck!" Tristan was humiliated and angry, and the other guys were all looking at him, but Uma didn't stay around to wait for him to get up. She took the chance to run off again and heard him shout after her that he wanted to murder her. The school was close and she sprinted with only one thing on her mind. *Get to safety.*

Euphoria spread in her body when she entered through the gates and saw an adult standing close to the entrance doors. Without stopping she ran directly in that direction, hoping for backup.

The adult was an older woman who was talking to another student and didn't see Uma until she was close. Uma recognized her as the librarian and slowed down and smiled with relief.

"Hello," the old woman said in a friendly fashion and furrowed her brow when she saw the five young men approach them at great speed.

158

"Slow down, gentlemen, you don't want to run someone down."

The guys slowed and came to a stop and all of them scowled at Uma.

"Excuse me, I'm feeling unwell. Would you mind helping me to a glass of water?" Uma asked the librarian in a low voice and the old woman nodded and signaled for Uma to go inside.

Uma didn't have to look back; she knew she had just made five enemies at school and that she would have to look over her shoulder from now on. She swallowed hard and made a fist without looking back.

CHAPTER 16
Wedding Day

Nina had come by early and helped Sybina get ready. She was skilled with make-up, and she arranged Sybina's hair elegantly in a braided bun on top of her head with white roses and a few artistic tendrils hanging down. Sybina hardly recognized the beautiful lady in the mirror, but she wanted Aston to be happy with her and she trusted that Nina knew his taste best. At least the dress was beautiful and simple, with a white flower pattern on it. Sybina looked almost royal, and Nina nodded satisfied.

"I will meet you later," she said and Sybina understood. After two weeks in England, she was beginning to understand the fundamentals of the language.

Sybina heard Nina leave the apartment, and with a last look in the mirror she took a deep breath and walked out to face Aston, who was pacing the living room floor.

"What do you think?" Sybina said, and to her surprise he didn't compliment her but laughed. This was not the reaction Sybina was hoping for, and she felt hurt.

"Come here," he said and led her gently back into the bathroom. She stood still as he started to pull out every pin in her hair one by one.

"Nina will be very disappointed," Sybina said, not understanding why he found her so displeasing.

"I don't care what Nina thinks. I want my wife to look herself, not a stranger."

Sybina gasped. The word wife felt so powerful. In a few hours she would be Aston's wife. At least for the next two years.

"There," he said and turned her so she could look in the mirror. Her long black hair cascaded around her shoulders beautifully.

"I love your hair like this. You are the most naturally graceful woman I know." He wasn't smiling, and it sounded more like a fact than a compliment. "You don't need all that make-up either."

Sybina fluttered her eyelids with the fake eyelashes that Nina had put on her. "I don't think we have time to undo the make-up," she said.

Aston took her hand. "That's okay. At least your hair is out again and I recognize you." He pulled her gently out of the apartment.

When they got to the city hall he parked the car and Sybina started to open her door.

"Wait," Aston said with a hand on her arm.

Sybina turned and looked at him. "What is it?"

"Are you sure?" He looked stressed and it made her nauseated. Was Aston backing out now? She swallowed hard and looked deep into his eyes. "Aston, you don't have to do this if you don't want to. You shouldn't throw away two years of your life because of me."

He blinked a few times. "Right! But that's my choice. What I'm asking is… are *you* sure?"

"Ohh. In that case—yes, I'm sure." Sybina smiled reassuringly, hiding how it bothered her to accept this huge sacrifice from him.

Aston bit his lip. "Remember you have to look like you are in love with me. It has to look real," he reminded her.

"Not a problem," Sybina answered.

"Then let's get married," he said with determination.

They walked quickly hand in hand to the city hall and were welcomed inside by Aston's closest family. It was a party of twelve with Aston's parents, sister, grandmothers, and his mother's two sisters and their husbands. His sister and mother had wanted to invite many more but Aston had refused to expand the guest list, as he had promised Sybina a small ceremony.

"What happened to your hair?" Nina asked, disappointed.

Aston shot Nina a wicked smile, taking the blame. She sent him a sisterly growl before she led them to the right room, where a marriage officiant was waiting and music playing. Everyone found their seats and sat smilingly while Sybina and Aston stood only a few feet apart looking anxiously at each other. Aston had rehearsed with Sybina when she was to answer yes, and Sybina waited for her clue when the officiant started talking. He talked for a long time before she heard Aston say "I do", smilingly, and then the officiant turned to her and talked. Sybina was so nervous she could hardly breathe, and then a motion by the door made her look up to see Tara standing there. Tara was pale and silent and staring right at Aston with deep longing in her eyes.

Aston pulled Sybina's hand to get her attention back, and Sybina looked into Aston's eyes and suddenly felt horrible for doing this to him. Maybe he was right when he said he didn't love Tara, but he deserved much better than to marry someone out of pity and obligation. And even if he hadn't met the right woman yet, it could happen any day and Sybina would become a regret in his life. *Speak up. Set him free*, her mind shouted. *Don't make him your slave and take away his freedom… you are being selfish when you know what it's like to long for freedom. If you say yes you will be the one trapping him. He will soon want his freedom and he'll come to hate you.* Sybina started hyperventilating and could only hear muffled sounds from the officiant.

Aston scowled at Tara and leaned towards Sybina. "Are you okay?"

Sybina looked down and closed her eyes with tears starting to press and a growing knot in her stomach.

"I'm sorry but I can't do this," she whispered, pushing away her fear of what was to become of her.

The wedding officiant stopped. "Sorry, what did she say?" he asked, looking at Aston.

Aston sucked in air and pleaded in a low voice. "Please, Sybina... don't do this."

Sybina looked up at him and with tears in her eyes and nothing but love for Aston she cleared her throat and said one of the few things she had learned to say in English.

"I'm so sorry, Aston."

CHAPTER 17
I'm Sorry

Aston

Aston stood pale and silent, like he had turned to stone. He was confused and looking for an explanation in Sybina's moist eyes, which were glowing with gentleness. Why would she back down now, right in front of the wedding officiant? They were so close to being married, and her timing made absolutely no sense to him.

The only reason he could find was Tara's presence in the room. Maybe Sybina had been reminded of the stupid fight they had over Tara a few days ago when she tried to make Sybina believe that Aston and Tara had sex while Sybina was out with her tutor. It was a lie, of course, and Aston shot a dirty look at Tara for showing up to stop his wedding. It had worked; Sybina had used the few words she could muster in English to tell him, and everyone else in the room, that she couldn't marry him.

Aston's mind was working quickly, and took him back to his conversation with Sybina only twenty minutes ago. When he had specifically asked her if she was sure she wanted go through with the wedding, her answer had been yes.

Aston could hear his family whisper nervously among themselves and sense them turn to look at Tara, whom they most likely knew from the articles about his kidnapping, where Tara had falsely claimed to be his girlfriend.

Aston took a step closer to Sybina, put his arms around her waist, and whispered in her ear. "Think of Uma. We are doing it for *her*, remember." Aston was a soldier at heart and saving Sybina and Uma was his mission, and even though this mission was different in nature from a military mission he was not about to give up and let Tara sabotage both Sybina's and Uma's safety.

Sybina reached out and caressed Aston's face, and he saw a tear run down her cheek.

She didn't look repulsed by him at all... and it confused him... why wouldn't she marry him when she was radiating nothing but empathy and care for him? No one had ever looked at him with greater warmth except maybe his mother.

"You can do this," he said with intensity and made Sybina look into his eyes.

"But..." she started but he interrupted her.

"Please, Sybina!"

She looked to his family and back to him, and he knew she was realizing the humiliating situation she was putting him in.

"What if you regret it?" she asked him with a pained expression.

Her words hit him right in the solar plexus. Sybina had nothing of a material kind, but still her empathy and integrity were greater than her focus on her own personal safety. This was not about him sleeping with Tara, this was about Sybina being worried about him for reasons he couldn't comprehend.

He took her hands and leaned his forehead against hers. "Sybina, this is what I want... please say yes."

Sybina took a deep long breath and whispered: "Okay."

The word was small but powerful and released a sigh of relief from Aston.

"Thank you," he said and kissed her forehead before he turned to the officiant and his family. "Just a little wedding jitters, everything is fine now."

"Tell them I was unsure of when to say yes and thought I had done something wrong," Sybina suggested softly and Aston translated to the others, who all laughed and smiled reassuringly to Sybina.

"You are doing fine, dear," Aston's father called out.

And then the officiant repeated his question to Sybina, who this time answered loud and clearly "I do."

They exchanged rings and everyone cheered happily after the words "I now declare you husband and wife," and Aston pulled Sybina into a kiss. He didn't mean for it to be anything than a quick kiss but once their lips touched he couldn't help himself and pulled Sybina closer, cupping her face with both his hands. Aston kissed Sybina in a way that was unfamiliar to him. The softness and gentleness of his kiss was that of a man kissing someone fragile and very precious to him.

Sybina put her arms around him and slid her hands up his back, returning his kiss with a tenderness and passion that surprised Aston.

"Don't forget to breathe," someone shouted, and it made Aston release his grip on Sybina's face and pull back to look at her with wonder. In his eyes Sybina looked more beautiful than ever, and he couldn't stop staring at her flawless skin, her sparkling eyes, and the radiant dark hair framing her pretty face. He was holding her hand and looked down at the simple golden wedding ring on her finger. His ring. The joy Aston felt about this significant symbol confused him. *It must be the pride of securing her safety*, Aston thought and looked up at Sybina again. She gave him a warm smile with those full lips that he had just kissed and all he could think was *more... I want more.*

Sybina

After the ceremony they were congratulated by everyone, and Aston's father even picked Sybina up and swung her around, giving her a full view of the room and a chance to notice that Tara was gone. Her new father-in-law said a whole bunch of things that she didn't understand, but she instantly liked him for his kind energy and his happiness for Aston.

Her new sister-in-law, Nina, and Aston's mother had arranged a wedding reception at his parents' home, which turned out to be a beautiful three-story house in a posh community. Nina showed Sybina around, and on the third floor she giggled as she opened the door to Aston's old room. Sybina took a few steps inside and stood still looking around. This was where Aston had lived when he was a child and a teenager. The room was fairly big, and besides a bed it had a desk, a couch, a chair, and something she had never seen before. She glanced at it, unable to understand what it was. Nina saw her confusion and broke into a grin. "Foosball table," she pronounced slowly and demonstrated how to use it. "It's fun." Nina gestured for Sybina to grab on to the handles and play a round. But before they could begin someone shouted for Nina downstairs, and it made Nina excuse herself and leave the room.

Sybina's eyes wandered the walls and took in the different posters. One showed five jet planes in formation. Another was a picture of a soldier in a jungle shooting around with two machine guns. He looked scary. A third poster showed a girl on top of a red sports car showing a lot of skin, and a fourth poster had a topless man flying in the air with white pants and a white band around his head. Sybina stepped closer to the poster trying to understand what the man was doing.

"Karate," Aston said from the doorway.

"Sorry?" Sybina turned and looked at him.

167

Aston pointed to the flying man on the poster. "The guy is doing karate. You know, fighting."

Sybina frowned... she knew fighting and war but she had never seen anyone dress like that guy on the poster. He looked ridiculous with his bare feet and completely weaponless. "He wouldn't last long in a real battle," she said dryly.

Aston smiled. "Do you prefer that guy then?" He pointed to the scary jungle man.

Sybina shrugged. "I prefer peace."

Aston moved closer and pulled her to his bed. "Come sit for a second."

Sybina sat down next to him.

"What happened back there?"

She knew he was referring to the wedding ceremony but she didn't know how to explain it to him.

Aston was fidgeting with a rubber ball that he had picked up from the bed. "I thought you wanted this, and now I feel like I've pushed you into something against your will."

Sybina leaned forward. "No, that's not it. I just feel that *you're* doing it for the wrong reasons and that you're paying too high a price," she explained.

Aston frowned. "Let me worry about that, okay?"

"Okay."

"Look, Sybina, I know this is hard with everything that happened to you in your past and I'm not asking you to love me; that would only complicate things anyway." He chuckled awkwardly. "But I'm hoping we can be friends... and that you'll learn to trust me."

Sybina nodded but internally her heart was stuck on his words. *He doesn't want my love. He wants my friendship.* She tried to change the subject. "Why did you become a soldier?"

Aston leaned back on the bed and rested his head against the wall. "Actually, it was never in my cards to become a soldier. My father is a world-renowned scientist, and everyone looked at me like I was to be the new genius of the family. But books were just not my thing. All I ever wanted was to be an elite soldier, and I joined the military right out of boarding school at nineteen."

"What did your parent say?"

"They let me, but it was hard for them to understand my fascination. They never judged me but they never praised me for my choice either. Not even when I joined the elite corps or when I received my medals."

Sybina sensed that the medals were significant to him.

"I've spent more than six years of my life in war zones. Every time I returned from duty in some sad part of the world I promised myself it would be the last time. I wanted to stay home and live in peace. But it's like a drug to me." He paused. "Here, things are safe and people talk about mundane things that make me want to puke after a while. Like how awful the rain is or how they need to lose a bit of weight or how hard it is to decide on the menu for their next party... I always felt so restless here, so bored and alone. And then I would take the next assignment to get away. To at least feel alive again."

"War makes you feel alive?" Sybina asked.

"I suppose it does. Every decision matters. You feel adrenaline. People rely on you. It's a matter of life and death, not just convenience or entertainment."

"But you left the military."

"Yes. I was offered a good position with Spread Life as Director of Security and I took it. I figured it was a step in the direction towards a more normal life. Less action but still meaningful. And I already spoke the language."

Sybina hadn't even considered that working abroad was Aston's job and that he would eventually need to leave her again. The thought of being stuck in his apartment all alone made her dizzy. "So when will you leave for your next mission?"

169

Aston smiled at her with his sea-blue eyes and the charming dimples that only came out when he smiled like this. "I have no plans of leaving anytime soon, Sybina. I think I'm needed here with you... and Uma, when we get her up here."

Sybina gave him a relieved smile that made his face split into a grin. "You didn't think I was going to ask you to come here and then leave you stranded all alone, did you? Come on, it's time to go down and open the presents, Mrs. Tailor."

As they walked downstairs hand in hand Sybina tasted the sound of her new name. *Sybina Tailor.* At the foot of the stairs Aston pulled her close and kissed her. Sybina smiled and played along for the audience while her inner voice was beginning to say inappropriate things like *I wish it was real.*

Sybina couldn't remember ever receiving a present in her life, so when they opened the presents her hands were shaking. She felt so unworthy for accepting all these extravagant gifts. She kept saying thank you as well as she could in English, and she could see people answering in ways that made everyone laugh and at one point made Aston blush. It was frustrating for Sybina not to be able to understand.

Nina was grinning loudly and pointing to Sybina, who understood that Nina was forcing her brother to translate. Aston turned to Sybina. "Everyone's very excited that you are making me stay home and they're giving us gifts that will come in handy when we have children, which they hope is soon." He said it a bit apologetically. Sybina smiled politely and opened Nina's present. It was a weekend trip to a luxurious spa resort. Nina spoke and again everyone laughed. "A good place to make a happy and relaxed baby," Aston translated and rolled his eyes at Nina.

CHAPTER 18

Traditions

Sybina

Around midnight Aston and Sybina left the party and went back to the apartment.

"Wait, I have to carry you over the doorstep," Aston said.

"Why?"

"Because it's a tradition," he laughed and reached out his hands.

"Alright," she said smilingly and placed her arms around his neck when he scooped her up in bridal style. It felt silly being carried into the apartment.

"Am I too heavy?" she said apologetically when he made a sudden stop just inside.

Aston tightened his grip on her. "Hardly," he answered without looking at her. Instead he stared into the dark hallway and made a low growl: "Nina!"

Sybina turned to see what he was seeing. She narrowed her eyes, trying to make out what she was looking at but when Aston turned on the light, she gasped.

The hallway was full of balloons in every color and long rolls of toilet paper were hanging from the lamps and the walls were scribbled with endless hearts and flaming red letters spelling: *Aston and Sybina Tailor, now husband and wife. You may kiss the bride, again and again and again and again.*

Sybina put a hand to her mouth and shook her head. "Why?" was all she could mutter.

Aston set her down and touched a letter on the wall; it was foil and peeled right off without leaving a mark. He sighed: "It's a prank on the newlyweds, I should have known she would do this."

"But Nina was at the reception with us, she couldn't have done it." Sybina reasoned.

Aston chuckled. "Nina is behind this, believe me. I know my sister!"

Slowly they made their way through all the balloons and looked into the bedroom, where rose petals were spread around on the floor and forming a heart on the bed. It looked romantic, and Sybina smiled when she saw all the candles placed around the bed.

"Is this a tradition too?" she asked.

Aston wrinkled his brows and shrugged. "I guess so," he mumbled. "I'm not a wedding expert, so I'm not sure."

Sybina reached her arms up to him and waited.

He raised his eyebrows. "What?" he asked.

"Aren't you supposed to carry me over the doorstep?"

He laughed. "No, not every doorstep, only at the front door."

"Oh," she said, feeling stupid for having misunderstood the concept. She could sense him watching her as she walked into the bedroom, and the whole set-up in the room made her nervous. Everything whispered of lovemaking: the bed, the candles, even her own heart. Would Aston want to have sex with her, despite his earlier refusal? Sybina could feel a knot in her chest and recognized it as fear of rejection. Aston was in a different league than her. He was rich and ridiculously attractive but he was a man and men had needs. Maybe he wouldn't say no if she asked him. He didn't know of the rumors that had followed her and even if he did, he probably wouldn't believe them. He was educated and not superstitious, from what she knew.

"What are you thinking about?" Aston asked her and she blushed.

"Nothing... I was just thinking about wedding traditions," she lied while walking into the bathroom. Aston followed her and stood silently leaning against the doorframe when she started to remove her heavy make-up. She ignored him because she honestly didn't know what to say to him. She couldn't tell him that everything about the wedding had been perfect, even the lame jokes about sex and children, and the frustration he picked up on was simply because it bothered her that it was all pretend when she wished it to be real. She also couldn't tell him that today had been like stepping into a fairy tale and pretending to be the princess who found her prince. Only, there was no such thing as a fairy tale and in her case it was more like an alternate universe where she could see all her dreams, try them on, and take them home for a while, but she couldn't call them her own. They didn't belong to her. They belonged to someone else and in two years she would have to give it all back.

Sybina tossed the wipes into the trash can and washed her face. It felt good; her skin could finally breathe again.

"Are you okay?" Aston asked in concern and she shot him a vague smile.

"Yes, I'm fine," she nodded and brushed her teeth, rinsed her mouth, and spit out the water. When she looked back up she saw Aston standing only a few steps behind her, meeting her eyes in the mirror.

"Sybina, what's wrong?" he asked.

Why did he have to be so damn good at reading her body language? She would have to be better at suppressing her emotions—*Or just get over your unreasonable desires and be grateful for what he's giving you,* she argued internally. *It's not fair to him.*

"Everything is fine. Thank you for a beautiful wedding," Sybina said softly and gave him her most convincing smile.

Aston stepped a little closer. "Do you need help getting out of the dress?"

"Yes, if you can unzip me that would be nice." Sybina pulled her hair to the side and let him unzip her dress. She felt his fingers run down her spine and it spread small shocks of electricity, making her gasp. Aston looked at her with surprise and then he planted a soft kiss on her neck.

Sybina didn't move but just stood there waiting, keeping herself from turning to him and throwing herself at him. The only thing keeping her back was the strong fear-of-rejection knot in her chest that was now replaying his answer to her question about sex:

"What about sex?" she had asked him when he first suggested marriage and his answer had been firm. She could still see him shaking his head, telling her: "I don't want sex with you. It's not about that, Sybina... It's about getting you to a safe place."

He doesn't want to have sex with me, she reminded herself.

"What do you want, Sybina?"

"What do you mean?" she answered.

"Just promise me that you will tell me if there is something you want."

I want you to love me, she thought, but she couldn't say that out loud; instead she answered, "I don't know what to tell you. I'm happy."

Aston sent her a long glance. "Good, I want you to be happy."

Sybina stepped out of the dress in front of him. He had already seen her body, and her pride and vanity longed for the same reaction he had shown her the first time. He was still standing close behind her when she bent over to pick up her dress. Straightening again, she caught a glance of Aston in the mirror that made her blood run cold. It was a mere nanosecond before he regained his cool, but she had seen an animalistic, raw desire in his eyes and it didn't speak of lovemaking, it told of hard-core fucking.

She had misjudged him. Aston might not be attracted to her, compared to his usual type of women, but he was still a man and he had needs. Flashing her naked body in front of him was playing with fire. She was in his apartment and she was his lawfully wedded wife. He could do to her as he wanted. She didn't know the laws of England, but where she came from a wife couldn't be raped; her body belonged to her husband. Sybina had seen what men could do to women sexually, and it scared her. Images of all the women she had treated for sexual injuries ran through her mind: ripped anuses and vaginas, bruises, and broken bones. Quickly she grabbed the dress, hurrying back into the bedroom where she hung it in the closet before she went to bed.

Aston came five minutes later, and by then Sybina had calmed herself and come to the conclusion that if he wanted to rape her, he would have done it already. After all, she had been in his bed and he hadn't touched her. Aston was a good guy.

She watched him strip down to his boxers and found it hard not to stare. Aston got into bed beside her and propped himself up on his elbow, taking her hand on the top of the covers. "Sybina... you know I would never hurt you... right?" He was looking into her eyes.

"Hurt me?"

"That I would never rape you."

Sybina had been too afraid to ask the question, but since he brought it up, she had to know: "Have you never raped a woman?"

"*No!*" His answer came immediately. "I didn't become a soldier because I loved violence but because I wanted to protect people. I could never rape a woman."

She could see he was telling the truth and relaxed again. Aston wouldn't hurt her.

175

"Good... How many women have you been with?" Sybina asked curiously, even though part of her really didn't want to know.

"More than I like to admit," he sighed, lying propped up on his elbow, facing her.

Sybina turned around on her stomach with her head resting on one hand and the other holding his hand. He was so beautiful, and she felt so foolish for having been scared of him, even for a moment. She would have given herself freely to this amazing man; he had no need to be rough with her, if he wanted sex. Without knowing it Sybina bit her lip and wrinkled her forehead.

"What is it, Sybina, are you still thinking of the stupid wedding traditions?" Aston asked.

She looked down. "I've never been to a wedding in Spirima, I only know one of the wedding traditions of my country."

"And which one is that?" Aston asked and stroked her hair. His kindness gave her strength to look into his eyes.

"The marriage is traditionally consummated by sex," she said and flushed red.

Aston pulled away a little. "Listen, Sybina, I promised I wouldn't ask that of you. You really don't need to."

"In this country, is it not tradition to have sex on your wedding night?" she asked him challengingly.

He smiled amused. "I believe it is."

"So...?" She raised an eyebrow.

Aston shook his head. "You don't have to, Sybina. Really it's okay."

If Sybina hadn't seen his raw expression of lust in the bathroom she would have turned away in shame and defeat. But now that he had revealed himself, she knew he had fleshly desires and she wouldn't give up so easily.

"But do you want to?" Her eyes were completely focused on reading his expression.

Aston blinked rapidly but it took a long time before he answered. "Yes, I want to."

"Really?" she couldn't help her giddy smile.

"You sound surprised," he said with a soft head shake. "I wanted you since the first day I met you... How could I not?... I'm only human."

More color spread in Sybina's cheeks, butterflies swarmed around her stomach, and she was sure that if butterflies had a voice, hers would be giggling with deep joy and feminine vanity. "I think we should have sex," she said softly and squeezed his hand.

Aston was hesitant for a few seconds before he leaned closer, softly placing a kiss on her lips almost like he was testing if this was a joke.

"Would you mind lighting the candles?" she asked him in a low voice.

Aston pulled back slightly and turned his head towards all the candles around the bed. Was he counting them? He narrowed his eyes and Sybina tried to swallow a chuckle; he was like an open book to her in that moment and she knew he couldn't care less about candlelight, but wanted to stay close to her. It warmed her heart.

"Just a few will do," she whispered and watched him get out of bed to light six of the candles, making the room glow in a soft, romantic, flickering light.

Sybina hungrily admired his strong naked back; the thought that he was going to make love to her was both exhilarating and frightening. Sybina had no doubt Aston was an experienced lover and she didn't want to disappoint him. She thought about telling him about her lack of experience but she feared that if he knew she was a virgin, he might start interrogating her to understand why, and then she would have to reveal the rumors. No, she wouldn't tell him, at least not now; she wanted this one night, even if it was the only one she ever got to experience.

Aston was quickly back in bed and kissed her again, this time letting his hand slide behind her head, thrusting his fingers into her hair and pulling her towards him in a deeper and more passionate kiss. He sucked on her lower lip and smiled before his tongue entered her mouth and playfully teased her. The thought of someone else's tongue in her mouth had always grossed Sybina out but with Aston it wasn't disgusting at all; it was intimate and right and he tasted sweet from his mint toothpaste.

Overwhelmed by the way Aston playfully nibbled her lips and tasted her mouth, Sybina followed his lead with a pounding heart and carefully drew the tip of her tongue along the inner edge of Aston's lower lip. The breathy noise that escaped from the back of his throat encouraged her to be braver, and she sucked his upper lip and let her hands weave into that delicious golden hair on his hard chest.

"I knew kissing you would be amazing," Aston groaned into her mouth, doubling her desire and giving her enough confidence to entwine her tongue with his.

A tingling sensation spread in Sybina's lower belly from the kissing and the fact that Aston's hand was traveling down her side and brushing her breast. Through the fabric of her t-shirt Aston's touch felt like little jolts of electricity and made every nerve ending in her body alert, and her sensitive nipples hardened into tight buds. When Aston pulled her left thigh over his hip and cupped her behind with a low growl of raw desire, a small gasp of excitement escaped Sybina.

Aston immediately pulled back. "Are you okay?" he asked hoarsely and when she nodded he leaned his forehead against hers. "Tell me if you want me to stop."

"Don't stop," was all she could say with her heart pounding and her longing for more of that delicious warmth that spread down between her hips every time he kissed her. To her own astonishment she began to rub

178

herself against him and let her hands move to his strong shoulders—almost like an ancient ancestral predisposition was kicking in and telling her how to progress in this encounter. The last three weeks had been one long buildup to this moment, and Sybina leaned her head back giving in to all the suppressed feelings and desires she had for Aston, thinking of his words: *I wanted you since the first day I met you.*

"You have no idea how beautiful and sexy you are," he muttered in her hair and planted kisses all the way from her mouth down to her collarbone, where he was stopped by her t-shirt. It took Aston only seconds to get it off her, so he could continue down to her breasts. Aston pushed Sybina gently onto her back and with his hands, tongue, and teeth he played with the full breasts that filled his hands perfectly. Sybina arched her back in a strange torturous tug of war between pleasure, whenever Aston whisked his tongue over her sensitive peaks, and pain when he took them between his teeth.

"I've wanted to play with these for so long," Aston muttered while sucking on her pebbled tips.

Sybina wanted to tell Aston that she had desired him from the beginning too, but talking about her feelings was not something she knew how to do and instead she let her fingers run through his short hair and wriggled her butt with a seductive smile.

"Is that an invitation?" Aston grinned and moved his hands down to her panties. He lay on his side wearing only his black boxers, bulging with his erection that Sybina had seen in all its glory when she helped him take a shower in Spirima. Back then, it had taken her by surprise but now she was curious and wondered what Aston would do if she touched him.

Before she could act on her thought, an intense feeling made her close her eyes and sigh with delight. Aston's hand had reached down to touch her most sensitive spot and with his slow circling movements, goosebumps spread up and down her legs and arms. Even her head was spinning and she couldn't think of anything but pleasure. Pure pleasure that she never dreamed existed.

With her eyes closed she lifted her arms in a gesture of surrender and felt Aston move in between her legs and pull her panties off. She cracked open an eye to see a satisfied smile on Aston's face telling her that this was his game and he knew exactly how to play it.

"Just relax," he told her before she felt his warm breath on her inner thigh. The area was so incredibly sensitive that she pulled back from him. Like a maestro controlling the pace of the music, Aston put a hand on her lower belly and eased her, before he continued.

His tongue worked skillfully and slowly towards her most sensitive spot, and when he reached it Sybina couldn't lie still anymore. It was such a powerful sensation, unlike anything she had ever been able to evoke by touching it herself.

Her hips started moving and Aston steadied her with a firm grip on her hips.

"I love how responsive you are to me," he said and eased a finger inside her. Sybina tensed up, overwhelmed with the many impressions and new things from the kisses to the touching, licking, and now this. It was too good to be true and a rush of fear flooded over her, with a roaring thought shouting: *What if I'm not good enough?*

"Relax. I won't hurt you," Aston said and returned to kiss her mouth again. This time she was more skilled and welcomed him by pulling him close and using her teeth to gently tug at his lower lip. Aston positioned himself between her spread legs; still in his boxers, he moved his erection against her and pulled her hands to the side of her head, lacing his fingers with hers. It felt amazing with him all around her, his weight on her, and his mouth close to her ear with erotic breathing that made her open her mouth in awe.

"Ahh," she breathed before he dampened her sweet noises of pleasure by kissing her again. Sybina lost herself in the kiss, and when he pulled back to look at her she lost herself in his beautiful blue eyes and heard her heart shout words of love, words that couldn't be said out loud. Nothing crossed her lips other than sweet moans.

His breathing became faster and she could feel his heart rate speed up against her chest and his hands squeeze hers. "I promise I won't hurt you but I really want you," he said in a hoarse voice.

"I want you too," she whispered back and Aston didn't need further encouragement, but removed his boxers and pressed his rock-hard cock against her belly. Sybina looked down and from the look of it she was certain he would never fit inside her, but his closeness, his masculine fragrance, and his arousal for her created a deep pull to feel him inside her.

"Tell me you want this," he asked and she responded by lifting herself to kiss him.

"Sybina, I need to hear you say it. Do you want me?" he asked.

"Yes, I want you." *To be my first*, she thought, but left out that last part.

She felt him press himself against her entrance. Sybina's eyes were wide open and her nails boring into Aston's upper arms as she lay still, waiting for the pain she had heard about.

"Relax," Aston whispered in her ear and started kissing her earlobe, then her neck, and then her lips.

"You need to relax first, beautiful," he whispered in her ear, magically distracting her from her fear with his skillful fingers that expertly pushed her buttons of raw lust and desire. Sybina's chest was moving up and down with her low moans and she opened her eyes, connecting with Aston, who was radiating desire and tenderness. When he pressed against her entrance again Sybina gave him a smile of lust and curiosity.

The first sensation of his tip inside her made her widen her eyes but there was no pain. Slowly he started rocking back and forth, and for every move he pushed a bit deeper.

"Christ, you are tight," he said and continued to work his way in.

Painful pressure built inside her. It hurt, and she bit her inner lip suppressing her pain.

"You've got to relax, Sybina. You are too tense. I don't want to hurt you," Aston whispered into her ear.

With a deep breath Sybina spread her legs further, arched her back, and pulled him closer. Aston pressed harder and deeper and a moment of sharp pain made her gasp out loud.

"What's wrong?" he asked when she stiffened, but Sybina just shook her head and signaled him to continue. He continued gently, carefully examining her eyes for discomfort.

"Relax, you're safe with me," he whispered and kissed her forehead, the tip of her nose, her cheeks, her lips, her chin, and her neck. His gentle affection swelled her heart, and with a deep breath she let go of the tension and pain and welcomed the slow-growing pleasure that took its place.

"That's it," he smiled at her and picked up the pace of his thrusting. It was such a strange and wonderful sensation having him fully inside her, and after losing herself in Aston's kisses, his rhythm, his fingers massaging her soft spot, his hoarse moans, and compliments about how much he wanted her, Sybina experienced her first orgasm. It started as a tingling and ran through her body with a force she couldn't control or compare to anything she had ever felt in her life. Without realizing it, she was calling his name, and the sound of her euphoria pushed Aston to climax and come inside her.

Aston lay on top of her with all his weight and she nuzzled his hair, dreamily, while enjoying the sensation of him still inside her. Then he kissed her and rolled down beside her, leaving Sybina with a new view on the world. For minutes they didn't speak and myriads of thoughts ran through her: she had treated female slaves for sexual injuries as long as she had been at the Masi headquarters. It had disgusted her and made her angry with the Masi warriors, but she had also seen a world outside the Masi headquarters and knew there could be love between men and women. Her parents had loved each other. And in the village where she had lived with the old healer, she had helped cure the village people and bring their babies safely into the world. She had seen love and affection between the married couples. But nowhere had she heard of such a thing as sexual pleasure for a woman. No one had prepared her and she wondered if she was an anomaly. Wasn't sex something men took and woman gave in exchange for the joy of motherhood?

Aston turned and looked at her. "Wow, I've never seen that expression on your face before... what are you thinking?"

Sybina raised both her brows and the only word that hit her was "wonderful," but it didn't begin to describe the revelation she felt inside. If Aston wouldn't mind doing it again then she would like to experiment with this part of life that was so unfamiliar to her.

She was twenty-seven. She never had a boyfriend; she never had prospects of having a family of her own, even though it was her biggest dream. She hadn't dared to dream about sexual gratification but now that she knew it existed, she felt like she was on fire. "Well, I'm glad you liked it," Aston chuckled and kissed her again.

Sybina grabbed him and kissed him back, demanding, signaling that she wanted to go again. Aston pulled back and gave her a curious look. She felt a raw hunger and started moving towards him, pressing him down on his back. He watched, surprised, as she climbed on top of him and started kissing and licking his chest. It was as if she were hypnotized, fixated on her prey, wanting to experience that addictive feeling of sexual pleasure again. Aston didn't speak; his face changed into a quietly observing expression, like he was trying to understand what was happening to her.

Sybina's eyes locked with his and communicated her desire and intention. He swallowed hard and closed his eyes as she grabbed his shaft and instinctively moved her hands up and down, excited to see it quickly grow again. Sybina was a small woman and when she eased down over him she wanted to take all of him, but found pleasure enough in the first half of his length. With her strong legs she rode him, chasing that same feeling her orgasm had given her before. She could see him opening his eyes, smiling at her, and she leaned back her head, letting her long hair fall behind her. Aston put his strong hands on her waist and slowed her down, then he forced her to be still. Sybina waited, wondering if she had done something wrong.

"Go deeper," he said and coaxed her down further, filling her even more.

"I can't," she whispered afraid he was going to tear her. She felt one of his hands move up behind her head and pull her down to him. With a gentle kiss he whispered into her mouth. "You can... trust me."

He waited a few seconds for her to expand before he thrust deeper inside her again, and again, until the fifth time she felt him stretch her and go all in. It hurt and she tensed. Aston held her still and didn't move inside her, but just kissed her deeply and waited for her to get used to his size. As soon as the pain lifted Sybina's hunger returned. She wanted to experience the brief feeling of euphoria that her orgasm had given her before and she started moving again. Aston took the hint and lifted her butt just enough that he could slide in and out of her in a fast pace that made her shiver. "Yes," she moaned, completely in her own bubble of delight. "Yes!" Aston kept going relentlessly and then it happened again... the same sweet feeling of liquid sunshine came flooding through Sybina's body and filled her with intense joy and satisfaction. "Yes, yes, yes, Aston," she breathed when she felt her insides convulse in small cramps of pure ecstasy.

"Yes, come for me," Aston exclaimed hoarsely and turned her around. Sybina was like clay in his hands—so content and happy that she would have allowed him to do anything at that point. "I want more of you," he groaned and pushed himself into her from behind.

Sybina was lost for words; her mind was no longer working and she was reduced to only feelings and sensations. With her female parts swollen and still pounding from her orgasms, all her nerve ending responded to Aston's every touch with heightened sensitivity making her gasp from his slightest touch. She heard herself moan in pleasure and bit her lips from the arousing sounds of his ragged breathing.

Sybina looked back and saw Aston glowing with raw lust for her. Little drops of sweat formed on his forehead; his eyes were hooded and his mouth open. "It. Feels. So. Good," he groaned, staccato, before he tightened his hands almost painfully around her hips, rolled his eyes back, and uttered a deep guttural sound that sounded almost like her name. She was fascinated with the way his face went from almost pained to angelic and peaceful, with a deep and long exhalation of air. Sybina could feel him inside her as he held on to her and pulled her body down to a position of spooning.

185

"I didn't expect a wedding night like this," he panted while trying to catch his breath.

They lay still together, breathing slowly, cooling off and falling asleep.

CHAPTER 19
Rude Suggestions

The next morning Sybina woke up with a full bladder and headed for the bathroom. Images of last night came back and made her yawn and smile at the same time. She peed and washed her hands and then she looked at her reflection in the mirror. She saw beauty. Feminine beauty. Sensual beauty. Sybina had never spent much time in front of a mirror. Her looks had been irrelevant and so had her femininity and sexuality. For the woman looking back at her from the mirror those things were very relevant. They were her new favorite things in life.

Sybina felt sore and sticky between her legs, and the thought of why made her smile. She took a quick shower without getting her hair wet. Her eyes were closed as she felt the warm water and let scenes from yesterday play in her mind. With a finger she found that place Aston had touched her yesterday. Immediately she felt her blood rushing warmly through her body and she decided to return to the bedroom and wake up Aston with some morning sex. But Aston was already awake and he looked all... wrong.

Sybina looked from his face down to the white sheets and saw what he was seeing. Blood. Smeared blood. She sat down on the edge of the bed.

"I thought you said your period wasn't until next week?" he asked, concerned.

"It isn't," Sybina said

"Then why did you bleed? Did I hurt you?" He ran his hands through his hair and looked like he was trying to think everything through.

"I don't know. I don't think so." She thought of how he had hurt inside her. "Maybe you're too big for me?" she pondered out loud.

Aston gave a small smile. "Even though I would like to flatter myself, I don't think that's the problem. Did you bleed before?"

"Before?"

"After sex with other men."

"What other men?" Sybina asked, puzzled.

"The other men you had sex with," Aston clarified but she was clueless as to where the blood had come from.

"Sybina... you told me you had sex with other men."

Sybina shook her head. "No, I didn't."

"You told me that the female slaves had duties and were expected to service the soldiers."

"Yes." She remembered having said that.

"Well..."

"Ohh." Sybina suddenly understood that Aston thought she had been including herself as one of the slaves with those duties. "They didn't want me," she said matter-of-factly.

His mouth dropped open. "What?"

Sybina nodded.

He snorted. "Listen... there is something you're not telling me...I refuse to believe any guy in his right mind wouldn't want you."

Sybina smiled and started to find this amusing... Aston was so amazing with the things he saw in her, what other men never had.

"They were afraid of me."

He looked suspicious. "What do you mean?"

"They all believed I'm a witch." Sybina waited for Aston's reaction.

He tilted his head slightly and narrowed his eyes. "I still don't understand."

"Then let me explain it better." Sybina pulled a blanket around her bare shoulders. "You remember I told you I was bought by the village healer, right?"

He nodded.

"People believed she was a witch, and after a certain incident with a man's penis they came to believe I was a witch too and that I could make men impotent by touching their penises."

"Ha!" Aston snorted and shook his head and then he signaled for her to go on.

Sybina rubbed her nose a little and then she spoke. "When I was sixteen an old man came to my house and when he realized the old healer wasn't home he tried to rape me. Before I understood what was happening, he forced me to touch his penis and I ripped my hand away. Maybe I could have knocked him out, but I didn't want to hurt him, so I told him I could make him impotent with a touch. He didn't believe me and I couldn't convince him to give it up until the old witch came home and saw him chase me around the house. She didn't like men to begin with, so she threw him out, shouting about his foul behavior toward me and making sure all the neighbors heard.

"Weeks later his wife spread the rumor that my curse was making her husband impotent. In reality the old healer had added some new things to his heart medicine, but she wanted to be sure he left me alone and started the rumor that if I touched a man's private parts he would be impotent. The rumor followed me to the headquarters and I never tried to argue against it, because it gave me protection from the soldiers."

"You're joking?"

"No."

Aston was looking down at the bloodstain again. "So yesterday you'd never had sex before."

Sybina shook her head.

"Wow," Aston said and rested his head in his hands for a moment before he looked up with a slight head shake. "And all this time I was worried that you had been tormented and abused by the soldiers."

Sybina gave him a smile in response and it made Aston loosen up and break into an infectious laugh. "Thank God Masi soldiers are so stupid."

Sybina laughed with him.

"I really had no idea," Aston looked at her like he was seeing her for the first time. "Wow, I literally took your virginity on our wedding night without knowing it. That explains why you were so bloody tight... I just thought you were afraid and tense."

Sybina bit her lip. She had been frightened and tense for a while, but there was no need to talk about that now.

"What about other things?" he asked.

"What other things?" Sybina frowned.

"Maybe in the village? Surely there must have been someone you made out with... you know, kissing... heavy petting?"

Sybina shook her head. "I'm afraid not."

"Didn't you ever want to?" he asked perplexed.

Sybina shrugged. "I don't think you understand what my situation was like."

"What do you mean?"

"Even if I had found someone to like we wouldn't have been able to see each other. The healer didn't allow me to walk around freely, and the only times I was out was when I was with her. Sometimes she would leave me home alone, but not for long. When I was sold to the general I was picked up by two of his soldiers and taken directly to the headquarters and placed in the basement. In the beginning a few soldiers tried to come on to me, but they were easily scared with warnings of loss of potency."

"So… you were completely untouched - ha, imagine that," Aston pondered out loud before he suddenly became serious. "Listen, I'm sorry I came inside you… that was reckless," he apologized. "There's a pill you can take to be sure you won't get pregnant; we should get one for you."

Sybina pulled back, clearly showing that she would never take such a pill.

Aston kept pushing until he finally gave up and threw his hands up in the air. "Fine, hopefully nothing happened, but we can't have sex again without protection."

"Protection against babies?" Sybina asked.

"Yes."

Sybina didn't speak. She only knew one sort of contraception and that was sterilization. The general never took chances after Uma was born. He almost lost his favorite slave in childbirth, and he had no need to breed more slaves when he could freely hand-pick from the infidel women the Masi warriors kidnapped. On his orders Sybina had operated on all the female slaves and made sure they wouldn't get pregnant, just like she had done with so many women in the village who had too many children already.

With the slaves it was different though, and the youngest girl had been only sixteen when Sybina made sure she would never conceive. The girl had thanked her after the procedure but that night Sybina cried herself to sleep. She knew the Masi headquarters was no place for children or pregnancies, but being forced to take away the women's ability to bear children, when it was her biggest dream herself, had been one of the worst experiences in her life. She couldn't believe Aston would ask that of her.

"No," she said firmly.

"But Sybina, you don't want to get pregnant."

"No protection," she said again.

"I don't understand, I thought you liked it yesterday."

"I did. But not that much."

Aston narrowed his eyes. "There's no way I'm having a kid. Either we use protection or we won't have sex."

"Then we won't have sex," she concluded.

"You can't be serious... Tell me you're joking." He threw his hands in the air and exhaled forcefully, but she really didn't care how frustrated he was. She wouldn't get a sterilization to have sex with him. It was out of the question. Sybina could tell Aston wasn't done debating this, and she found him rude to have even suggested it in the first place.

Offended, she got up and turned her back on him, clearly showing that to her, this conversation was over. "I want to check up on Uma," she said and left.

From the bed behind her she heard a loud growl coming from Aston.

It was nice talking to Uma, as it helped Sybina take her mind off her own problems. Uma tried to put on a brave attitude and only spoke about the good things at the school—the library, her dance teacher, and the morning runs. Sybina asked about her new friends, but from the way Uma quickly changed the subject Sybina understood that she hadn't connected with anyone yet.

Uma asked about the wedding and laughed at some of the funny things Sybina told her. "I wish you could have been there. I can't wait till you can come and stay with us?"

"When is that?" Uma asked.

"Aston says that it will take a while, but you can come visit us on a tourist visa in a few months. How does that sound?"

"I would love that," Uma said dreamily, and Sybina finally heard genuine happiness in her voice again.

When they broke off the conversation Sybina called the counselor at Uma's school. Only he and the headmaster knew of Uma's background, and Sybina was hoping that the counselor, Mr. Tollon, would be helpful in working through some of the emotional wounds that Uma was left with.

"How is she doing?" Sybina asked.

"Well, it's only been two weeks and she's still settling in. Academically she's far behind, of course, but all her teachers report that she is determined and bright. Uma really wants to catch up and we are all impressed with her work ethic." Sybina sensed a *but* coming. "Socially Uma is challenged, though. She has no social skills to make friends and the other kids find her hostile."

"Hostile?"

"Well, yes. The boys seem to be a bit scared of her. I mean it's understandable that she doesn't trust men and boys, but the problem is that the more she resents them, the more it becomes a sport for them to get close to her."

Sybina raised her eyebrows thinking of the few men that she had seen try to get close to Uma. "And how is that working for the boys?" she asked, interested.

"Well... let's see... there have been a few incidents."

"Care to elaborate?"

"Hmm... yes, one got kicked in his private parts during dance class."

"Oh no, I hope he's not seriously injured," Sybina asked worriedly, thinking that violence like that might get Uma expelled.

"No, no, he's fine now and I had a talk with Uma about the incident."

"Anything else?" Sybina was afraid to ask.

"Yes... She regularly threatens any boy that comes near her and although it hasn't been confirmed yet, there's a rumor saying she might have been in a fight with some older boys yesterday... but the details are unclear as none of the boys will admit it."

"Do you know why they got in a fight?"

"Not in detail, but I've had a conversation with the guys and asked that they leave her alone. Can't say that it's been working, though. She seems to be attracting them like flies... it's become their favorite game of the day, I'm afraid. To test her and challenge her."

"That doesn't sound good... And have you made any progress with her in your sessions?"

"Hmm." Mr. Tollon sighed. "I wish I had, but my gender is against me. From a professional standpoint I find Uma very fascinating and would very much love to get inside her head and understand what she thinks; but in the two sessions I've had with her, she's been completely closed off and won't answer any of my questions about her past. Last week she just looked bored with my attempts but this week I pressured her a bit too much, and she stared at me like she was figuring out the best way to kill me. It was very disturbing, to be honest."

"I see. I'll talk to her about it, I promise."

"Yes, please do. We all want her to be happy here."

"Thank you, Mr. Tollon, I appreciate it."

When Sybina put down the phone she felt sad for Uma. The girl had been through enough, and she wished the boys would just leave her alone. She wondered why Uma hadn't told her about the incidents. *Probably because she doesn't want me to worry. Everything will be much easier when she moves up here,* Sybina thought and sighed.

She wanted to talk to Aston about it, but she was still upset with his rude suggestion and decided on a walk in the park to clear her head instead.

When she got there, people were enjoying the nice weather playing games or just relaxing on picnic blankets. She walked around trying to organize her thoughts but then a sight caught Sybina's eye and made her sit down on the grass, quietly observing from a distance. It was a family with three children. The youngest girl was chasing a butterfly and got upset when it flew away. Her brother, who was eight or nine, sat up and yelled at his little sister when she ran over his magazine. They had an older sister with long brown hair, not much older than twelve, and Sybina saw how she tried to solve the conflict between her siblings and was rewarded with only rude faces. After a while the girl gave up and complained to her parents. Sybina saw the mother look annoyed and give reprimands to the two small ones from the picnic blanket she was sitting on.

Sybina was mesmerized because this was just like the image she remembered from her childhood, the family picnic she had drawn on the wall of the infirmary. But unlike this family picnic her memory was idyllic; she couldn't remember ever fighting with her siblings. *Did we never fight?* The answer came from deep within. *Of course we did.*

A realization hit her: *I must have glamorized my childhood. Forgotten about anything bad and held on rigidly to the happy memories.* It made sense to hold on to the happy memories as a way to get through her sixteen years as a slave.

She couldn't take her eyes off the family, and watched how the parents returned to a conversation and the older daughter challenged her younger siblings to a race. The older girl was so eager to please her siblings that she didn't run full speed. Her legs were longer and she could have easily won, but her brother was running full speed and beat her to it. And then it happened. The boy was so focused on running and looking back to see how far ahead he was, that he didn't see the stone in front of him. He tripped head first and rolled around on the grass before he lay still—unnaturally still. The scream from the older sister was loud, and immediately Sybina jumped up and sprinted to the boy, called by instinct.

She got there just before his parents and shouted "*No*" when his father reached out to pick the boy up.

"Wait!" she said with her limited vocabulary and kneeled down by the boy's head, letting her fingers run over his head, neck, and spine. The boy was breathing but unconscious, and Sybina already knew he had injured his back and neck; she could feel several of his vertebrae pushed out of place. She considered treating him here, but she was a stranger to these people and if they mistakenly thought she had caused him harm she would be in trouble.

The mother came running and was trying to get to her boy too. Sybina shook her head and pointed to his head.

"No," she said and wished she had the words to explain to them what was wrong.

"Call an ambulance," the father yelled and the mother pulled out her phone while Sybina took a position on her knees, letting her legs hold the boys head stable while she gently used a fingertip to open the boy's mouth and make sure his breathing was unhindered.

Sybina didn't say anything but she understood the panic and fear they expressed and could hear voices around them as a crowd gathered.

"You should place him in recovery position," someone shouted and the father leaned forward again, wanting to turn his son onto his side. Sybina leaned forward, placing her hands on the ground on each side of the boy, shielding the boy with her body. "No," she said with an authoritative tone and looked directly into the father's eyes. He was very close to her and with a quick movement she reached up and put her hand behind his neck, pressing on his spine. "Not good" were the only words she could find in English. She couldn't explain it better, but he nodded with big frightened eyes.

"I think she's saying that there could be a spinal injury," the father said, pale and with tears in his eyes. She saw him grab his son's hand and sit quietly beside him.

When the ambulance arrived, Sybina stepped aside and watched the paramedics work. They asked questions and put a device around the boy's neck to support his head before they lifted him gently to a stretcher. Sybina turned around and left. Her work here was done and she only hoped the boy would be all right.

Walking away from the site she thought about the father and the love and protectiveness he had shown towards his son.

Why didn't Aston want children? To Sybina, children were small miracles, and she was sure Aston would be as loving and protective as the father who was now in the ambulance. Aston was such a mystery to her.

When she returned home Aston wasn't there, and she turned on the TV. She had found it was an excellent way to learn English; she picked up new words all the time.

Aston walked in four hours later when she was chopping a salad, and she didn't bother asking him where he had been. He tried to make small talk about the fabulous weather and asked her if she wanted to go for a walk.

"No thank you, I already did," she answered dismissively.

"Listen, Sybina, I don't understand why you got so angry earlier. It's not like I'm being unreasonable for wanting to use protection. I mean it's in your interest too," he said with a deep sigh.

Her response was a blazing look of dislike.

"Wow," Aston raised both his brows and palms. "Is it a religious thing?"

Sybina just snorted, offended. She wasn't religious. The only religion available to her had been Masi, and she stopped believing in him when he took her family and made her a slave. No god could be that cruel.

"I don't want to discuss it," she exclaimed in annoyance and turned away.

Aston raised his voice slightly. "Yeah, well, that's too bad, because I'm not done discussing it and I can tell you two things for sure." He walked closer to her and stopped just in front of her, almost taking her breath away with his raw masculinity and the heat radiating from him. Sybina leaned back to create greater distance. She wanted to ask him which two things he could tell her, but she couldn't speak—couldn't focus on anything but the way Aston was gazing at her mouth and swallowing hard. Involuntary she wet her lips expecting him to kiss her; she wanted him to kiss her even though it made no sense to her. She was angry at him for good reason, and she wanted him to know that. Kissing him would send the wrong signal.

Aston kept stoically still when he said: "I want to have sex with you."

Now it was Sybina's turn to swallow hard. She put down the knife in her hand and looked up at him. "What's stopping you?" she heard herself say. Aston gasped and then he kissed her, hard and needy.

Sybina returned the kiss, mentally kicking herself. *Stop it. Just pull away now. As in any time now...* But her mouth and body overruled her mind and kept kissing Aston, who lifted her onto the kitchen counter and pressed himself between her legs.

"I want you so fucking bad, Sybina," he moaned, and she felt him tug and suck at her lips.

"I want you too," she said into his mouth and leaned her head back.

He gave her a heated, sexual laugh. "I knew you would come around."

198

His words made her stop and look at him. "I'm not coming around," she pointed out. "You are."

Aston pulled back and snapped his head up. "There's no way in hell we're having sex without protection. *I don't want a fucking baby.*" The last part of his sentence came out with a sneer.

Sybina sent him an icy glance and moved her head close enough that they were nose to nose. He was still standing between her legs but the temperature had just dropped from hot and steamy to cold and challenging. "Then get your hands off me."

Aston kept his ground and his jaw was as stiff as his erection pressing against the v of her thighs. "I don't think so. You want this as much as I do."

Sybina pushed him but his hard chest didn't move an inch. *I'll never hurt you*, she remembered him saying and from the look in his eyes she wasn't scared. He was frustrated but not dangerous.

"I'm not afraid of you," she said "You never raped a woman… remember?" Her words were unnecessary mocking, and internally she was shaking her head. She wasn't herself around him. The calmness and intellect she had practiced to perfection when it came to handling conflicts with Masi warriors felt out of reach around Aston. He got under her skin and she couldn't think clearly.

Aston narrowed his eyes. "Yet. But I might, if you keep provoking me like that."

Her head tilted a bit, scanning him. "You wouldn't dare," she pointed out, knowing he was bluffing.

Aston's nostrils were flaring, and with an arrogant movement he leaned closer and spoke against her ear in a low-pitched voice. "Maybe you'll think it's a dream when you feel me inside you, and I bet that when you do, you'll surrender to me like you did yesterday."

She snorted but didn't move away. He smelled so good, almost intoxicating, and if it hadn't been because the bastard expected her to choose between him and motherhood, she would have surrendered right then and there.

"You wouldn't sink so low," she hissed.

"You want me as much as I want you... don't think for a minute I don't know it," he said hoarsely and didn't move a muscle when she pushed him again. "I'll have you again, Sybina. Count on it!"

Sybina squared her shoulders. He had told her he was bad with relationships and now she could see why. The man was a Neanderthal, and so competitive that he didn't want to give up in a fight. He wanted the last word and said things that were completely out of character and that she didn't think he meant for one second. *I hope he means the last part, though*, she thought.

For a second the impasse between them was physical, with him still between her legs and with both hands firmly gripping her thighs, and with her leaning back to create distance. They were bluntly staring at each other with narrowed eyes in a wordless power struggle.

Think Sybina, think. But it was almost impossible with Aston oozing with testosterone so close to her; for some unfathomable reason it turned her on to see him so demanding and masculine.

You can do this, she chanted internally and a calmness fell over her. Aston might be bigger and stronger physically, but she had a different type of strength. Once, Hunilla—Uma's mom—had called her a mental warrior and complimented her for her way of dealing with the Masi soldiers using only her verbal skills. If Aston thought he could pressure her into something against her will, he was mistaken. With a deep sigh Sybina centered herself and smiled sweetly at him. Her voice became soft. "I know you would never hurt me or make me do something

200

against my will. I see it in you, Aston. You are noble and brave and have no need to use force against a woman." Her hand caressed his chin and she saw him open his mouth to speak but then he closed it again.

"This is really silly. You're the one who saved me and protects me, not an abusive Masi warrior." Ignoring his perplexed expression, Sybina leaned in and hugged him. Soon she felt his arms hugging her back and a deep sigh coming from him as well.

"You would never hurt me, Aston. Would you?" she whispered with her head leaning on his shoulder.

His voice was thick when he answered. "No, Sybina, I would never hurt you."

She pulled back and gave him a peck on the chin. "That's why I trust you so much."

Her words worked magically; when she gave him a discreet push he pulled back and let her down from the counter. She smiled as she moved away from him and then she turned. "Aston."

"What?" he asked, and this time civilly.

"Thank you for being good to me."

He blinked and nodded a short "You're welcome" before he moved in the other direction.

Calmness, kindness, and courage were truly super powers.

CHAPTER 20
Emotional Outlet

Uma

Maybe it was a good thing for Uma that she had nothing to compare her new school to. She had hoped to meet new friends but after three weeks of trying her best to connect to girls she met, she made a decision to focus on her studies instead. After all, she had lived thirteen years without a friend her own age and it wouldn't kill her to live without one now.

Today was Saturday, and it had been a week since Sybina and Aston were married. Uma was going to meet up with her dance teacher Miss C, who had offered her a private lesson. She figured the young teacher had taken pity on her after the dramatic events that happened this past week, but she would take all the kindness she could find at this point.

Uma looked over her shoulder as she moved out of the school and to the side building where the dance studio was located. She was always watching out for potential threats from groups of students. *Not that any of them could take me down in a fair fight,* she boasted to herself with a youthful snicker. But her enemies traveled in packs and she was only one person. The worst of them all was Tristan, who always walked around with his girlfriend Simone like the two of them were freaking royalty or something. The guy even walked with a swagger... a bloody big swagger. Uma scoffed with contempt just thinking about him and wished for the millionth time since she got here that Tristan, Simone, and everyone else would just leave her alone. But no; Tristan still held a grudge from the dance class where Uma kneed him in his balls. *Wasn't my fault the idiot pulled me so damn tight; one should think that would have taught him to keep his nasty hands to himself.*

It wasn't that Uma was afraid of fighting Tristan... at least not one on one. Despite his size and strength Uma considered herself much faster and more ruthless than him; Tristan was a pampered schoolboy, who at best had a few schoolyard fights under his belt. Uma on the other hand had grown up among the worst of men, watched warriors train, and fought for her life several times. The only real danger she perceived from him was that she could get expelled for hurting him. For that reason alone, she would avoid him at all costs.

When she arrived at the dance studio Miss C was already there and to Uma's surprise she met her with a hug.

"I heard what happened to you and I figured it was time for you to experience something good at this place."

Uma smiled and nodded. "Thank you."

"Before we start dancing, come sit for a second." Miss C led Uma to a windowsill, big enough for them both to sit facing each other, leaning against the frame with their feet up.

"I know you've had a tough start here at school, Uma." Miss C smiled sympathetic. "Dancing can be a great outlet for your frustrations, so I figured it would be healthy for you to come here today."

"Okay," Uma said.

"How do you feel?"

Uma forced a smile. "I feel fine."

"Really?" Miss C's way of saying the word revealed that she didn't believe Uma one bit. "Do you want to tell me what happened?"

Uma sat still looking out the window, seeing the forest in the distance and thinking about what to tell Miss C.

"Okay, let's try something else. I'll tell you what I know and you'll correct me if something isn't right. Alright?"

Uma nodded and looked at Miss C.

"I heard that you used to be a slave for general Mantonis and that you grew up among the Masi warriors. True or false?"

"True," Uma said and looked stern. "Did you know the general?"

Miss C shook her head. "Only from the newspapers."

Uma looked down. "What else did you hear about me?"

"I heard you were born a slave and only just escaped this month."

"True."

"You don't like boys and men because they hurt you in the past?"

Uma nodded.

"And on Tuesday morning some students overheard a conversation between the headmaster and Mr. Tollon discussing your past and now everyone at school knows about it."

"True."

"The girls in your dorm threw you out?"

Uma crossed her arms. "They didn't throw me out," Uma corrected Miss C, who leaned a little closer to Uma with a tilted head.

"Then what happened?"

"Simone and the others told the headmaster they didn't want to share a room with a slave and their parents called him too."

"So?"

"The headmaster said it was my choice to stay or go, and he showed me an alternative to the dorm that I decided to take."

"And where are you sleeping now?"

"In the attic."

Miss C turned her head away and Uma could see she was biting her lip. "Do your parents know about this?"

"No and I don't want them to," Uma insisted. "It's nice of you to care, but it's really not bad at all. The slaves used to live in the attic and now that locals from the village work here instead, they don't use the beds up there. I think it's been empty for the last five years since the slaves left. You don't have to feel sorry for me. I've got more space and freedom up there than any of the other students and I can have my lights on as long as I want. I actually prefer it this way."

Miss C shot her a small smile. "If you say so, Uma. But what about the pasta?"

Uma pushed her jaw forward, annoyed that Miss C had heard about that.

"It wasn't a big deal," she said softly.

"From what I heard some kids poured pasta and tomato sauce all over you at dinner... Uma, look at me... They humiliated you and degraded you and you say it's no big deal?"

"You know, Miss C, kids at this school come from rich families and they all grew up with slaves in their household and feel that I shouldn't be allowed to be here. They think being born a slave means I'm stupid and less of a human being, and the only way I can prove them wrong is to work hard and be better than them.

"Better how?"

"Better at everything," Uma said defiantly.

"Listen, Uma, you don't have to be anything but yourself. The kids that did this to you are shitty brats and they should be ashamed of themselves... there, I said it... but don't you dare quote me on that." Miss C pointed a finger at Uma.

"I won't." Uma broke into a big smile and felt elated that Miss C took such an interest.

"Now, Uma, I'm not saying your reaction was unjustified but slamming one student's head down in the table and forcing another to his knees to beg for mercy isn't an acceptable solution to solving your problems either."

"I just wanted them to leave me alone," Uma defended herself.

"I know... but there's two hundred students and only one of you with nowhere to hide, so stop making more enemies than you already have, please."

"Alright."

"I know you haven't been to the dining hall since the incident on Wednesday, so what did you eat?"

"Stuff."

"What stuff?"

"There's a lady in the kitchen, she used to be a slave too and she lets me eat with the staff."

"Okay... and that works for you?"

Uma nodded. "Yes, they're nice and they let me eat as much as I want."

"Good. I talked to Mr. Tollon about your after-school activities and we agreed that dancing won't work for you."

"But..." Uma started, feeling upset because Miss C was her favorite teacher.

"Hear me out, Uma. Ballroom dancing requires a partner, and after what you did to Tristan no one wants to dance with you, especially now that they know you were born a slave."

Uma's head fell forward.

"With the way they've treated you these past three weeks I can't imagine you want to partner up with any of them anyway. Instead, we are going to do something different. I'm taking you under my wing over the summer, and luckily for you we only have a week left of this school year. I understand that you'll be staying at the school over the summer and so will I on the weekdays, so you're adapting to my schedule. From now on we go running in the morning, and when the other kids go to their after-school activities this week, you do your homework and get something to eat. At seven you meet me here Monday, Tuesday, and Thursday and then we dance."

Uma lit up with excitement.

"But I should warn you, Uma... the dancing I do for myself is not ballroom dancing, it's... something else."

"Thank you... thank you... thank you." Uma was hardly able to contain her joy.

"Alright then, let's get this party started—and by the way, when we're alone you are free to call me Jasmin."

Jasmin got up and moved across the room to the hi-fi system and with another smile to Uma she called out, "Just watch first and then you'll try to imitate me, okay?"

"Okay." Uma turned to watch Jasmin position herself in front of the mirror while a completely new type of music filled the room. The bass alone was enough to make Uma feel the music in her belly... the beat made her move her head, and when a female voice started singing her eyes widened. It sounded amazing, and she couldn't help tapping her foot to the entrancing music.

Jasmin was snapping her fingers and looking serious as she pushed her jaw forward and brushed her hands across her shoulders before bending forward and shaking her head around in a circle that made all her hair swing... Uma was hypnotized by Jasmin's assertive attitude and her sliding dance moves, which looked so effortless, graceful, and different from the waltz that Uma had seen the students dance. Jasmin looked tough and almost a bit aggressive with her serious facial expression occasionally accompanied by a raised eyebrow, narrowed eyes, and sly smiles. There was nothing cute about this type of dancing; it was raw and cool and when Jasmin ended her dance routine Uma was gaping.

"Wow... that was amazing,"

Jasmin broke into a huge grin. "Good, but now it's your turn."

They practiced for an hour, and when Uma returned to the attic later that day she was the happiest she had been since coming to the boarding school. In Miss C she had found a new friend, a running partner, and someone to look up to and learn from.

With a smile plastered on her face she picked up her English book and started reading.

CHAPTER 21
Aya

Sybina

Sybina woke to find blood in her panties. It had been eight days since they had sex and she knew Aston was worried she might be pregnant. They hadn't had sex since their wedding night but he had tried seducing her a few times, and every time it ended with him being more frustrated than before. It was hard to use calmness and kindness all the time when she wanted him so badly too, and twice they had ended in arguments about it.

One time he had pressed her against the wall and kissed her heatedly. She had given in to him and kissed him back. But then he had suggested they could play around in other ways that wouldn't get her pregnant.

"You mean kissing?" she had asked.

"Uh-huh..." he had moaned against her neck. "And oral and anal."

Aston was the only lover Sybina had ever had and the idea of oral and anal sex didn't sit well with her. She had seen too many women being raped, and memories of female slaves being forced into oral sex repulsed her. She remembered Hunilla's choking sounds from when the general raped her mouth and her red eyes from his sperm smeared across her face. And anal sex was the most painful kind of sex, from what the female slaves had told her; she didn't doubt them one moment. She had heard enough soul-crushing screams from the young girls to consider murdering the brutal men who penetrated them roughly and didn't give a damn about ripping their tight anuses. It didn't help that their desperate screams had mostly been dampened by another man filling the slave's mouth. In no part of her imagination did Sybina imagine that oral or anal sex could be anything but awful to a woman.

"No, thank you," she had said but Aston had still carried her to the bed and started undressing her. "Don't say no to things you haven't tried." He had teased and kissed her belly, while pulling her pants down. It had freaked her out and before he could get her undressed, she had pushed him away harshly.

"I said, no!" she yelled. "What kind of man takes a woman against her will?"

Aston had reacted as if she had cut his face open with a broken bottle. "I was going to give you oral sex. Not take it," he had told her angrily.

The adrenaline from being afraid had still been pumping inside Sybina when she attacked him again. "And then what? You give me oral and then I'm supposed to let you choke me."

"Choke you?"

"I said no, Aston. I've seen oral and anal sex and I *don't* want it."

"You talk about it like it's something dirty and wrong," he exclaimed. "I told you I won't hurt you and you said you trusted me. I gave you oral sex on our wedding night; you didn't complain then."

"I don't want it—end of discussion."

"Then what do you want, Sybina?" he asked, exasperated. "You're killing me here..."

"Just regular sex like we had on our wedding night," she said frustrated. "I want to feel you inside me."

"I want that too... but not until you accept that we need to use protection," he argued.

"Never!" she bit him off.

The next time they fought about it had been last night. Aston had been restless in the bed, and his tossing and turning had woken her up in the middle of the night.

"What's wrong?" she asked.

"Nothing," he exclaimed forcefully.

"Are you sick?" She reached to touch his forehead but he pulled away from her.

"I'm not sick, I'm just going crazy. I keep covering you up and you keep pushing the covers away. It's driving me insane to be so close to you, knowing I can't have you."

Sybina had felt flattered and thought that maybe he would drop the sterilization thing.

"You can have me, Aston," she said in a silky smooth voice and saw his eyes widen. "You can have me as many times as you want." She let one finger slide over his jawline.

"With protection?" he asked hopefully.

Her eyes and voice changed back into being firm and non-negotiable "No protection."

"Arghhh." Aston had growled and turned away from her, leaving the bedroom; but somehow he had come back after she fell back asleep, because he was here now, sleeping on his stomach with his hand reaching to her.

Sybina looked down at him and started to shake him lightly. "Aston, wake up."

"What is it?" he asked and rubbed his eyes.

"I got my period," Sybina said

"Thank God," he sighed with visible relief on his face.

Sybina ignored the feeling of rejection in her stomach and started to get dressed while Aston headed for the shower. He was whistling happily and when he got out he was exceptionally chirpy.

"Listen, Sybina, I have a few meetings today, but how about we go out for dinner tonight? There's something I want to tell you."

"I don't mind cooking," Sybina told him.

"I know, and I appreciate how you always keep this place immaculate and all your good food, but I want to take you out tonight. Okay?"

"Okay," Sybina agreed and went back to her project of the day. When they arrived in London three weeks ago Aston had given her full permission to decorate the apartment to her liking, and she had already spiced up the bedroom with a beautiful modern wallpaper on the end wall, a red colored rug, new lampshades, and cushions that made the room look much warmer.

Today she was working on the living room, and new furniture was arriving to compliment the few pieces Aston already had when she arrived. Sybina enjoyed the creative process of decorating and Aston was very pleased with the results so far. It also gave Sybina something to do, other than clean, cook, and study English.

She often felt restless and unfulfilled in a way that was new to her. She was good at keeping herself busy but her thoughts kept going back to the night of the wedding. It was as if she'd been allowed a glimpse into an erotic world with sexual pleasure she never knew existed, but now the window was slammed shut with his demand for her to get sterilized. That was so not happening, and she was still angry with him for insisting on it. And yet she couldn't turn off her attraction to him or tune out the sexual energy that still surged between them.

The way Aston looked at her and his small hints of invitations didn't go unnoticed, and the hardest part was the nights: having him so close that she could feel his warmth, smell his masculine fragrance, and hear his deep breathing. It was tempting to just reach out, and ironically his own words about seducing her in her sleep had played in her mind... a lot. She had considered doing that exact thing to him. Would he stop her if he woke up with her astride him? She had been awake some nights and watched him sleep—letting her fingers slide down his

212

body without actually touching. She had heard him mumble in his dreams, hoping to hear her own name on his lips. But she never had.

Two years seemed like an eon to sleep next to the most gorgeous and sexy man she knew, knowing that the only way she could have him was to either trick him or give up her dream of becoming a mother, but she would not yield.

As they sat in a restaurant that evening not far from his apartment Aston started talking.

"I've accepted a new position with Spread Life."

No! Fear filled Sybina and her heart started racing.

"What's wrong?" he asked. "Why do you look so sad?"

"You! You told me you wouldn't leave me here alone." She suddenly felt nauseated.

"Sybina, you are jumping to conclusions. I never said anything about leaving. The position is at the headquarters. It's only forty minutes away." Aston seemed surprised at her strong reaction. "For the first time in my life I'm going to try out a desk job and if it drives me insane, you'll be the first to know." He said.

"So you're not leaving me then."

"No, I'm going to stay here as we agreed," he assured her.

"Until the two years are up?" she asked and wished for him to say... *no, forever*, but he nodded seriously... "Yes, until the two years are up."

"And then what are you going to do?" Her question was unreasonable. It was none of her business what he did when he had fulfilled the contract, but she needed him to tell her anyway.

"I don't know. I don't want to think that far ahead. It all depends, I guess."

213

Aston felt silently into his own thoughts and then he leaned forward with an earnest expression. "Can I ask you something, Sybina?"

His question made her uneasy, as Aston never asked for permission to speak; she found it ominous, but nodded.

"How did you cope when you were... ehh... sold? I mean, you were just a child and your whole family had died. It makes me sick to think about the suffering you must have gone through."

Sybina thought about it, trying to think back to a time that was for the most part suppressed. Her eyes glazed over and she answered with a distant expression. "I can remember making rules of happiness... I peeled away everything and built my happiness on the very fundamentals. If I got food and sleep then it was a good day. I would tell myself that if the sun came out it was a good day, or if I got to go outside in the garden, or if I saw a butterfly. I made sure to set the criteria for a good day so low that almost every day was a happy day, in my definition.

"I also made a pact with my older self. I was only eleven, but I promised myself that when I got older and stronger, I would be free again. It must sound strange to you, but I was so alone that I developed a bond with my older self. I would talk with her in my mind and she would guide me, protect me... She was my invisible friend."

Aston took Sybina's hand. "Didn't you have any friends at all?"

"No, the witch was eccentric and not very caring. People didn't like her and she never socialized with anyone. We came into people's houses only when they needed our help. And later of course, there was also the rumor that I could make men impotent."

Aston blinked, clearly affected by her story. "I can't imagine how lonely you must have felt."

"Don't be sad for me, Aston. I had a dog and three cats in the house. They were my friends. I spoke to them and gave them lots of affection. I even named the dog—Ollito, like my little brother—and pretended he could understand what I was saying. When I was most frightened or sad I would replay scenes from my life with my family, but so detailed that it was extreme. I would focus on every insignificant detail to be sure I never would forget them, or forget who I really was. The colors, the words, the atmosphere, the sounds, and smell... It was so vivid in my mind that reliving my memories felt real."

"Why did you get sold to the Masi warriors?" Aston wanted to know.

Sybina sighed. "Even though nobody liked the witch, she was much respected for her results and she had helped the general in the past, so he knew her. He wanted her to join the resistance; after all, she was a slave owner herself, and she was a great believer in Masi, but she didn't want to leave her home in the village. She was too old, I guess, but she couldn't keep me with the new laws of freedom for all slaves, so she quickly sold me to the general, who didn't care for the king's new rules and refused to free his slaves."

"How old were you then?"

"Twenty-two. I spent five years in that basement taking care of Masi soldiers, but on a positive note, I met other slaves and they became my friends."

"Are you okay talking about this?" Aston asked.

"Well, it's my life. I wish things had been different and that my family were still alive and that my father never owed that money, but it is what it is. I can't change any of it." Sybina forced a smile. "I'm sure you have seen your share of horror too."

Aston nodded and looked like he didn't want to go down that path, and Sybina agreed that this conversation was serious enough without his violent memories.

215

"I'll tell you some other time," he murmured.

When they were done eating, Aston paid the bill and they left the restaurant, strolling down the street to his apartment. Sybina was unusually quiet.

"What is it?" Aston asked her.

"You said something in the restaurant," Sybina started. "We spoke about what you'll do after the two years are over and you said that it all depends... What did you mean? What does it depend on?"

Aston was just about to answer when a woman shouted his name. They both looked up to see someone come running towards them, and instinctively Sybina took a step back. Aston put his arm around Sybina and shouted out to the woman.

"Aya, is it really you... how are you?"

As soon as Aston said her name, Sybina recognized Aya, who was clearly distraught with her eyes wide open and her lips trembling.

"What happened, Aya... are you okay?" Aston asked her and she responded by talking so incredibly fast that Sybina had no chance of understanding anything.

Aston slowed her down and invited her to come have tea with them, and Sybina understood when Aya swallowed hard and nodded. "Yes, please."

They were very close to the apartment; Aya went with them. While Sybina went to make some tea, Aya and Aston took seats in the living room. Sybina knew that Aya and Aston had been colleagues, and she understood their need to talk about the kidnapping and everything that happened to them in captivity. It wasn't hard to see that they cared for each other. Sybina gave them some time to talk before she entered with the tea and saw them sitting on the couch. She could tell that Aston was disturbed and Aya was still distressed, and Sybina gave them both a warm smile when something caught her eye. The way Aya held her hands over her stomach made Sybina speculate

The Healing Slave

that she was pregnant. Part of a healer's job was to be a midwife, and life in the village had given her plenty of practice. She could often spot a pregnant woman before the woman knew it herself.

Sybina poured Aya a cup of tea when suddenly Aya exclaimed, "You are married." She was looking at their wedding rings.

Aston started explaining how he couldn't leave Sybina in Spirima and that the only way to save her was to marry her. Sybina understood that much, and soaked up the protectiveness coming from Aston.

Aya kept looking back and forth between them and Sybina heard her mention the word love. *Did Aya just ask Aston if he loved me?* When Sybina saw him shaking his head no, she felt sure. *Aston doesn't love me. He never said that he did.* Sybina pushed an unwelcome feeling of sadness away. Instead she focused on Aya, who looked completely lost and was calling out the healer in her. Sybina picked up a blanket and went over to tuck Aya in. She sat down next to Aya and grabbed her hand, rubbing it and sending her vibrations of calmness and clarity. Whatever Aya had going on in her life she needed to be strong for the child inside her.

"Uhhm, it feels good," Aya whispered and closed her eyes.

"Good for the baby," Sybina said in Spiri and Aya instantly opened her eyes to gape at her.

"What baby?" Aston asked in confusion.

"Aya's baby," Sybina said, still smiling.

Aya swallowed hard and flushed pink.

Aston leaned toward her. "You better start talking, Aya... what's going on?"

Aya sighed and started telling the story of her and Kato. This time she was talking slowly; Sybina understood parts of it and Aston translated the rest.

"So what are you going to do?" Aston asked.

"I don't know." Aya said and sniffled. "What do you think I should do?"

Aston shook his head and refused to give advice, and they talked some more. In the end it was decided that Aya would sleep on the couch and early tomorrow morning Aston would drive her back to Kato's place. After a bit more catching up between Aston and Aya, Aston got out sheets for Aya and apologized that he didn't have a bed in the guestroom yet.

Sybina went to bed and lay awake thinking of Aya's pregnancy and her own situation. She remembered the way Aston had been shaking his head when Aya asked him if he loved her. *What did you expect, Sybina?* She blamed herself.

"Are you awake?" Aston tugged at her softly. She turned and faced him in the almost dark.

"How did you know Aya was pregnant?" he wanted to know.

"I was a midwife in the village. I know the signs."

"But there were no signs. Her belly didn't show anything," he argued.

Sybina turned around to face him. "So what... now you think I'm a witch with supernatural powers too?"

Aston propped himself on his elbow. "No, of course not. I just don't understand how you could possibly know."

Sybina wasn't in the mood for long talks; she was tired and sad. "Listen, Aya's belly might not have shown but her body language did."

"Okay, I trust you," he said.

"Thank you." She gave a soft snort and closed her eyes.

"Is something the matter?" he asked.

"No, everything is fine." She sighed and turned around, holding back her thoughts. *You wouldn't understand it anyway.*

CHAPTER 22
Immigration Services

Sybina

Aston and Aya were gone before Sybina woke up. Sybina took a quick shower and was going to the kitchen to make tea when she heard the doorbell ring. It was still seven in the morning and too early for visitors; thinking Aston had left without his keys, Sybina went to open the door and froze to the floor at the sight of a man and woman, looking so odd together that they couldn't possibly be a couple.

The woman was in her late fifties and dressed in a tent of a dress accompanied by sensible shoes and a brown leather bag. The man couldn't be more than in his late twenties but his long-limbed body in his ill-fitting brown suit, combined with his grave expression, made him look much older; and the briefcase he was holding by his side made Sybina sure that this was the feared visit from the immigration service.

Hot and flustered, Sybina greeted the couple, fully aware that the outcome of their visit would determine her future.

"How do you do." The woman gave Sybina what was probably meant to be a calming smile, but because it never reached her eyes it had the opposite effect. "My name is Mrs. Fletcher and this is Mr. Graham. We are from the immigration services and would like to speak to Mr. and Mrs. Tailor. Are you Mrs. Tailor?"

Sybina swallowed excessively and nodded.

"May we come in?"

"Aston not home," Sybina said, hoping they would come back when Aston was home, but the voluminous woman took a small step forward with the words: "That's okay, we'll just ask you a few questions then." Her determined expression automatically made Sybina step aside, allowing the immigration workers to enter.

"May we look around?" Mrs. Fletcher asked, and with a type of sign language to clarify her question to Sybina she gestured at her eyes and pointed around. Sybina had understood her words just fine and nodded.

Mr. Graham disappeared down the hallway, peeking into every room. Sybina didn't like his prying light gray eyes; the man had almost no color with his blond hair and pale skin, and it didn't help that he was wearing a beige shirt under the brown suit. *He looks like a cardboard box*, Sybina thought.

"Is there somewhere we can talk?" Mrs. Fletcher asked and started walking towards the living room, where she stopped abruptly. Sybina followed her eyes to the couch where Aya had slept. It still had the sheets and the pillow and blanket. It was evident that someone had been sleeping on the couch.

"Did your husband sleep on the couch last night?" Mrs. Fletcher asked softly, and Sybina got an internal image of a spider eyeing a fly in its web.

Sybina's heart was racing. This was such bad timing. She remembered her first night here and Aston's words on how important it was for them to be sleeping in the same bedroom. "No, not Aston. Aya sleep here," Sybina said with the limited vocabulary she had in English and used gestures to make herself understood.

"Who is Aya?" the woman asked.

"Aya is Aston's friend."

"Does this Aya sleep here often?" Mrs. Fletcher asked with a smug smile and an arched brow.

"No, one time. Aya home today."

Mrs. Fletcher was scribbling in her notebook and then she pointed to the dining table. "Why don't we sit here?" She took a seat and pulled out a long list of questions.

"So how did you and Mr. Tailor meet?" she asked, interested.

Sybina felt frustrated that she could understand what the woman asked her but was unable to give intelligent answers. She needed Aston to translate.

"I don't speak good English," she said apologetically.

"Don't worry, Mrs. Tailor, you did fine before. Just try to tell me."

Sybina frowned for a second and then she pointed to herself. "Me healer. Aston hurt in head."

Mrs. Fletcher nodded. "Yes, we know Aston was kidnapped and assaulted. Is that what you are referring to?"

Sybina nodded. "I help Aston. I like Aston."

"From your papers it says that you are from Spirima. Did you meet Aston in Spirima?"

"Yes."

"Okay, so from what I understand your husband was injured and you helped him and that's how you first met. Is that correct?"

"Yes." Sybina nodded.

"And you didn't know Mr. Tailor prior to the kidnapping?"

"Prior?" Sybina repeated unsure what the word meant.

"Did you know Mr. Tailor before the kidnapping?"

"No."

Mrs. Fletcher was taking notes, and all the while Sybina was twisting her wedding ring on her finger.

"When did you first kiss Mr. Tailor?"

Sybina thought about it. There had been small kisses on the forehead and cheeks in the refugee camp but the first real kiss had been on their wedding day.

"Wedding," she said, nervous and afraid she would misunderstand something or give a wrong answer.

Mrs. Fletcher raised an eyebrow. "Really? Your first kiss was at your wedding?"

"Yes."

"What is your favorite color?"

"Green."

"How did your husband propose to you?"

"In Spirima."

"Yes, but how?"

Sybina thought about it. "In tent. He ask. I say yes."

"In a tent," Mrs. Fletcher repeated and noted it down.

"What is the name of his sister?"

"Nina."

"How old is Nina?"

"Like me." Sybina shrugged; she didn't know for sure. This interrogation was exhausting.

"What is the name of his brother?"

Sybina rubbed her arms and looked around. Was this a trick question or had Aston somehow failed to mention he had a brother?

"Aston has Nina. No brother."

Mrs. Fletcher nodded and wrote down some more.

"When was your last period?"

"Now. Two day." Sybina held up her index finger.

"You'll be done in two days?"

"No, two day." She pointed behind her.

"Ohh, you mean this is your number two day... your second day?"

Aya nodded.

"Alright... You were married two weeks ago. How many times have you slept with your husband since then?"

"Sleep every night," Sybina said.

Mrs. Fletcher smiled vaguely. "Let me rephrase that. How many times have you had sex?"

Sybina flushed. She didn't like to answer questions this private to complete strangers.

"Two times," she said uncomfortably and saw Mrs. Fletcher scribble it down.

The questions kept going and going, and then to Sybina's relief she heard keys in the door and the sound of Aston walking in. There was an awkward moment when Mr. Graham came out from the bedroom and Aston demanded to know who he was in a very unfriendly way.

Luckily Mr. Graham was quick to jump back and shout "Immigration services." It made Aston back down and hurry to join Sybina in the dining room.

Mrs. Fletcher presented herself and Mr. Graham again and continued with her questions. Sybina saw Aston send a displeased glance at the couch.

"How do you feel about your husband?" Mrs. Tailor asked.

Sybina smiled at her with confidence. "I love Aston." There was no wavering, and Aston squeezed her hand.

"Would you mind if I ask you a few questions, Mr. Tailor?" The woman looked at Aston who smiled politely.

"Not at all, go ahead."

"What is your wife's favorite color?"

"Green," he said and Sybina smiled, relieved.

"When is her birthday?"

"October 12," he said, quick and short.

"When was the first time you kissed her?"

Aston leaned back. "Hmm... that depends on what you define as kissing... I believe the first real kissing wasn't until we got married."

"Interesting," The woman said and noted down. Aston shot Sybina a worried glance but she smiled at him.

"Now could you tell me how many times you have had sex since the wedding?" She looked at her papers.

"We had sex twice on our wedding night," Aston stated and the woman nodded for him to continue. But he didn't.

"That's two weeks ago. How many times would you say you've been together since then?" Mrs. Fletcher asked, interested.

"We haven't," Aston said and Sybina felt a slight irritation coming from him.

"Why is that?" Mrs. Fletcher said and tilted her head with a smug smile.

"Sybina has her period and we've been really busy," Aston explained.

"Is that why you sleep on the couch?"

Aston narrowed his eyes. "I never sleep on the couch. A friend of mine was in trouble and spent the night. I believe she's flying home to Norway today; you may have heard about Aya Johansen, my colleague who was also kidnapped in Spirima. I'll be happy to give you her number and you can have her confirm it herself.

Mrs. Fletcher narrowed her eyes a bit. "Yes, I heard of Aya Johansen and yes, I would like her to confirm your story."

"It's not a story," Aston insisted.

"Uh-huh... I still have a few questions. Why did you marry Mrs. Tailor?"

Aston looked at Mrs. Fletcher and then he looked at Sybina. "Because I fell utterly in love with her the first day I saw her. She not only saved my life twice but she also gives me a reason to want to live."

"How very poetic." Mrs. Fletcher said dryly. "How did you propose?"

"It wasn't fancy. I just asked for alone time with her and proposed in my tent."

"You hadn't known each other very long when you proposed. How long exactly?"

"About a week."

"That quick?" She said it like there was a statement in the words.

Aston leaned forward. "Listen, Mrs. Fletcher. Sybina and I met in a war zone. Things are raw and honest there. You don't play games, you don't hold back. Sybina has been a slave since she was eleven and not known freedom for sixteen years. I've been a soldier since I was nineteen and never known love. We found each other and it just clicked between us. A week, a month, a year... it would have made no difference. When you know... you know."

Sybina flushed red, and even Mrs. Fletcher looked a little taken by Aston's description of true love; she put down more things on her list.

"What type of contraception do you use?" she asked and for once Aston's eyes flickered.

"We haven't decided yet," he said slowly and looked at Sybina.

"Oh," Mrs. Fletcher said and wrote down again.

"And what are your plans regarding children?" Mrs. Fletcher looked at Aston and Sybina could almost feel his mind racing. He couldn't know that Mrs. Fletcher hadn't already asked Sybina the same question. He would be wondering what she had answered.

"We've only known each other for five weeks so for now we are still focusing on our marriage and getting to know each other." He was being completely authentic and honest.

"All right. I think that's it for now. Good luck with everything—you'll hear from us again within the next six months, and I should warn you that more unexpected visits might occur."

"You're always welcome. We have nothing to hide." Aston stood up, held Sybina's hand and didn't let go as they both walked Mr. Graham and Mrs. Fletcher to the door.

Just before they left, Sybina thought she saw Mrs. Fletcher look at her with a kind smile.

225

After Aston closed the door, they rushed back into the living room and frantically went over every question, comparing answers. They couldn't find anything alarming.

"You were amazing when you talked of true love," Sybina said, impressed.

"And you looked so convincing when you told her that you love me," Aston laughed. "For a moment there I thought you really meant it."

Sybina smiled. "Maybe it's because I like you so much."

Aston took a step closer, still glowing with excitement from the aftermath of having successfully overcome the first encounter with the immigration services. He looked at her with beaming eyes and reached out to grab her hands. "How much do you like me?"

Sybina chuckled... "I don't know... how do you measure something like that?"

"Do you like me enough to have sex again?" he flirted

Sybina stiffened. *If he's bringing up the sterilization again, I'll hit him in his handsome face."* What do you mean?" she asked, trying to sound casual, and sat down to create a little distance between them.

Aston sat down in front of her. "Listen, I know I said sex wasn't part of the deal but I'm losing my mind here. What happened on our wedding night... I didn't expect it but it was phenomenal... to me at least... and I can't stop thinking about it. You can't imagine how tortured I've felt lying next to you these past fifteen nights and not being able to touch you... it's killing me, Sybina." His eyes were begging, and she had to look away to resist kissing him right then and there. She knew exactly what he meant.

"I think about that night too," Sybina admitted.

"Then explain to me again why we're not having sex." Aston threw his hands in the air. "You say it's not because of religion, you say you want me too and yet you refuse. Sybina, we are married, for God's sake. How can there be anything wrong in making love between man and wife?"

226

"Making love?" Sybina snapped her head back and narrowed her eyes. "How dare you talk about love and then ask me to get sterilized. I'm not doing it!" Her hands were shaking with the anger, disappointment, and indignation she had carried around since the morning after their wedding.

"Wait... what?" Aston looked dumbfounded. "Back up again... I want you to get what?"

"Sterilized," she repeated.

He looked completely lost. "When have I ever said anything about sterilization?"

"You told me so. Remember how you said we needed protection against pregnancies?"

"Yeah, but I was talking about condoms..."

She looked blank.

"Oh, come on Sybina, you do know that there are other ways of protecting against pregnancies than getting a sterilization."

"Like what?" she asked, feeling stupid for being clearly clueless.

"Come with me." Aston took her hand and pulled her with him to the bedroom, where he grabbed something from his nightstand. "Condoms."

Sybina watched with curiosity as he unwrapped a condom and explained how it worked.

"So you understand that we can have all the sex we want without you having to be afraid of getting pregnant." He looked like all the world's trouble had suddenly disappeared.

"What makes you think that I'm afraid of getting pregnant?" Sybina's question was so brutal and honest that it clearly caught him off guard.

"But clearly you wouldn't want a child with... I just figured that..."

"That what?" she interrupted him.

"That you would want to wait until your new life starts."

Sybina felt her lips quiver and the need to scream at him... He was such a tease; one minute talking about true love and wanting to make love to her, and the next minute reminding her that this was only a temporary thing between them. *You are the stupidest man in the history of mankind... I hate you*, she growled internally and turned her back to him.

"What did I say wrong?" He pulled her around, and she couldn't help it—she felt humiliated and hurt and she spoke with great intensity.

"You know, Aston, I may be clueless about most things in your world and I'm sorry that I didn't have parents very long or people who cared, or schooling... but you. You had all those things and you're still clueless."

Aston pulled back a little. "Then enlighten me. Tell me what I'm missing. I'm trying hard here, but I can't read your mind. Tell me what you're thinking."

"Are you sure you can handle the truth?" she snorted and felt horrible inside.

He looked pale and a bit unsure about how to handle this emotional side of her.

"Yes I'm sure," he said, not sounding convincing at all.

"My biggest wish is to have a child!"

Aston blinked a few times. "Okay... but..." He seemed to be thinking. "Listen, Sybina, you don't want a child with me."

"Why not?"

He frowned. "I'm not exactly father material, and a child is a big commitment. And besides, Sybina, shouldn't it be with someone you love?"

She sighed and calmed herself before she spoke again. "Aston, will you answer a question for me honestly?"

"Of course"

"Did you sleep with Aya?"

228

He looked like he didn't understand the questions, didn't know the answer, or didn't get why she was asking in the first place.

"Did you ever sleep with Aya?" Sybina repeated, and her question surprised even her; but the thought had been with her ever since she found out Aya was pregnant, and she needed to know if it was Aston's child.

Aston shook his head confused. "What does that have to do with anything?... I'm married to you."

"I told you that you're clueless," she cried and ran to the bathroom, slamming the door behind her. This was so unlike her. She was embarrassed about her loss of emotional control. *Think, think, think*, she ordered herself but she couldn't organize her thoughts. *Why didn't he just answer the question? Because he did sleep with Aya, of course. She's the one he wants and now Aston is stuck with me, when he really wants her... oh, what a mess.* She was crying so hard that she didn't even notice Aston enter the bathroom. He sat down next to her and pulled her into his lap.

"I'm so sorry, Sybina," he said and held her in his arms.

Sybina looked down and sniffled. "What do you want?"

"I want to make you happy."

Why does he have to be so damn lovable?

"Sybina, listen, you have to be really specific with me. When it comes to relationships I have no experience, and you're right, I'm clueless and half the time I don't even know what I'm feeling myself, so to think I can guess or understand what you're feeling is to overestimate me greatly."

She listened, waiting for him to say more.

"Like right now, I can sense that you want something from me but I'm not sure what it is, so help me out. Talk to me."

"Okay. I asked you a question and you didn't answer me. Did you sleep with Aya?"

229

"No, I never slept with Aya," he answered earnestly.

"Did you want to sleep with Aya?"

Aston squirmed uncomfortably under her. "Okay, listen, I'm not going to lie. Aya is attractive. But I never wanted to sleep with her as much as I wanted to sleep with you."

"Do you love her?"

"No," he shook his head. "I'd only known Aya for a few months when we were captured. I mean, I like her very much and I care for her in a protective way, but only as a friend. I don't understand your interest in Aya. What does she have to do with us?" And then she saw realization hit him: "Are you jealous of Aya?"

Sybina started crying again and nodded, feeling ashamed.

"Why in the world would you be jealous of Aya? The woman's a mess. You saw that for yourself."

"But she's loved and she's pregnant."

Aston was frowning like none of this made any sense to him. "But soon you'll have Uma to care for. She's kind of a child."

Sybina sniffled. "I know.... But Aston, when your time with me is over... Do you think you want to have children with someone else? I mean do you want to be a father some day?"

Aston shook his head. "No, it's not for me. I would only mess it up. Marriage and children is something I gave up a long time ago."

"So you wanted it at some point?" Sybina asked.

"I think, what I tried to say is that, as a child I figured it would happen naturally someday, like it did for my parents, but it's been years since I thought like that. I've turned my back on that kind of lifestyle. It's just not for me."

"Why."

"Because I've seen the world and I don't think it's a place I want to bring children into."

"And yet here you are... married," Sybina concluded.

Aston nodded and stroked her hair calmingly. "You know, if someone had asked me six weeks ago if I would ever marry, I would have said one hundred percent no."

"I know." Sybina looked down, feeling sad. She was his obligation. "Are you looking forward to having this marriage over with?" Her question reeked with sadness and she couldn't control the tears running down her cheeks.

Aston leaned into her hair when he answered. "When it's over, I'll probably disappear into a desert somewhere, as far away from here as possible."

Sybina turned on his lap, looking directly into his eyes. Her eyes narrowed. "That is a cruel thing to say."

Aston blinked a few times, confused. "Why... I won't leave before you have everything you need, and Uma will be here with you."

Sybina looked down, feeling exhausted from trying to communicate her feelings with him. She felt like they were caught in a dance but never really in sync. With a last effort she took a deep breath and looked up with complete honesty. "But Aston, what if it's you that I need most of all?"

He opened his mouth to speak but nothing came out His eyes were asking if she was being serious and she answered him with an honest expression.

"You need me?" he whispered hoarsely.

Sybina nodded and kissed him softly.

It took him a few second but then he kissed her back. The force behind the kiss surprised Sybina. There was a primal hunger in his kisses and he was all over her at once—pulling off their clothes, touching her breasts, biting her neck. Sybina felt the intensity in his desire and it aroused her like crazy.

"I'm right here... take all you need," Aston groaned into her mouth and kissed her passionately. She kissed him back and he picked her up effortlessly and carried her to the bathroom tabletop, where he placed her on the edge. Sybina leaned back and enjoyed the sight of him standing between her legs with a burning desire in his eyes and a strong grip on her hips. He undressed himself in between kissing her. When he pulled down his pants his erection sprung free and when he slid it over her belly, she remembered the delicious feeling of being completely filled by it. Aston traced kisses from her lips, down her neck, teasing her nipples, and continuing down to her lower belly.

"Wait, Aston, I'm bleeding, remember."

He looked up and gave her a wolfish grin. "Good, then we won't need condoms," he said and pulled her with him into the shower, where he pressed her against the wall, kissing her and biting her nipples lightly. Sybina gasped so loudly that it made him look up and give her a satisfied smile. "Relax, baby..." he smiled. Sybina was taken aback with how different he was from on their wedding night. He was rougher and more demanding, like the time they argued in the kitchen, and it did incredible things for her libido. With a soft moan she closed her eyes and leaned her head back in surrender.

"I've wanted you every freaking minute since our wedding night," he hissed and pulled her legs up around his hips. "Tell me you wanted me too."

"Uh-huh," she moaned into his mouth but it wasn't enough.

He cupped her face with an intense glare. "Say it, Sybina. Say you longed for me too."

"I want you, Aston," she said in English and it made him blink and enter her smoothly. She was so wet that he slid right in and started taking her against the shower wall while warm water flushed down and created steam around them.

"Oh, Aston," she groaned and fisted her hands into his hair. He varied his movements by pulling out of her, circling her sensitive spot only to enter her again, making her arch and gasp from the feeling of being filled up completely. Now and then Aston kept still, allowing her to feel every inch of him pounding inside her like an extra heartbeat. It was an intense feeling of being fully connected with him, and when he leaned down and kissed her passionately, she felt like he was claiming her as his woman. Then he started moving again, faster, harder, and her eyes grew big as the energy built between them. It was raw... honest... nothing but desire and longing, expressed without words. He pumped in and out while his hands and eyes explored her body. Her breasts, her hips, her arms, her strong legs surrounding him.

Aston looked down at her face and she smiled, enjoying the sight of him taking her deep and fast. Then he pulled out and came on her stomach. Sybina found it the sexiest thing she had ever seen, not because of his strong and trimmed body or his good looks but because of the way he made her feel *wanted*.

"I could do this all day," Aston said, slightly out of breath, and tightened his grip around her. Sybina wanted to stay close to him. *I could do this all day too*, she thought and kissed the golden chest hair that she so adored. After a while, Aston pulled back and lifted Sybina gently down onto the floor.

"Thank you," he said and kissed her on the top of her head. Sybina shot him a sexy grin, feeling on top of the world.

"Why did you tell Aya that you didn't love me?" Sybina asked

Aston frowned. "What do you mean?"

Sybina smiled "I heard Aya say the word love while looking at me. And I saw you shaking your head no."

Aston was thinking back and then he smiled. "Aya didn't ask me if I loved you. She told me that she thought you loved me."

"And you didn't believe her?"

"I told her that you were just a very warm and generous person."

Sybina chuckled. "That I am... normally, but still you must have known."

"Known what?" Aston asked and his question made Sybina's heart skip a beat. She looked at him, stunned. *After what just happened between us, don't tell me you are still clueless...*

"What?" Aston said. "Now you are doing it again. You're looking at me like I'm supposed to read your thoughts. I can't!"

Sybina didn't speak. She just looked at him like he had to be joking.

"Are you saying that Aya was right?" Aston sounded doubtful.

"What do you think? What do you see when you look into my eyes? What do feel when we're together... like just now or on our wedding night?"

Aston looked frustrated, turned off the water, and stepped out of the shower. He took a towel and handed it to her before getting one for himself. "Just because you enjoy the sex doesn't mean you love me, Sybina," he said in a matter-of-fact tone.

Sybina blinked at him. "Why would I enjoy the sex if I didn't love you?"

Aston's smile widened into a grin. "Oh, believe me... sex and love isn't the same thing. I would know."

Sybina gaped at him, trying to suppress the massive pressure she felt in her chest; she had just declared her love for him and the idiot was lecturing her that she was confused and that he had no feelings for her. She wanted to stay cool and collected and keep her pride, but inside her an emotional volcano erupted in tears and she fled.

"No, wait, Sybina. I didn't mean it like that... Don't go," she heard him call behind her, and then he caught her and pulled her back. "I'm sorry. That came out wrong. Listen to me."

Sybina raised her eyebrows "All I'm hearing is *you* telling me that sex has *nothing* to do with love and that you would know..." Tears, anger, and her raised voice were all out of her control. "Are you referring to *all* the women you've had sex with or just *me*?"

Aston closed his fists and took a deep breath. "You misunderstood."

Sybina glanced down at herself: naked and wet. She didn't want to have this conversation right now and went back to pick up her clothes, which Aston had tossed all over when he almost ripped them off her just ten minutes ago. She could see him follow her every move and she could sense he wanted to say something, but she ignored him and was relieved when he left the room. It was so hard to communicate with him; every time she thought they were moving in the right direction he took a turn and pushed her into a web of doubt and confusion.

In silence Sybina dressed, all the while her mind was thinking about Aston between other women's legs. *Who taught him to make love like that? How many has he made feel as wanted and desired as me? When I said I needed him, he thought I meant physically and now I stupidly complicated things by telling him I love him. How am I ever going to look him in the eye after exposing my feelings like that?* Sybina's pride was hurt. She had given Aston every chance to reveal his true feelings but once again she was left disappointed. *You keep thinking your feelings are mutual... when will you get it into your thick scull? Aston doesn't love you—get over it!*

235

After dressing Sybina returned to the kitchen, where she found Aston.

"Listen, Sybina, I want to explain myself," he said and stood up.

Sybina held up her hand. "Don't, Aston, it's alright. I think you're right. I was just confusing sex with love... It's all new to me. I apologize."

"Ohh," Aston blinked rapidly and sat down again. "Yeah, that's what I thought."

CHAPTER 23
Unwanted

Sybina

"I'll see you when I get home." Aston gave Sybina a smile and half a hug before he left for his first day at work.

"Have fun," she said in English and received an impressed nod from him.

"You're a fast learner."

"Thank you," Sybina said and returned to her laundry.

The last three days had been the most awkward in her time with Aston. Saying she didn't love Aston had been the easy part. The hard part was pretending it was true.

Aston was back to normal and had initiated sex several times since Monday, when he taught her about condoms. Sybina had pulled back from him in an attempt to protect her heart and she was more quiet than usual, but when he started kissing her and touching her, she found it impossible to say no. Sybina had decided that she would allow herself to have sex with Aston but never again expose her true feelings for him. According to him it was possible to separate sex and love, and with a bit of practice Sybina was hoping to learn how to master that. Condoms were practical but Aston didn't like them and she had agreed to take pills instead—another way of preventing pregnancies that she wished she had known about in Spirima.

After pushing the start bottom on the washer Sybina turned and walked through the apartment. It was spotless, as Aston had already made the bed and done the dishes while she sorted the laundry. Sybina started whistling and put on her sneakers with unhurried, relaxed movements.

She locked the door behind her as she left for her daily walk. She was a creature of habit and had survived on discipline and routine since she was eleven, and she was already creating new habits and routines here in London. Her days started with a morning walk before Jacob, her tutor, came to teach her English at noon. In the afternoon she did her homework, went grocery shopping, and prepared dinner, which was always served at seven. It felt good to Sybina that an everyday routine was starting to kick in; she was starting to know all the names of the shops in the neighborhood and recognize people and dogs on the streets. That all gave her a sense of familiarity.

Sybina walked to Lincoln's Inn Fields, one of her favorite parks in the area. She came here most days and only varied the route to and from the park. The old buildings, the green grass, and the many people who lay or sat on it fascinated her.

After walking for about an hour Sybina sat down on a bench and watched the people walk by her. Some looked very busy and were talking on their phones but others like her seemed to have all the time in the world. Sybina tilted her head and squinted her eyes to block out the sun and get a better look at the man who'd just passed her. He seemed so familiar, and she was trying to remember where she had seen him, but from his back it was impossible to say. She needed to see him from the front and started to follow him, hoping he would turn around.

When he did she almost bumped into him and immediately knew who he was.

"How are you?" Sybina said with a small smile.

The man's eyes widened in recognition. "You? I remember you."

Sybina nodded and her smile widened. "How is your son?"

A smile grew on the man's face and he reached out to touch Sybina. "I'm so happy I bumped into you because I wanted to say thank you... the doctors said you saved Harry from a life in a wheelchair."

"Is Harry your son?" Sybina asked and felt happy she could actually have a small conversation with a stranger. Three weeks of intensive training was paying off.

"Yes, yes, Harry is my son," the man said, and with a hand on Sybina's elbow he led Sybina to a bench next to them. "What's your name?" he asked in a friendly way.

"My name is Sybina."

"I'm John," he said and held out his hand.

Sybina shook it and gave him a bright smile. "I'm happy your son is okay."

"Your English has improved since the last time I saw you," John said.

"Yes. I practice every day," Sybina said with a strong accent.

"Where are you from?" John asked. "No wait, let me guess... are you from Brazil?"

Sybina laughed. "No."

"Israel?" he guessed while laughing.

"Spirima," Sybina revealed and saw his eyes shoot open in surprise.

"Wow, I don't think I've ever met anyone from Spirima. That's rare."

Sybina nodded and hoped he wouldn't be asking her about the civil war.

"But you live here in London now?" he asked.

"Yes."

"Do you come here often?"

"In the morning, yes," Sybina said and smiled again.

"Then maybe I'll see you some other time." John said and stood up. "I just want you to know how grateful we all are that you were there that day when Harry fell."

"My pleasure," Sybina said.

Sybina did meet John again. In fact she started meeting him most mornings and he would join her on her walks in the park. She learned that he was an author and had been divorced from his wife for the last three years, and that they still did many things together with the children such as picnics like the one Sybina had seen them on.

"It means a lot to the children," he told her and she agreed.

On the ninth day after their first meeting John announced that he was so inspired by Sybina that he was going to write a book about her.

"Really?" Sybina asked surprised.

"Absolutely! I don't think anyone really knows what happened in Spirima, and you could be my inspiration for a thriller. Did you hear about the English upper-class guy who apparently was a part of the terrorist organization down there? It was on the news this morning," John said.

Sybina shook her head. "Which guy?" she asked.

"I don't remember exactly... he's some sort of IT entrepreneur with a short name—K something."

Sybina stopped. "Try to remember. What was his name?"

John rubbed his forehead. "I don't remember, but hang on." He pulled out his phone and did a short search. "See, it's this guy Kato Mantonis. Do you know him?"

Sybina stared at the phone with a picture of Kato, and even though he was shaved and wearing a tuxedo in the picture Sybina recognized him right away and read the headlines with big eyes.

"Are you okay? You look pale," John said and put his hand on her shoulder.

"I think I need to sit down."

John led Sybina to a bench and gave her time to collect herself.

"I know him," Sybina said.

"You know Kato?" John asked.

"Yes." She nodded but left it at that.

"I'm a good listener if you want to talk."

Sybina frowned. "Thank you, John, but I have to go home to Aston."

"Your husband?"

"Yes."

"Okay, I can take you," he said and offered his arm to her. Without thinking Sybina took it and walked with John to her building.

"Thank you, John," Sybina said and gave him a small hug. Nine consecutive days of talking had made them friends.

"Any time, Sybina."

Sybina nodded before she went inside, feeling grateful to have a new friend in John.

As soon as she came into the apartment she saw Aston on the phone and the news channel running on the TV. Aston looked grave.

"I don't want to be part of this circus. I already did a press conference," he said into the phone and hung up.

"Are you okay?" Sybina asked him.

"I tried calling Aya and she's not picking up. I feel sorry for her and Kato... this is a mess." He pointed to the screen.

Sybina sat quietly watching and reading the headlines flashing over the screen. She felt sorry for Kato and Aya, who had been chased much more by the press than Aston had.

"What are you going to do?" she asked.

"I don't know." Aston paced the floor. "Apparently it all exploded yesterday evening but we escaped it because we went to the movies with our phones on silent. This morning after you left I looked at my phone and there are a ton of unanswered calls and messages... I wish they would just leave me the fuck alone. Sybina took the remote and turned the TV off. The room went silent.

"We have to help Kato," she said.

"He *was* a Masi warrior," Aston pointed out. "They're right about that part."

"True, but he was also the one who helped Aya escape and who unlocked your chains, not to mention killed the general."

Aston rubbed his forehead with his palm. "Do you know how hard it was to keep you out of the media when we first arrived? I don't want to get you dragged into all of this and have them turn up here to write stories of your time as a slave. We don't need that kind of exposure."

Sybina folded her arms in front of her. "So you would rather let Kato get executed for being a terrorist?"

"There's no death sentence in England. He would only get life in jail."

Sybina widened her eyes. "If you don't speak up, then I will. I'm not letting Kato become the next victim in this ugly war and spend his life in prison when his baby needs its father. Enough people have suffered, don't you think?"

"But what if he deserves it? You don't know what he did as a warrior. Don't you want revenge for what the Masi warriors did to you?" Aston argued. "And besides, the guy was a jerk to Aya when she came to see him, remember."

"I don't hold any anger towards Kato. I'm grateful to him and I'm dead serious, Aston. Either you tell what he did for us or I will. Aya loves Kato and he's the father of her child. If you won't do it for him, do it for her."

Aston was deep in his own thoughts for a while. "All right, you're right, we probably wouldn't be here if not for Kato, and I suppose I could spread the word without exposing you."

Sybina smiled. "Thank you, Aston, it's the right thing to do."

"I know," he said and picked up his phone with a heavy sigh.

Later that day Aya gave an interview in Norway that was transmitted to all news channels in England and Aston went on the nine o'clock news, where he confirmed her story.

Journalists kept calling, and the next day Sybina was saddened to see in the headlines that Kato had hurried to Norway, where Aya had been admitted to the local hospital with bleeding. She prayed to the higher powers that Aya wouldn't lose her baby and was relieved when Aya and Kato returned to London that same week. Aston had already spoken to Aya on the phone but Kato wanted to personally thank Aston for the positive things he had said about him in public, so Aya called Aston to let him know that she and Kato would swing by.

Sybina was delighted to have their first friends over and took the opportunity to make a superb dinner that surprised Aya and Kato, who didn't expect anything other than a cup of coffee.

"This bread is delicious," Kato said as they sat and enjoyed Sybina's home-cooked meal.

"So is this... what is it again?" Aya asked and took another bite.

"It's just a traditional Spiri dish with lamb, potatoes, garlic, and a bunch of herbs."

"Uhhm," Aya said. "It tastes amazing."

Sybina soaked up every compliment and was pleased to see Aston thaw to Kato. His resentment about Kato's being a Masi warrior and a jerk to Aya faded quickly and they fell into conversation easily. She saw them both laugh together and touch upon serious topics while she and Aya bonded over the food, the baby, and the fact that they were both with English men and new in a city without any friends.

Aya spoke broken Spiri and Sybina spoke enough English for them to have conversations that had meaning and heart, and made Sybina appreciate that in Aya she had an ally in this big city.

Over the next weeks Sybina and Aya hung out often when Aston and Kato went to work. Aya wanted to see all the tourist places and Sybina was happy to come along. She still did her morning walks but her tutoring with Jacob changed to two days a week instead of five. It gave her and Aya time to see the city by tube and the double-decker busses. They talked nonstop and commented on everything they saw, and it made Sybina's English stronger and more fluent. Kato and Aya stayed over for dinner, often, since Aya was a terrible cook and Sybina enjoyed making dinner and having them around. No one had to pretend with each other. All four knew about Spirima and the things that happened back there. Luckily Aston and Kato didn't seem to mind spending time together. They had learned that they had more in common than they thought when it turned out they had both gone to the same posh private school and knew some of the same people, even though Aston was four years older than Kato.

"I'm actually going to Liam's stag party this weekend," Aston said while they were eating Sybina's incredible chicken pie with salad in the kitchen.

Kato looked up. "Liam Addams?"

"Yeah, he's getting married to the youngest of the Diggins sisters. Do you know her?"

Kato shot Aston a smug smile. "I know the middle sister, she used to date a former friend of mine."

"You mean Oliver?" Aya asked.

Kato nodded. "He's into the gold-digger type, and the Diggins sisters don't date anyone without money... stacks of money."

Aston laughed. "I heard that rumor too. We can't make it to their wedding as it's the same day as yours, but I'm looking forward to a night out with some of the old gang this Saturday."

"Speaking of that... can I just say how excited I am that your wedding is only three weeks from now?" Sybina interjected.

"Almost four," Aston corrected but was ignored by the two women, who were now going over the guest list.

"I can't wait for you two to meet my family and my crazy but amazing friend, Sofia," Aya said excitedly and stuck out her tongue at Aston, who dramatically banged his head down the table.

"Who started the wedding talk?"

Aya broke into an infectious grin. "You did, with your talk of stag parties."

Aston looked lost. "Christ, I need to keep my mouth shut. I'm going to shoot myself if I have to sit through another evening and listen to you two talk about colors on napkins."

"But you're so good with colors and decorations, we really need your feminine input on important matters like that," Aya mocked him.

Aston puffed out his chest and squared his shoulders. "I'm getting a beer... do you want one, Kato?"

Aya pretended to cry and dry her eyes while suppressing a grin. "Ohhh, the girls are being mean to me, I need to suck on a bottle of beer." It made Sybina and the others laugh. It was hard to resist Aya's positive personality and the way she was fearless around Aston. Whenever he became grumpy she made fun of him and got him to loosen up on the big mean alpha male attitude.

245

The jealousy Sybina had once felt towards Aya was gone now that she saw Aya around Kato and the love that they shared. Instead she felt a deep connection of solidarity and friendship with Aya.

"I forgot to ask you about Uma," Aya said. "How is she and when is she coming?"

Aston took a sip of his beer and looked at Sybina. She knew the mention of Uma always brought up in him the feeling of having failed. When they escaped the Masi headquarters Aston had promised Uma he would go back and get her mother out too, but with the explosive fire burning down the house, Aston had chosen to get Sybina and Uma to safety instead. She knew he still had people looking for Hunilla in Spirima, but so far no one had made any progress in the search; and in the meanwhile Uma was left alone in a boarding school with no friends or family around.

Sybina forced a smile. "We might be able to get her up here on a tourist visa at the end of August, but school starts again on September 1 and they don't look kindly on absence."

"To hell with the school." Aya exclaimed forcefully. "The girl needs some solid hugs and love. Just get her up here as fast as possible."

Sybina looked at Aston, who she had been discussing the situation with earlier today. They were torn between the school rules and the desire to have Uma with them. Aston gave her a silent nod and she knew he agreed with Aya.

"She can fly in on the twenty-fourth and if she stays two weeks she's only missing out on one week of school."

Aya clapped her hands... "That's in twelve days."

Sybina felt tears pressing. The thought of calling Uma to tell her to pack her things made her heart flutter.

"It's finally happening," she whispered. "But what if she doesn't like it here?"

Aya gave Sybina a hug. "Oh, sweetie, we're going to make sure she loves it."

Sybina was tugged into Aya's hug and caught a glimpse of Aston frowning and was unsure of what he was thinking; maybe he thought her too emotional or maybe he wanted to be the one hugging her. She never knew what he was thinking; communicating with Aston was still a challenge.

CHAPTER 24
A Letter for the General

Uma

"Again from the beginning... one, two, three," Uma heard Jasmin shout over the loud music and started dancing again. Uma did the routine as Jasmin had taught her and tried to focus on stretching her arms like Jasmin wanted her to.

"Good," Jasmin shouted, and the encouragement made Uma try even harder when she got to the tricky part. "Right, right, left, spin around, head down, look up, roll up slowly, slide to the side, hands up, twist, and pose."

Uma ended in a pose with one hand in the air and the other resting on her side. Looking into the mirror she saw she looked funny with her serious expression and the unnatural body posture, but Jasmin applauded. "That's it, now you got the steps and we can start on improving the way you move."

Uma frowned and it made Jasmin laugh. "Don't worry, you're already doing amazingly... but we can all improve, Uma... you and me included. Come on, let's do it again and make sure the steps are drilled into your brain."

They practiced for another hour and then Jasmin stopped the music.

"It almost nine o'clock, we should wrap it up—but before we do it's time for that show I promised you." Jasmin's eyes sparkled.

"Your first dance routine?"

"Yes, the one that I practiced at home and copied from the music video. This is Thriller, the song that started my love for dancing."

Uma moved to the side, and Jasmin pushed play and took a position with her head down waiting for the music to start. Strange sounds of a creaking door, footsteps, and howling wolves started and then the singing began. Uma wasn't sure if the person singing was male or female, but she was highly entertained by Jasmin's dance that made her look retarded with the way she held her head and hands. She almost looked scary with the way she made big eyes and opened her mouth with her head tilted. It was completely different from Jasmin's other type of dancing, normally graceful and sensual. This was just odd and funny. When she was done she bowed and Uma clapped politely.

"What kind of dancing was that?" she asked.

"It was 'Thriller' with Michael Jackson."

"It looked... different."

"It's supposed to look different, it's zombies dancing." Jasmin started packing her things.

"What's a zombie?" Uma asked.

"A dead person awoken from his or her grave."

"But that's impossible," Uma pointed out.

Jasmin emptied her water bottle. "Of course, but it makes a good story."

"It must have been nice to dance around like that as a child. I bet you had a perfect childhood." Uma walked out of the dance studio, waiting for Jasmin to turn off the light. The dance studio was in a side building, and they walked slowly towards the main building where their rooms were.

"You know, Uma, I don't know what happened to you before you came here, but I know enough of a slave's life to not want to compare my misery with yours, but just know this. Not everything that shines is gold."

Uma wrinkled her forehead. "What do you mean?"

"Just that I might have grown up in a wealthy family with connections and a powerful family name, but behind the façade things happened that shouldn't be happening to any child."

Uma stopped and stared at Jasmin, who in her eyes was the picture of perfection. "Were you beaten?"

Jasmin looked at her and sighed. They had reached the entrance to the main building, and she took a seat on the large stone steps leading up to the front door of the school. "Let's just say my childhood wasn't the fairy tale people think it was."

"I don't understand."

"My brother was four years older than me and he would come to my room at night."

"What did he do to you?" Uma asked with her mouth gaping.

"At first he fumbled at me and later he forced himself on me."

"Didn't you fight him?"

"I did, but he was much stronger and I was so young when it started. Eventually it just became a nightly ritual that my brother came and did his thing."

"He raped you?" Uma's voice rose to a high pitch and Jasmin hushed her.

"Yes, every night for many years."

Uma narrowed her eyes. "Men are pigs. If I ever see him I'll kill him," she said decisively.

Jasmin shook her head. "My brother joined the Masi warriors and was killed four years ago. I think he got what he deserved and besides, the secret got out eventually."

"How?"

"We received a last letter from him where he wrote an apology and after that I had to explain to my parents about what happened."

"I know about last letters, I saw the recruits write them when they joined. Some of them cried like babies writing those letters," Uma said in a mocking tone. "But what did your parents do then?"

"Uma, I have to be honest with you. Incest is not that uncommon in this country and my mother experienced it too. It's a taboo that people just don't talk about, and my parents reacted by sending me to a psychologist to deal with it.

"A what?"

"It's like a doctor who helps you feel better when the thing that is wrong is in your mind and not your body."

"Oh, okay. So did he heal you?"

"I don't think you ever completely heal from something like that, but he did help me forgive my brother."

Uma's eyes narrowed and she leaned her elbows on the step behind her. "Really. And how did he help you do that?"

"He had me write a letter to my brother and tell him about my feelings, and that helped."

"But your brother was dead," Uma said, confused.

"I know, but writing the letter made me feel better, like I got rid of some of the anger I had been carrying inside me."

"Hmm."

"Maybe you should try it too."

"What, write a letter to the general?"

"Yeah, and every other person who hurt you."

Uma snorted. "That would be a long list of men."

"Well, make that list and work your way through it. What do you have to lose?"

"Time. I'm studying to catch up to the others, and all my teachers gave me assignments to keep me busy all summer."

"Okay, but then why don't you write one letter tonight, and see how it feels."

"Okay, one letter and no more," Uma agreed and got up from the stairs. "I'll see you tomorrow for the run."

"Yep, seven-thirty as usual," Jasmin said and smiled. "And you did good today, your dancing is really coming along."

"Thanks." Uma waved and ran into the house and up the stairs to the attic where she could be all alone.

That night she wrote a letter to the general and was happy that no one was there to hear her growls and her sobbing as she worked her way through it.

To you. The general. The cruelest man in this world.

I hate you! I hate you! I hate you!
I hate everything you did to my mom and me, and I wish you would die in hell with the worst death possible. You deserve it and I would go to hell to torture you myself if I could.
I would stab you with a knife, burn you with a torch, and make markings on your skin like you marked me and every other slave you owned.
I would whip you until you didn't know your own name.
I would cut your fingers and toes off like you did with the hostages and I would do it slow to prolong the pain.
I would choke you, hit you, kick you, and break every bone in your vile body with pleasure just like I was choked, hit, and kicked into a coma in your bedroom.
I would cut your head off like you did with the soldiers and prisoners you sacrificed to Masi and while we're at it I would cut your chest open to see how black your heart must look.

I would put a bullet to your head and splatter your brain on the wall with a laugh like you did with others.

I would have the devils rape you in all your holes and pull your hair out and spit on you and call you useless trash because that's how you treated others yourself.

Basically, I wish I could use my summer vacation from school to come down to hell and kill you again and again with as much pain as possible. I would do it for the hostages, the prisoners, the deserters, your personal slaves, and for every other slave you kept a slave longer than legal by starting that stupid war. I would do it for my mother who you raped, beat, and whipped more times than I can count. And I would do it for Sybina who you kept in a basement as your slave for five years when she could have been free. And for me because I was an innocent child born into your sick world of evil and you never once showed me any kindness. There is no excuse for behaving like you did!

My mom once told me that you were not always like this but I don't believe her. I know in my heart that you must have been born evil and the war was just your excuse to kill as many as possible. May you rot in hell with the other devils and may every day bring you the same amount of pain that you caused others in your miserable life.

Umbra

The next morning Uma met with Jasmin by the front door like always, and she handed her the letter.

"I wrote the letter to the general," she said. "Do you want to read it?"

"Do you want me to?" Jasmin asked.

"It was your idea, so you might as well see what came out of it."

"All right." Jasmine took the letter and read it silently, and then she folded it and handed it back to Uma, who put it in the pocket of her sweatpants.

"Well, you certainly didn't hold anything back... there's a lot of anger in that letter. How did it feel to get it out?" Jasmin asked and started running towards the gates like they did every morning on schooldays.

"Good." Uma followed Jasmin without sharing about the many torn-up pages she had written before that one and the pain of going over all the horror the general had caused in her life. She had cried and screamed into her pillow but afterwards there had been a bit of relief.

"You know, my psychologist told me that in order to get to acceptance and ultimately forgiveness we have to cross the bridge of anger. That's what the letters are for. To get it out of your system so you can move on."

"That might take a thousand letters in my case," Uma said dryly.

"Was the general your father?"

"No, I don't think so. He had brown eyes like my mother and mine are green. Also he wasn't a tall man, and I'm half a head taller than my mom and far paler than both her and the general."

"Do you have an idea who your father might be?"

"Yeah."

"Who?"

"A tall, pale, green-eyed swine who used my mom, that's who." Uma scowled and picked up the pace. Uma was faster than Jasmin and could easily run an hour without getting tired.

"Take it easy, Uma, I just want to jog today," Jasmin called after her and Uma slowed down again. She didn't like jogging, she liked sprinting full pace, but Jasmin preferred to talk while they ran.

On her first morning run with Jasmin they had met Tristan and his group, who had questioned why Jasmin was running with a student. Jasmin had gracefully disarmed the young men by telling them that she would have been running with them if they weren't so damn fast. That boosted their egos and they gallantly offered to slow down their pace if Jasmin ever wanted to join their group.

After they were gone Uma told Jasmin about her encounter with Tristan and his group, and Jasmin had assured her that there were no dangerous animals in the area. "If you're lucky you'll meet a deer, a cow, or a goat, but that's about as exciting as it gets around here."

The next time Uma and Jasmin met the group, Uma had to swallow her grin when Jasmin called after them, "Be careful about the bears and the snakes, will you, boys? The school wouldn't be the same without you." Most of the guys had no idea what she was referring to and just smiled and waved at her, but Tristan narrowed his eyes and pinned Uma with intense hatred. Uma didn't mind; she just hoped he got Jasmin's message about leaving Uma alone.

There had been forty days of running since that first time and it was now mid-August, with almost all the students vacationing. Uma enjoyed the quiet and spent her time in the library and on the lawn studying when she wasn't running or dancing with Jasmin or cooking with her only other friend at the school, Martha, who worked in the kitchen and lived in the village.

"I hope you don't mind me asking this, but did you have slaves in your house when you grew up?" Uma asked Jasmin.

"Yes, we had four, but so did every other family we knew. I never thought about it until the war broke out. Tradition is a peculiar thing, isn't it?" Jasmin said, out of breath.

"I suppose so," Uma answered.

"Uma, about your letter. I was wondering if the general did to you what my brother did to me, but it wasn't really clear to me."

Uma furrowed her brows and looked away; she didn't like to think about it. "My mother protected me as much as she could and made a pact with him of some kind that meant he had to wait until I was thirteen. When my birthday came he wanted to have sex with me, but I refused."

"What happened then?"

"He and another man beat me up and almost killed me."

"Bastards," Jasmin hissed.

"I told you. All men are swine," Uma said again.

Jasmin shook her head. "I hope you're wrong about that; I would like to believe there are decent men in this world and that I'll find someone special soon."

"Why?" Uma asked with a frown.

"What do you mean why? I'm tired of going out with the wrong kind of men, I want to meet someone who treats me with respect and loves me."

Uma stopped running abruptly and turned to face Jasmin in absolute horror. "You go out with *men*?" Her strong reaction made Jasmin laugh and run back to her.

"Yes, Uma, I do," Jasmin said and stood opposite her with a hand blocking the sun.

"What for?"

Jasmin pointed her index finger at Uma's nose tip. "You're funny, you know that?"

Uma didn't respond, but kept looking at Jasmin to understand why Jasmin would want to go out with men when she knew what men were capable of and what pigs they really were.

"Okay, I'm going to tell you a secret, but you can never tell anyone, all right?" Jasmin lowered her voice.

Uma nodded.

256

"This teaching job is my cover. I do this to keep my parents off my back and to make money, of course, but I make most of my money on the weekends as a go-go dancer in the city."

"What kind of dancer is that?" Uma said suspiciously, wondering why it was a secret.

"I work in a large night club and dance on a high podium where no one can touch me. I get the people hyped and on the dance floor."

"So you strip for them?" Uma asked, knowing how often her mom had been asked to strip for the soldiers to music. Her mother had told her she always found that a humiliating experience.

Jasmin shook her head. "No, Uma, I'm not a stripper. I'm a go-go dancer, and my job is to get people on the dance floor and make them have a good time."

"And that pays well?"

"Yes, it pays *very* well because of all the tips I get, and whenever I'm on break I get free drinks from the guys and invitations to expensive restaurants. I never pay for a meal when I'm in town."

"And you like those men?"

"No, of course not, but I use them to make money and I hope that one day I'll actually meet a man who is different."

"Sounds like you believe in fairy tales," Uma said with her arms folded.

"Don't be such a cynic." Jasmin elbowed Uma. "I see the boys looking after you at school. They may be afraid of you, but no one can deny that you are very pretty; I'm sure you could get a boyfriend if you wanted to," she joked.

"Are you drunk, Miss C?" Uma asked with a raised eyebrow.

"No." Jasmin grinned.

"Are you high on something then?"

"Absolutely not," Jasmin said and started running again. "You can pretend that all men are evil and bad, but one day, one of them is going to sweep you off your feet and change your mind."

"Ha. Never!"

"I hope it happens… for your sake. And I sure as hell hope it will happen for me too."

Uma shook her head. "It won't happen to me. I know that as surely as I know my name is Uma."

"Well, in that case you have nothing to worry about, do you?" Jasmin said with a beaming smile.

CHAPTER 25
Opportunities

Sybina

Sybina looked up and down the street. John was late, and it was very unusual for him to be so. Every morning he met Sybina on her walks and always on this corner, only five minutes from where Sybina lived. They would walk together around the area and he would show her parks and streets she hadn't seen before. John had a good sense of humor, he was easy to talk to, and he made her feel like the most interesting person in the world. He asked her about Spirima, her childhood, traditions, her work, her passions, what she missed, what she thought about London, the Brits, the food, the traffic, and the candy. Whenever she said, "I don't know, I haven't tried it," he would go out of his way to introduce her to it. Last week he had taken her to taste ice cream and she had tried a little taster spoon of all twenty-three sorts that the tiny store carried. She now knew that her favorite ice cream was raspberry.

Another time he had brought licorice for her to taste and yesterday he shared a bag of jelly beans with her.

Meeting with John was always entertaining and he was good at telling stories from his life. Before he met his ex-wife and had his three children he used to travel a lot, and he told stories from exotic places that made her want to explore the world herself. John talked about his children, and Sybina took joy in seeing his pride of their achievements and growth. John was a good father and she didn't understand why his ex-wife didn't want to be married to him anymore. He seemed so nice, kind, and loving.

Maybe he wasn't particularly handsome but he had a kind heart, and Sybina hoped he would soon find a woman who would appreciate his gentle manners and humor.

"Sybina, dear." John's calling out got her attention and she turned to see him hurry towards her.

"Please forgive me for being late today... it was only because I stopped by that place I told you about—the holistic health clinic where I have my allergies treated—and I told Cindy about you. She's the owner and she said she would like to meet you tomorrow."

"Tomorrow?" Sybina exclaimed with excitement.

"Yes, we'll go there tomorrow morning and you two can talk about work."

Sybina clapped her hands and gave a little jump. "Yeah... this is so exciting."

"I know, but listen, we have to make it a quick walk today because I've got a deadline with my editor, who wants to see the first three chapters of my new book."

"And you're not ready?"

"Almost. I just need a little finishing."

"Okay, that's fine. I'm meeting Aya for lunch today anyway."

"How is Aya?" John knew Aya only from the media and from Sybina's chitchat about their friendship.

"She's good, I think. The wedding is close now."

"And the pregnancy."

"The baby is fine."

"Wonderful, and Uma?"

"I'm calling Uma today and telling her to come."

"What do you mean? Did the papers go through?"

"Yes."

"That's amazing. So she's finally moving here."

Sybina shook her head.

"No, not adoption. Just the tourist visa. Uma will come next week, Sunday."

"Okay, I understand. But still, that's amazing, Bina. I'm so happy for you."

Sybina smiled. John called her Bina and sweetie and darling and many other things, and every time they bumped into someone he knew he would most often call them sweetie and darling too. It was one of his charms.

They walked for forty minutes before they went different ways and Sybina half flew home, feeling so happy about this morning's walk.

When she got home she called Aston to tell him the good news but he was in a meeting and would call her back.

In the meantime she showered, changed her clothes, put on a bit of mascara and some lip gloss, and combed her hair before she left the apartment to meet with Aya for lunch.

When Aston called her she was on the bus and the connection was bad. She tried to tell him about the holistic health clinic and Emily but he seemed distracted and busy.

"Listen, can we talk about this when I get home?"

"Okay."

"I got the ticket for Uma, so call her today, okay?"

"I will."

"Okay, see you later," Aston said.

"See you." Sybina put the phone away. She would call Uma when she was somewhere quieter; and besides, she needed to pay attention not to miss her stop. Riding the bus was still new to her.

She got out by London Bridge and went up the escalators to the Rooftop Café, where the view was fantastic; Aya was already there.

"My god, Aya, you look fantastic—it's like you're glowing."

261

"Thank you, sweetie, I feel wonderful and you look beautiful too."

Sybina gave Aya a huge smile. "Thank you. It's a good day today."

"Tell me." Aya said and leaned in when Sybina took a seat at the table.

"I might get a job tomorrow."

"As what?"

"I'm not sure. But it's a holistic health clinic so a healer or homeopath would be my guess. Honestly, they could hire me to clean or cook and I would take it. I just really want to make my own money."

"Seriously?"

"Yes."

"Then I would like to hire you as my magical fairy," Aya said, laughing.

"Your what?"

"My magic fairy to keep our house presentable and inviting. Now that we're moving to a bigger place I could really need some help, and you know I'm just not good with the whole cleaning and cooking thing. If you're serious I would love to hire you to help, and when the baby comes you could be the nanny."

Sybina tilted her head. "But I would do all that for free, Aya; just tell me what you need."

Aya waved a finger in the air. "No, no, I insist on paying you, and it really would be you doing Kato and me a huge favor. Let's agree that once you know if, and how much you'll be working at the clinic, then we can figure out how many hours you can work at our house. And I can guarantee you that I will pay you a generous salary."

"Don't you think you should ask Kato first?" Sybina asked.

"Absolutely not! I have my own money."

"Are you rich like Kato?" Sybina asked in surprise. "Does a nurse make a lot of money in Norway?"

"No, I'm afraid not, but the insurance company paid me a small fortune when I came back to Norway because of the physical and emotional pain I went through."

"Really." Sybina couldn't believe what she was hearing. Aya had been a hostage for six days and been paid a fortune, and Sybina had been working as a slave for sixteen years and never seen any money at all.

"Yes, and now that I live with Kato I'm selling my apartment in Stavanger, and that means more money coming in and no expenses, so I would *love* to do something useful with that money and pay you triple for helping me out."

"Well, in that case, you've got yourself a deal," Sybina said and shook Aya's hand formally.

Aya didn't leave it with a handshake but pulled Sybina into a big hug before she leaned her head back and started laughing all the way from her belly. "I wonder what Aston says when he discovers that I snatched you for my household. I'll have him on the phone two minutes later."

Sybina laughed with Aya. "I suppose you would... under normal circumstances." They both knew Aston was a rich man and wouldn't want his real wife to clean other people's houses for money. But the agreement he and Sybina had was that she would use the two years' safety net that he offered her to build a life for her and Uma. That meant an independent income, learning English, and eventually finding a place to live on her own.

Aya was the only person who knew the truth about Sybina and Aston's marriage, and Sybina appreciated that they could speak openly about it.

"Don't fool yourself, Sybina. As long as you are officially Aston's wife, everything you do will reflect on him. He won't like people thinking he isn't providing for all your needs.

"Hmm... we'll see," Sybina said.

A waiter approached them and asked for their order. Sybina hadn't had a chance to look at the menu but Aya recommended the risotto, so she went with that.

"Is Uma still coming on the twenty-fourth?" Aya asked.

"How did you know that?" Sybina asked.

"Remember at your house when you were unsure about whether or not to bring her up here, and Aston said she could fly in for two weeks."

"Oh yeah, that's right." Sybina placed the napkin on her lap like Aya had done. "And yes, she is. I'm calling Uma later today to tell her the good news."

"Let's drink to that." Aya raised her glass and they toasted in sparkling water.

For a moment Sybina took in the beautiful view of the London skyline and then she asked a question that she had been meaning to ask Aya since the first time she met her.

"Aya?" she started.

"Yes."

"Were you there when the general died?"

Aya took a sip of her water and nodded. "Yes, I was there."

"Would you mind telling me how he died?" Sybina asked.

Aya took a deep long sigh and then she told Sybina in a low voice about the night she had been whipped by the general and Kato, and the way Kato had stabbed his uncle in the back.

Sybina didn't say a word while Aya talked. She just listened, and only when Aya was done talking did Sybina look up with teary eyes and take Aya's hand.

"Thank you, Aya. I wanted to kill him myself for all the misery he caused the people around him."

Aya blinked away a few tears. "I can only imagine what you've gone through and the horrors you've seen," she whispered and then she cleared her throat. "And Uma, of

264

course, poor girl... Kato told me stories about her, you know."

"Really? What stories?" Sybina immediately felt uneasy.

Aya lowered her voice. "Kato remembers Uma from the Masi headquarters, and he told me that his uncle once killed a soldier because of her."

"He told you that?" Sybina knew the episode; she had just never spoken of it. "What exactly did he tell you?"

"Well, according to Kato every soldier knew that Uma was off limits. She belonged to the general and was not to be touched, but when she was nine or ten one of the soldiers tried to rape her, and the general got so furious that he shot the guy."

"Most of it is true," Sybina said.

Aya's eyes grew big. "There's more to the story?"

Sybina's chest rose in a long, deep sigh. "I'm only telling you this so you understand what Uma went through as a child. There were several incidents around Uma, but the one Kato is referring to happened almost four years ago when she was nine and a half. Uma was one of the slaves serving food in the soldiers' dining hall the day it happened. The soldiers were celebrating a victorious day and they had been drinking for hours. One of the soldiers grabbed Uma as she walked by and forced her down on his lap, trying to kiss her. She was disgusted by him and much to the men's amusement, she fought back. The guy wanted to put her in her place, or show off perhaps, and while the other soldiers cheered him on he threw Uma down on the table and ripped her clothes off. He would probably have succeeded raping her because she had no way of fighting him off, being only half his size.

"But Uma is resourceful, and she found the only weapon she could in her position. She grabbed a wine bottle and smashed it into his head as hard as she could. It worked to get him off her, but the guy was drunk and didn't feel the pain as much as he normally would have, so he attacked her again. She used the broken part of the bottle to cut him, but he hit her hard several times and broke her collarbone. That's when the general arrived." Sybina was far away in her memories and stopped talking.

"And what happened then?" Aya asked.

"The general broke up the fight and made sure everyone understood that Uma was off limits by setting an example."

"The general shot the soldier," Aya said, making it sound like a question.

"Yes. First he shot him through both his hands so he would never touch the general's slaves without permission. Then he shot him twice in the crotch and left him for the others to deal with. One of them ran to get me and I came to help, but by then the soldier had already shot himself through the head."

Aya shook her head violently. "Psychopaths and sociopaths."

"I know. I can't wait to get Uma up here to live among normal people and experience a better life. I know the school is a big step up, but it's so far away and I think she's lonely."

Aya suddenly made a small jump in her seat like she had the best idea ever. "We should bring Aidan to meet Uma next week."

"You mean Kato's younger brother?" Sybina asked.

"Yes... he's only seventeen and he's adorable."

"I don't know... Uma is kind of hostile to boys," Sybina warned.

"Ha, don't worry. Aidan is extremely popular with the girls. He's just as handsome as Kato and so unbelievably charming and funny. I'm sure she'll love him." Aya picked up her phone and showed Sybina a picture. "Look, can you see the resemblance to Kato? I imagine this is how Kato looked when he was a teenager."

Sybina looked at the phone and saw a picture of Kato with his arm around Aidan.

"What a cute smile he has," Sybina commented and noticed that Aidan had the same beautiful brown eyes as Kato's. "He has nice eyes," she said.

Aya nodded. "They both do. I've noticed that Aidan has slightly lighter eyes than Kato, though, more like hazel brown. But anyway, what do you think?"

"I don't know, Aya. Uma is not your average thirteen-year-old girl. I know that you mean well, but she really doesn't like guys."

"Oh, don't get me wrong, I didn't mean it in a romantic way or anything. Aidan is always surrounded by girls; he wouldn't be interested in anyone that young anyway... I just thought that he was the closest person to her own age who speaks Spiri around here, and it might be good for her to make a friend before she moves here permanently."

Sybina thought about it. "Alright. Maybe you're right. But I'm warning you, Uma can be a feisty handful. There have been several incidents at her school where boys got too close to her."

Aya looked curious. "What does she do to them? Hopefully the place doesn't have wine bottles standing around."

"No, but she still beats them up."

"You're joking?"

"Nope."

"Beat them up how?"

"Okay, maybe 'beat up' is the wrong description, but last month she twisted a boy's arm because he wouldn't leave her alone. She broke his thumb."

"She broke his thumb?"

"Yes."

"Didn't she get in trouble with the school then?"

"Yes, but she didn't get expelled because the security footage showed that the boy grabbed her hair and made suggestive gestures at her to provoke her."

"Stupid boy," Aya said. "Does she fight girls as well?"

"Uma doesn't fight anyone she doesn't feel threatened by. She never did. She's just so on guard and used to having to protect herself that I think she forgets that these are just kids and not dangerous soldiers. It really pains me that Uma is having such a hard time at the school too. She doesn't connect with the other kids, and who can blame her? She hasn't met much friendliness in her life. Sometimes when I talk to her, I feel like she's a thirty-year-old person stuck in a thirteen-year-old body. But in other ways she's like me, completely clueless about what other people consider normal."

"Any news on her mother?"

"No, still no sign. I believe she died in the fire. But Uma still has hope and we'll do whatever we can to find her mother again, if she's alive."

"Well, just let us know if you need anything. Kato can sponsor a search if needed. I'm sure it'll help him feel better, if he can be of any service."

"I'll tell Aston. But honestly, I just want Uma to come and stay with us already."

"How is that going?"

"Not well. We can't adopt until her mother has been officially missing for two years and we can't be foster parents because we live abroad. For now we're waiting, hoping to find her mother and bring them both here somehow. Uma really needs love from family and friends."

"I know," Aya said determinedly. "And that is why we'll bring Aidan. He's such a happy kind of guy. Ahh, stop looking at me like that, Sybina... Aidan is a big boy, he doesn't scare easily." Aya smiled.

"If you say so." Sybina grinned. "But don't say I didn't warn you."

CHAPTER 26
Jealousy

Aston

To Aston, life was good. It had been two months since he brought Sybina back to London with him; his mission was on track with Uma flying in for a two-week visit in only eight days; and Sybina was already speaking English well enough to carry a conversation.

He was lying in bed and listening to the water running from Sybina's shower. He knew her morning routine, as she was always sticking to the same thing all seven days a week. A quick shower where she didn't get her hair wet, then a light breakfast followed by a morning walk. He didn't understand why she showered before she walked since she always showered again when she came back, but from his days spent in Sybina's infirmary he knew she was a little obsessed with cleanliness.

Aston didn't mind; after more than ten years in the military he liked routines himself and he actually appreciated that Sybina was so predictable.

He heard her turn off the water and knew she would soon be walking through the bedroom in only a towel, and that if he stayed in bed he would have a ringside seat for watching her dress herself. The thought made him smile. Even though he had just taken her this morning, the thought of her smooth naked skin and the perfect handful of her perky breasts made him hard again. Sybina was divine and she never said no to sex. His cock jerked at the

269

thought of her small whimpers and her body shaking with her orgasm.

Sex with Sybina was nowhere as advanced as what he had previously shared with Tara and other women before her, but it made him burst with masculine pride that he was the first to do it all: the first to take her on the floor, the sofa, the counter, in the shower, in the car; and the first man to make her beautiful body shiver with orgasms and give her goosebumps because of a simple ice-cube melting on her hot body or him licking ice cream off her. He was the first to come on her breasts, her belly, her thighs, and her cute little ass. Sometimes he felt like he was branding her with his semen, and the primitive thought made him shake his head in wonder.

Most of the sex they had was downright boring compared to the things he had done in the past. He had to restrain himself and be gentle with her, which was difficult for someone like Aston who wasn't normally a gentle lover, but someone who liked to fuck hard and dirty. He would have sworn he wasn't into virgins and innocence; he always chose women who were kinky, open-minded, and got turned on by rough sex. Women like that threw themselves at him and begged for more because he was freaking expert at making his women scream with ecstasy. A lazy smile spread on his lips and he folded his hands behind his head, leaning back in the soft pillows and indulging in memories. Several of his lovers had called him addictive and one had him on speed dial with the name Mr. Sex God.

A small chuckle escaped him thinking of the rough, uninhibited, hard-core sex from his past and then he shook his head to pull himself together. He couldn't have that with Sybina, as he suspected even a smack in her butt would freak her out. No one could blame her; even though she hadn't been raped by the Masi warriors herself, she had seen and experienced brutality from men for years.

No, his job was to gently show her that sex with him was a safety zone where she never had to worry or be afraid. He had willingly put aside his need for rough bed-play and indulged in plain sex, which was still better than no sex and surprisingly satisfying, come to think of it.

In the beginning he had felt sure he would soon tire of her like he had tired of every other woman he had ever been with. It hadn't happened yet; in fact he felt insatiable and kept wanting more from her. He had wondered why that was and had come to the conclusion that it was because he had an end date. He had committed to a two-year scam marriage and felt sure that when the time was up and he didn't have to share his bed with Sybina any more, he would automatically lose interest in her. Steadfast, Aston dismissed the nagging thought inside him that questioned his logic.

When the door opened and Sybina came out with wet hair and a towel around her, Aston stayed in bed and returned Sybina's careless smile. *Beautiful*, he thought.

"I have to hurry," Sybina said over her shoulder as she bent down to put on her panties. Aston was too focused on her bent position and the free view of her two perfect round curves to listen.

"John is taking me to meet a friend of his who has a holistic health clinic; maybe I can work there," Sybina said and pulled a t-shirt over her head and jumped into a pair of soft pants that fell perfectly around her hips.

Aston pushed himself up in a sitting position. "Who is John?"

Sybina turned and placed her hands on her hips. "Honestly, Aston, do you ever listen to anything I say? John is the author who is writing a book with me as his inspiration... remember?"

Aston shook his head. "No, I don't remember. How do you know... this John?"

"We walk in the mornings. He's an author."

271

Aston's face tightened. "And how long have you been walking with him?"

Sybina shrugged. "I don't know exactly... a little over a month, I think."

It felt like a vein had popped in Aston's head. *Why the hell didn't I know this... who is that man and is he a threat in any way?*

"Why didn't you tell me?" Aston said, trying to control the irritation he felt inside.

"I *did* tell you, but you must not have paid attention."

"And John is getting you a job?"

Sybina put her hair up in a ponytail. "I hope so. He's introducing me to the lady who runs the clinic. He told her about me and she wanted to meet me." Sybina smiled and turned around. "I'm late, but I'll see you later."

Aston heard the front door close behind her and jumped out of bed. In no time he put on running clothes, a cap, and sunglasses and went after her. He needed to check out this John. He ran down the stairs to the street. He could see Sybina walking down the street and followed her discreetly. After a five-minute walk Aston saw a man wave at Sybina and when they came close enough, they hugged. Aston narrowed his eyes and moved closer to get a better look at the guy. He was older than Aston, but not by much, and he looked like a traditional academic with square black glasses, a white shirt, and gray trousers. Aston only got a quick look at his face but felt pleased to see that John had a receding hairline, a large nose, and thin lips. Aston felt confident that Sybina couldn't possibly consider John nearly as handsome as himself, and with the man's weak shoulders and thin body he couldn't be much of a sight with his clothes off.

Aston kept close enough to hear bits and pieces of their conversation and understood that John was talking about his children; Aston hated how interested Sybina seemed to be, knowing that children were a soft spot for her.

They laughed a lot and Aston couldn't help making a fist after noticing how often John touched Sybina with his shoulder and arm, simply by walking too close to her.

It wasn't hard to follow two civilians like John and Sybina who had no clue they were being followed. John was doing most of the talking and he spoke loud and clear, making it easy for Aston to follow most of the conversation.

"Do you have any exciting plans for tonight?" John asked Sybina, who shook her head.

"No, Aston is going out with friends."

"You don't need him to have fun, do you?"

Aston saw Sybina shrug.

"I could take you to see a movie or we could go to a restaurant or something."

Sybina laughed and shook her head but her reply was too low for Aston to understand.

"No, really, Bina, I don't think Aston would mind. If you were my wife, I would want you to have friends and to enjoy yourself." John's words made Aston clench his teeth and yell at John internally. *Shut the fuck up, you bloody retard, and stop calling my wife Bina.* Aston's heart was racing and most of all he wanted to pull Sybina with him back to the apartment and explain to her what a creep John was, but he knew she wouldn't take that well. Instead he followed Sybina and John to the holistic clinic on Earlham Street, where they went inside.

Twenty minutes later they came out and from the way Sybina radiated excitement, Aston knew the meeting had been successful. He followed them back and heard John talk about celebrating and once again offering to take Sybina out. This time Aston didn't hear her say no because a family passed them and forced Aston to fall back a bit.

When he did catch up they made a stop and Aston turned around to look at a window display. He could see their reflections in the window and was still close enough to hear John say: "Here, darling, take my new card, it has the new number." John leaned in and kissed Sybina on the cheek... "Until tonight then."

Something close to rage broke out in Aston. *Darling? Tonight? What the hell is going on?* John had already walked on and Sybina looked like she was heading home, but Aston decided to beat her to it and ran a shortcut. He was still upset and angry when Sybina returned, and it took all his willpower to smile when she came in with the exciting news.

"The owner of the holistic clinic is going to take me on for a three months' trial period... can you believe it? I'm starting after Uma's visit."

"That's great. Congratulations."

"Thank you." Sybina came over to give Aston a hug, and even though he really wanted that hug he was stiff and tense. Aston and Sybina were not very physical around each other, except in bed. There was no kissing, holding hands, back rubs, or spontaneous hugs between them, so for Sybina to come and hug him was a big thing.

"So how are you going to celebrate?" Aston asked and looked down, disguising his tense jaw.

"Maybe we could go out for lunch and celebrate it?" Sybina asked.

"I can't, I'm leaving in thirty minutes for Liam's stag party."

"That early?"

"It's a whole-day event."

"Alright, never mind then."

Aston looked up at her happy face and tried to bite his tongue, but the question was eating him up and he had to know. "Are you going out with John tonight?"

Sybina took a step back and her joyful expression faded. "What?"

Aston could feel the fire in his chest. "Oh, come on, *Bina*. I heard him invite you out… did you say yes or no?" There was accusation in the words.

Aston hated the way Sybina was looking at him, as if she was seeing him for the first time and not liking what she saw.

"John is just a friend," she said slowly with a low-pitched voice.

"Ha," Aston snorted. "He wants to be more than your friend. You know John wants to fuck you… right?" He threw the words at her with force.

Sybina blinked and didn't speak and her silence made Aston's blood boil. "What? Am I missing something… did he fuck you already?" Aston instantly regretted saying it and looked away. He knew Sybina hadn't slept with John from the way they had interacted, but his anger got the better of him and right now he was furious at John, Sybina—and the whole world, to be exact.

Sybina was speechless and Aston was trying to hold back the unnecessary cruel words playing in his mind. "Say something, *darling*," he said in a mocking tone, referring to John's words. Aston had never used loving nicknames with Sybina or any woman. He hadn't even considered it before today, and now he was annoyed that he hadn't come up with Bina or addressed Sybina with darling first. John was such a pest.

Finally Sybina spoke and her voice was thick with disgust. "You followed me?"

Aston straightened his back, crossed his arms, and raised his chin slightly just like he had done thousands of times with recruits in the army. He knew he looked fierce and powerful in that position. "Good thing I did; at least now I know what's going on," he said in a rough voice.

"I can't talk to you when you're like this," Sybina said and turned around.

"Come back here and explain yourself," Aston shouted after her, but she went to the bedroom and slammed the door, leaving him completely powerless and frustrated.

Thirty seconds later Sybina came stomping back into the living room with teary eyes glowing with anger. "You know what... you only had to ask if you wanted to meet John. I've kept *no* secrets from you and you make me feel like I'm a criminal who did something wrong. John is just someone who appreciates my company and finds me interesting. I don't have many friends, so I'm grateful to have him at least. Honoring you doesn't mean I have to hate every other man, and I never broke our agreement. I only had sex with you."

"Good!" Aston shouted back at her. "And that's how it's going to stay."

"No, it's not how it's going to stay. Soon you'll be rid of me and you don't have to worry about who I date or sleep with," Sybina shouted with tears running down her cheeks.

"That's right, but until then, you are my wife and I'm the only one who has sex with you. Do you understand?" The knot in his chest made it hard to speak and at the end of his sentence his voice had sounded almost brittle, like it was going to break. Aston pulled back, realizing that he had been pointing his finger and leaning forward in an aggressive way. He closed his eyes to shut out the image of Sybina with eyes so full of sadness and tears. *I'm such a jerk*, he told himself and swallowed hard. *I'm practically pushing her into the arms of John, who's going to be there to pick her up after I destroy her... I'm so stupid, stupid, stupid.* With a growl Aston pulled his shoulders back and left Sybina, who was crying. He went to the bedroom and picked out the clothes he was going to wear for the stag

276

party and took a quick shower, all while admitting to himself that he wasn't cut out to be anyone's husband.

Aston considered canceling the stag party but that would mean staying home and talking things over with Sybina; somehow going out and getting drunk was more appealing. Hopefully things would go back to being normal between them tomorrow. After all, he and Tara had fought all the time and still continued having sex.

Before he left, he went to see Sybina, who was lying on the couch curled up with a blanket and looking into the TV with glazed eyes,

"I'll see you tonight when I get back."

"Okay," she answered in a dull voice without looking at him.

Aston took a step towards her. "Hey... I'm sorry I shouted at you."

Sybina didn't react, and for a while Aston just stood there waiting for her to speak before he turned around and left the apartment.

CHAPTER 27
Liam's Stag Party

Aston

Aston and nine other men spent the day shooting at each other with paintball guns, and obviously Aston was superior on the field. Some of the guys were hit numerous times and Liam, the groom, got a large bruise on his neck where he was hit by accident.

It was a warm August day, and after running around for two hours the group went to a spa hotel owned by Liam's future brother-in-law, who had a chain of hotels and had reserved a spa for the men's private party. It gave them a chance to shower, swim, and relax in the spa while being served with all the beer and champagne they could drink.

Liam had to sit through a pedicure and manicure and complained that he ended up with pink nail polish on both hands and feet, but he completely forgot about it when two strippers showed up and gave them all a sexy show and Liam got a double lap dance.

Out of the nine men in the party, Aston knew five of them already as they had all gone to the same boarding school as teenagers and were now highly successful in their separate fields. The four other men in the party, Aston had only met today. They were three bankers that worked with Liam and Liam's future brother-in-law, who came from a wealthy aristocratic family with old money. The constant flow of beer and champagne made them all talkative and loud and when they went to dinner at a prestige gourmet restaurant many intimate details were spilled.

"You know I hate that you guys married before me... right?" Liam said, a bit drunk and looking ridiculous with his pink nail polish. "Joanna is constantly comparing our wedding to all of yours and it's costing me a bloody fortune to top your extravagance."

"That's women for you. It's always about the fanciest dress and the longest guest list. We ended up having more than four hundred people at our reception... I honestly didn't know half of those people," Liam's brother Max said and held up his glass of wine. "Women! Can't live with them... can't live without them."

"Hear, hear..." some of the other men chimed in.

"Look at the bright side. At least you have an all-you-can-eat-buffet of sex available to you." Daniel, one of the few single guys, argued. Most of the men broke out in collective laughter.

"Just make sure you get as much sex as you can the first year, Liam, because once she gets pregnant the show is over," one of the men said.

Liam looked pale. "No way, Joanna isn't like that. She loves sex."

"A baby will change that... I guarantee it."

"Surely it's not like that for everyone," Liam insisted.

"Ha!" His brother-in-law-to-be snorted. "If Joanna is like her sister, you better get some painkillers for all her migraines."

"But you look so happy together," Liam said and his brother-in-law chuckled and held up his glass.

"Oh, we're very happy... she gives me heirs and freedom and I give her luxury and status. Cheers to that."

Aston heard the men discuss the price of trophy wives. He knew several of the women in question and they were always stylish and fashionable and definitely pretty, but

279

he never realized exactly how much money these women were spending to stay that way.

"It's not just the household and my wife's personal allowance... now there's the kids with all their nannies, private schools, private tutoring, riding and tennis lessons—and don't even get me started on the vacations to St. Moritz, the Bahamas, and Spain... Women of this caliber expect to be treated like royalty," Rory, one of Liam's colleagues, said and emptied his glass of expensive wine with a hint of pride.

Aston was slightly fascinated by the men's pissing contest over who had the most expensive wife.

"What do you mean when you say *women of this caliber*?" Aston asked, leaning back in his chair and folding his arms. He knew exactly what Rory had meant but after meeting Sybina he had a different view on qualities in a woman.

"You know, it's all about beauty and class," Rory explained.

"Hmm... interesting," Aston said and frowned.

Liam, who was sitting next to Aston, patted his shoulder. "I see a ring on your finger, old chap, but I don't recall any wedding invitation. What happened?"

Aston smiled slightly. "My wife wanted a small ceremony. I had to pressure her to spend money on a white dress. In fact, the only money I see her spend is on the groceries she buys to make her incredible home-cooked meals every night—and the twenty Euros she tried to give a skater at the park because she mistakenly thought his torn Calvin Klein pants were due to poverty and not fashion."

The men laughed. "Did the skater take the money?"

"No, he got confused or maybe offended, I don't know."

"That's too funny. Who is your wife, do we know her?"

"No, she's from abroad."

"Ohh, so you married down, maybe that's the smart thing to do," Max said and took a big bite of his lobster.

"Does she clean too?" Rory chuckled.

Aston turned red. "To be honest, Sybina keeps the place spotless, never has a migraine, and never asks for money... She is smart, beautiful... even without make-up... and the kindest, warmest person you'll ever meet."

"Does she have a sister?" Daniel asked with a smile.

"No, she doesn't have any family," Aston answered.

"So no mother-in-law either... you've got to be joking... fence her in and be sure you never lose her... she sounds too good to be true," one of the others jested.

"How did you meet her?" Daniel asked.

"She saved my life in Spirima when I was captured."

"Saved your life how?" Rory asked and leaned closer.

"She nursed me back to life when I was beaten half to death and she stepped in front of me when a Masi warrior pointed his gun at me, and when we broke out of the Masi headquarters she saved my life again."

"Wow... I can see why you fell in love with her," Daniel said and nodded his head enthusiastically. His words made Aston look down. He couldn't tell them he wasn't in love with Sybina but only married to her in order to protect her. It would jeopardize the whole thing.

"Yes, she sounds like an angel, but I bet it's just a matter of time before she becomes like the rest though," Rory said. "Every woman likes expensive things... it's just a matter of time before they find their niche. Maybe jewelry is her thing."

Aston grinned. "I don't think so. I gave her a diamond necklace for the wedding but she's not wearing it. I don't think she likes that sort of thing. She doesn't like me to spend money on her and I don't force things upon her she doesn't want or like. And about your comment that I married down, Liam, I really don't see that there's anything *low* about her."

Liam grinned. "No, no, I didn't mean it like that, old friend. I just meant that you could have married someone from high society, if you wanted to. I mean with your family's status and all."

Aston raised his brows, once again reminded why he had kept going abroad for so many years. His friends were impossibly snobbish and trivial, and normally he would let it fly; but now he felt their judgment on women was a direct attack on Sybina. "High maintenance is not a sign of class to me. Loyalty, integrity, and kindness are far more important in my book," Aston pointed out.

The nine men around the big round table went quiet and then one raised his glass. "I salute both Aston and Liam, for marrying the women of your dreams. Cheers to true love."

"To true love." Everyone cheered and raised their glasses but Aston couldn't help adding in his mind, *And to scam marriages.*

Around midnight the group of men entered Black Diamond, a posh nightclub in central London. A table was reserved in their name and a waitress brought over three coolers with alcohol and soft drinks to mix with.

"Help yourself," someone shouted over the music and Aston went for a soda, thinking he needed to take a break on the booze. He was already more drunk than he liked to be, and the flashing lights and loud music in the nightclub didn't help.

The men's stylish clothing, expensive watches, and attitudes smelled of money and even though only a few of the nine could be considered good-looking, the group instantly attracted women who came to sit with them. The girls were all young and pretty with heavy make-up and tiny dresses. A girl sat down next to Aston. "Hi, I'm

Tiffany," she said and flashed a set of teeth so white they looked almost bluish in the fluorescent lighting.

"Hi," Aston shot her a vague smile.

"So what are you guys celebrating tonight?" Tiffany asked with a strident voice that was loud and unpleasant.

"Stag party," Aston said politely and pointed to Liam. "Hence the pink nails."

"Ohhh, that's so funny," Tiffany purred. "When my sister got married her husband's friends got him drunk and gave him a tattoo."

Aston eyes narrowed. "Did he want a tattoo?"

"Noooo... that was the whole joke. And it was big too," Tiffany laughed.

Aston shook his head and picked up his phone, trying to signal that he wasn't really interested in her. A few months back he would have gladly danced with her and taken her home for a fun night, but tonight all those club girls seemed over-the-top glittery and artificial, and he wasn't sure if it was really the girls that had changed or just his taste in women in general.

"Do you want to dance?" Tiffany asked and turned her face in a way that showed the shimmer in her make-up.

Aston shook his head. "No, I'm married."

"Well, married men dance too you know," Tiffany laughed.

"Not this one." He was glad to have an excuse that didn't offend women.

"Oh, okay, your loss." Tiffany shrugged and moved over to Liam's brother Max instead.

Aston checked his phone to see if Sybina had called him. He had left a few voice messages, saying he was sorry, but she hadn't responded. Aston rubbed the back of his neck and put down the phone. He needed to clean up the mess with Sybina tomorrow; he thought about buying her flowers and chocolate. Wasn't that what married men did when they screwed up?

283

With a sigh he pushed the thought away and picked up the soda, leaned his head back, and emptied the bottle in one long slurp.

"Hey, handsome," a honeyed voice said and Aston felt hands on his chest.

He looked to his side and saw Tara sitting next to him and leaning against him; before he could say anything a camera flash went off.

"Get off me," Aston said and got up. His reaction made the others around the table look up to see the commotion.

"Don't be mean," Tara said with a pout followed by a smile.

"Just leave me alone," Aston hissed at her and pulled away from the table when she tried to touch him again.

Tara wouldn't give up and followed Aston, who harshly pushed her away when she tried to rub herself against him in a sexy dance to the loud music.

Liam's brother Max, whom Aston knew from school, stepped between them. "Hey, Ash... let's go shoot some pool."

Aston nodded to his friend and scowled at Tara, who blew him a kiss. He was still angry with her for trying to destroy his wedding and couldn't believe how persistent she was. The woman just wouldn't take a hint.

Max was a lousy pool player but at least there was less noise in the upstairs poolroom, and they could have a conversation and get away from Tara. Aston stayed until two in the morning and then he took a taxi home, genuinely missing Sybina and hoping she would forgive his stupid outburst of anger earlier. He knew she wouldn't screw around with John, she wasn't like that; but he was just very protective of her and wouldn't allow anyone to hurt her like the Masi warriors had hurt her.

They didn't rape her, you only thought they did, he remembered and rubbed his eyes. *So why does it matter when this whole thing is fake anyway?* Aston shook his head, confused by his own logic around Sybina. *It matters because I care for Sybina and she's so damn innocent and needs my protection from men with dirty minds.* With a sigh he looked out the window, chewing on the irony that he himself was exactly the kind of man she should avoid— incompetent and hurtful when it came to relationships and with an always burning sexual desire that would give her physical pleasure but never the fulfillment she longed for. Someone like Sybina needed to be loved, something he wasn't capable off.

CHAPTER 28
Double Standard

Sybina

The void in Sybina's stomach grew. She had accepted that Aston didn't feel about her like she felt about him. She took what he gave freely and tried to be grateful for the conversations, the movie nights, the walks, and the friendship.

Every time they had sex Sybina tried to put a layer of protection around her heart and keep her emotions separated from her sexual drive, but there were moments of blissful lovemaking that felt real to her, and it took immense will power to never let a word slip about how she felt when she was on cloud nine with all the endorphins released by her orgasms.

Sybina had convinced herself that although her marriage to Aston was fake, it was still a good marriage with mutual respect, sex, and friendship.

But Aston's harsh accusations today when he accused her of sleeping with John had been so unfair, and she was shaken by his unjust anger with her. Sybina felt judged and convicted for a crime she didn't do, and she had spent the evening crying her eyes out in bed. Aston had showed her a side of himself today that she hadn't seen before and she didn't understand it or like it.

Around ten in the evening Aston had called a few times. Sybina wanted to answer but in the end she sat with her phone and watched it go to voice mail. She didn't know what to say to him, and even after listening to his apologetic messages she still didn't want to talk to him. At least not on the phone.

Around 1:30 in the morning the doorbell rang and woke Sybina up. She went to the door wearing a long t-shirt and opened it prepared to meet a drunk Aston but outside stood Tara wearing full make-up, high heels, and a tiny black dress.

"What do you want?" Sybina asked, annoyed.

Tara spoke with a sugary voice and waved a phone in the air. "I just came to drop Aston's phone off."

Tara might as well have kicked her in her stomach but Sybina managed to put out her hand with an indifferent expression and Tara placed the phone on her palm.

"Give Aston a kiss from me," Tara said and turned to leave. "Oh, and don't look at the pictures, it will only upset you."

"What do you mean?" Sybina asked, not sure she wanted to know.

Tara mimicked zipping her lips and throwing away the key and then she threw her head back, laughing, before she went down the stairs.

Sybina closed the door and walked back into the bedroom. For minutes she debated whether or not to look at the pictures Tara referred to. Sybina didn't like the idea of snooping in Aston's private things but after the way he attacked her earlier today, she was still angry and disappointed with him for following her, and felt that she somehow had a right to know what pictures Tara was talking about. If Aston had done something he shouldn't have, she wanted to know about it. *Or do I?*

In the end she picked up the phone and typed in his code. She had seen him type the code often enough to know it was his birthday. With shaky hands and a pounding heart she opened his camera roll and starting scrolling through his pictures. There were five pictures from tonight. The first one showed Tara looking into the camera and Aston sitting next to her. Aston didn't look into the camera or smile but Tara was hanging on him and blowing kisses at his camera. The next picture was blurred, and after turning the picture upside down and around a few times Sybina decided it was a close up of Tara's cleavage. The next one showed Tara lifting her dress and showing her thong. Sybina wrinkled her nose up, hating to admit to herself that Tara had a beautiful body. She scrolled on to the next picture and blinked when she saw Tara looking up at the camera while giving Aston a blow job. Sybina's hand went to her mouth and she took a deep breath before she scrolled to the next picture and saw Tara bent over a toilet with her dress up her hips, being taken from behind. In the picture Tara was looking back over her shoulder with an open mouth and narrowed eyes—looking straight at the camera.

Sybina kept staring at the repulsive pictures again and again. Apparently Aston was a man with double standards when it came to fidelity.

Sybina was shocked and hurt. *Why Tara, of all women? Why her?* She got up and paced the room while shaking her arms, as if to try and shake the feeling of the total humiliation and heartbreak she felt invade her body like a dark, flesh-eating parasite eating at her heart.

The pressure in her chest was so intense that she became dizzy and had to sit down. Aston had been very clear about not sleeping with others and she had considered him trustworthy. She had put her life and Uma's life in Aston's hands and depended on him, and now her trust was tumbling down like domino pieces falling in line. If he could lie to her about this, then what else could he lie about and what if he backed out of their agreement? *Two years is a long time to live with someone you don't trust or like, and we're only two months in.*

Sybina put a hand on her chest and bent forward with a sob. Long-hidden pain of being let down in her childhood returned with a vengeance and she fell back on the bed with a scream of pain. She had trusted Aston. Just like she had trusted her father. But she had fooled herself to believe in a lie, and now the truth was staring her in her face. Aston was not to be trusted and she was trapped. This time not as a slave but as an immigrant depending on Aston to get her permanent residency. She wanted to leave but didn't know where to go. She curled up into a ball; her whole body was shaking with despair because of all her dreams shattering around her. The blind love she had felt for Aston had been ripped away violently by the disgusting pictures of his cock inside Tara. It wasn't just his betrayal but also the realization that she herself wasn't enough and never would be Aston's kind of woman. He wanted women like Tara, who were Sybina's direct opposite. Women who didn't say no to oral or anal sex and who were confident and gorgeous.

Sybina didn't know how long she'd been lying on the bed crying when she heard the key in the lock and the heavy footsteps of Aston coming home.

She pushed the phone to his side of the bed and took a few deep breaths to get her breathing back to normal before she turned around, pretending to be sleeping.

Aston stood in the doorway for a while before he entered. She could hear him move around and brush his teeth before he came to bed. From his movements she knew he had found the phone.

"What the fuck..." he mumbled and then he shook Sybina gently.

"Are you asleep?"

"No," she said softly.

"How did my phone end up here? I lost it," Aston said with words slurred, clearly drunk.

Sybina dried away a tear in the darkness. "Did you lose it before or after you had sex with Tara?"

Aston giggled and lay back again... "She wishes, but I don't want her."

His arrogant dismissal of what happened between him and Tara made Sybina furious and she sat up, turned the lights on, and scowled at him. "At least be man enough to stand by your actions," she hissed at him.

Aston blinked and pushed himself up into a sitting position too. "What are you talking about?... You know I never lie," he said assertively, and it made Sybina want to scream. No wonder she had been sucked into his web of lies with his convincing act.

"Aston, you're such a hypocrite. First you accuse me of sleeping with John and then you go out and bang Tara... Why did it have to be her of all the women in London? Why her?" Sybina was speaking fast with a wobbly voice from part crying, part screaming.

Aston held up his palms and shook his head with a complete look of confusion. "I'm telling you I didn't sleep with Tara... or anyone else for that matter."

"*Liar!!!*" Sybina screamed and pointed to his phone. "If you didn't want me to find out you shouldn't have taken pictures of the whole thing."

"You checked my phone?" Aston said in disbelief and opened it to see the pictures. His head pulled back and his eyes widened in surprise. "What the hell is this?"

Sybina got out of bed and stomped to the bathroom. It was impossible for her to stay in bed with him when he couldn't even acknowledge it or apologize.

"Sybina, this isn't me," Aston shouted after her.

"Right. Of course it's not you. Tara just took your phone and filmed herself having sex with someone else to set you up," Sybina said in a mocking tone.

Aston got out of bed too. "I told you she's crazy."

"Pssss. Please, don't even go there!!!" Sybina snorted

She grabbed her toothbrush and went to her closet, where she started packing things without any plan.

"Sybina, stop." Aston grabbed her shoulders, but she shook them loose.

"Don't touch me. Never, ever, touch me again with those lying, cheating hands," she hissed through gritted teeth with tears in her eyes.

Aston pulled his hands away. "Where are you going?"

With forceful movements Sybina threw more clothes into the bag. "I'm going to someone who appreciates my company."

"John? You got to be joking, Sybina. You're *not* going to his place. You're *staying* here."

"I'm a free woman, I can go exactly where I want to go and you can't stop me."

"Oh, yeah... well, how about this?" His eyes darted the room as if desperately searching for a way to make her stay. "If you leave this apartment the marriage is over and you know what that means, don't you?" Aston waved a hand. "Goodbye England, hello poverty and homelessness for you... and Uma."

Sybina closed her eyes and took a deep breath before she turned to look at him. "You are not who I thought you were. I think I'll take my chances."

Aston leaned against the closet and looked shaken. "Okay, then go see if John wants to marry you and adopt Uma... because I'm sure as hell not going to when you don't even believe me," he said, words slurred.

Sybina picked up her bag and took a last look at Aston. "It would have been easier to believe you if you hadn't told me yourself that drinking, gambling, and *whoring* is what you do best. Goodbye Aston."

Aston gaped at her, and without waiting for him to come back with some other cruel comment Sybina left the apartment.

291

Aston

Aston sunk to the floor with the phone in his hand, his mind blank.

Only much later did he realize he should have run after Sybina, but by then she was gone and he had no idea where John lived or even what his last name was. His prophecy from earlier came back to him. *I pushed her into John's arms. I lost her!*

Images of Sybina crying in John's arm and John comforting her with his hands caressing her, calling her Bina and darling, kissing her, exploiting her fragile state and taking her to bed, made Aston get up and kick the bed in a state of powerlessness. He hurt his foot and jumped around cursing. Limping to the kitchen, he got ice to cool his hurting foot and opened the fridge. Inside was a plate with leftovers from Sybina's dinner. He slammed the fridge door shut and went to sit on the sofa and looked around. The place was so different since she moved in. Her warm personality was in the paintings, cushions, and blankets that gave color to the room; even the flowers on the dining table were a testament to Sybina's ability to make any space more welcoming.

Flashbacks to his life before Sybina left him cold. His empty, colorless apartment had been the representation of how he had felt inside; he couldn't go back to that, he wouldn't go back to that. The loneliness and emptiness would kill him.

A noise startled him and to Aston's surprise he realized that the sound was coming from him. It was a deep sob followed by many more. For the first time since he was a boy, Aston wept and held nothing back. The release of emotions brought a tide of suppressed pain with them. Aston cried for the misery he had seen in the war, the loneliness he had felt, the dreams he had lost, and he cried for Sybina, who had gone through so much pain and yet rose above it all like a goddess of goodness. She had not only saved his life, she had loved him...

And I dismissed her... I told her she confused love and sex, but she was never the one who was confused... I was. That's why the sex with her is so amazing. We're not just screwing, we're making love. His realization made him gasp out loud. The discussion he had with the other men at the bachelor party should have made him realize how special Sybina was to him. He could never be with a superficial high society girl, he needed something else... he needed Sybina... *she* was the perfect woman for him... "I love, Sybina!" he said out loud as a statement to himself.

Waves of regret washed over him, making his hands shake and his heart race. *Why didn't I tell her that I loved her? Why did I let her go out the door without telling her how I feel?* The answer came abruptly: *Because you're a fucking retard, that's why, and now she's with another man.*

Aston punched a fist down on the floor. Waves of jealousy rolled over him, taking his breath away and making his stomach hurt like the worst food poisoning. At least this time he saw the jealousy for what it was: fear. Aston was terrified of not being enough, and of losing Sybina to another man. It didn't matter that John wasn't as handsome as Aston; he was a family man, and Sybina's greatest dream was to become a mother herself. John would have that as leverage, and after the mistrust Tara had created between them now, it would be easy for John to make his move.

Aston's head fell into his hands and more sobs escaped him with the thought that he would never talk with Sybina again, eat with her, snuggle with her, laugh with her, make love to her, shower with her, or just walk through the park with her. *Why didn't I ever hold her hand when we walked? Stupid, stupid, so unbelievably stupid.* He blamed himself. God, it hurt to cry. He had forgotten how every muscle tensed and how draining it felt to cry so violently.

After the tears came the rage. Tara had destroyed the best thing in his life: his relationship with Sybina. Because of Tara, Sybina, now hated him. In his alcohol-fogged brain only two thoughts stood out clearly. One: Tara was going to pay for this. And two: He wanted Sybina back, desperately, and it would be a cold day in hell before he allowed another man to snatch his wife from him. He was a warrior, after all, and he would go to war to get her back, if needed.

CHAPTER 29

Hiding

Aya

"I can't believe he did that. What an unbelievable bastard. God, I just want to take a punch at him myself," Aya exclaimed and hugged Sybina who was crying in her arms.

Kato stood in the doorway, his eyes asking Aya if he should stay or go. They had been sleeping when Sybina woke them up with a bag in her hand and now, five minutes later, they knew why.

Aston had cheated on Sybina with his ex-girlfriend Tara. Sybina had just explained how Tara had even brought Sybina the proof herself by returning Aston's phone and casually dropping a line that "Sybina probably shouldn't look at his photos, it would only upset her." Of course Sybina had done just that and from her description, the photos on his phone left no doubt; Aston really had been with Tara and banged her in a lousy nightclub bathroom. *Ew, how low is that?* Aya wrinkled her nose remembering Tara from her time in Spirima; the girl had been something of a nymphomaniac, so she shouldn't be surprised, but still...

Sybina had confronted Aston when he finally got home drunk, and he had denied everything and called Tara crazy. Aya couldn't deny that Tara did do some crazy things but it took two to tango, and Aston was a huge prick to deny everything when there was hard proof to show his guilt.

"Just go," Aya mouthed to Kato, who looked relieved and moved away.

"I trusted him," Sybina sobbed. "Did you know that it was Aston who insisted that we were exclusive… not that I would have slept around anyway, but still." Her voice was full of indignation.

Aya stroked Sybina's back, waiting for her to continue.

"And then it turns out that what he really meant was that I have to stay true while he can screw around. He's such a hypocrite."

"I know." Aya continued rubbing Sybina's back gently.

"And you know what the worst part is?" Sybina looked at Aya with big teary eyes.

"No." Aya shook her head.

"Yesterday Aston had a rage of jealousy because I walked with John. Can you believe that?"

Aya shook her head again. Aston had to be the stupidest man in all of London to treat Sybina like this. Scam marriage or not, he was fortunate to have Sybina in his life and for Aya, who had seen Aston before he met Sybina, the change in him was evident. He was much more gentle and soft around Sybina, and even if he didn't realize it himself he cared very much for her. Aya had seen the way he looked at Sybina with pride and protectionism.

"He told me the marriage is over." Sybina started crying again.

"He told you what?" Aya raised her voice.

"He told me that if I walked out the door the marriage was over and he wouldn't adopt Uma."

Aya narrowed her eyes. "What an asshole."

"And Uma is flying in next week. *What am I going to do*?" The last part came out in a long sob.

Aya bit the inside of her cheek and made a fist. *When I get my hands on him…* She promised herself that she was going to tell him exactly what a buttfuck he was, but for now she had to suppress her anger and be strong for Sybina. "Don't worry, sweetie, you and Uma can stay in a hotel. I'll pay for it."

"I can't ask that of you," Sybina said in a low voice, looking up at Aya.

"I would offer you staying here with us, but we only have the couch and that won't work for the both of you. I wish we were in our new place, then we would have a guest room..."

Sybina pulled back to look at Aya. "Thank you," she said, heartfelt, and mustered a small smile. "I don't know what I would do without you, Aya."

"It's not that long ago, I slept on your couch and I was the one crying over my man... I know how it feels," Aya reminded Sybina and pulled a blanket and a pillow closer. "Will this do or should I go search for some sheets?" she asked.

"Thank you, it's all I need." Sybina assured her.

"Good, then let's continue our talk tomorrow. For now, try to get some sleep, dear.

Sybina thanked her again and Aya went to bed herself, hoping that tomorrow would be a better day for Sybina and making plans for how she could help Sybina if Aston was serious about divorcing her.

Sybina

Sybina tried to fall asleep but her head was full of thoughts, memories, and images... ahh, those damn photos kept flashing before her eyes. The picture with Tara's lips around Aston's cock disturbed her more than the others. She had never allowed him oral sex herself. The idea alone repulsed her after seeing so many female slaves forced and choked by Masi warriors stuffing their erection down the woman's throat. Tara had looked like she enjoyed it and her make-up hadn't been running at all. That had Sybina puzzled because whenever Sybina had watched the young sex slaves getting fucked in their mouths it had always ended up with mascara running from their tears and from the semen smeared over their faces. Maybe the photo had been taken before the oral sex really began, but even when Tara brought the phone by, her make-up had looked perfect. Was it possible that Tara truly did find oral sex pleasing or that Aston hadn't been as brutal with Tara as the Masi warriors had been with the slaves? No matter what, Aston was clearly not satisfied with what Sybina could give him. Tara seemed like the kind of girl who had no inhibitions... she was a wild thing, and maybe that was why Aston had stayed with Tara longer than with any other woman.

Sybina could hear muffled voices from Aya's and Kato's bedroom. She knew they were talking about her and for a fleeting moment Sybina's envy of Aya was back. Aya had Kato, who loved her unconditionally. They were so good together and expecting their first child, not to mention getting married, for real, in less than a month. Sybina wanted all of that too. And until a few hours ago she would have said that she wanted it with Aston. But not now. Not after his betrayal and his lies.

If he had only admitted and apologized then maybe she could forgive him, but he didn't even have that much respect for her. Sybina closed her eyes and sighed deep and long with mental exhaustion. Her chest hurt from all the crying, and she wondered what Aston was doing right now and if he even cared at all. It took a while, but finally she drifted off to sleep.

Aston

In the west end of London Aston was roaming through his apartment.

"Where is it?" he muttered and slammed yet another drawer closed.

He had found things he had forgotten he even had, and his military dog tags, which he thought he had lost. He looked at the chain with the two metal tags stating his full name and birthday. He would have to find a place for it so he didn't lose it again; the damn thing had no monetary value, but it had followed him through a decade of hardship and held significance for him.

"Where did you put it, Sybina?" he said almost inaudibly and continued searching.

After an emotional breakdown over losing Sybina and a realization that there was no way in hell he would let another man have her without a fight, a thought had penetrated his alcohol-infused brain. John had given Sybina his phone number. Aston knew for certain because he had followed them on the street yesterday and seen John hand her a card, telling Sybina it was his new number. Aston was sure Sybina had gone to John and feared that she might have taken the card with her, but on the off chance she hadn't he would find the card... and her.

Aston had been searching for the card for twenty minutes; it was a mystery to him how anything could hide in this place with the immaculate order that both he and Sybina kept. It took him another fifteen minutes of frantically searching before he found it—in the trash. "Ha!" He should have known. Sybina had the number in her phone now; she wouldn't want unnecessary paper lying around. She was a minimalist in that way.

Aston looked down at the card in his hand. *John B. Michaels, Author.* Sybina had spoken the truth about his job and maybe the man really was writing a book about Sybina, but Aston had seen the way John looked at her and had no doubt he would like to do much more to her than write about her. He ground his teeth at the thought alone.

There was no address on the card, only a phone number and email address, but with that information it should be easy to locate him. Aston popped open his laptop to do a search.

He quickly learned that the man had actually received several awards for his work and published seven books. Pictures on the website confirmed that it really was the man Aston had seen Sybina with, and a simple search on the yellow pages gave Aston John's address. He considered going right away but it was four-thirty in the morning and he was in no shape to confront Sybina. He would sleep a few hours, shower, and get his wits together before he went to bring his wife back home.

Sybina

It was the smell of coffee and bacon that woke Sybina. She sat up and saw Aya in the kitchen.

"Good morning," she said and stretched.

"Good morning." Aya smiled. "Did you manage to sleep a little?"

"Yeah, a little." Sybina yawned.

"I'm making you breakfast," Aya informed her and started cracking eggs in a bowl.

"Do you want me to cook?" Sybina asked, feeling she should be doing something.

Aya rolled her eyes lovingly. "I think I can handle breakfast, I'm not *all* that hopeless in a kitchen..."

Sybina got up from the couch and put on her pants, and then she folded up the blanket she had used for sleeping.

"Would you like some coffee?" Aya asked her. "Or juice?" She was holding the juice in her hand.

"Juice please," Sybina said and after a quick visit to the bathroom, she joined Aya in the kitchen.

Kato joined them. "Good morning," he said and walked towards the fridge. As he slipped past Aya he unconsciously let his hand slide over her behind, like a salutation from one lover to the other.

Aya shot him a smile. "Good morning."

Kato stopped in his tracks and, like a magnet pulled to its counterpart, he turned to hug Aya from behind, resting his hands on her pregnant belly and kissing her neck. "Uhm, bacon. It smells good," he said smilingly.

Aya turned her head and gave him a quick kiss.

Sybina's stomach churned when she saw Kato's eyes beam at his woman, so full of admiration. She and Aston had never had that sort of ease around each other. The only place they had been physical with each other was in the bedroom when they had sex. Outside the bed it was polite and courteous, but always guarded somehow. She knew why now. While she had been keeping her distance merely to protect her heart, he had kept his distance because he had no bloody heart to give to her. Maybe it was occupied by Tara or whomever else he had been screwing, while she naively thought they were exclusive, but she doubted it; her guess was that Aston only loved himself.

"I was thinking," Aya said and poured juice into a tall glass. "If we can convince Aston to not officially file for divorce then Kato and I can help you find a place to stay. If for some miracle the immigration workers don't find out, then you can stay in London and get your permanent residency." Aya handed Sybina the glass of juice.

Sybina looked at the frying pan. "I think the bacon is done," she pointed out.

"Oh, shoot." Aya hurried to get the bacon of the pan and both she and Sybina ignored the fact that they were clearly overcooked.

Without asking for permission Sybina took over on the eggs that Aya had already mixed with milk, salt, and pepper in a bowl. Expertly Sybina started whisking the eggs while Aya found yet another frying pan for Sybina to use.

"Aston was angry yesterday, but I'm sure he can be persuaded to let you stay; it's not like you did something wrong," Aya continued and started toasting bread.

"I don't know, Aya, he was very specific and made it clear that the marriage is over."

"Aston being responsible for sending you back to Spirima... that's not going to happen," Aya declared defiantly.

"Can I just say something for a minute?" Kato asked and snatched a piece of the bacon.

"What? Careful, it's hot," Aya warned him.

"Before you two go search for apartments and stuff, maybe talking to Aston would be a good idea. I mean, call him up and tell him you're coming home to talk things through."

Both women stared at Kato and then at each other before they shook their heads. "I don't want to talk to him," Sybina said firmly.

"Why?" Kato asked.

Aya raised her eyebrows. "The man lied to her, cheated on her, and threatened her about being able to stay and you don't understand why she doesn't want to talk to him?"

"Maybe there's an explanation. Maybe he didn't really cheat at all... did you consider that?"

"Oh, please, Kato. Sybina saw the pictures herself," Aya argued.

Kato shook his head and broke into a boyish grin, and it hit Sybina how different this Kato was from the gloomy Masi warrior she had first met him as. "You two are impossible."

"We're not and it's not funny, Kato. Sybina's world is falling apart. You're being insensitive," Aya scolded him.

Kato loc
that... it's ju
accused of i
forehead. "I
Sybina
into a fine l
"Not re
Kato n
"That's be
with lies o
"What
didn't... yo
"If it h
would hav
Sybin
you didn't do anything... right?

"Right!"

"So your situation is completely different... Kato, I saw the pictures of Aston's dick in Tara's mouth." Sybina's cheeks flashed red. She didn't like to be vulgar, but the situation called for it.

"Maybe you're right Sybina, but there is such a thing as photo manipulation, you know."

"Oh, please." Aya snorted. "Listen, we respect your bro code or whatever you have going on, defending Aston, but right now we need to come up with a plan so Sybina can stay in England.

"And what about Uma?" Sybina felt her tears well up again.

Kato pulled back, snatched another piece of bacon, and left the room quietly.

"We'll work out something." Aya assured Sybina "But first the pregnant woman needs breakfast, or I might get so hormonally disturbed that I go visit Aston and use him as a verbal punching bag."

They sat down to eat.

want breakfast?" Sybina

bedroom door. "He'll come if
not being very supportive," she
t that."

ght. Maybe I should go back and talk
said slowly.

her head. "I don't think you should go talk
t him come to you." She picked up a piece of

t what if..."

Aya interrupted Sybina with a gentle hand on her arm,
nd a serious expression. "Let's face it; if Aston lied to your
face, he's just gonna lie again. Why don't I go over and get
your clothes for you and let him stew... maybe in a few
days he'll realize what a jerk he is and apologize."

"You think so?"

"He'd better... and that's when you can ask him to at
least not file for divorce but let you live somewhere else."

Sybina looked down, overcome with sadness. "Why
Tara? Of all the women in London, why her, Aya?" Tears
flowed again.

Aya handed Sybina a napkin with a sympathetic pat on
her arm. "Here, sweetie, you'll be alright, I promise."

Sybina blew her nose and sniffled: "I think it's because
Tara will do things I won't do... sexually. He's bored with
me... you know."

"In that case he's a fool, because sex isn't everything
and Tara is not even remotely the woman you are. I never
liked her."

Sybina knew that Aya and Tara had been roommates
in Spirima, where they had both worked as nurses in the
refugee camp.

"Why would she do something like that?" Sybina asked
quietly.

304

Aya sighed. "Tara feeds on drama and she and Aston... well, they fought all the time but..." She trailed off.

"What?" Sybina asked, drying her tears away.

"Well, let's just say that the one thing they could agree on was... sex." Aya wrinkled her nose and sucked in her lips like she wanted to take the inconvenient truth back.

"Tara told me that Aston loved her. Do you think that's true?" Sybina asked in a small voice.

"Nooo," Aya exclaimed forcefully. "Aston never loved Tara and he never told her that he did."

"How do you know?"

Aya took a sip of her juice. "Because I had to listen to all her complaints about it. She longed to hear him say it. She longed to make him commit to her, but he never would. Did you know Tara asked him to marry her?" Aya asked.

Sybina snapped up her head. "Really?"

Aya nodded.

"Well, what did he say?" Sybina hurried Aya.

"He said no, of course. He said he would never marry anyone..."

The door to the bedroom opened and Kato came out with a smug smile.

"So, ladies, have you solved the situation or come up with a battle plan on how to destroy Aston completely?"

"That's not funny," Aya retorted.

"No, but you know what is?" He took a seat at the table.

Both Sybina and Aya held their gaze on him. "What?"

"I called my friend Liam." Kato took his time and spread butter on his toast with no hurry in the world.

"And?" Sybina said impatiently.

"I asked him if he had seen Aston with anyone yesterday at his stag party."

Sybina's heart started thumping like it was breaking out of her chest to get to the truth faster. "And what did Liam say?"

Kato took a deep breath. "That he lost sight of him when Aston went to play pool with his brother."

Sybina was confused. "But Aston doesn't even have a brother."

"When Aston went to play pool with Liam's brother," Kato clarified.

Without knowing it Sybina had moved to the edge of her chair, and his words made her close her eyes. For a second she had hoped Kato had good news and that by some miracle, Tara had been wrong. But Liam's words only cemented that Aston had left the stag party. *Shoot pool, my ass!* A sarcastic voice in her head snorted.

"So… I called Max, Liam's brother," Kato continued, only to pause again.

"And?" Aya impatiently tapped her foot under the table. "Could you speed it up a bit, you're killing us here."

Kato laughed. "Yeah, well… that's what you two get for being so bloody gullible and believing everything Tara and Diana tell you."

Aya narrowed her eyes. "Say that again?"

"Relax, babe, I'm just trying to prove a point here."

"Well, prove it faster then." Her voice was now high-pitched.

"Okay, okay." Kato held up both palms. "According to Max, he and Aston played pool until they went home around two o'clock, and he also said that Aston was searching for his phone before they left. I asked him about Tara and the only thing he could think of was a brunette that Aston got into a fight with. He said that she came on to Aston but that he got aggressive and pushed her away. That was actually why they ended up playing pool… Max was afraid Aston would get kicked out for fighting with the woman, so he pulled Aston away."

Complete silence fell over the room. Only the low humming sound from the fridge and the distant sound of traffic noise from the street could be heard.

Sybina and Aya gaped at Kato, who took a big bite of his toast, eyes dancing with triumph.

"So he didn't?" Sybina asked, unable to finish the sentence.

"Wow... this changes things," Aya said slowly.

Sybina's head fell into her hands. "Tara tricked me."

"That little bitch," Aya hissed.

"Yep..." Kato confirmed.

"But why?" Sybina sniffled.

Aya spoke slowly. "You know why, Sybina. Tara wants you out of Aston's life. She's jealous."

Sybina raised her head. "I need to talk to Aston." She got up to find her phone. It was on silent, and she could see several unanswered calls from him.

"Don't call him. Just go home and talk to him face to face," Kato suggested.

For the first time in twenty-four hours, Sybina smiled. "Thank you, Kato, thank you so much."

CHAPTER 30
Behind the Black Door

Aston

Aston got out of the taxi and looked at the townhouse in front of him. It had three floors; the two top ones were in red brick stone while the lowest was painted white and made the elegant front door stand out with its black shiny surface that matched the black railing on the six-step staircase leading up to it.

Steadying himself, Aston went up the staircase in a few agile steps and looked at the sign on the door. *Michaels*, it read. This was the right house, and Sybina was inside.

Aston tensed his jaw and pressed the doorbell, listening for voices on the other side of the door. He had already called Sybina numerous times, but all he got was her voicemail.

Aston pushed the doorbell again and this time he kept it pressed in, making a long continuous ringing sound; he would not be ignored. It was only eight-thirty in the morning but he didn't care if he woke them up.

When the door finally opened John stood there looking like he had been sleeping a minute ago. His hair was messy and again Aston noticed how weak the man looked. He didn't plan to use any force or aggression, but his reptile brain took pride in the fact that he could take down the man in front of him in one punch... if it came to that.

"Yes?" John said and rubbed his eyes. "What can I help you with?"

"I want to see Sybina," Aston said firmly and tried to get a look behind the man, who narrowed his eyes and pulled the door closer to limit Aston's view. *So Sybina is here,* Aston concluded.

"You must have come to the wrong house, no one with that name lives here," John said with strained politeness and tried to close the door.

Aston was prepared; he put his foot in and pushed the door open. "I said..." he repeated slowly, "I want to see Sybina."

"And who are you?" John asked, agitated.

"Her husband." Aston's voice was icy.

John wrinkled his noise. "Yes, she told me about you... the soldier!" he said in a flat tone. "Seems that blow you suffered to your head left you a bit... delusional."

"Delusional?"

"I told you, Sybina isn't here," John insisted.

"Ha," Aston snorted. "How stupid do you think I am? Call her down here or move aside and let me get her myself."

"Get her yourself?" John laughed condescendingly. "What do you think this is... the Stone Age? Did you remember your club to hit her in the head before you drag her home?"

A low growl escaped Aston. "Move aside, *author.*" Aston hissed the last word.

"Author?" John jerked slightly and frowned at Aston. "Is that supposed to be an insult... *soldier*?"

They glared at each other in a battle of testosterone, and Aston was surprised that the weakling didn't just roll over and die.

"Move aside or call Sybina down here. This is my last warning."

With a defiant look John turned his head and shouted. "Bina darling, the soldier wants to talk to you. Wanna come down here, babe?"

"Don't you fucking talk to my wife like that, you little shit," Aston yelled at the man.

"Or what?"

Aston took a threatening step closer. "Or I'll break your fucking neck."

John shook his head. "No wonder she left you... you clearly have an anger issue."

Aston formed his hands into fists, provoked by the smug ass in front of him, and without any further hesitation Aston pushed himself past John, who yelled at him to stop.

Running, Aston took the stairs up in a few steps, and looked into every room until he found the bedroom. The bed was undone, but Sybina wasn't there. Aston kept calling for her, but even though he looked in every room, she wasn't anywhere to be seen. Exasperated, Aston stormed down the stairs and looked around the living room and kitchen. Sybina was nowhere.

Finally he went back to John, who stood with an annoyed expression still holding the door open.

"Where is she?" Aston asked and this time there was a slight pleading in his voice.

John sighed. "I don't know."

"She didn't come here last night?"

"No, she didn't."

"But she told me she was going to you." Aston's mind was already running over worst-case scenarios. *Did she do something stupid? Was she attacked in the night? Is that why she never made it all the way to John's house?*

"Did she now?" John shifted his weight from one leg to the other. "Well, I wish she had come here," he added dryly.

Aston snapped his head back to look at John. "You *will* stay away from my wife, do you understand?"

"Stop pointing your finger at me and get the hell out of my house before I call the police," John shouted back.

310

Aston left and ignored John's insults behind him. He had been called worse than scoundrel, bastard, and imbecile; his focus was on finding Sybina, and there was only one other place she could be. In a quick movement he pulled up his phone and called Aya.

"Hello."

"Did Sybina come to you last night?" he blurted out.

"Yes."

"Tell her I'm coming."

"No, Aston, Sybina..."

Aston hung up. He had no need for Aya to finish that sentence: he already knew Sybina didn't want to see him, but he wouldn't take no for an answer.

It took him fifteen minutes to get to Aya's and Kato's apartment and all the way he regretted calling first. It had been stupid and there was now a big chance that Sybina would have left to avoid him.

When he rang the bell he was prepared to meet Aya's wrath, but he couldn't care less. If Sybina was in that apartment he was going to talk to her, explain to her that she had it all wrong.

When the door opened he was met by Aya, who stood there with open arms. Aston was so taken back by this unexpected sight that he completely froze when she hugged him.

"Sybina knows," Aya said. "I tried to tell you on the phone so you didn't have to come all the way here."

"She knows what and where is she?" Aston asked in confusion and looked down at Aya.

"Kato called Max, who confirmed you didn't cheat on Sybina, and she went home to talk to you about an hour ago."

Aya's words sank in and the significance made him blow out air with a loud "hooo."

"It's all good," Kato said, coming to the door. "Sybina knows Tara tried to set you up and she's pissed at Tara, but not you."

Aston reached out his hand to Kato and with a tug he pulled Kato into a masculine hug and patted his back. "I owe you one, man, thanks."

Kato returned the patting on Aston's shoulder. "My pleasure."

For a few seconds they all stood looking at each other before Aya exclaimed, "Well, what are you waiting for? Go home and talk to her."

Aston lit up in a smile and turned around. "Ohh, I will."

Sybina was sleeping when Aston got home. He found her on top of the bed with one hand under her chin and the other folded against her chest. The sight of her so peacefully sleeping in their bed made him stop and stare for a minute. He considered waking her up, as he had so much to tell her; but he couldn't bring himself to disturb her, knowing that she was probably as sleep-deprived as him.

With a soft movement Aston sat down next to her on the bed, quietly stroking her hair and finally feeling his muscles relax a bit. The way Sybina's hand was folded in a fist and positioned on her heart made him suspect that she was holding something; gently he opened her fist. The sensation in Aston's stomach was far more than butterflies whirling around, it was a freaking giant albatross taking off and flapping its wings with so much force that it created waves of euphoria from the top of his skull, out his arms, and down to the tip of his toes. Sybina was holding his dog tags, and it almost made him cry with relief. *Sybina still loves me.*

Carefully Aston took the chain from Sybina's hand and without waking her up he placed it around her neck. He kissed her cheek and lay down behind her, spooning her with an arm protectively around her, and closed his eyes. The smell of her hair, the sound of her quiet breathing, and the warmth from her body was intoxicating, and he surrendered to sweat dreams of making love to her.

CHAPTER 31
Waking Up

Sybina

It was warm, much too warm, and Sybina opened her eyes, slowly adjusting to the light. She was in her and Aston's bedroom and for a moment she wondered if it had all been a nightmare: Tara, the pictures on Aston's phone, the fighting with Aston, and her night in Aya's and Kato's apartment.

Aston's arm was tucked protectively around her, and as she moved to her back he furrowed his brow and muttered something in his sleep. For a moment Sybina lay still, watching Aston with his mouth slightly open and his strong features. He was the most attractive man she knew; not even Kato, who was indisputably handsome, came close to Aston in her opinion. Aston was strong and tall, and his dark blond hair was getting long enough that she could lace her fingers through it. He truly was a fine specimen of the male gender, and Sybina recalled the way his blue eyes shone with intelligence and confidence, but most of all Aston oozed sex in the way he moved, talked, and acted. She didn't blame Tara for wanting him back, but she couldn't forgive the way Tara had gone about it.

The chain around her neck caught Sybina's attention. She knew the chain had been in her hand... Had Aston put it around her neck? And if so, why? Softly she raised the dog tags to her mouth and kissed them. She had found the chain on top of the drawer when she got back to the apartment and been immediately drawn to it. Aston had carried this chain right next to his heart for years, and that made it special to her. Maybe he would let her borrow it for a while.

Pressure on her bladder made Sybina get out of bed to use the restroom. She was washing her hands and brushing her teeth when she heard Aston cry out her name.

Sybina opened the bathroom door with her toothbrush in her hand. "What is it?" she asked.

Aston stared back at her with wild eyes and unruly hair. He was fully dressed but clearly disoriented. "I thought you left me again," he said and reached out to her.

Sybina tilted her head. There was something radically different about Aston. The last time she had seen him he had been drunk and mean, threatening her with divorce and poverty. Now he was uncertain and looked almost... needy for her.

Sybina moved back to the bed, fascinated with the look in his eyes and his hands reaching out to her.

"I'm here," she assured him and Aston sat up to hug her tight.

"I'm so sorry. I didn't mean what I said. I don't want this marriage to end."

Sybina pulled back from Aston's tight squeeze and blinked up at him.

"You don't?"

"No, I don't," he said, shaking his head.

"Not now... or not in two years?" she asked, unsure if he was referring to his threat from yesterday or when the contract was up in two years.

Aston looked deeply into her eyes with a pained expression. "Ever."

Sybina opened her mouth to speak but she had no words.

"I mean it, Sybina. I don't want our marriage to end in two years or ever. I want to stay married to you."

Sybina was baffled by this change in Aston, and it was impossible for her to articulate the myriads of thoughts in her mind that spoke of confusion, caution, and hope. The best thing she could come up with was a simple "But... why?"

"What do you mean, why?" Aston cupped her face. "Because I love you, of course."

"You love me?" Sybina asked doubtfully. "Since when?"

Aston closed the gap between them and planted a long kiss on her lips. "I just do," he said when he pulled back.

Sybina took in a deep breath. "Right, um... listen, Aston, you don't have to say it; I'm not mad at you anymore. I know what Tara did."

Aston ran a hand through his hair and blinked rapidly. "Christ, Sybina, I'm telling you that I love you, and now you don't believe me?"

Sybina cleared her throat and fiddled with the dog tags on the chain around her neck. "I don't know what to say, Aston... I mean it's nice that you think you love me and all, but it's just the timing of it and the fact that you can't even tell me when it happened. All I know is that you certainly didn't love me yesterday."

"I *did* love you yesterday and the minute I lost you, I realized that I've loved you for some time now."

"Really?" Sybina wondered why the thought that Aston loved her was so hard to believe.

Aston took her hand. "Sybina, look at me."

Sybina shot him a quick glance before she looked down again.

With a finger under her chin, Aston lifted her head. "No, Sybina, I want you to look into my eyes like you did that time in the infirmary."

They were very close when he started speaking in a husky voice. "As long as I live, I will never forget the morning I woke up in your infirmary to find you on a chair by my bed. I couldn't believe someone like you existed, someone so pure and good that they would give up their bed and sleep on a chair for a stranger. You had the most amazing look of warmth and bravery in your eyes. A better man would probably have recognized that you stole my heart in that moment, but I'm a cynic and tried to deny it until yesterday, when the thought of losing you made it undeniable: I'm nothing without you.

Sybina's eyes widened. "I remember that moment. To me it felt like recognizing an old friend. Like I had known you always and only just found you again."

Aston nodded. "So you felt it too?"

"Yes... but if you felt that way about me, why wouldn't you give me more than two years?" Sybina asked.

Aston's face split into a grin of disbelief... "That was for your benefit... not mine! Look... I didn't think you felt that way about me... that you would want to be with me."

She leaned her forehead against his.

"Why not?"

He kissed her nose. "Because most of the time I don't even want to be with myself."

Sybina didn't speak; she just stayed close to him—kissing him, caressing him, loving him.

Aston hugged her tightly. "I'm sorry for messing things up, Ina."

Sybina hugged him back. "My mother used to call me Ina."

Aston smiled at her. "And now your husband calls you Ina."

Still leaning her forehead against his, Sybina whispered: "I want to hear you say that you'll be my real husband... not just a pretend one."

She observed him closely to see his reaction and found his eyes suddenly dancing playfully with a flirtatious grin. "Why don't I tell you that you're my wife and that I'll never let you go, while I do to you what only your husband has ever done to you?"

She giggled when he pushed her down on the bed.

"I love you, Sybina, and I'll keep telling you that until you believe me." Aston told her.

Sybina reached up to hug him. "Just hold me, will you. I just need a minute to let it sink in," she whispered and heard Aston chuckle into her hair.

"Take all the time you need, I'm not going anywhere... and I'm never letting you go, either!"

Sybina stayed in Aston's arms for a few minutes before she pulled away to look at him. "So Uma can still come?"

"Of course."

"Ohh..." Sybina blinked again. "And what about Tara?"

Instantly Aston's face tightened "I'll deal with Tara, don't worry."

"How?"

"I haven't decided yet... do you think you could cook me up a poisonous apple or something."

"What? What do you mean?"

He smiled. "You know, like in 'Snow White.'"

Sybina didn't blink. "'Snow White'?" she asked.

"Never mind... it's a fairy tale, just forget it."

"Okay... but this is not a fairy tale and you can't kill Tara."

"No, I suppose not." He smiled sardonically. "But yesterday I was tempted to."

"Aston, you're scaring me. You wouldn't physically hurt Tara, would you?"

He sighed. "No, I won't physically hurt her, but I do intend to make it crystal clear to her that if she ever comes near you or me again, I'll make her life a living hell."

"Just don't do something stupid..." Sybina warned. "Besides, the universe will make sure she gets what she deserves."

"Ha," Aston snorted. "I don't have patience for that sort of thing. I'll go talk to her myself."

"I'd prefer you didn't. Your attention would be her prize for all the hard work she did yesterday. It's what she's waiting for. I think it would be much more efficient to ignore her."

"What hard work? And what do you mean, ignore her?"

"Well, think about it. Clearly she had to seek out a man and have sex with him and then come all the way over here to drop off your phone. She's poking the bear and waiting for you to come running to her; it's what she wants."

"I hardly think fucking a stranger in a restroom is what Tara considers hard work," Aston said flatly. "And this bear definitely wants to roar and rip her head off. Are you seriously asking me to ignore her instead?"

Sybina nodded. "Yes, I don't even want us to talk about her. It's a waste of oxygen when we could be kissing instead." Sybina smiled. "Tara can never come between us again, I should have trusted you, Aston. I'm sorry."

Aston kissed her again. "I forgive you," he whispered and pulled her closer, letting his hands explore her features like it was the first time he was seeing her. Sybina lay still, watching his eyes move along with his fingers, taking her in with touch and sight. She smiled when his mouth opened slightly and hunger played in his eyes. Hunger for her.

"You want me." Sybina chuckled, voicing her observation.

Aston lifted his eyes to look at her. "You have no idea. This is..." His words were swallowed in the kiss she planted on his lips, and she pulled away regretting that she didn't get to hear what he was about to say.

"This is what?" Sybina asked, a bit out of breath and overwhelmed with the emotion welling up inside her. She

319

had tried so hard to suppress her love for him, convinced that he felt nothing; and now that he finally admitted he loved her, Sybina's love for Aston was shaking the bars of its prison, demanding to be set free, but... what if?

"This is it," he said.

"It?"

"You know what I mean."

"I don't think I do."

"Love," he said.

Sybina tilted her head. "Are you sure you don't confuse love and lust?"

Aston narrowed his eyes and squeezed her hips, making her laugh. "Don't use my words against me."

"Why not?"

"Because I was a moron who screwed up big time."

"Really?"

"Yes, really."

"How so?"

"I should have realized that everything was different with you. We don't fuck, we make love—and I never make love."

Sybina lowered her voice to a whisper: "We do?"

Aston tucked a strand of her hair behind her ear. "Yes, Ina, we do. With you it's soft and innocent, and normally I would be bored out of my mind, but with you it's like I can never get enough."

"You think sex with me is boring?"

"No, the opposite. Sex with you is amazing because it's pure and..."

"Spiritual?" Sybina suggested.

Aston's head snapped back. "What? No, I'm not religious,"

"To me it's spiritual."

Aston looked confused. "Like you hear church bells ring or something?"

Sybina shook her heard. "Of course not... but I feel that I'm connecting to you on more than a physical level, that's why I use the word spiritual."

"Yeah, well, you can call it what you want. All I know is that you're doing something to my head and heart, because I long for more than your body now. I want all of you and it started long before we began having sex."

"Maybe I put a spell on you?" Sybina suggested with a wink. "Maybe I truly am a witch?"

Aston raised his brows and pushed her down on the bed. They were both fully dressed; with slow catlike movements he got on top of her and lifted her legs around him. The ancient game of bump and grind made Sybina open her mouth and moan his name.

Aston leaned down and spoke with a low sexual growl into her ear: "If you did cast a spell on me, I'm not complaining. I've never been happier and I'm all yours."

Sybina put her arms around his neck, reveling in the weight of his body covering hers. Inside her, emotions pressured and bubbled up, and with a quick hand movement she dried away a tear from her eye that was rolling down towards her ear. She wanted to tell Aston that she was all his too. It was right there on the tip of her tongue but the words didn't come. Instead she spread her legs wider, signaling what she couldn't say in words, and like the hunter he was, he picked up on her message and started to undress her with slow movements, as if he was unwrapping a precious gift. When he removed her pants he held on to her left leg and spread kisses over her foot, calf, and thigh before letting it go.

"Promise, you'll never leave me again," Aston said and peeled off her panties with ravishing lust in his eyes.

I love you, Aston, her inside voice told him, but the man wasn't a mind reader and she would have to say it loud for him to know.

"Promise me," he repeated.

"I promise," Sybina said and smiled when Aston made sure she was wet and aroused before he pushed himself inside her and started moving. Both his hands found hers and laced together, and she watched hypnotized as he turned their laced hands and kissed the back of her hand only to move on to kiss her chin, her nose, and her mouth. She couldn't stop staring into his bright blue eyes that were completely fixed on hers, and in his eyes she saw so many emotions that it was hard to pin one down—they spoke of fear, caution, awe, surrender, and need.

The connection between them was strong and raw, and Sybina felt like every one of Aston's thrusts inside her was directly aimed at her heart. If the energy of his body had a voice it would be roaring: "Let me in, accept me, love me."

Sybina couldn't help her tears. This was spiritual and beautiful to her. This was far more than physical; this was two souls merging and making promises of friendship, loyalty, protection, and companionship for life.

Aston kissed away one of her tears and Sybina saw a flash of confusion on his face. "Do you want me to stop?" his eyes asked.

"Tell me again that you're mine," Sybina asked in a brittle voice, fighting her last bit of inner doubt.

A smile grew on Aston's face and he lifted their hands and kissed her wedding ring. "I'm all yours," he whispered and turned their hands to her, waiting.

Sybina could see his hand in front of her, his wedding ring on his tanned finger, and without hesitation she kissed it. "And I'm all yours." The look on his face was indescribable and more powerful than a thousand words, making all her doubts evaporate into thin air.

"I love you, Aston."

This time it was Sybina's turn to kiss one of his tears away.

They didn't say more for a long time. They only kissed and touched and made love until they came together, holding each other tight and whispering loving promises.

"That was amazing," he declared afterwards.

"Uh-huh," was all Sybina could mutter as she lay sated and sweaty on top of Aston's chest, listening to his pounding heart.

"What are you doing?" she asked when she saw him raise his phone and take a picture of her.

"You are so beautiful," he said. "I want a picture of us kissing for my screen saver."

"But my hair is all messy and so is yours," Sybina pointed out.

"Exactly... we have sex hair and post-orgasmic looks on our faces; this is what I want," he declared and pulled Sybina up to kiss her. Snapping sounds from the camera told Sybina that he was shooting pictures.

"I want to see them," Sybina demanded, and when Aston scrolled over the pictures she marveled. They both looked so relaxed, in love, and completely at ease with each other, and she had never seen Aston more sexy and hot than when he was kissing her and looking straight into the camera. His expression saying "Mine!"

"Wow, this picture is amazing," she exclaimed and turned to kiss him again. "You take my breath away."

"And you take mine," he added, and while Sybina lay her head to rest on his chest again she heard him fiddling with his phone, tapping out a text. A whooshing sound made her look up. "Did you send me the picture I liked so much?"

"Nope. I sent it to Tara."

Sybina raised her head. "You did what?"

Aston arched an eyebrow defiantly and handed his phone to Sybina. She looked at it and saw the photo of Aston kissing her with a subtitle saying. *Hey Tara, just wanted to thank you for bringing back my phone. Since you shared pictures of your new lover, I thought I would return the favor with a picture of the most beautiful woman on the planet: my wife and best friend. I hope you love your new man as much as I love my soulmate. Take care, A.*

Sybina lips curved up. "I'm your soulmate now?"

"Absolutely," Aston growled and bit her neck softly. "And my best friend."

"You are a wicked man... this is going to make Tara throw her phone into the wall in pure anger."

Aston shot her a devilish grin. "I hope so."

"I told you to just ignore her," Sybina tried to scold him, but it was impossible with him tickling her.

"It was either this or a poisoned apple, and since you insist I can't kill her, a little mental torture will have to do instead."

A vibrating sound made Aston look at the phone, Aston held it up and opened the message for them to see. It was a close-up photo of Tara's hand flipping a finger with a subtitle reading: *Fuck you!*

Aston broke into laughter. "Tara got the message," he managed to say.

Sybina shook her head. "Good, but it ends here. You had your fun, now leave her alone, I don't want you to provoke her further."

"Yes, ma'am." Aston put up his hand and saluted her, army style.

"At ease, soldier," she said, amused.

Her comment made Aston close his eyes in regret. "Shit, there's something I need to tell you and you're not going to like it."

"What is it, Aston?" Sybina asked. "What did you do?"

"I might as well tell you before you find out," he admitted. "I was sure you had gone to John's house so I went to get you back."

Sybina's eyes widened and she swallowed hard but kept quiet.

324

"You have to understand that I thought you'd slept with John and I was hurt and wanted you back," Aston explained.

"Yes..."

"Well, John wasn't exactly welcoming or helpful, so things got a little heated."

"Please tell me you didn't hit John?" Sybina pleaded.

"I didn't hit John," Aston said firmly. "I wanted to, but I didn't."

"Good!" Sybina sighed.

"But you might prepare yourself for him telling you I'm a lunatic, a caveman, an imbecile, and a whole bunch of other things that I don't remember. He used a lot of words, that man."

Sybina smiled. "He's an author... words are kind of his thing."

"Yeah, well... now you know.... So do you still love me, even though I'm all those things?"

Sybina grinningly pressed a firm kiss on Aston's lips. "You went to get me back?"

"Yes."

"Even though you thought I had slept with John?"

Aston nodded and played with her hair.

"Would you have forgiven me if I had?"

"No..."

"Then why even bother to come for me?" she asked, curious.

"Because you're my wife and you belong here. In my bed, not his."

"Interesting. So you would have slept with me even though you wouldn't have forgiven me?"

Aston gave her a lazy smile. "I would have brought you home and punished you by keeping you in my bed for days, given you so many orgasms that you couldn't walk or think straight and made you completely addicted to me.

I would have made sure you had no energy left to think of another man than me."

Sybina gave a low melodious chuckle. "If that's your idea of a punishment then couldn't you just pretend that I slept with John and go ahead and punish me?"

He pulled at her hair. "Don't put images in my head. I don't want to think about you having sex with John... ever."

"I'm sorry, Aston... you really should punish me for making you think of me and John?" Sybina laughed seductively.

CHAPTER 32
Uma's Visit

Uma

Jasmin released Uma from her hug. "I'll see you in two weeks."

"Thank you for taking me to the airport, I appreciate it," Uma said and looked down to hide her moist eyes. Annoyance overwhelmed her one minute, sadness the next, and other times she found herself laughing without a reason. Right now she felt emotional about saying goodbye to the best friend she had, her dance teacher Jasmin, who had become something like the big sister Uma never had.

"I'll miss you," Jasmin said and touched her shoulder.

Uma bit the inside of her cheek and nodded her head. If she spoke now Jasmin would hear how emotional she was, and Uma never cried. She hated crying. It was for weak people. Uma wasn't weak!

"Did you remember the package I gave you?" Jasmin asked and that question saved Uma from her emotional minefield. Suddenly her thoughts were directed back to the fact that she was caring a package with menstruation pads in her hand baggage. Her sadness over leaving Jasmin was instantly replaced by shyness, and her cheeks heated up. Only two days ago she had started bleeding for the first time and freaked out. Luckily it had happened during dance lessons and Jasmin had been there to save the day with her sisterly explanations and support.

"You're a woman now and you can get pregnant," Jasmin had said, and the idea alone had horrified Uma. She was never having children; that was for certain. Children meant sexual relations with a man, and no man in the entire world would ever get near her. She would rather die.

Anger sneaked up on her, and her shyness and sadness were gone. Lately her emotions were all over the place and she hated it. She had even had thoughts about what other people thought of her, and that was the stupidest thing ever. Jasmin had explained about puberty but it didn't do her much good to understand that the emotional roller coaster was normal for kids her age; she still wanted it to stop. There was no room for feelings in her life. She needed to focus, study, and keep out of trouble, and with these, 'hormonal disturbances', as Jasmin had called them, Uma would have to work doubly hard at keeping her cool when the school year started. Already now some students had returned to the school, and their attitude toward her was still hostile and arrogant. She was the former slave no one wanted to talk to.

Last year had been hard enough. Now she felt like a bomb ready to blow most of the time, and the thought of what problems that would get her into when the school year started made her form a fist. A public display of emotion was horrifying to her. No one would ever see her cry—and she couldn't show her anger either, because that would only get her in trouble with the headmaster and possibly expelled. She needed to get those damn emotions under control or she would be in serious trouble. Her only safe zone was when she was alone in the attic, the only place she could give in to her tears and let them flow. But Uma hardly ever cried. It was rooted deeply into her, compliments of the general. Every time Uma cried she was back to being a toddler watching the general whipping her mother because of her childish tears. Uma hated tears as much as she hated the general.

"See you soon." Uma waved a hand to Jasmin, who blew her a kiss. "Don't do anything I wouldn't."

Jasmin waved back. "Ditto," she said smilingly, looking pretty.

Uma had never been on a plane before and was so excited about the journey that it went far too quickly. Everyone was overly kind to her and treated her with politeness and care. The stewardesses smiled and kept asking if she needed anything, and they brought her sodas, nuts, and candy. It was paradise being the kid that everyone looked out for and complimented for flying alone. None of them spoke Spiri, so Uma was forced to use the English she had learned in school and was proud that she could make herself understood.

When Uma arrived in London she kept gaping around at the big signs in the airport and hurried to follow the crowd of passengers to the baggage claim area. Sybina had explained everything in detail, but Uma was still on her toes and constantly nervous that she would miss something important. The minute she had her bag and walked through customs to see Sybina with her arms reaching out to her, Uma felt those damn tears again and quickly blinked them away. Sybina gave her the longest hug and even Aston tried to hug her. That didn't work. Uma was stiff as a board and pulled back. Aston didn't force it but patted her shoulder instead, and shot her a smile.

They took her home to his apartment and it was the nicest place, smelling of homemade food and cake. Sybina had been at it all day preparing Uma's favorite dishes. She ate too much and got a stomach cramp, or maybe that was the menstruation; hard to say.

The next day Sybina took Uma for a walk around the neighborhood, and she was astonished and could hardly comprehend how different this place was. Uma had been isolated all her life. Even at the school she was isolated. Traffic, busses, baby strollers, bicycles, roller skates, and skateboards were all new to her, and she pointed and stopped more often than not. Sybina understood and took time to explain. They sat on the grass in the park, just watching people and talking. It was the best day ever. When they got hungry they walked to an outdoor café and sat down to have delicious food served. Uma tasted her first burger with fries and looked like the happy kid she never got to be.

Uma loved spending time with Sybina. She would lie on the green grass with her head in Sybina's lap and Sybina would caress her hair and speak of all the things she had experienced since coming to London. They talked for hours and when they walked Sybina held Uma's hand, just like her mom would have, if she had been here.

Uma had asked Sybina why she married Aston. It was still a bit of a mystery to her why Sybina would chose to be with a man. Sybina had spoken about love, trust, and respect, and Uma had nodded like she understood but the reality was, she never would understand.

On her second day Uma was introduced to the TV and she loved it. She knew TV from the school but her access to it had been limited, as it had only been used for educational purposes,—showing documentaries and such.

Aston's TV showed films and had amazing sound. He had asked her if she wanted to see romance, comedy, or action. He had even explained the categories to her and she had wrinkled her nose when he described the concept of romance. Eww.

In the end Aston put on a slapstick comedy, and Uma was laughing more than she could ever remember. Sybina came over and sat down next to her.

"It's so good to hear your laugh."

Uma smiled. It felt good to laugh.

"They will be here in thirty minutes," Sybina said. "I can't wait for you to meet our friends. Kato is even bringing his younger brother, who speaks Spiri."

When a shadow fell over Uma's face, Sybina stroked her hair. "I know you're not fond of guys but I hope you will be nice to Aidan. He could turn out to be a friend for you when you move here. Or at least someone who could introduce you to new friends."

Uma frowned. "We are talking about Kato's younger brother... also known as the brother of Jonul and nephew of the general... right?" Her voice sounded cold.

Sybina inhaled sharply. "I know, Uma, but remember that Kato was the one who killed the general and helped us escape. We can't blame Kato for his brother's and uncle's behavior. And Aidan knows very little about what happened in Spirima, so please avoid the topic, okay?"

"What does he know?"

"Well, about a month ago all the news channels discovered that Kato and Jonul were Masi warriors and that Kato killed the general, so I assume Aidan knows that part. But as far as I know not much else came out, and I'm not sure Aidan understands the details of his brothers' lives in Spirima."

"Does he know they kidnapped and killed people? Does he know Jonul and the general raped women for the fun of it?"

Sybina took a deep sigh. "I don't think so."

"Why can't I tell him what a scum family he has?" Uma asked with fire in her eyes.

"Because Kato will have to give Aidan the details himself; it's his secret to tell."

"Ha," Uma snorted.

"Uma, I need you to promise me that you can keep it secret."

"I'll be on my best behavior," Uma said convincingly and bit down on her tongue to keep from saying what she really felt.

Sybina looked skeptically at her and then she nodded. "I trust you are mature enough to understand the situation." Her words made Uma scowl inside. She wanted to be mature and grown up. No more teenage emotional wobbly stuff; that was for losers. She would show Sybina that she wasn't a kid anymore. She was a woman, and she had the blood in her panties to prove it. "Don't worry," she muttered.

"Thank you," Sybina said and walked to the kitchen, where the loveliest smell from a cake in the oven was spreading. Uma shot a glance at Sybina's back and saw her preparing coffee and tea and setting out cups and plates.

Half an hour later their guests arrived. Uma heard the doorbell ring. Social gatherings were out of her comfort zone; she didn't know exactly what she was supposed to do with herself and figured that the best thing was just to keep in her seat.

Aston went to open the door, and happy voices filled the foyer and followed him into the kitchen and living room that made one big room. Sybina signaled for Uma to stand up and come closer, and she suddenly felt enormously aware of herself and the way she looked. She lowered her head and let her long dark hair cover more of her face in an attempt to hide. She didn't know what to do with her hands and arms, and folded them in front of her a few times.

"Uma, this is Aya, my best friend here in London," Sybina said with a bright smile and led Uma closer to the three people who were filling the kitchen with their presence.

Aya stretched out her hand and Uma shook it politely, even mustering a smile. She had heard so much good about Aya.

"And Kato," Sybina said and Uma looked up to see Kato, who looked so different without his black Masi uniform. Her brows narrowed as she noticed that the Kato in front of her was handsome and had a smile on his face. *A smile? Really?*

Uma didn't give him time to shake her hand; she let her attention move to the last person in the room and looked straight into a pair of friendly golden eyes.

Aston continued his introductions. "Aidan, this is Uma, who will soon come and live with us."

Aidan smiled and reached out his hand politely. Uma took a small step back. *I'm not   touching the general's nephews—no way!*

Aidan's smile turned into annoyance and Aston tried to smooth out the situation by leading their guests further into the room, offering them tea and coffee.

Aidan moved but shot a glance over his shoulder that hit Uma straight in her belly. He had spoken without words and his message was clear. "You're just a small child."

"Aidan, why don't you teach Uma to play cards?" Aya asked ten minutes later, and a sharp look from Sybina told Uma that she'd better play along and be polite. Aidan didn't look pleased, but he shrugged and signaled for her to follow him to the table in the dining room, and then he sat down and expertly picked up a deck of cards, shuffling them while looking back at her. "Are you coming or what?"

Aston gently pushed Uma in the direction of the table and closed the door to give them privacy. At first Uma sat quietly, alert, watching Aidan pass out cards to both him and her. He spoke Spiri with an English accent, but well enough for him to explain the rules of the card game to her. She never answered.

"So when are you coming to stay here?" he said, semi-friendly.

"I don't know," she told him in a bored tone that she'd learned pissed off grown-ups, and hopefully Aidan too.

"Are you always this pleasant?" he asked her bluntly.

Uma narrowed her eyes and felt her heart race. Being in an enclosed room with him felt suffocating and the emotional roller coaster was taking her in loops.

"Only when I'm around creeps like you," she hissed and instantly regretted it. *So much for being mature as Sybina trusted I would be.*

Aidan raised his left eyebrow. "Don't waste your charm on me, *little girl*." He emphasized "little girl" and it made Uma furious.

With her blood boiling she lowered her head. "I'm not a little girl," she said forcefully and then lowered her voice. "I'm much older than you are."

"Really. Then how come you look like you're eight?" He gave her a smug smile, unimpressed with her anger.

"How old are you?" she asked.

"I'm an adult," Aidan answered.

She snorted. "As if."

"I am!" he insisted.

"Of course you are, in your own little dream world."

"I'm seventeen... I can drive a car, I can work, I can have sex. I'm an adult," he argued, clearly irritated. "I'm almost ten years older than you."

Uma snorted and leaned forward. "I think you must be right. You are old. So old that your eyesight is aged and making you blind. I'm thirteen, not eight, you moron."

"Same, same," he muttered. "You play with dolls. I drive cars."

"I may only be thirteen but you are not even slightly as mature as I am. In years of matureness I'm 396 and you are two. That's how much we differ, pretty boy," Uma muttered.

With a thick layer of sarcasm Aidan leaned forward and their noses were almost touching now. "Yeah, you really do come across as old and wise, real balanced and mature... very impressive."

Uma tasted blood on her tongue; she had bitten down so hard that it was actually bleeding. Under the table both her hands were formed into fists and every natural instinct in her told her to pull her head away. She could smell his minty breath and feel the heat from him, and knew that if she pulled back now he would take it as a victory. She was too proud and angry to give him that satisfaction and focused on letting her hatred for him, his uncle, and his brother Jonul shine through her eyes when she spoke slowly. "You. Disgust. Me!"

Aidan's expression changed into amusement. "You don't know me well enough to feel that strongly about me. I think you must be in love with me."

Uma's lips pressed into a thin line. "I wouldn't touch you if you were the last boy in the world."

"Man, not boy," Aidan corrected.

"Ha. You're no man. You are just a little self-obsessed boy who thinks that every girl finds you attractive."

"I *am* attractive." He sounded confident.

"You are repulsive," Uma spit out, keeping her narrowed eyes piercing him with only a few inches between them.

"I bet that you would like it if I kissed you right now," Aidan said challengingly.

"I know that if you did, you would die," she threatened.

"I'm not scared of little girls." He leaned back, pretending to look her over, but Uma felt victorious for having stood her ground. Aidan had retreated, not her.

"Good for you, *pretty boy*," she whispered, keeping the same position, hoping he would give up and leave. But Aidan just narrowed his eyes like her and leaned forward again.

"So you think I'm pretty, do you?" He smiled. "I thought you said I repulsed you."

Uma's jaw clenched. "Oh, you are pretty alright. As pretty as a girl. I bet your gay lovers like that about you." She looked triumphant, when she saw how her words upset him.

"I'm not gay!" he exclaimed, insulted, and then he composed himself. "But if I had to choose between a guy and you, I would chose the guy any day. You are so nasty you could make any man turn gay."

Uma sat there frozen, but inside her head a vein popped and the force of a volcano was pressing on her chest. *Keep it cool... don't let him win*, she kept saying to herself, and her years of training in suppressing emotions kicked in. "Good," she said slowly. "I wouldn't allow any man to touch me anyway. So I guess it's a win-win."

He nodded. "Don't worry, no man will ever want you. You are ugly both inside and out."

Uma stared at him and there was something in his eyes... a flash of regret? If so, it was quickly gone, and Uma was fighting with every bit of restrain she had to avoid tipping the table over and hitting him in the head with whatever she could find. Uma pre-puberty couldn't have cared less about his opinion of her, but Uma the teenager was hurt and confused. Was he right? Jasmin had told her a thousand times that she was pretty with her green eyes and long hair, but maybe English boys had a different taste in girls. Who the hell was this loser to call her ugly? Uma was so angry she could spit but she could never show him that. She put on the "You are boring me to death" mask and leaned back, picked up her cards, and shot him a patronizing look. "So how did this game go again?"

Aidan looked at her with a mixture of respect, worry, and disbelief, and then he started to explain again.

Uma won the game, and it felt good to beat Aidan. She would have preferred to punch him in his stomach but beating him at gin rummy was better than nothing.

"Do you want to play again?" Aidan asked and looked at her.

Uma looked away. She had been studying him for the last forty minutes when he wasn't looking at her. He looked so much like Kato, only younger and less muscular. He had clean skin for a teenager and his hair was thick and dark. Not that she cared how he looked; she just rarely had a chance to study a sample of the enemy up close—and he was very close. The table between them was narrow and their feet under the table had touched several times. Every time they both pulled away as if the other was poisonous.

"Can't get enough of me beating you, or what?" Uma asked sarcastically.

"I let you win. Isn't that what grown-ups do with children?" Aidan said coolly.

"I don't know, go ask the grown-ups if you want an answer. But I'm no child. I'm a woman."

"Ha... here we go again." Aidan rolled his eyes.

"I am!" Uma felt like stomping her foot and screaming at him. "I got my period and that means I'm a woman." She instantly blushed red; she felt it herself. It was humiliating enough that she had just told him a secret that not even Sybina knew, but that she blushed red in front of him was the closest thing to a public display of emotion she had come to in months, and it was unacceptable.

He laughed at her. He didn't even say anything. He just laughed and it was the most horrible sound in the world.

"What's so funny?" she spit at him.

"You are. All puffed up trying to convince me you're a woman, telling me about your period. You crack me up."

"Stop laughing."

"Or what?" he snickered. "Are you going to tickle me to death?"

Murder. Murder. Murder. All Uma could think was how much she wanted to make him stop laughing. It was humiliating.

"I already told you, I wouldn't touch you even if you were the last boy in the world," she said with flaring nostrils.

"Man," Aidan corrected her again when Aston popped his head in.

"Good to hear you're having fun together. I brought you some more cake, do you want it?

"Sure," Aidan said with a big smile and when Aston left the room Aidan started laughing again. "I suggest you eat the whole tray of cake. With a little luck it might go to your hips and boobs and make you look like the woman you so desperately want to be, kid."

"I think I might. At least I'm slim and can eat as much cake as I want to. You wouldn't want to get any chubbier; I can imagine you're having problems picking girls up as it is."

Aidan stopped laughing. "I can have any girl I want to," he stated.

A smile spread on Uma's face and she gave him a sly smile. "Liar!"

He tensed his jaw. "Ask Aya or my brother. Girls swoon around me."

"Not this girl. You can *never* have me." Uma took a big bite of Sybina's cake to hide the grin playing on her lips. If this was a game of chess she had just told him, "Checkmate, pal." There was no way he could win this one. Ever!

Aidan ignored her and took a piece of cake himself. They sat quietly munching on the cake, avoiding looking at each other, and yet she felt him look her way a few times. He was probably brewing up mean comments to throw at her, but it would never dampen the amazing feeling she had in her belly. He might be bigger, stronger,

338

and older than her, but he was not her superior; she had stood her ground and she felt damn good about herself.

When it was time for Aya, Kato, and Aidan to leave, Aston approached them and asked: "Did you have fun, kids?"

He received a lethal glance from Aidan. "I'm not a kid," he said.

"I'm sorry." Aston smiled. "Didn't mean to offend you. So, Aidan... Maybe when Uma moves here you can come by and hang out with her sometime; she'll need friends and you speak Spiri." Aston sounded light and hopeful.

Aidan wrinkled his nose and looked at Uma. "I have a lot going on and I'm sure Uma would rather find someone her own age. You know how *little girls* like to play with dolls and ponies." Uma scowled back at him. She had never owned a toy in her life, and if Aidan had known her situation better he would have understood how hurtful his insult really was. She wanted to punch the smug grin off Aidan's face but she quickly regained her controlled posture and walked by the two men with a casual remark. "That's okay, Aston, Aidan isn't into girls. He's more into *playing with boys*." Uma suppressed a grin when she turned and saw Aston shoot a surprised glance at Aidan, who scowled at her. And then she heard Aidan whisper to Aston, "Are you sure you want that demon child in your family?"

Uma wanted to laugh at how easy it had been to wipe the smug smile off Aidan's face. He was no match for her.

CHAPTER 33
The Wedding

Sybina

The days with Uma went much too fast. Sybina wanted time to slow down so she would get the most of it. Around Sybina, Uma was relaxed, loving, and had a wonderful humor. With Aston in the room she clammed up. Aston tried his best and patiently exposed Uma to small doses of his presence. Uma accepted his company on daily morning runs, and apparently she surprised him by outrunning him every time he challenged her.

"She's like a freaking cheetah, you should see her run. Sybina, I've never seen anything like it." Aston had said after returning the first morning.

At the end of week two Sybina thought she saw improvement. She even heard Uma laugh at one of Aston's jokes.

Aston took Sybina and Uma on a road trip to Scotland, and it had been wonderful to see the old towns and the beauties of nature. They had gone to Edinburgh and visited the old castle, and both Uma and Sybina had been fascinated and a little creeped out by a picture of a woman who looked straight at you no matter what angle you viewed her from. They had also done an underground ghost tour and seen the part of the city that had been barricaded when the plague came and killed almost half of Edinburgh's population in 1645. People had simply been left to die.

Uma had shown no signs of fear on the ghost tour and shot amused smiles at the group of Japanese tourists that were clinging to each other in the dark underground as if monsters were going to jump out at them from the walls. It didn't surprise Sybina that Uma showed no fear. The girl had lived with monsters all her life and she had become a tough person in many ways.

Aston had told them stories of the highlanders of Scotland and the many wars between England and Scotland. He was a great storyteller and had tried to teach Uma to say a few words with a Scottish accent. Sybina had a hard time understanding the locals but she found their singsong accent intriguing.

Today was the day of Aya and Kato's wedding. They were in the English countryside at a romantic and idyllic estate in old English style; chosen because it was the place where Kato had proposed to Aya three months ago.

Sybina felt beautiful in her new dress and high heels; she was even wearing the diamond necklace Aston had given her, and Aston had a hard time keeping his hands off her. With Uma in the house they were toning down their love and tried to keep the touching to a minimum, but like always, the forbidden held a double attraction, and even though they made love quietly and gently every night to not wake Uma, it wasn't enough. Something was starting to bother Sybina. There was a part of Aston that she didn't know. A part that he had shared with his other sexual partners and not her. He had told her that he would normally have considered their sex boring, and it made her think that he had needs which she didn't fulfil... Sybina wasn't delicate or fragile, and her curiosity was beginning to raise questions about his past and his sexual fantasies.

Sybina hated that Uma had to fly back to Spirima tomorrow, but if she were to find one single positive thing about the situation it was that she could start to explore with Aston.

She took a proud look at Uma, who lit up her surroundings in her dark purple dress, with her long dark hair and sparkling green eyes. She was not yet a woman, but gorgeous in her youthful way.

Aston looked proud too when he escorted Sybina and Uma to the tent where the party was set up with impressive round tables, white tablecloths, golden chairs, candles, and the finest cutlery. There were even chandeliers hanging from the ceiling of the huge white tent and an elegant lady giving a magical touch to the whole thing with her captivating harp music softly lifting everyone's mood.

It was impossible not to be affected by the romantic setting, and Sybina was happy that Uma got to experience this extravagant wedding and see for herself that good and beautiful things happened in the world too. It wasn't all religious fanaticism, slavery, and violence. The world offered hope, love, and romance as well, and miracles happened all around. The baby growing inside Aya was a sure proof that even in the darkest moments miracles happened.

Aya looked stunning in a white dress that didn't hide her pregnancy but enhanced it elegantly. The wedding ceremony had taken place in a local church from the seventeenth century and offered a perfect setting with its atmosphere and history.

There had been photographers outside the church and Sybina had tried to explain to Uma that Kato and Aya had been in the media a lot, but Uma didn't understand the concept of media and had more questions than Sybina had time to answer. She and Aston had been asked to pose for a picture too and Aston had done so and hurried along. He didn't like the attention and when the press asked who the pretty girl was, he didn't answer.

Uma had looked down and Sybina feared that Uma thought Aston was embarrassed by her, when in truth he was just trying to protect Uma and avoid stories of her past as a slave in the media. It was up to Uma how much she wanted to share with others, and Sybina could understand if that part of Uma's life was something she would rather leave behind and walk away from. Moving to England would be a clean slate for Uma, a new chance of happiness.

"Have a glass," a voice from behind offered and Sybina saw Aston reach for three flutes of champagne. She thought about protesting Uma's drinking alcohol but it seemed foolish. Uma was the youngest person present, and one thing that had changed since she had last seen Uma was that the girl was becoming self-aware and easily embarrassed. She was thirteen and a half, and a full-blown teenager in puberty. The changes were happening fast and right in front of their eyes. Uma was taller than Sybina and starting to get curves. She would be a fine woman with her bright green eyes, thick hair, and full lips, but Sybina couldn't decide if Uma's beauty would be a curse or a blessing. She would no doubt attract attention from scores of young men and if she didn't overcome her hatred for them, she could easily be forced to live a life like a hedgehog with all its spikes raised. Sybina would do everything she could to help Uma find joy and happiness.

They were seated at a round table with three others. Sybina had Aston on her left side and Uma on her right. Aston sat next to Lisa, Aya's cousin who studied in Oslo; and next to Lisa, and right across from Sybina, sat Sofia, Aya's best friend from Norway whom Sybina had heard so much about and looked forward to getting to know. The last person at the table was Aidan, who, even though Sybina had warned Aya against it, had been chosen to sit next to Uma. Aidan had Sofia on his right side and was very polite and charming when he greeted her. When he turned to acknowledge Uma, Sybina saw the two teenagers greet each other with disdain, and she knew putting them next to each other had been a mistake. Aidan might be charming and friendly but everyone had their limits, and a thirteen-year-old ice queen was more than he wanted to deal with.

Sybina was soon in a conversation with Sofia, whom she found interesting and knowledgeable, but her senses were very aware that Aidan and Uma didn't say a word to each other. Aidan kept texting on his phone and Uma kept looking bored, which Sybina knew was an act on Uma's side since her eyes had been glittering until Aidan came. There was no doubt that Aidan's presence bothered Uma.

At one point Sofia took an interest in Aidan and conversed with him. Sybina was flabbergasted to see the difference in the young man, who clearly found Sofia interesting and immediately put his phone down. Sofia was twenty-four years old and good-looking. Sybina took a better glance at Sofia and decided that maybe she wasn't beautiful like Aya, who was one of those tall Scandinavian girls with long blond hair and big blue eyes, girls that had just won the gene pool lottery, but Sofia had style and charisma that made her interesting. Her hair was brown and reached just below her shoulders, styled in curls for the evening, but her best features were her feminine curves, especially her round breasts that had Sybina wondering if they were fake or real—and then there were her sparkling eyes and the way she spoke. Sofia was smart, to the point, and had humor. There was power radiating from her. Personal power and independence, and it was very attractive. Clearly, Aidan thought so too, because he was flirty and Sofia was playing along, amused by the young man's adoration.

Aidan leaned towards Sofia, giving her a charming smile that would take the breath away from most young girls, but not a woman like Sofia.

Sybina smiled as she watched them interact. Aya had spoken of Sofia, and Sybina felt like she already knew her. Aidan might be entertaining and charming but Sofia was way out of his league; she was not into young men, they were only fun distractions.

Sofia needed someone who would challenge her and although Aidan had the potential to become a fine man one day, he was only seventeen and not man enough for Sofia.

When Sofia took a bathroom break Aidan immediately returned to being a disinterested teenager texting on his phone. Sybina tried to make small talk with him and to involve Uma to get a conversation started between them, but nothing seemed to work.

"Who are you texting?" Sybina asked in an attempt to get Aidan to stop and pay attention to his dinner partner. He looked up with a smug smile. "One of my girlfriends."

"One of?" Sybina asked. "How many do you have?"

He laughed and shrugged. "Right now, only two."

Uma yawned provocatively.

"Aren't you afraid they are going to find out about each other?" Sybina asked, confused by his open admittance to betrayal.

Again he shrugged and returned his attention to the phone that was vibrating discreetly.

Kato stood up to make a speech and Sybina whispered to Aidan, "Would you please translate?" She could have asked Aston, who was on her other side, but she wanted Aidan to interact with Uma at some level, even if it was just to translate Kato's words into Spiri so Uma would understand.

Aidan sighed with exasperation before he started to whisper.

"I can't hear you," Sybina whispered back and Aidan leaned closer, but with Uma sitting between them Aidan was now in Uma's personal space. Sybina wondered if she had pushed Uma too far when she saw her close her eyes and press her body as far back in her chair as possible. Sybina looked down and saw Uma clench the edges of her chair, while Aidan spoke in a whisper and translated Kato's speech of finding true love, overcoming challenges, believing in the impossible, and trusting in each other. It was a beautiful speech, and looking at Kato's love shining from him to Aya was breathtakingly romantic and had Sybina tearing up.

Uma had been holding her breath and suddenly Sybina saw her chest rise and fall rapidly. Aidan ignored it and Sybina looked at him speculatively. Was he enjoying the effect he clearly had on Uma and leaning closer than he needed to? His left arm was resting on the back of her chair, and with Uma pressed all the way back his arm was touching her hair. His other hand rested on the side of her chair just next to her hand. Although he didn't touch Uma's skin Sybina knew Uma was uncomfortable with him so close, and she wondered if she should ask him to pull away from Uma. She would no doubt seem hysterical to him since he wasn't even touching Uma, and Uma would no doubt be embarrassed by her, so Sybina kept quiet, listening to Aidan's soft voice translating Kato's words.

"We had a rough start and I don't blame you for feeling like I was the last man you wanted close to you."

Uma opened her eyes, and Sybina didn't miss the way she turned her head and looked at Aidan as if the words were his own. If her eyes could speak they would be saying, "You're damn right, so back the fuck away."

Aidan ignored her. "I cannot thank you enough for taking a chance on me. For loving me. For trusting me," he whispered in Spiri, and this time he had the nerve to smile at Uma.

Sybina put a hand on Uma's hand to calm her down, fearing that Uma would explode in the middle of Kato's romantic speech. Aidan was either incredibly insensitive and blind to the way he affected Uma or he was toying with her. But Aidan just took it up a notch by looking directly into Uma's blazing eyes and translating Kato's words: "I love you now and forever and you are beyond comparison the most beautiful and amazing woman in the world."

Sybina smiled at Kato and Aya, who were now kissing, and they all raised their glasses to the newlyweds and drank a toast to them.

Aidan had pulled away and had all his attention again directed at Sofia, who had returned to her seat. Uma left the minute the talking resumed around the tables, and she was gone for more than twenty minutes.

If she had stayed away longer, Sybina would have gone searching for her, apologizing for asking Aidan to translate, but Uma came back smiling, looking on top of the world, and when she sat down she completely ignored Aidan and spoke only to Sybina. They went over the decorations, the dresses, the love between Aya and Kato, the estate they were on, and how this wedding was like something out of a fairy tale. Uma was relaxed again and even smiled and laughed a few times. Sybina felt proud of her. The girl had felt cornered but she had pulled through without a scene.

When the dancing started, Aidan asked Sofia to dance and they left the table. Aston wasn't around, and when a handsome man from Aya's side of the family came to ask Sybina to dance, she politely accepted.

As they danced he told her in his charming Norwegian accent that this was his first visit to England. He was tall and had broad shoulders and was clearly not a skilled dancer but neither was Sybina, so she didn't mind that they only swung from side to side while talking. He told her that Aya had talked about Sybina and he presented himself as a second cousin to Aya. Sybina smiled up at him until she heard Aston's voice next to them. "Do you mind if I cut in? I would like to dance with my wife," he said flatly and the Viking pulled back. "Of course," he said and let go of Sybina's hands.

Aston stared the man down and Sybina shook her head. "Was that necessary?" she asked. "We were just dancing."

"No one gets the first dance but me," Aston said and whirled her around and pulled her back into his arms. "I don't share well."

"And I don't do well in cages," Sybina pointed out.

Aston looked disturbed. "What are you implying?"

"Nothing, Aston, let's just dance."

Sybina felt his tension and pulled him down for a kiss. "You have nothing to worry about, you know that, right?"

He gave her a small nod but it wasn't in sync with the expression in his eyes.

"I won't leave you again," Sybina said close to his ear and smiled when he lifted her from the ground.

"You better not," he said and kissed her hard on the mouth.

"But I'll dance with whoever I want to," Sybina insisted. "That is non-negotiable."

Aston gave her a small smile. "If you insist, but not too close."

"Caveman," she teased.

"Witch," he teased back before he broke into a laugh and swung her around again.

Sybina beamed at her husband. Over her shoulder she saw other women looking at Aston and she didn't blame them; he was eye candy with his black tuxedo and killer looks—a combination of style and bad-boy attitude that worked as an aphrodisiac on most women.

Sybina lifted her head and smiled up at him; it was all it took for her to get a kiss.

"Maybe I should be the jealous one; you're attracting a lot of attention from the women here," she said.

Aston shrugged "I wouldn't know; I only see you."

"Good, because you're mine and they can't have you." Her tone was sultry.

A boyish grin broke out on Aston's face and it shot his sex appeal through the roof, making Sybina wet her lips instinctively.

"Come with me," Aston whispered in her ear and with decisive steps he led Sybina away from the dance floor.

"Where are we going?" Sybina asked, "And what about Uma?"

Aston looked down at her with eyes glowing with lust. He scanned the room and pointed to Aidan, who stood close by. "Look after Uma for ten minutes. We'll be right back."

Aidan didn't get a chance to answer before Aston was gone and pulling Sybina with him. "What are you doing?" Sybina said laughingly, wondering what his rush was.

Aston pulled her with him into the forest and soon pushed her up against a tree. "I need you so fucking bad I could scream," he rasped in a hoarse voice and started kissing her passionately.

He had been drinking, and he was different from his normal controlled self. This Aston was hungry and wanted his woman. He pulled up Sybina's dress and used his hands to feel her.

"People might see us," Sybina objected.

"I don't care..." His hands moved down between her legs and he gave a satisfied moan. "You are dripping wet for me,"

Thoughts of Uma and other people potentially seeing or hearing them flashed through Sybina's mind, but Aston's kisses and his lust for her were intoxicating. He wanted her and he couldn't wait. It did something to her, and she felt a rush of desire when he pulled her around and pushed her up against the three again, this time biting her neck and shoulders. "I have to fuck you, Ina," he growled.

Sybina pushed her ass back against him. "Then take me," she said and heard him make a guttural sound.

"It's not going to be slow and pretty," he warned her. "I'm going to fuck you hard and fast."

Sybina closed her eyes and smiled. His words turned her on. She trusted him and knew he wouldn't harm her. This was the kind of raw sex Aston had shared with other women, and the thought that she was here to meet his need, aroused her. Sybina turned her head and gave him a challenging smile. "Are you going to talk all night or actually do it?" She saw him widen his eyes in surprise before he grabbed her hips hard and pulled her back. "Lean on the tree," he ordered and penetrated her with one long deep push. Sybina let out a deep moan from the explosive feeling of being filled so completely.

Normally Aston allowed her time to get used to his size and took it slow with her, but not tonight. He held an arm tight around her waist and slammed himself into her again and again. She could feel every inch of him pounding against her flesh and held on to the tree for support. She was on her toes and he was bending his knees, but every time he pushed himself inside her he went deeper, slamming his cock against her cervix. He was too big and too aggressive, her rational brain told her, but another part shouted for him to fuck her senseless and never stop.

If someone had walked by, they would have heard them. Even the music couldn't block out the loud moans that Aston made or her panting.

It was so dirty and primal, and poked at an unknown part of Sybina. She liked outdoor, impulsive, rough sex with Aston, even though it was a bit uncomfortable to be standing like this and slightly painful with the way he took her hard and rough. It was a revelation to experience the major satisfaction of meeting his needs and feeling so desperately wanted by him.

He made a suppressed roar. "Fuck... I'm coming!" Aston's body convulsed in jerks and he squeezed her hips tightly while pumping his sperm inside her.

350

Sybina looked back at Aston. He was still inside her and standing with his eyes closed and a dreamy smile on his face. She might not have reached her orgasm, but she was highly satisfied with herself for giving Aston that beautiful expression on his face.

When they walked back to the party, Aston had his arm around her shoulder and leaned against her. "I wish I could stay with you in a room and not leave the bed for days... I'll never get enough of you, Ina."

Sybina answered him with an intimate squeeze. "I wish that too, handsome."

They returned to the tent with shiny eyes and red cheeks. Uma was still sitting in her seat and Aidan sat next to her, with his phone. Sybina suspected the two of them hadn't spoken a word to each other in the ten minutes she and Aston had been gone, but she was too high on sex to be bothered. Uma was young and there would be time to help her; today was about celebrating romance.

CHAPTER 34
Boundaries

Aston

Sybina was quieter than usual. Two hours ago they had taken Uma to the airport, and Uma was now on her way back to the boarding school in Spirima. Sybina had kept drying her tears away when she hugged Uma goodbye but the girl hadn't wept a single tear. Aston had observed her closely these past two weeks and he wasn't fooled by the kid. She had been sad to leave, but had played it cool. Probably to spare Sybina.

Aston was an expert observer, and these past two weeks had allowed him a better picture of the child; he had gained much respect for her.

Uma didn't speak much with him, but she spoke with Sybina and had pretty much succeeded in convincing Sybina that she liked it at the school and was looking forward to going back. Aston knew better; he saw the subtle signs that betrayed Uma when she spoke. She was a world-class liar; her eyes didn't drift and her breathing didn't change; she didn't dry-wash her hands or get red cheeks from the emotional stress of lying. In fact Uma didn't betray herself with any of the typical signs of lying that Aston knew so well from his time in the military, where he had interrogated grown men and women.

Uma was able to look Sybina straight in the eye and tell her what she thought Sybina needed or wanted to hear. At first Aston had found it disturbing until he realized that Uma's lies were always altruistic in nature. She was covering up the truth to make the situation easier for Sybina. She didn't lie in general, only when she didn't want Sybina to suffer on her behalf. Aston had concluded that despite her traumatic childhood she did have a conscience.

Uma's signs of lying were so subtle that he had only seen through them by coincidence. What gave her away was the perfection with which she delivered the lie. Normally Uma, like most teens, were only mildly interested in her surroundings and even when she spoke with Sybina her eyes would scan the room and flicker around. It was her nature to be constantly observing and thinking, but when Sybina asked her a difficult question that required a lie to comfort her, Uma looked straight at her, held her voice calm, and delivered the words with conviction. The only thing that gave Uma away was that she didn't know that her counselor at the school gave them reports about what trouble she was in.

Sybina had asked Uma on one of the first mornings: "So how are the other kids treating you."

Uma had said: "Fine." That was her first lie.

Sybina also asked if there had been any problems with the boys and Uma had cryptically replied that it was nothing she couldn't handle. That wasn't a lie, Aston could see; she meant it.

"What about the girls, are they being nice to you?" Sybina had asked, and Uma had lied for the second time and pretended that the girls were nice and everything was fine.

If Aston hadn't known better from the counselor, he would have believed her—she was *that* convincing. But he knew from the school reports that Uma was being excluded by the other students, and because he had been on the outside of Sybina's and Uma's conversation he had the luxury of being able to observe Uma without having to respond.

Sybina would have called Uma's bluff too if it weren't that she wanted to believe Uma's lies so badly.

Aston had wanted to make Uma aware that she was a child and it was okay for her to lean on Sybina and him; she didn't have to be the strong one. But he needed to build rapport with her first and it took time. Hopefully when she moved in with them he could start helping her build trust in adults in general and men in particular.

Aston wasn't good with emotions himself either, but he was older and understood that suppressing them came with a price. There were only so many things a human could do to numb themselves, and personally he had used sex, gambling, and alcohol to do it in the past. If Uma didn't find a way to cleanse her system and get the anger and hurt out, she would be a candidate for all sorts of destructive behavior in the future, and he worried about her. At the same time he saw immense strength and resilience in her. But strength, intelligence, and hatred were a dangerous cocktail and Uma seemed like one of those people who could swing either way.

Aston rubbed Sybina's neck and kissed her on the top of her hair. "How about a movie?" he asked but she was deep in her own thoughts and hard to reach.

"I know you miss her. But look at the bright side. Uma likes it here. Now all we have to do is wait for the papers to go through."

"That's the problem, Aston. The wait is killing me," Sybina sighed.

"I know. The lawyers have tried everything but until her mother is declared dead, Uma is not considered an orphan and cannot be adopted. All we can do is sponsor her at school."

Sybina sighed. "If only we could find Hunilla."

"I still have people looking for her, if she's alive, we'll find her... But in case we don't, I promise you that we're prepared and ready with all the adoption papers. Only problem is..." He trailed off.

"What?"

"Even with the best lawyers it might take time... I was warned that the system is slow and rigid, not least because there's an overload of cases after the war. I've told my people to pressure, bribe, and do everything in their power to push the adoption case through but these things can take a long time."

Sybina paled. "How long?"

Aston took her hand. "No one can say for sure; worst case—years."

"Years? You mean on top of the two years before she is declared ready for adoption?"

He nodded with concern. "They won't start working on our adoption case until the two years are up."

Sybina's eyes welled up. "What's wrong with these people? Don't they see that they are hurting Uma?"

Aston dried away a tear that was escaping Sybina's eye and she buried her head against his shoulder.

"Oh God, I feel so horrible for leaving Uma alone at a school with no real friends and no family."

"I get that, but don't underestimate Uma. She's strong and resilient. She'll make it through. At least she has someone waiting for her and caring for her. That's more than many other kids in her situation have."

"You're right." Sybina sniffled and forced a small smile.

"Why don't you come to bed with me and let me distract you a bit?" Aston suggested and took her silent smile as acceptance. With a loving smile, he picked her up from the couch and carried her towards their bedroom. Sybina leaned her head against him. "I love you," she whispered.

It didn't take long for Aston to get her undressed, and just as he had promised he distracted her by making love to her. Yesterday he had been drunk and horny and fucked her against a tree. His brave Sybina had let him but he regretted being so rough on her. Sybina was a lovemaker and she liked it gentle and soft. For some reason he had come to appreciate that sort of sex although he would have sworn it wasn't for him. If sex could be compared to exercise Aston was into hardcore CrossFit training with loud rock music and sweat dripping from pushing himself and his partner to their limits. Sybina on the other hand was more of a yoga type of girl and all about their spiritual connection and smooth controlled movements. Metaphorically speaking, Aston had joined her yoga classes to be with her and it wasn't bad at all. Yoga was really nice, at least with Sybina. But yesterday... he had longed for a quick, hard fix of CrossFit and she had given it to him. Maybe seeing her dancing with that big blond dude had been what made him crave her, maybe it was a territorial thing and his craving for her had been about marking his scent on her... it sure felt that way, but now it was different. He had all the time in the world and just wanted to satisfy his woman and make sure she experienced pleasure.

A few weeks back he had almost lost Sybina, and the suffocating fear that had filled him then had helped him push through his fear of commitment. Aston smiled at the irony that he was now married and unwilling to let his wife go. Hell, she turned him into a bloody primitive Neanderthal whenever other men got too close to her. It was ridiculous. All his adult life Aston had been avoiding any sort of commitment to women, dodging one bullet after the other, leaving a trail of beautiful but pissed-off women behind him. He had turned down marriage proposals and broken off contact with any girl who was stupid enough to bring up the subject of moving in together or even worse... marriage and kids.

Aston was not a poet or a particularly verbal man, and since last week's big confession he hadn't told Sybina in words that he loved her. He told her with his eyes, his hands, his actions, and his permanently hard dick for her, and right now he was giving her the best of him. His full attention and gentle care. If she was hurting, he was here to heal her, distract her, and fill her up with lust and laughter.

Sybina

"I love you," Sybina whispered into Aston's mouth while kissing him deeply and passionately. Aston interlaced his hands with hers and moved down, placing kisses along her neck, and cupped her breast before he suckled on her nipple playfully.

He was so controlled and gentle, in comparison to yesterday when he pulled her from the dance floor because he couldn't wait another second to be inside her. Memories of being grabbed and slammed into from behind made Sybina bite her lip and smile. She closed her eyes, listening to the soundtrack of Aston from yesterday, so incredibly horny for her that he couldn't control himself. He had growled, moaned, cursed, and roared out his orgasm and it had been the most erotic experience of her life. Raw, unleashed, and uninhibited—and she hadn't cared one bit that he was aggressive and rough; in fact it had been a turn-on.

Sybina was confused by her own reaction and desire to experience Aston like that again. She wanted to give in and let go of her need for control. No more worrying about Uma, no more judging right sex from wrong sex, or doubting her own ability to be as good in bed as the women from Aston's past. She needed him to be strong for her and be that safe zone where she could set it all free with no fear of falling—trusting that if she did, Aston would be there to catch her, to never hurt her, to never ridicule her, to never judge her. She was tired of being strong and aware, she wanted passionate, blissful fucking.

And why shouldn't she? It had felt deeply frustrating to see all the women at the wedding yesterday sending long glances at Aston while she knew he was compromising his sexual desires for her. He had told her that he had never made love with other women, only her. She didn't want to give up on the lovemaking, but she wanted to experience the other side of him as well. He was like a fine racecar, strong and potent, and she was forcing him to drive in slow motion. She was holding him back. There were so many things she had refused to even consider doing with him and it was nagging her, scaring her. How long would slow motion be enough for him before he pushed down on his gas pedal and took off, leaving her behind?

Sybina looked down and smiled, seeing Aston's tongue and lips playing over her body. "Do you love me?" she whispered, greedy to hear him say it again.

He answered her by sending her a flashing smile and licking her belly button.

"I need to know... do you love me?" she asked again.

"Uh-huh." He groaned and closed his eyes. She knew what it meant. He didn't want to talk, he wanted to touch and feel; but she needed him to say the words that would tell her she was safe with him.

"Then say it," she said pleadingly.

Aston opened his eyes to look at her. "I love you, Ina."

Sybina sucked in his words with an explosive gasp and tasted them on her tongue. They were sweet and addictive, and the gnawing monster in the pit of her belly that had two heads, anger and self-doubt, cuddled up like a purring cat at peace. With a satisfied grin she grabbed Aston's hands and placed them on her breasts, showing him she wanted him to squeeze them. "I want it hard," she growled in a seductive voice that was very different from the loving and pleading voice she had just used.

Aston looked up at her and tilted his head. "Hard?" he asked.

"Hard!" she said in challenge, wondering where this confident, sexually aggressive part of her had been hiding.

Aston's breathing became slightly quicker, his eyes sparkled more brightly, and he laughed huskily. "How hard?" he asked, curious, and held her gaze.

Like a split personality Sybina heard the new confident woman in her chuckle, in a smoky, mysterious, silky voice with a twist of demand. "I'm a strong girl, I won't break easily." She slid her nails down over his shoulders, leaving red marks, while she fixed on him a sexually provocative glance.

Aston's reaction was priceless with his mouth opening slightly, his eyes widening, and his Adam's apple revealing he was swallowing hard. He looked edible and a ferocious appetite took her over, pushing the last part of her normally restrained, controlled self into an inner closet and slamming the door hard. "I liked it yesterday and I want you to give me more of that. Tell me how you want to fuck me..." Her words made Aston drop his mouth. "I want to hear you say it," she continued and got up from the bed. Aston moved back in a sitting position, looking incredulous at her.

Slowly Sybina walked to her closet and pulled out a scarf. She was naked and made sure to give him time to enjoy her body moving as sexily as possible. With the scarf in her hands she moved back to the bed and without losing eye contact she crawled up and kneeled in front of him. "I want to tie you up," she said.

Aston raised an eyebrow. He didn't speak a word but they had an entire conversation just by keeping eye contact.

Never going to happen, his eyes said.

Why? hers asked.

359

I don't have a submissive bone in my body, that's why, his eyes told her, and while communicating this to her Aston took the scarf from her.

"Lie down and leave the control to me," he said, this time using words, and when she didn't do it fast enough he pushed her back on the bed and placed her where he wanted her.

"But I wanted to..."

"Shhh," he hushed her.

A warm feeling spread in Sybina's body, filling her from head to toe. There was no fear. No shame, only trust and surrender. With a lazy movement she lifted her arms and inclined her head, giving him permission to tie her up.

He hesitated for a moment. "Ina, maybe this isn't the best idea. I don't think that..."

She cut him off. "I don't want you to think, I want you to take me till I can't remember my own name."

Aston's eyes narrowed and with a slight head shake he tied her hands together and secured the rope to the headboard. He worked fast and knew what he was doing. When he was done his eyes were constantly locked on hers with complete focus. "Are you sure?" he asked her.

Sybina laughed again, silky smooth, and wriggled her hips. "Less talk—more action." She wanted the Aston who had taken her yesterday. He had been ruthless and animalistic, not hesitant and uncertain. She could feel the beast in Aston just underneath his surface, but he was holding back. "Stop holding back, Aston. I said I wanted it hard," she whispered seductively.

Aston went down on her and started kissing her inner thighs, moving up to her magical, sensitive spot. She moaned and then she shook her head. "No, I want you inside me." Aston had given her oral before and it was always amazing, but it wasn't what she wanted today. She wanted it hard and dirty, and he was procrastinating.

She knew he was thinking, analyzing, and assessing her. She could see it in his eyes, and she wanted to scream at him to stop thinking and just do it. Desperate she poked at him to provoke his inner beast to come out and play like yesterday.

"What is it? Are you not up for the task? Do you need me to find someone else to fuck me?"

Aston froze for a second. "What did you say?"

"I need a strong man to take me and I want you... so give it to me already."

It took Aston a nanosecond to position himself and penetrate her, all gentleness forgotten.

"Don't provoke me," he hissed and she laughed. *Mission accomplished, the beast is out, time to play.*

"There you are... I like this part of you." Sybina bit his earlobe hard and he pulled his head out of her reach and bit her nipple in return. The pain aroused her.

Like yesterday, he was aggressive and pounding hard into her and his eyes were now glazed with wild lust. Sybina wanted to take a picture of him right now: capture him mouthwateringly masculine, horny, and beautiful.

"Don't look at me like that or I'll come too quickly," he managed to say and slowed down.

"I want more," she gasped and pushed against him like an addict for heroin. "Tell me that I'm yours," she ordered.

"Oh, have no doubt," he whispered into her ear. "You are mine and only mine."

"Then fuck me hard."

In a quick movement he turned her around and ordered her up on her knees. Her hands were still tied together and the rope attached to the headboard forced her to lean forward. Behind her, Aston, pushed himself into her and with a strong grip on her hips he picked up his pace again. His stamina was amazing and again and again he pounded hard into her.

"Yes." She felt her orgasm build inside her; it was getting closer. She couldn't see him and she wanted the connection with him, not just physically but mentally too. "I belong to you," she insisted. Aston didn't answer; he was thrusting fast now.

"I want to belong to you," she moaned again.

"You are mine," he panted through gritted teeth.

Sybina felt out of control. Her desire was so raw and she wanted even more. "Smack me," she demanded without knowing what dark corner of her soul that had come from. She didn't have time to question it, it was irrelevant where it came from; all that mattered was that it felt right to say it. Sybina wanted more of that sweet arousing pain he could offer her to push her over the edge.

"Smack you?"

"Yes..." she said demandingly and wriggled her butt, protesting that he was slowing down.

The sound of his hand against her naked behind was loud but there was no pain, only pleasure flowing through her.

"Again..." she hissed and felt him smack her butt again. This time it made her scream out his name.

"Harder," she cried out, feeling her orgasm come rolling.

But instead of pushing her over the edge to euphoria, Aston pulled away from her.

Sybina looked back to see what he was doing and instantly realized that something was very wrong. Aston's eyes were dark and without speaking he untied her and she sat down staring at him.

"What are you doing?" she asked, annoyed—cheated just seconds before her orgasm.

"No, what are *you* doing?" he replied with a raised voice.

Sybina grew cold. *Is that judgment in his eyes? Repulsion? No... please, Aston, don't look at me like that.*

"What do you mean?" Shame flared in Sybina and, suddenly self-aware, she covered herself with a sheet, confused by Aston's sudden anger.

"You want me to be like them... to hit you, to own you... what is wrong with you?"

Sybina opened her mouth trying to find words. But there were none.

"I'm not a fucking Masi lunatic. I don't get turned on by causing you pain and I don't understand why it's suddenly a turn-on for you." Aston was oozing with frustration and ran his hands through his hair. "I don't know what you're trying to prove here, Sybina, but I don't want to play this game." He got up and started dressing.

Sybina didn't speak; she just stared at him with horror. "I'm sorry, Aston, I don't know what came over me. It just felt... good."

"Good?" He snorted. "How far would you have gone? Do you want me to fucking whip you, is that it?"

"No," she protested. "I... I..."

"I think you need to see a professional. There is something seriously wrong with you." His last words were followed by a slamming door, and then he was gone.

Sybina fell back into the bed, surrendering to her tears. *I'm a pervert and a freak like the people I lived among. A monster.* She felt deeply ashamed of herself and cried herself to sleep.

CHAPTER 35
Poets and Cavemen

Sybina

Aston was still not talking to Sybina the next morning. He left for work without so much as a goodbye, leaving Sybina with a deep hole of despair in her heart.

Aston was right of course; she was deeply disturbed and horrified about the things she had said and done. "Smack me?" *Where did that come from? I hate violence. I hate men who hit women. Why would I want Aston to smack me?*

"There is something seriously wrong with you." She heard his words again and again in her mind, and every time they were followed by the repulsed expression on his face. Sybina's chest trembled with another sob and she sank to her knees, covering her face with her hands. She wanted to vanish into thin air, too shameful to ever face Aston again. The only man she wanted to think highly of her now thought of her as a freak, a twisted pervert, a disturbed woman. Would he despise her enough to ask for a divorce? He had insisted she get professional help. Did that mean someone could help her get rid of this inner devil that spoke through her and used her body to become an abomination?

She had planned to walk with John today. She hadn't seen John since Aston paid him a visit. They had texted a few times, but she had been too busy with Uma's visit, the trip to Scotland, and the wedding to meet with him. Okay, so maybe she had also waited for things to calm down between her and Aston before resuming her daily walks with John.

The thought of facing anyone right now was impossible. Rationally, she knew mental disease wasn't visible on the outside and if she controlled herself and locked away that crazy part of her she could hide it— except from Aston. He already knew her shame... he would always know.

Sybina's limbs felt too heavy to move but she wanted to shower. *As if you can wash away how dirty you feel,* she thought and got up from the floor slowly. The door buzzer rang with an insistent humming and she had no idea who that could be. For a moment she considered ignoring the person at the door, but that would be rude.

Sybina forced herself up and got to the little white box on the wall. "Hello?"

Aya's voice flowed through the device. "Hey, it's me, I brought cake."

Sybina sighed but pushed the button, knowing there was nothing she could say that would seem like a plausible excuse to turn Aya away. She would just have to pull herself together and act as normal as possible.

When Aya made it up the stairs she was glowing with happiness. Her hair was styled, her skin perfect, and she had the biggest smile on her face—until she saw Sybina.

"What's wrong, dear?" Aya hurried to hug Sybina and that was enough to make Sybina cry again.

"Come on, sweetie. Let's make a pot of tea and then you'll tell me everything, alright?" Aya led Sybina to the kitchen and placed her on a high chair while she started to prepare the tea.

"Is it Uma?" Aya guessed.

Sybina didn't answer. Could she lie to Aya and tell her it was all about Uma?

"So it's Aston then," Aya concluded before Sybina even got to try and make up a lie. "Tell me what he did this time."

Sybina sniffled some more and took the tissue that Aya held out to her.

"He didn't do anything. Let's talk about your beautiful wedding instead. How about the honeymoon?" Sybina insisted.

Aya came over and sat down next to Sybina. "We're leaving tomorrow for Paris, but I don't want to talk about that right now. Look at me. What happened?"

For a long time Sybina didn't speak. She didn't want Aya to look at her with repulsion too. But Aya was her friend and she didn't want to lie to her either. "It's me. I'm sick," Sybina finally admitted.

"Sick... what do you mean you're sick?" Aya caressed Sybina's hair. "You are scaring me here, Sybina. How bad is it?"

"No, it's not that kind of sickness. I won't die of it." Tears began rolling down her cheeks, and because she was both crying and drying her nose at the same time she was hard to understand when she said: "I'm a sick pervert."

"Come again?" Aya looked baffled.

"I'm a freak."

Aya shook her head. "You lost me. Take it from the start. I want to understand."

Sybina sighed and buried her head in her hands. "I don't want you to hate me too."

Aya pulled Sybina's hands away so she could see her face. "Sweet Sybina, there is nothing you can say that will make me hate you. Just spit it out."

With a moan of defeat, Sybina started talking. She told it in as much detail as she could remember and Aya just sat still, nodding and listening.

"And now he won't even talk to me. He's so disgusted with me," Sybina finished.

"Really?" Aya didn't sound disgusted or upset; she moved calmly to pour the hot water into the teapot. "Care to hear what I think about it?" she asked and took Sybina's nod as a silent yes. "I think Aston's a jerk who's missing the obvious."

Sybina felt such a rush of relief that Aya didn't seem disgusted with her. "What do you mean?"

"You said it happened just after he told you he loved you... right?"

"Right." Sybina nodded.

Aya looked speculative. "So maybe that's what it took for you to finally be you and show your deepest desires to him. You needed him to make you feel completely loved and respected."

"But it wasn't gentle lovemaking at all," Sybina argued.

"No, I know it was more raw sex and dirty talk. But think about it, Sybina: the trigger was his declaration of love. Maybe this was your way of giving him freely what you have witnessed other men take with force. I can relate to that!"

Sybina blinked a few times. "Are you saying that because I lived in an extreme environment I can only associate love with brutal sex?"

"No, that's not what I'm saying. I just think you are like the rest of us."

"Of whom? Slaves?" Sybina was confused.

"No, silly." Aya smiled. "Women."

"What do you mean?"

"Listen, Aston is your first lover, right?"

"Right."

"But Kato wasn't my first. I had a few boyfriends before him, and I can remember being turned on by some of the same things you experienced last night. It's not uncommon… in fact it's rather primal in most women to want to be taken and desired and… claimed."

"*No!*" Sybina gasped in disbelief.

"Definitely. Kato had to get used to it too. I think what won him over was when I explained to him that it only works for a woman when she feels completely safe with the man. So in some ways getting to that point in your relationship where you can let out the dirty talker is a great compliment to the guy."

Sybina eyes were wide open. "So you have rough sex with Kato and he likes it?"

"Sometimes; it all depends on the mood. Sometimes we tease, play, and laugh. Other times we snuggle and make love quietly… sometimes we stay in bed for hours and other times it's just a quickie in the shower. There's no right or wrong sex… I like variation and yes, Sybina, I like rough sex too."

"But Aston was disgusted with me."

"I have a hard time believing that. I think he was more disgusted with his own reaction than with yours. He's probably confused because he doesn't want to hurt you, yet it turns him on."

"So you don't think I'm perverted then?"

"No, hon, you are no more perverted than me and the women I know."

"Even Sofia?" Sybina dared ask.

Aya broke into a laugh. "What do you mean, *even* Sofia? She's probably the worst of us all. That girl is a wild one, and she might not have lived it out but she once told me about some of her erotic fantasies and phew, she is kinky."

"Kinky how?"

"The woman is so strong and independent but she always goes for the bad guys, and I suspect it's because she's looking for a man who's strong enough to stand up to her. Problem is, he also needs to be wicked-ass intelligent to not bore her, and how easy do you think it is to find a man like that?

"Not easy?" Sybina said without knowing for certain, since she had never searched for a man in her life.

"More like *impossible,* and that's why she's still single. She's got a lousy taste in men.

"So does she have kinky sex then?"

"I don't know, but I think she would like to." Aya shook her head softly. "Sofia is very picky... she won't just take anyone. She might be a cynic on the outside but she's got a heart longing for love just like the next girl..." Aya smiled lovingly and made a little chuckle. "Enough about Sofia, but where I come from we have a saying that sex is the playground of adulthood."

"I don't understand." Sybina said and thought of the playgrounds she had seen around the parks of London. How did that even compare to sex?

"It means that sex is about having fun and experimenting to bring out all sorts of otherwise hidden parts of yourself."

"Like what?" Sybina asked, confused.

"I don't know... maybe giggly, girly, submissive, dominant, horny, playful, silly, slutty... you know... sides of you that you would never show others around you, except for your partner.

Sybina nodded for Aya to go on.

"When I'm with Kato, I put aside my responsible adult and become playful with no worries or concerns. I need that. It always makes me feel better, like it's this wonderful outlet of stress for me. Even in Spirima I was able to lose myself in Kato's arms and forget all my worries. Sex is powerful that way, right?"

Sybina nodded and looked down. "But Aya, did you ever ask Kato to smack you?"

Aya took Sybina's hand. "It doesn't matter what I asked Kato to do, Sybina. You shouldn't compare yourself to others, and I promise you that I've done things far worse than ask Kato to smack me."

Sybina's head snapped up. "You have?"

Aya looked away and then she sighed deeply. "Remember that time when you asked me how the general died and I told you Kato stabbed him in the back?"

"Yeah."

"Well, there's something that I didn't tell you."

Sybina didn't speak; she waited for Aya to continue.

"After the general had Kato whipping me and he took over himself... I thought I was gonna die from the pain." Aya was shaking slightly and she wet her lips as if her mouth had gone all dry.

"But Kato stabbed him... right?" Sybina asked softly.

Aya gave a stiff nod. "Yes, but the general was still alive when I... I picked up the whip and I... became someone else... I was so angry."

"So you whipped the general?"

Aya's eyes glazed over and her forehead was furrowed. Tears started welling up in her eyes. "He pleaded for his life, Sybina, but I didn't stop." Aya sat passively and didn't react when a tear ran down her cheek.

Slowly Sybina leaned into Aya and hugged her. "Thank you."

Aya waited for a second. "For what?"

Sybina took a deep breath and sat back to look into Aya's eyes. "I already told you, the general was a dead man. If you hadn't killed him, I would have. I'm glad he felt pain when he died. He needed to see what he had done to others."

"Kato says his uncle had it coming," Aya looked away.

"The man had raped, molested, beaten, and killed more people than you can imagine. Don't ever... *not for a second*... feel guilty about what you did, Aya."

Tears were still running down Aya's cheeks. "It wasn't just the general, Sybina, I made Jonul kill himself too."

Sybina sighed. "Then I owe you a thank you for that too."

Aya shook her head. "They were human beings, Sybina; how can you say that?"

Sybina's eyes became hard. "Because I treated their victims again and again. Because I put tags on the toes of the dead men and women they discarded like they were nothing. Did you know Uma almost died because of those two monsters?"

Aya's eyes grew big. "Uma?"

"It took me a month to bring her back to life after they went at her and if you hadn't killed them, they would have destroyed her completely."

"So you don't think I'm a cold-blooded monster then?" Aya asked.

"No, Aya, I don't." Sybina handed Aya a tissue.

"Good." Aya sniffled and dried her nose. "And I don't think you're a pervert."

A soft laughter broke out between the two women as they sat revealing their darkest secrets to each other, receiving acceptance.

Sybina got up, poured the tea into cups, and cut the cake Aya had brought. They moved on and talked about the wedding, the honeymoon, and Uma's departure yesterday when Aya's phone rang

"Sorry, hon," Aya said and got her phone out of her bag. "It's your confused husband."

Aya's expression hardened. "Hello, Aston."

"Hey, Aya... Thanks for the great party and all, but listen, I've been trying to reach Sybina for the last hour; she's not picking up... I'm on my way back to the flat but I'm just slightly worried... have you heard from her?" Aston's voice was loud enough for Sybina to hear clearly.

"You sound really concerned... did something happen between you two?" Aya said sweetly while rolling her eyes theatrically at Sybina.

"Ehh, no, just an argument... I'll try calling her again. I just figured maybe she had called you."

"No, Sybina didn't call me." Suddenly Aya's voice grew deeper and darker. "However I did stop by your place and found Sybina here alone with swollen eyes from crying, so we've had a little talk."

Aston was quiet and then he spoke in a flat tone. "What kind of talk?"

"Oh you know... the kind of talk women have when they have been made to feel like they are sick perverts, by the one person they trust and love."

Sybina sucked in air and shook her head with wide eyes, signaling to Aya to stop provoking Aston. Aya ignored her. "How dare you make Sybina feel that way?" she snarled into the phone.

Sybina looked in horror. She really didn't want her best friend and her husband fighting like this, even if they had been friends before she came into the picture.

"It's none of your business, Aya. She shouldn't have told you that." Aston raised his voice and Aya followed his lead.

"Of course she should tell me, that's what friends are for. She needed to hear that she's perfectly normal and no more sick than any of the other women you have been with."

"You don't know what you're talki..."

Aya cut him off. "Remember who you are talking to? Tara was my roommate when you *dated* her..."

"So what?"

"I know what happened between you two..."

"What is that supposed to mean?"

She scoffed. "You're no boy scout, Aston."

"How the hell would you know?"

"Because Tara liked to share intimate things about her sex life with you and because I *heard* you—it was a tent camp, you idiot, everyone heard you. Tara was a screamer, remember... you are into some pretty rough shit, admit it.
"

"So, it's not my fucking problem she liked it."

"I don't recall you calling Tara sick or perverted..."

"You don't know shit!!!"

"Don't shout at me..."

"I'll shout as bloody much as I want to and you better stay the hell out of my sex life, Aya Johansen."

Aya raised her voice too. *"I know your sex life is none of my business, but when you hurt my friend and step on her then I have a bloody damn duty to step in and pick her up..."*

"Do you have any idea how fucking mad I am at you right now?" Even through the phone Sybina could hear Aston's voice tremble.

"I don't care if you're angry at me, I'm angry at you too..."

"This conversation is over."

"Fine!" Aya looked at Sybina, who sat frozen on her chair. "Your husband says hi. He's on his way home and he's... pissed."

"Tara was a screamer?" was Sybina's only remark.

Aya closed her eyes and collected herself. With a deep exhalation of air she brushed her hair back and sighed for a second. "I'm sorry, I shouldn't have mentioned that in front of you, it's just that I get so mad when Aston pretends he doesn't like rough sex, because I know he does."

Hearing Aya talk about Aston's rough sex with Tara, while Sybina felt unsure about her own worth, was painful. Sybina pictured him with Tara and then she pictured Aston on his way home, fuming with anger. She would be the one to face his wrath.

"Do you want me to stay when he gets here?" Aya asked.

"No, I think it's better I talk with him alone." Sybina answered.

"Okay, but don't let him bully you—and call me afterwards. I'm here for moral support." Aya got her things and moved to the door. "Don't be scared of him, Sybina. He's the lucky one for having found you. Not the other way around."

Sybina knew Aya meant well and gave her a brave smile, but inside she was petrified.

It only took thirty minutes before Aston stormed in, but in that time Sybina had showered and prepared herself to meet his anger.

"Is Aya still here?" he said with narrowed eyes from the doorway where he had stopped with his legs spread and his arms crossed like a true soldier.

Sybina sat on the couch and looked at him. "No. She left," she said as calmly as she could.

"Good. Why did you even involve her in the first place?" he said accusingly and moved closer.

"Aya came over and she could see I'd been crying… it just came out… I didn't mean to," Sybina explained herself.

"Well, next time, don't talk to Aya about it, talk to me about it."

"But you weren't here."

Aston stopped in front of her but kept his arms crossed. "I'm here now, so talk to me. What the hell happened yesterday? You want to be my submissive, obedient sex slave now?" His words were as harsh as yesterday and made her blink.

"No." she whispered in a weak attempt to defend herself, and hated how he towered over her with his big muscled body.

"Then what do you want from me?"

"I don't know. I wasn't thinking. It just happened."

Aston squatted down in front of Sybina… "But why *that*? I mean with your background and all." His voice was

374

no longer hard and accusatory but soft and thick with emotion.

Sybina found it hard to look directly at him; instead she looked at her hands while she tried to explain. "I think it was my way of showing you that I felt safe with you. That I loved you and trusted you completely."

Aston swallowed hard.

"And because I was curious and wanted to explore."

"Okay," he said more softly. "I'm listening."

Sybina took a deep breath and tried to organize all the thoughts she had been going over while waiting for him to come home.

"I like making love... but I liked it when you took me hard at the wedding too. I just wanted more of that."

Aston watched her closely. "Okay. I'm just surprised that rough sex turns you on."

"Yeah, it surprised me too, but I don't think it will happen again."

Aston frowned, "Why do you say that?"

"Because I saw how disgusted you were and because it's a turn-off to feel judged."

Aston closed his eyes and rubbed his hand over his face. "Please don't say that," he whispered.

"Why not?"

"It makes me feel awful about myself... Aya was right. There's nothing wrong with you wanting to have rough sex. It's just me being a hypocrite." Slowly Aston got up to sit on the couch next to her and took her hand. "Listen, my biggest fear when we got together was that you were severely damaged by the Masi warriors. Back then I thought they had raped you, remember?"

Sybina nodded.

"I swore to myself that I would prove to you that not all men are beasts. Then yesterday you pushed me to smack you and I resisted it but did it anyway and it... it felt good, and you had me really confused. I got angry at you for making me treat you violently. I know I said some really mean things and I'm sorry about that. I just don't want you to see me like the Masi warriors."

Sybina kissed his hand. "You are nothing like them, Aston."

"No, I'm not. I want to protect you and respect you, not beat you."

Sybina smiled softly. "Ironically, I think it was your words of love that unlocked that horrible part of me."

Aston leaned in and kissed Sybina's hair and pulled her into his arms. "Don't say that; there's no horrible part of you."

Sybina listened to his heartbeat for a moment, savoring his warmth. "I promise I won't ever ask you to smack me again or surrender myself like that. We can go back to before it happened."

Aston pulled her head up to kiss her. "Why?" he said and nibbled on Sybina's lip. "All this talk about surrendering has made me hard, and we never did finish what we started yesterday."

Sybina wasn't sure what to make of this twist of events but she couldn't resist his deep kisses that worked miracles on the wounded part of her soul.

"This is all new to me too, Ina, give me time to learn," Aston said quietly.

"Sex isn't new to you," she pointed out.

"No, but love is, and navigating my sexual desires alongside my need to protect and respect you is hard."

"Why?"

"Because you're my wife, not just a chick I met in a nightclub. What if I hurt you? What if I overstep your boundaries?"

"I'm not that fragile, Aston."

Aston cupped Sybina's face. "Okay, but promise you'll tell me if you don't like it."

"I promise."

Aston was looking deeply into her eyes. "You know that plain sex is good enough for me, right? You know I love you either way?"

Sybina put a hand on top of his. "I know, but I like the beast in you and I trust you to not hurt me, Aston. You have to trust me too—trust that I'll be honest with you and tell you to stop if you move too fast or go too far."

"Alright, we'll take it slow. And just so you don't get the wrong idea, I'm not into sex clubs, gagging you, or whipping your cute little ass with canes. I like rough and dirty but I don't share and I don't torture... if it doesn't turn you on, we're not doing it."

Sybina nodded in agreement and pushed forward to kiss him but was stopped when Aston grabbed her hair and pulled her head back. With a wicked grin he licked her neck and sucked her earlobe. "This is going to be fun." Electric impulses shot down between Sybina's hips.

"You are mine." He emphasized the words. "I'm the only one who gets to touch you like this... is that understood?" he commanded in another low sexual growl.

"Yes," Sybina moaned.

"Do you remember what I was doing to you before we stopped?" he said in a low sexual tone.

"You were taking me from behind," Sybina whispered with every nerve cell on alert just waiting to see what his next move would be.

"That's right." He kissed her deeply and with a low groan he started undressing her.

"Get on your knees and prepare to be fucked hard," he said huskily and she did as told, pushing back her ass and looking back expectantly.

Aston licked her, making her burst into sweet moans, but when his thumb pressed on her anus she tensed.

"Relax, Sybina. I won't take you there today, but soon."

"I don't think I can do that," she exclaimed and again the idea of not being enough entered her mind.

"Shhh, babe, breathe," Aston said with authority and Sybina focused on his voice and took a deep breath. "Trust... remember?" The words sounded gruff but Sybina heard the pleading underneath the words.

She turned his question around. "Do you trust me?" she asked.

"Of course," he said, muffled because his mouth was busy biting her ass cheeks and hips.

"Will you let me tie you up then?" Sybina asked.

Aston stiffened. "What? Why?"

"I've been thinking and I want to experiment with oral, but I don't want you to move."

"I promise I'll keep still," Aston said quickly with a happy grin. Before Sybina knew it he had positioned himself naked on the couch.

Sybina could feel her heart race. She had been wondering for weeks how he tasted down there and whether she could give him the satisfaction of oral sex. She wanted to, but it pushed every fear button in her mind.

"Okay, no rope then, but put your hands to the side," she instructed.

Aston pulled her into a hug. "You don't have to do this if you don't want to. I'll never hurt you. You know that, right?"

She nodded and pushed him gently back on the couch. *Here goes.* Slowly she moved forward and placed her hands around his proud erection and lowered her head to kiss his foreskin. Aston kept completely still.

A bit braver, Sybina opened her mouth and placed her lips around him and let her tongue lick a little. He tasted slightly salty but pleasant. She looked up at Aston and saw love shine from his eyes. *I'm doing it for Aston,* she told herself, and suppressed the internal resistance and let her mouth slide over his cock, taking in as much as she could.

He sat perfectly still but leaned his head back and moaned in pleasure. Encouraged by his reaction, Sybina found a rhythm and worked him in a steady pace.

"Fuck, this is good, Ina," he groaned and then she felt his hands in her hair.

He didn't press her head against his groin, he just weaved his hand into his hair, but it ignited Sybina's fear and made her stiffen and pull away.

"What's wrong?" Aston asked

"I told you to keep your hands to the side."

"Yeah but…" His words faded. "You've got to trust me, Sybina."

She wanted to, but her heart was racing and her hands shaking.

"Shit. Come here." Aston slid down on the floor and took her in his arms. "Fuck, Ina… you're shaking… shhhh… relax, I've got you," he whispered and stroked her back.

Without wanting to, Sybina started crying against his neck, and he patiently held her and caressed her until she was only sniffling.

"Want to talk about it?" he asked softly and pulled down a blanket from the couch and covered them both.

From deep within her, words came and she told him about lying under the general's bed and listening to Hunilla being raped and choked. She told him of the soldiers' idea of oral sex and her own fear of it, and he let her talk without interrupting her. It was horrible to talk about but also cleansing in a strange way.

"Those guy were brutal rapists, Sybina, they deserved to be castrated for the things they did, but you never ever have to do anything with me you don't want to. I promise,"

"But I want to give you everything your other lovers have given you."

Aston kissed her forehead and smiled. "You've already giving me so much more, Ina. I'm planning to stay with you for the rest of my life; we have plenty of time to figure this out. Rough sex, anal sex, oral... I mean, honestly, don't stress about it. As long as I can make love to you, I'm a happy man."

"Okay."

"How do you feel?"

"Surprised."

"What do you mean?"

Sybina wiped her eyes and gave him a small smile. "When did you become so good at talking about emotional stuff?"

He broke into a big smile. "I'm getting better at this shit... right?"

"I think so."

With a tight hug Aston buried his head in Sybina's hair and sniffed her in. "It's because I love you so damn much."

"Ditto."

"And because I want to fulfill your every need." He kissed her jawline. "I'm going to make sex the most amazing thing in the world for you and help you push out every bad memory you have."

Sybina smiled dreamily.

CHAPTER 36
The Lake

Uma

Uma was excited to meet up with Jasmin for their morning run. She hadn't seen her for two weeks and was dying to tell her about London.

They met outside as usual and the first thing Uma noticed was that Jasmin looked better than ever. Normally she ran with a worn t-shirt and morning hair, as they always showered afterwards, but today she looked smart with a tight tank top and shorts, a high ponytail that was arranged and make-up. *Make-up for a run? What's up with that?* Uma wondered.

Jasmin was happy to see her and they hugged.

"Welcome back, Uma. I can't believe it, but I think you grew while you were gone."

Uma grinned. "Yep, I think I did."

"How was it?" Jasmin smiled.

"It was good," Uma assured her. "Did anything exiting happen here while I was gone?"

"All the kids are back, new kids have arrived… and a new teacher."

Uma frowned. Was Jasmin blushing? Whoa…

"But I want to hear all about London." Jasmin quickly said.

"Okay."

"Hey, ladies, do you mind if I join you?"

Uma turned to see a man approaching them. She didn't know him and looked at Jasmin, expecting her to reject the man. After all, running was their thing and they had a lot to catch up on.

But Jasmin didn't say no. She smiled at the man and greeted him politely… no, kindly.

"That group over there is the school's fastest runners, you might want to join them," Uma said and pointed to the fast trackers.

"But you're also more than welcome to join us if you want," Jasmin added.

The man, who was around thirty and looked rather fit, turned his head, looking at the fast track group with Tristan and five other young men leaving the school grounds. He shrugged. "I'm not that fast a runner. I would love to join you ladies, if that's okay."

Uma wanted to say, "No, it's not okay." But Jasmin's eyes sent a silent message: "Be nice!" while her mouth said: "Uma, this is the new teacher I told you about, Mr. Raffen."

The man walked closer and reached out his hand. Uma's heart started racing, but she forced herself to politely shake his hand. He was a teacher after all.

"I'm, the new math and physics teacher, and who might you be?"

"I'm Uma," she said flatly.

"Good, let's get to it, shall we?" Jasmin started running and looked back with a grin. "Show us what you've got, Mr. Raffen."

He grinned back at Jasmin, and Uma watched the two adults find a comfortable pace alongside each other. Uma quickly overtook them and was constantly forced to wait up for them with their slow pace. Uma was annoyed; she had been looking forward to running with Jasmin—alone! And now she was jogging alone listening to Jasmin and Mr. Raffen talking behind her. It was driving her crazy to hear her cool, confident friend Jasmin giggle over things that weren't even remotely funny. Mr. Raffen was clearly trying to impress Jasmin with his wit and humor and talked about physics experiments gone wrong and his time at the university in Germany.

Jasmin actually *liked* this guy; she was *flirting* with him. *That's just so not cool.* Uma turned and ran backwards, to signal how slow they were running.

"It's okay, Uma, go run yourself tired, but only the normal route. We'll see you back at the school."

Uma nodded, understanding that she had just been ditched by Jasmin, but thankful that at least she could let out some steam by running full sprint. After two weeks of running with Aston she was faster than ever. That man could move seriously fast for someone his size. She was quickly so far ahead that she could no longer hear them, and she didn't look back. In her mind she went over details from England: Sybina's hugs, kisses, homemade food, a hand to hold, and their trip to Scotland. For a short while, they had looked like a regular family and she had felt part of something normal. Coming back to the school was... Uma pushed the thought away; nothing good was going to come out of feeling sorry for herself. She had spent two wonderful weeks in London and in time she would be living there or her mother would find her and she would be living with her.

It was almost mid-September now and although it was still very warm, the trees were starting to show yellow and red colors. Uma was fascinated by nature and wished she could spend much more time outside investigating what she had been denied all her life.

Jasmin had told Uma to run the normal route, which was a 5K loop taking her back to the school, but like most teenagers Uma felt compelled to go her own way; and with her speed, she could run the 8K loop and still be back at the school before Jasmin and Mr. Raffen. They would never know.

Uma ran down her favorite trail and made good speed. The miles flew by her and brought her through the forest and down to a beautiful lake that Jasmin had promised her they would go swimming in one day. Everything was quiet except for her own panting and a few ducks quacking grumpy at her for disturbing their peace and quiet. She wondered if she could drink the water; it looked clean enough, but if the ducks pooped in the water it probably wasn't such a good idea. Uma dipped a hand in the lake and ran her wet hand across her forehead to cool her down from the running. The water looked so inviting with its glistening surface that reflected the sunshine and the trees around the lake.

She really wanted to jump in, and this was probably her last chance for a swim this year before the summer was completely gone. So what if she was a bit late for school today; she had been behind walls her whole life and, today, she was choosing to celebrate her freedom with a dip in the lake. *I don't have to ask for permission, there's no one around for miles*, she decided, and without further hesitation she stripped naked and jumped in the lake. The water was cool but wonderfully smooth and refreshing. Uma made a small howl of happiness and splashed around in the lake. She couldn't swim but that didn't matter. The water wasn't deeper than her navel and she indulged herself in this moment of blissful happiness, jumping around and having fun.

She played with leaves that flowed on the water, she hit the water with a stick and saw how the water reacted by splashing up. Uma had never been in a pool or a lake before and she was in a bubble of exploration and exaltation.

When she heard them it was too late. They were already too close for her to hide.

Six tall young men strolled towards her all looking at her with amusement and interest. They were the fast trackers with Tristan in front. Uma looked to her clothing on a nearby tree stump; she could get to it before them, but it would mean exposing her nudity to them. Instead she ducked down, leaving only her head and neck above the waterline and covering her breasts under the water.

Tristan was the first to speak. "Where's Miss C?" he asked and looked around.

"She just needed to pee, but she'll be here in a second," Uma lied.

He smiled and walked slowly to the stump with her clothes.

"You forgot a towel," he said.

Uma kept her mouth shut and scowled at him.

"You know guys, we should leave and let the young lady get dressed," Tristan said smoothly. None of them looked like they had any intention of leaving. Tristan lowered his voice slightly and smiled sardonically. "But then again, you are no young lady, are you? You're a slave."

Uma spit in his direction, making them all laugh.

"If you want your clothes, you're going to have to come up here and get them," one of the guys called out.

Tristan picked her clothes up. "Or we might take them with us and let you run naked back to school."

Uma turned her back to them and let her right hand feel over the bottom of the lake, searching for a weapon of some kind. Her hand found a stone that she picked up.

"So what is it going to be?" Tristan asked impatiently. "Are you going to get out of the water and dress in front of us or are you going to run back to school naked."

She looked over her shoulder, calculating her options. In her mind she had already seen plenty of ways she could hurt the guys; she wasn't afraid of a fight, but several things about it made her hold back. One: Jasmin would find out she had broken her trust and run a different route. Two: She would be expelled from school for being violent, and three: There were six of them in running shoes, she was naked and barefoot; she wouldn't be able to outrun them nor would she be able to beat up all six of them. She would most likely be the one that got beat up the worst.

Surprising herself, she released the stone in her hand. Surprising the young men, she walked proudly out of the water with her head held high. She was beautiful and had nothing to be ashamed of. If they touched her, she would kill them.

She heard several gasps from the boys and saw them exchanging glances. They were staring at her, their eyes sliding up and down her body, and a thought made her raise a brow and suppress a smile. If only Aidan was here to see these guys, he would see that she was no child. They certainly didn't look at her as a child. But then again, this culture was completely different from Aidan's. In Spirima girls were often married before puberty and typically to men twice their age. Uma had pubic hair and although she was tall and slim she had breasts as well; the guys were making comments about her body that she chose to ignore. There was no need to reward their rudeness.

Uma frowned. Aidan certainly wasn't right that no man would ever touch her—one of the young men had just shouted that he wanted her to ride his dick. She wasn't even sure what that meant exactly, but she got the idea and arched a brow, grateful after all that Aidan wasn't here to see her naked and humiliated like this. He would probably have enjoyed the show and been on the boys' side, and six enemies was plenty to deal with as it was. Occupied with thoughts of Aidan and her annoyance with him, Uma walked straight up to Tristan and reached out her hand. "Give me my clothes," she said coldly.

He eyes slid up to meet hers. "Or what?" he said alarmingly softly.

Uma arched a brow. "Or you'll be on the ground, crying for your mommy in a second." She placed her other hand on her hip, while continuing to reach out for her clothes.

Tristan shook his head. "There's six of us, what do you think you are, Catwoman?" All the guys laughed.

"Just give me my damn clothes," Uma hissed.

"Look at her nipples, she's sexually aroused," one of the young men commented and both Uma and Tristan looked down at her breasts. Her nipples were pointy, but she knew for sure it had nothing to do with being aroused; she was just cold from the water. Tristan gave her a puzzled look.

"Quit looking at my tits," Uma demanded and folded her hands into fists when the guys moved closer to her. One of them reached out and touched her hair; she bashed his hand away and scowled at him. Another one touched her back, and a hand slid down her behind. Every time she turned to bash their hands away a new hand touched her from another direction. She was tempted to do more than just bash their hands away, but smart enough to know that fighting one of them meant fighting all of them; that was a bad plan, it was better to avoid fighting in the first place.

When she had made a full circle the guys were laughing and the atmosphere was threatening. Uma considered snatching her clothes from Tristan but the young men formed a wall around her and Tristan's eyes were alert, he was waiting for her to do that: waiting for her to show emotions. She had already shown anger; that was a weakness. She wouldn't show that she was afraid of being raped. Uma wasn't stupid, she knew there were enough of them to hold her down and take turns; she knew what men were capable of. Fear was pumping through her body but she kept her head cool and turned to face their leader again. Tristan's eyes lifted slowly from her breasts to her eyes.

"What is this really about? Are you still angry that I'm a better runner than you?" She tilted her head and pinned him.

Tristan tensed. "You wish."

"You wanna find out if you can take me?" she coaxed him on.

Tristan narrowed his eyes, "I can take you any day." His eyes slid provocatively down her body.

"Prove it!" Uma challenged him. "You and I will race back to the school... fully dressed."

"And when I win?" he said with mild interest.

"You mean when you lose."

"When I win, you are going to be my slave for a week."

Anger deep in the pit of Uma's stomach made her snarl. "I'm no one's slave."

"You'll be mine. Carry my books, polish my shoes, and get me my dinner. You will make sure to meet all my needs." Some of the boys where whistling suggestively in the background.

"Not going to happen," Uma declared firmly.

Tristan moved close enough to whisper in her ear. "Or I could let the boys have you right here."

Uma's nostrils flared. "Fine. Whoever wins the race will be the other's slave for a week. But *no* sexual stuff."

Tristan chuckled condescendingly. "Don't worry, I wouldn't fuck you if you begged me to. My girlfriend would be too jealous." He threw Uma's clothes at her with force and signaled for the others to move back, allowing her space to dress herself. Uma took her time, not showing how affected she was from their ogling her.

"How did you even find me here?" she asked while dressing, wondering if they had somehow spied on her.

"If you didn't want company you should have been quieter," one of them pointed out and again they all laughed. Uma rolled her eyes. Teenage boys were the most annoying category of the male species she had ever met.

She didn't ask them any more questions, but focused on tying her shoelaces. She started walking away from the lake and towards the trail. She heard them follow her and stopped when she was back on the trail. She waited a minute until Tristan was next to her. The trail was narrow and his arm was touching hers.

"See you at the school... *slave*," he said.

"Swine," she reciprocated.

They took off and started running fast. Because he was taller and bigger he used his elbows to push her behind him, but Uma used the same courtesy and elbowed him right back and quickly snaked in front of him. He cursed but she settled into her turbo gear and got ahead just enough that he couldn't reach her. She was angry, she was scared, and she was never going to lose this bet. Flying through the forest, Uma didn't take a second to look back. Tristan was a strong runner with years of experience. He had longer legs, stronger muscles, more power, but Uma was lighter, had less to carry, more to gain, and she was pushing herself to outrun him.

"Keep going at that pace, and the victory is mine," she heard him call out to her behind her. Uma considered his words. No one could sprint the distance to the school... unless... it was either that or become Tristan's slave. Uma didn't slow down for one second, but kept running like the devil was chasing her. She couldn't hear him anymore. After a long sprint she knew Tristan wasn't close any longer but she still kept pushing forward. When she finally saw the school, her heart was pumping faster than ever and she was sweating from every pore on her body. *Keep going, keep going,* she repeated in her mind and shut out the immense pain from her chest, her neck, her shoulders, her legs, and feet. Her body was shouting at her to stop, but she didn't have a choice and kept running.

Just when she entered through the gates an explosive cramp in her right leg made her leg fold under her and she found herself on the ground, whimpering in pain.

She couldn't think. Couldn't breathe. It was as if her leg was filled with a million fire ants biting at her simultaneously. Uma forced herself up on all four and dragged herself towards the stone staircase. It took everything she had but she got there just in time to see Tristan come running, tomato red and foaming at the mouth. He threw himself on the stone step and leaned back, trying to catch his breath. Uma was too pained, out of breath, and exhausted to talk and luckily so was Tristan.

Slowly the significance of what had just happened dawned on Uma. She had avoided being raped in the forest and she had outrun the fastest runner at school. She shot a grateful thought to Aston for pushing her every morning for the past two weeks.

They sat for a few minutes without speaking, cooling off and catching their breaths until the rest of the runners came back, all wanting to know who had won.

Tristan was scowling when Uma stood up, now recovered enough to speak. She dusted the dust from the stone step off her butt and smiled in a superior way.

"Tristan lost and will be my slave for the nest weak."

She turned to leave but leaned down and whispered loudly, "Don't worry... I wouldn't fuck you if you begged me to... my boyfriend would be too jealous."

Tristan didn't reply, but behind her she could hear his friends ask him what the hell he was doing losing to a girl. Uma smiled and walked away. It was time for a quick shower before school—and time to come up with ways she could humiliate her new slave.

CHAPTER 37
Slavery

Uma

Rumors travel fast in a school, and before lunch Uma was confronted by Tristan's girlfriend, Simone.

"Is it true that you won a bet with Tristan?" she asked indignantly, hands on her hips and her three best friends behind her.

"Ask him," Sybina responded coolly.

"I can't, he won't talk to me."

Uma shrugged and walked on.

Simone and her minions got in her way. "Stop right there. You're not going anywhere before you tell us what's going on," Simone demanded.

Uma yawned and rested all her weight on her right foot. She was drained and wanted nothing more than to skip lunch and go take a nap. She had arrived back from London late yesterday evening, slept poorly, and this morning's run had sucked out all her energy. "It's between Tristan and me," she said, dismissing Simone.

"There is nothing between Tristan and you!" Simone warned.

"Right," Uma said, annoyed, and finally managed to push herself through the group of girls. She had one hour before her next class and swung by the kitchen to greet her friend Martha in the cafeteria, where she grabbed an apple and a bun. Uma never ate with the other students; it was better this way. Eating in the hallways wasn't allowed, nor was running, but five minutes later Uma was in her attic room, munching on the food and taking off her clothes. She was going to get a quick power nap while the others enjoyed lunch.

She was down to her underwear when a voice spooked her. "I suggest you keep the rest on."

Uma turned around trying to locate the voice and saw Tristan leaning against the wall in a dark corner of her room.

"What are you doing here?" she said, annoyed that he was stealing time from her nap.

"I'm at your service, remember." His tone was flat.

"Then go eat your lunch and leave me alone," she said and crawled into bed.

Tristan's eyes narrowed. "Why do you sleep up here?"

Uma scoffed. "Because it's peaceful. How did you even find me here?"

"I followed you..."

Uma was too tired to grill him about why. "Okay, whatever, Tristan. Just let me sleep."

"Aren't you going to take me up on our bet?"

Uma rubbed her eyes. "Absolutely... my first command is for you to leave me alone."

His eyes narrowed and he stood watching her for a while. "Seriously?"

"Now," she added and turned her back on him. After a minute she heard the door close. She desperately wanted to close her eyes and sleep but a thought kept bothering her. If Tristan knew where she was, what would stop him for bringing his friends up here and continue what they had started in the forest? She didn't trust Tristan, or any man for that matter. Quickly Uma got up and locked her door.

Uma got through her afternoon, and at seven in the evening she went to dance with Jasmin as usual. Jasmin was happy and wanted to hear all about London. They talked more than they danced, and all the time Uma wondered if she should tell Jasmin about this morning. If she did, she would have to admit that she went swimming in the lake, and Jasmin had specifically told her to take their usual short route. Jasmin would be disappointed in Uma and furious with Tristan and his friends. The boys would blame her if they got into trouble and hate her even more. She kept her mouth shut.

Jasmin talked about Jasper, the new teacher that Uma had met as Mr. Raffen. He had complimented Jasmin's hair and although she denied it, Uma could see Jasmin was smitten with him.

"You're not going to go out with him, are you?" Uma asked.

"Don't be silly, Uma, he hasn't even asked me."

"But isn't there some rule against staff dating?" Uma asked.

Jasmin laughed. "We're not dating, and besides, teachers can date each other, just not students."

"Hmm," Uma scoffed and changed the subject.

Time flew by with all the catching up, and they didn't realize they had missed the curfew before it was too late. It was past ten and lights would be out in the dorms by now. It made Uma even happier that she had her own room up in the attic. She still had homework to do since she'd missed the first week of school, and her growling stomach reminded her that she had forgotten about dinner... again. It didn't worry Uma; she had a care package from Sybina in her room full of cake, candy, and chocolate, and she could always go steal fruit in the kitchen if she needed to. She'd done it before.

When she got up to the attic, she was relieved to see it was all dark. She had been afraid Tristan would be in her room again but it was empty; luckily he had a curfew too. Normally she showered after dancing, but it was too late now. The plumbing always made loud noises in the old bathroom down the hall. Uma went there anyway, letting a slow jet of water run silently and using a washcloth to wash herself. Her hair would have to wait until the morning, but she felt on top of the world when she walked back to her room, softly whistling. She had gotten her worst enemy off her back. Now all she had to do was go to her classes, study hard, stay away from the other kids, and keep to herself in her own little kingdom up here in the attic. She had Jasmin, Sybina, and Martha; she didn't need more than them to be genuinely happy. With a satisfied smile she picked up the book on World War II she needed to read as homework and hung her towel on the back of a chair.

His voice startled her as it was so unexpected, and she gave a shriek.

"Déjà vu," Tristan said.

Uma turned around and held up her fists, ready to fight. All her defenses were rising throughout her body.

"I'm not here to fight you," he said and stepped out into the light.

"What the hell is wrong with you?" Uma lowered her fists and folded her arms in front of her, refusing to give Tristan the satisfaction of knowing her nakedness made her feel vulnerable. "I asked you to leave me alone, didn't I?" she hissed.

"You do realize that folding your arms like that only makes your tits look bigger, right?"

Uma's heart was racing but she played it cool, rolled her eyes at Tristan, and went to her dresser. "Why do you keep coming to my room?" she asked in annoyance and put on underwear.

"Where were you?" he asked. "I waited for you until curfew, and you weren't here."

"None of your God damn business where I go, and curfews don't apply to me." It wasn't entirely true, but Uma didn't follow the same schedule as the other students and with her own room in the attic she did have a lot more freedom than most.

"Well, sit down, because we're going to have a talk."

"Aren't you afraid you'll get caught outside your dorm after curfew?" she said with mockery.

Tristan didn't dignify her question with an answer.

Uma sat down on her bed, now wearing underwear. "I'll sit only because I want to," she pointed out.

"Whatever. Just tell me what you're planning to do. I'm a senior, I don't need this kind of ridicule to stain my reputation." He sat down on a stool but his foot was tapping up and down and showing how tense he really was.

The big lion hates being on a leash, she thought.

"I was hoping we could establish some ground rules," he said.

"Like what?"

"Like you not bossing me around in front of the others... Maybe I could meet with you in secret here and you could tell me what you need and I could give it to you, without the others knowing about it."

Uma laughed. "Oh, I see, to save your precious reputation."

He nodded. "Yeah."

A slow smile grew on Uma's face. "Tristan, did you have slaves when you grew up?"

"Of course," he said without any sign of shame or regret.

"Did you ever meet with them in secret to spare their reputation?"

He didn't answer.

"Didn't think so," Uma said dryly. "Let me ask you this then. If you had won the bet, what would you have me do?"

395

He looked away.

"I would have been on my hands and knees, wouldn't I?" Uma asked but again she received no answer. "You would have done your best to break me, and humiliate me... for the fun of it, wouldn't you?"

Tristan shot her a challenging glance and she saw that she had nailed it. The reason he was here, pestering her, was because he expected her to be as mean to him as he would have been to her; he was terrified.

Uma sighed. "Well, I can assure you that other men tried to break me all my life. Tristan. You wouldn't have succeeded, and do you know why?" Slowly she rose to her feet and moved to stand right in front of him.

He shook his head. "Why?"

"Because unlike you, I don't give a flying fuck about what the other students think of me. Their opinion of me doesn't define me. Your opinion of me is irrelevant too."

She was in her underwear, but given the fact that she had been naked in front of him this very morning and five minutes ago, she didn't care. She wasn't afraid of being alone with Tristan; if he tried to touch her, she would break his arm. But she was concerned what would happen if she pushed him too far as her slave for the week. It surprised her that he was even willing to own up to the bet; she would have expected him to blow it off with the excuse that it was just a joke. Uma wasn't stupid. She might have power over him this week, but what about next week and all the weeks after that? Was one week of humiliating Tristan worth what he would do to her to get even, if she took it too far?

"So tell me what you want from me," he said softly.

Uma gave him a speculative glance. "Alright, here's the deal. I never wanted you as a slave, I just wanted you to leave me alone. If I agree to make this week easy on you and never boss you around in public, then you have to promise me something in return."

Tristan waited for her to continue.

"You'll never tell anyone about this place and you'll never bring anyone up here."

"Why would I?"

"I don't need you to carry my books, fetch my food, polish my shoes, or anything that will humiliate you in public. The only thing I really want is for you and your minions is to leave me alone. No comments, no touching, no threats… nothing."

"Okay," Tristan agreed.

"Try to get your girlfriend to leave me alone too," Uma said, knowing it was a long shot.

"I don't control Simone," he protested.

Uma arched her brow. "I'm sure you can find some way to persuade her, or do you want me to let it slip that you came to my room after curfew and I was… naked? I thought you said she's the jealous type."

"She wouldn't believe you. She knows I ha…" he stopped himself.

"That you hate me?" Uma asked.

Tristan nodded.

"I don't care how you feel about me. Believe me, I understand hate, but if you're angry about losing this bet, remember that you were the one who set the prize, and consider what you would have made me do, if I had lost."

Tristan sat for a minute and his eyes stayed on her face. "You don't talk like a child, do you know that? How old are you anyway?"

"How does a child talk?" she asked, momentarily thrown off by his comment.

"I don't know, less serious… more giggles and silliness, I suppose. You talk like a grown-up."

Uma shrugged, "To answer your question, I'm thirteen and didn't meet a child until a few months ago; and even now, you're the only child I talk to."

"I'm not a child," Tristan said, insulted.

"Student then... anyway, I grew up among adults and believe me, I never saw giggling or silliness before I arrived here. I am what I am, so deal with it."

Tristan held up both palms. "I was just making an observation."

"And I was just giving you an explanation," she replied dryly.

"So all you're asking of me is to keep others from harassing you."

Uma smiled smugly. "You say that like it's an easy task."

"So I basically have to be your bodyguard for the week?"

Uma turned her back on him, offended. "As if I needed a body guard. I can take care of myself."

When she looked over her shoulder, Tristan's eyes were on her ass.

"Don't look at my ass," she reprimanded him.

"I'm not," he said, annoyed. "Besides, it's not as good as Simone's."

"Ha, is that supposed to hurt my feelings?" She shook her head, indicating he was an idiot—she honestly couldn't care less about what he thought of her ass. "In that case, why do you keep popping up when I'm naked?"

Tristan folded his arm and gave her a smug smile. "I like to mess with you... and I like your breasts."

Without wanting to, Uma flushed red, unsure what to do with his unwelcome compliment, "I'm sure Simone's breasts are better than mine," she said sarcastically.

"Of course," he answered.

Uma snapped around and faced him with fiery eyes. "And you know what's good about Simone too?" she said with contempt.

"What?"

"She's such a warm and loving person." Uma didn't hide it when she rolled her eyes.

"So are we done here then?" Tristan asked dryly.

"Yes, we're done. Just make sure your girlfriend, and all the minions that you two royals keep, leave me alone."

"And that's all? You won't talk to me in front of others then?"

"Unlike you, I never aspired to be a slave owner. I have no need to humiliate you to feel better about myself, so yes, that's all... *for now*." She added the last part to make him sweat.

He growled low and got up.

"Oh, and Tristan..."

He turned and gave her an impatient stare.

"From now on, you'll knock. I'm tired of you sneaking up on me."

He scoffed and left.

Uma swallowed a grin. The guy had no idea what he had just agreed to; Uma was the most hated person at school and getting the others off her back would take an army. She didn't expect him to succeed, but she would enjoy seeing him try.

The next day was fun for Uma. She deliberately turned up early for her morning run and waited for Jasmin to meet her. Tristan came shortly after and so did four of the others in his running group. Tristan ignored her but the other guys kept making suggestive comments and catcalling Uma while waiting for their last member to join them.

"Are you going to strip for us again today?" one of them asked her.

"Shut up, just leave her alone," Tristan barked.

Uma suppressed a smile and stayed impassive. She didn't have to scowl at them, Tristan was on the job and it amused her to see his frustration.

Another one of the guys called out to Uma, "Are you sore, baby? Did I take you too hard in my dreams?" Tristan punched the guy who said it hard on his shoulder. "Cut it out, she's only thirteen," he hissed.

"What the hell, man? Thirteen is old enough to have sex."

"Yeah, my mother was thirteen when she had me," another of the boys said.

"What the hell is wrong with you, Tristan? The bitch is going to boss you around for a week and you defend her?" the guy who had taken the punch argued, and three of them started making chicken sounds and flapping their arms.

"What's going on?" Jasmin asked from the door, but Uma just shook her head softly. "Nothing, let's go."

A second later Mr. Raffen showed up and Uma was forced to endure another jog listening to the two talking tortoises. Their slow pace was killing her but even when they told her she could run along, she still kept with them until they were almost back to the school again. There was no reason to test her luck.

Tristan's tribulations weren't over by a long shot. He walked by when Werner and some of the other boys were following Uma and making hateful and loud comments about her past as a slave. Tristan helped her get away by simply honoring the younger boys with his superior presence and distracting them with a few questions. After lunch, however, Tristan's girlfriend Simone came storming towards Uma and this time Tristan wasn't around to interfere.

"Is it true you stripped for Tristan?" Simone asked and got in Uma's face.

"No," Uma said, honestly disgusted; she had never taken her clothes off *for* Tristan. He had seen her naked, but that was not by Uma's choice, and she wasn't stupid enough to poke the dragon and tell Simone any details about that.

"What the hell is going on then? Why are people saying that you did and why is Tristan asking people to be nice to you?" Simone spit out.

Uma wanted to leave, but Simone and her friends were making themselves wide and blocking the hallway. "Look, I didn't strip, and I don't know why he's asking people to be nice to me. Maybe your boyfriend is just a nice guy with a big heart?" Uma suggested and did her best to keep from laughing at the absurdity. Tristan was an asshole, but Simone didn't think so, and maybe she would buy into Tristan's good motives.

Simone wrinkled her nose, spun around, and walked away with her chin up high and her friends following her lead. With a loud voice she declared, "Yeah, well, don't think we'll be nice to you, slave, *because we won't.*"

Uma was used to this type of harassment from students and shrugged it off. Only one thing from Simone's mean words stood out for her, and it made her smile with amusement: Tristan was actually asking people to be nice to her. In what alternate universe had she woken up? She was both surprised and impressed with him.

Unfortunately Tristan's efforts didn't help at all, they only seemed to make things worse. On the second day rumors and speculations were running like wildfire, going from one extreme to the other, and even Jasmin started asking questions.

"What's up with you and Tristan?" Jasmin asked.

"Nothing."

Jasmin raised a brow. "I heard you two are dating now."

Uma coughed violently and could hardly breathe. "That's ridiculous."

"That's what I thought, until I saw Simone and Tristan in my class today. Simone had red eyes and they kept fighting, so I had to split them up and have them dance with others.

"Really?" Uma hid a smile. She didn't like either of them and felt no guilt.

"Yes, really... and what's even stranger, I heard Tristan defend you today, Uma."

"Hmm, cool." Uma smiled satisfied.

"Is there something you want to tell me?" Jasmin's beautiful brown eyes were sparkling with curiosity.

"Nope, nothing is changed," Uma said firmly. "I still hate boys and men... every one of them, and especially Tristan," she said honestly.

"Well, it doesn't sound like he hates you though."

Uma swallowed her need to say, "Oh, he hates me alright." Instead she gave Jasmin a head shake. "I give it a week until he becomes the same mean Tristan again... besides, I want to dance, not talk about stupid stuff."

Jasmin laughed. "Okay, fine with me."

That night, Uma went back to her room with her head held down. At the end of their session Jasmin had told her she was now dating Mr. Raffen, or Jasper as she called him. It was a hard blow; she couldn't understand how Jasmin would let herself fall into a man's trap. It made no sense to Uma that Jasmin looked so happy when she spoke of Jasper. It felt almost like a betrayal from Jasmin—that she was fraternizing with the enemy. Jasmin should know better; her own brother had molested her and shown her what swine men are. How could Jasmin be so naïve, to think that Mr. Raffen was any different?

Uma had tried to convince her it was a mistake but Jasmin had only made it much worse by saying that one day Uma would find love too.

As if.

Uma loved Jasmin, but the woman had clearly lost her mind; Uma had snapped back at her and left in anger. She was still upset and disappointed when she came back to her attic, and it didn't make things better that she found Tristan sitting outside her room, waiting for her.

Uma felt tempted to take all her frustrations out on him and just shout, scream, and hurt Tristan, but she restrained herself and walked past him with a sigh, leaving the door to her room open. Tristan entered and closed the door behind him.

"I can't do it," he exclaimed.

Uma crawled onto her bed, crossed her legs, annoyed, and looked up at him. "Can't do what?"

"Simone says that if I defend you one more time, she'll break up with me, and everyone is making assumptions and starting rumors about me."

"What are they saying?" Uma asked, wanting to see him squirm.

"Just shit."

"What shit?"

"Doesn't matter."

"Tell me anyway?"

"That we're dating and that I *like* you." He spit out the words.

Uma gave him a blank stare. "So what do you want me to do about it?"

"Give me some other job I can do for you, that won't cost me my reputation and my girlfriend."

"Why would I do that?" Uma asked coolly.

"Because..." He didn't clarify but sat down on the stool and gave her a defiant look.

"Alright, I'll do it, but only because you're only making things worse for me too, and having Simone follow me around asking questions is butt-fucking annoying.

Tristan's eyes widened. "You shouldn't talk like that," he said dryly.

"Please forgive my lack of manners. I might have picked up a few bad words from the swine I was among in the Masi headquarters." She gave him a challenging stare and said, "You're welcome to leave anytime."

"So it's true?" he asked. "You were at the Masi headquarters?"

Uma nodded. "General Mantonis owned my mother."

"And you too?" Tristan whistled. "You must have seen some sick stuff."

Uma swallowed hard. "I did," she said and wondered: *Why am I even talking to my enemy?*

"Cool," he said, intrigued.

Uma's head snapped back up and she narrowed her eyes. "Cool? What part of sick stuff is cool, Tristan?" She moved fast and was in his face, making him stand up defensively. They were standing opposite each other and she was looking up at him with anger blazing from her eyes. "Do you like your mother?" she snarled softly.

"I love my mother," Tristan said, confused.

"Then imagine your mother brutally raped every day. Would that be cool to you? How cool would it be if you had to bathe her fragile body and help her clean the long marks from the whipping her owner gave her? And do you think it would be *cool* to see your beloved mother held down by five strong men taking turns with her, filling every hole they could find on her body while you were just a child and could do nothing to help her?" Uma's voice was arctic and her body shaking with fury. How dared this eighteen-year-old ignorant boy glorify the general and the horrible things he and his men had done?

404

She could see Tristan get paler as she spoke. "Do you have a sister, Tristan?"

"Yes," he whispered.

"How old is she?"

"Twelve... she's here at the school."

"How *cool* would it be if six boys did to her what you and your friends did to me by the lake? Or even worse, what you guys were going to do."

"That's different," Tristan defended himself.

"Why?"

"Because you were born a slave."

Uma closed her eyes, holding back her urge to take all her anger physically out on him.

"Right... and you believe that slaves are born to be used, destroyed, humiliated, and toyed with... You believe I'm fair game because unlike your sister, I have no feelings, no pride, no honor?" Uma stopped talking. The knot in her throat was threatening to make her voice break.

Tristan stared at her, his lips pressed into a fine line. He didn't deny it.

Uma blinked rapidly, still shaking with fury. She forced herself to take a step back to regain her self-control. "Alright," she said and exhaled forcibly through the nostrils. "Since you evidently don't have the power to get people off my back, I'm giving you another job. Tomorrow, you'll clean the bathroom and my room.

"No way!"

"Yes way." Uma pinned him with her green eyes. "If you won't keep others off my back and you won't do anything for me in public, then cleaning my room and bathroom are the only things I can think of."

Tristan broke into a wicked smile. "I could give you a massage."

Uma lowered her head and tightened her jaw. "When hell freezes over! And until then, you can honor the bet by cleaning as I asked you to, or go to hell, and leave me alone."

He didn't look pleased but he finally nodded in agreement. "Tomorrow," he said.

"Tomorrow," Uma repeated.

"And we're clear, I won't be protecting you anymore."

"You never did," Uma pointed out. "But that doesn't mean you can harass me either."

"Right." Tristan turned and walked towards the door and then he stopped. "Is it true?" he asked without turning. "Do you really have a boyfriend?"

Uma narrowed her eyes. "Why?"

Tristan turned around and faced her. "It just doesn't seem very realistic that anyone here at school would want you."

His words hurt, but Uma didn't show it. Instead she broke into a laugh. "Nor that I would want anyone here at school. My boyfriend lives in London."

Tristan crossed his arms. "Really?"

Uma arched a brow and met his skeptical look with calmness.

"What's his name then?"

"Aidan." The name flew out of her.

"How old is he?"

"Seventeen."

Tristan stopped and gaped at her. "That's almost my age."

"Good night, Tristan." Uma turned her back on him, pretending to be bored.

She heard the door close and let out a gasp of air. Why had she told Tristan that Aidan was her boyfriend? She disliked them both equally and didn't want a boyfriend, ever… so why lie about it? *Stupid pride.* She had wanted to get back at Tristan for that lame comment he made about not wanting to have sex with her even if she begged him. It had been her anger, her vanity, and her need to get even that had made her come up with that stupid, stupid lie. Now people would think she liked a boy. She hated all boys. All of them. Especially Aidan, because he had told her that no man would ever want to touch her. He had told her he would rather be with a man than her, and he had told her she was ugly inside and out. Uma threw herself down on her bed and buried her head in the pillow. She didn't want anyone to hear her cry. It was all because of those damn hormones.

CHAPTER 38
Independence

Sybina

"How do I look?" Sybina asked when Aston entered the bathroom meeting her eyes in the mirror.

"You look beautiful," he said and walked closer.

"I'm a bit nervous. I'm not sure what to expect from a nightclub."

For the first time in her life she was going to a nightclub. Aya and Sofia were taking her; Aya was on a mission to hook up Sofia, who hadn't had a boyfriend for eight months.

Aston turned her around and kissed her. "Expect men to look at you, offer you drinks, ask you to dance."

Sybina looked up at him. Aston and Kato had both suggested several times that they come too, but Aya and Sofia had insisted on a girls' night out.

"Say no to all of them," he instructed with a smile. "If you need to dance, drink, or fuck, you come to me."

"I'm not going to have sex with anyone," Sybina pointed out.

"Except your husband," Aston said and sucked her neck.

Sybina pushed him away and he shot her a wicked smile. "You didn't?" she said and turned to look in the mirror. A huge love bite was already showing on her neck.

"I'm wearing your ring, there's no need to mark me like that."

"Caveman, remember," he said with a grin and kissed her again. Sybina kissed him back, met his tongue, and immediately Aston pushed her up against the wall, lifting her legs around his hips.

"Don't, Aston, they are picking me up in ten minutes."

"That's all I need to remind you what you have waiting for you at home."

Sybina shook her head. "You're impossible."

"Then why are you undressing me?" he asked hoarsely.

"Because you got me all hot and now I want you."

"Your wish is my command, babe." Aston lifted Sybina up and placed her by the sink, pulling up her dress, sliding her thong to the side and his fingers inside her; she opened his pants.

"Don't ruin my make-up," she said.

He lifted her down and turned her around. "I want you to watch me fuck you." He pushed her forward while meeting her eyes in the mirror. Sybina watched as Aston took her hard from behind and kept eye contact with her. His eyes were claiming her, telling her again and again that he was the only man allowed to touch her.

"Remember this, tonight," he said when her orgasm came rolling and she called out his name.

When it was his time to explode inside her, she gave him an erotic smile and whispered, "Ditto, darling."

Ten minutes later, Aya and Sofia picked Sybina up in a cab. She got in the taxi with her face flushed red, and slightly out of breath. Sofia and Aya complimented her on how radiant she looked. Sybina smiled. It was what Aston liked to call her post-orgasmic look, but she couldn't tell them that.

Sofia looked good with her brown hair styled and her elegant make-up, and Aya... well, Aya had been born gorgeous, and looked so happy to be out with her two best friends.

"Aston got us on the list at one of the upscale nightclubs," Sybina said.

Sofia frowned. "I would rather go to a downscale fun place than hang with all those stuck-up rich people who are so full of themselves."

Sybina agreed. "Maybe you're right, I've never been to a nightclub and I'm not a good dancer, so I prefer some place where no one cares."

"No one cares anywhere, all they care about are themselves and how they look," Aya pointed out. "No more fuss from you two. We're going to give this club a chance, and if it's horrible, we'll leave and find another place, alright?"

Sybina and Sofia nodded in agreement.

"But first this pregnant girl has to eat, and I've booked us a table at my favorite steakhouse."

The restaurant was nice and the waiter friendly when Aya, Sybina, and Sofia sat down at a table in the corner.

"Oh, Kato told me to say thank you for keeping our house so clean and tidy... he's impressed with your work," Aya told Sybina.

"Tell him it's my pleasure." Sybina smiled back.

"Can you do my apartment too?" Sofia asked hopefully.

Aya laughed. "Sorry, honey, but you've got to find someone else. Aston is already pissed at me for hiring Sybina on as a domestic helper. He doesn't care that I pay her handsomely; he doesn't like it one bit."

"Really? Why? Isn't it just a few hours a week?"

Sybina shook her head. "It's about twenty hours a week with the shopping, cooking, and cleaning, and since I'm also working part time at the holistic clinic now, Aston thinks I'm overdoing it."

Sofia sat back. "What do you think?"

"I enjoy it. I've always been a busy person and I get to see a lot more of Aya and her beautiful big belly, not to mention that I have my own bank account with my own income, and that makes me feel independent."

"Then why isn't Aston just happy for you then?" Sofia asked.

"He tolerates it but he's mentioned several times that it's unnecessary for me to work if I don't want to."

"And by that he means he's happy to provide for you financially?" Sofia said with her arms crossed.

Sybina nodded. "I guess. He got offended when I wanted to pay him back for the many hours of tutoring and the clothes he bought for me when I first arrived."

Aya leaned forward. "He got offended how?"

"He refused to take my money and just told me that what's his is mine."

"That's actually kind of sweet," Aya exclaimed.

"Psst." Sofia smacked her tongue.

"Don't be a cynic, Sofia, you now Aston loves Sybina."

"So why can't she share what she earns with him? Why does he get to be too cool to take anything from her?

"Actually I did pay him back, he just doesn't know it yet," Sybina said and explained. "I put the money in a shrine Aston keeps in his closet. It's full of baby pictures and some personal letters that I haven't read. It's probably going to take him years before he finds the money, but to me it was all about the pride of paying him back. It means a lot to me that I have my own money. I never had that in my life and it's a sign that I'm with Aston because I want to be, not because I'm financially dependent on him."

"Hold on to your freedom and independence, woman... what about your permanent residency status, any news yet?"

"We had another visit, but it went really well and as far as I know all the signs are positive. The lawyers just told us to be patient; apparently these things take time. But I got good news." Sybina clapped her hands in delight. "Cindy at the clinic is helping me get certified as a naturopath. She says I already have the knowledge, so I might as well get the paper to show it. I'm studying all the English names for the plants and herbs now.

"That's great, Sybina." Aya toasted her.

"It will be my first formal education, and you know what's crazy?"

"What?" Sofia asked.

"A naturopath here in England doesn't even have to forage the ingredients themselves or make their own medicine. It all comes from a computer. Cindy showed me how she just orders everything and then it's shipped right to her door. Isn't that crazy?"

Sofia and Aya laughed. "You are too sweet, Sybina. But yes, I can see why that would seem magical to you. By the way, what happened to that guy who got you the job in the first place? The one Aston almost knocked down when he thought you were at his house," Sofia asked.

"You told Sofia about Aston storming into John's house?" Sybina asked Aya with a look of reproach.

"Of course I told Sofia, I tell her everything… was it supposed to be a secret?"

"No, but… anyway, Sofia, to answer your question: John is doing fine and we still walk now and then."

"Is he still angry at Aston?"

Sybina smiled. "He still thinks Aston was rude and primitive, but he told me that he respects Aston's determination to get me back. Well enough about me, Sofia, how is London working out for you?"

Sofia lit up in a big smile. "Great! Did you know it was Kato who first suggested I move here?"

"No."

"He said I could live in his and Aya's old apartment rent-free and he could pull strings and get me a consultant job."

"Wow, that's very generous of him," Sybina said, impressed.

"Yes. Getting time with Aya and being around when the baby arrives, what's not to like?"

Sybina raised her glass. "Kato has proven to be an amazing man, cheers to him."

The girls all cheered.

"And Aston, should we toast to him too?" Sofia asked and Sybina and Aya interchanged a quick glance.

"What? Sofia asked.

"Nothing, let's raise a toast to Aston, who was slow to realize how lucky he was to have Sybina, but who won points by going after her," Aya said and raised her glass.

"To Aston," they all chimed in.

It had taken Aston weeks to forgive Aya for meddling in his business after fighting with her on the phone. Aya was just as stubborn as Aston; even though Sybina had explained to Aya again and again that Aston had apologized for making Sybina feel like a pervert, Aya still held a grudge. Last week Sybina had finally managed to persuade Aston to go see Aya and they had talked it out. Sybina was relieved that everyone was back to normal.

"By the way, Sofia. I want to make it a tradition that we all meet on Wednesdays for a cozy meal at our place," Sybina said.

"I love that idea." Aya nodded.

Sofia lit up. "Me too. I'll bring wine."

"Great, then book your calendar for dinner at seven on Wednesdays."

"Thank God. I'm getting tired of cornflakes anyway," Sofia snickered.

The food was delicious and they laughed a lot; at one point they laughed so hard that Aya actually peed her pants a little, which made them laugh even more.

Around midnight they were ready to go dancing and sent appreciative thoughts to Aston when they walked around the long line of people and got let in like VIPs because he'd gotten them on the list.

The hostess in the club led them to a private table. "I want to sit in the bar," Aya said to the others. "It's easier to pick up guys in a bar than at a private table; it takes too much courage for them to walk over to us if we sit isolated." The hostess raised her brows in surprise and shot a glance at Aya's bulging belly.

"The guys are not for me, obviously," Aya exclaimed, offended.

"I'm happy to arrange seats in the bar if you prefer," the hostess said with a smile.

Sofia, Sybina, and Aya watched her approach a group of stylish young men and point to the table Aya had just rejected. The men nodded and lifted their beers, getting up from their chairs in the bar.

"Great," Aya muttered sarcastically. "Now she's cleaning out the bar of the best-looking guys. Why didn't she ask some of the girls to take the table?"

Sofia took Aya's hands and pulled her to the bar. "No more Mrs. Hormonella from you tonight. We want the positive Aya, who sees opportunities.

The men smiled politely and gave their seats to them. "Thanks for the upgrade, ladies, come join us at the table if you feel like it," one of them offered.

As soon as they were gone Aya turned to Sofia. "How about the one with the glasses? He looks good."

Sofia sneaked a peek. "I like the dark-haired one better."

"He's got a ring on his finger," Sybina pointed out.

"Which one? The dark-haired or the one with the glasses?" Aya asked without looking at the men.

"The dark-haired," Sybina said.

"Let's just forget about the men for a minute and have some fun, okay?" Sofia suggested. "I know you want to hook me up, Aya, but honestly that's second priority to having a fun night out with the girls. And besides, if this is Sybina's first time in a nightclub, then I want to make sure it's a fun one." Sofia leaned over the bar and gestured to the bartender. They ordered drinks and Sybina sipped her first Mojito ever while Sofia was entertaining them with colorful stories from her new workplace. Apparently English men were very different from Norwegian men, and Sofia sounded hilarious when she tried to imitate their pick-up lines in English accents she hadn't mastered one bit.

"Why don't you just go out with them to see where it leads?" Aya asked.

"You know me better than that; I'm not into nice guys in suits and I never date colleagues. I need someone tough and badass, like a cute firefighter, a police officer, or maybe a hot mechanic." Sofia grinned.

"Uh-huh." Aya rolled her eyes. "Only problem is that you get bored of them real fast when they aren't smart enough. So where are you going to find a hot firefighter with a membership in Mensa?"

"Aston is pretty smart and he's a soldier," Sybina said.

"Aston is a great guy and so is Kato," Aya agreed "But not even our amazing guys could live up to Sofia's unrealistic expectations."

"That's not true. I'm sure they would have been enough... maybe."

"Maybe?" Sybina asked, intrigued that anyone would find Aston or Kato lacking.

Sofia took a sip of her Mojito. "No maybe; Aston and Kato are definitely fine."

Aya scoffed. "You don't fool me. You've already found several things about them you couldn't live with... that's what you do, Sofia. You find mistakes, and we both know why."

"Why?" Sybina asked.

Sofia rolled her eyes at Aya. "Don't listen to her, Sybina... Aya just has this crazy idea that I only go for the bad guys because I know they never want to have a serious relationship anyway... she thinks I do it to protect myself."

"I don't understand," Sybina said.

Aya took over. "I'm just saying that for someone as smart as Sofia, it sure is strange that she keeps picking the same type of man, when she *knows* he's not what she needs. Sofia is attracted to men who don't give a damn, because that allows her to not give a damn either. And the few times the men actually start to care, she terminates the relationship quickly, making up flaws she can use as an excuse."

"But I thought you wanted a boyfriend?" Sybina asked.

"I do. It's just Aya overanalyzing me," Sofia defended herself. "I'll find him... someday."

"Whoa, the baby doesn't like this loud music too much. He's kicking like crazy." Aya placed a hand on her stomach.

"Maybe he's a dancer," Sofia suggested.

Sybina smiled. "He's a she."

Aya gaped at her. "You think, or you know?"

"I'm pretty sure,"

Sofia raised her palms. "Okay, before you two start swinging a pendulum or putting down tarot cards, can we do a little thing called dancing?" Sofia got up from her chair.

"Aren't we supposed to wait for men to ask us to dance?" Sybina asked in confusion.

"Hell no, we don't need men to have fun on a dance floor," Sofia declared and led the way.

Sybina was laughing more than she had in a long time. Sofia and Aya couldn't care less about looking good on a dance floor; the two long-time friends were dancing like no one was watching and showing Sybina dance moves from earlier decades. Each one looked stranger and funnier than the previous, and they constantly had Sybina imitate them. She liked the Charleston and the boogie, but found it impossible to do the moonwalk. They taught her the electric eel, the robot, something called the running man that was a lot harder than it looked, and when they started to do vogue movements with their hands the DJ rewarded them and put on the right song for it. Sofia and Aya squealed and blew kisses at the DJ. "That's Madonna," Aya shouted over the music and showed Sybina how to look all serious and move her hands in front of her face.

As they danced several men joined them, only to leave again when they didn't receive any attention from the small party. After an hour of dancing and several failed attempts of learning the butterfly dance Sybina gave up. "I need something to drink," she shouted over the music and made her way back to the bar only to see their seats taken. Aya and Sofia followed right behind her.

"I'm sorry, I think you took our seats," Sofia said to the girls.

"We didn't see any name tags," a blonde responded with a sassy tone.

"Could you at least give us one of the chairs for our friend who's pregnant?" Sybina asked politely. The girl turned her back to them.

"I'm sorry, girls, but to be honest I would prefer to go home and get my feet up." Aya pushed her hair back. It was damp from all the dancing.

"Of course," Sybina agreed and got ready to leave too. The thought of Aston waiting for her was incentive enough.

"Can't you stay with Sofia a bit longer?" Aya pleaded. "If you go, Sofia will go too, and I really don't want her night to end this early because of me."

Sybina smiled. "I can stay."

"Great. Thank you." Aya hugged them both and left to get a cab.

"Listen, Sybina, you really don't need to stay if you don't want to. I'm perfectly fine either way," Sofia assured her.

417

"Really?" Sybina smiled, thinking how much she wanted to go home to Aston. "Let's just have one more drink and call it a night then."

It only took another five minutes before they were surrounded by three guys, one of them hitting on Sofia pretty openly. He was a big guy with a scar over his left eye, making him look tough. Sybina could see Sofia was interested.

"What do you do?" Sybina asked him.

"I'm a professional stuntman," he answered and Sofia's smile grew bigger.

Sybina chuckled with satisfaction, and Sofia didn't object when Sybina bade her farewell and left her with Mark, the stuntman.

CHAPTER 39
Wednesday Night
Aston

Wednesday night Aston came home after a stressful stop-and-go commute to fall even more in love with his wife. Sybina had created a feast for the senses with the relaxed background music that instantly calmed him down and the warm colors that met his eyes looking around to see flowers, a nice table setting, and soft candlelight. God, his home looked like a commercial for blissful harmony! His nostrils automatically flared to soak up the fragrance of homemade bread, coq au vin simmering in the oven giving away the deliciousness of garlic and red wine, and a mouthwatering aroma from the chocolate she was melting into a bowl with vanilla, cream, and sugar.

"Are you making that chocolate dessert I love so much?" Aston asked while hugging Sybina from behind. He couldn't decide what smelled better, Sybina or the food.

"Anything for you." Sybina turned her head and gave him a warm smile.

He planted a kiss on her lips. "I think I won the lottery with you."

Sybina shook her head with a chuckle. "It doesn't take much to impress you, does it?"

Aston growled low into her ear and bit her neck gently. "How long do we have before they get here?"

Sybina chuckled. "Not enough for what you have in mind."

"But you look so hot in that apron, babe..." His hands were already pulling up her dress. "How about I slide up into you while you stir the chocolate?"

Sybina leaned her head back and rested it on his collarbone while his hands explored her soft skin under her dress. She moaned a little and spread her legs.

"We really shouldn't." she muttered.

"We really should," Aston insisted and slid a finger inside her. Fuck, the warmth and the moistness of his woman would never cease to entice him; his erection throbbed in his pants. The sound of the doorbell made Sybina tense up. Damn it, so much for the quickie Aston had in mind.

"Could you get the door?" Sybina asked.

He scoffed. "With a raging boner in my pants, not likely."

Sybina laughed and shook her head at him. "Okay, I'll do it, and you wash your hands and get that thing under control."

"How long are they staying?" he called after her... right now he wished they could be alone all night and continue what they had just started.

Sybina didn't answer him, she was already letting in Sofia, Kato, and Aya. They all came back to the kitchen happy and excited.

An hour and two bottles of wine later they were enjoying Sybina's meal and catching up.

"Sybina, you truly are spoiling us," Kato said and took another bite of the tender chicken on his plate. What is this again?"

"Coq au vin."

"It's delicious, and so was the soup," Kato said firmly. "I'm not a big fan of seafood but that lobster bisque was amazing."

"Thank you." Sybina was glowing and Aston couldn't take his eyes off her. Sybina made everyone feel welcome and relaxed in her company, and he knew how important this group of people were to her. They were the closest thing to a family she'd had since she was eleven years old.

Sofia nodded enthusiastically. "This tastes amazing, Sybina. If you ever get tired of Aston, I want to be your roommate."

Aston winked at Sofia. "She might get tired of me, but I'm never getting tired of her." Sybina shot him a private smile telling him *ditto*, and it made him fantasize about all the places he wanted to kiss her tonight.

"How is work, Sofia?" Kato asked, and she stopped eating and narrowed her eyes.

"You just had to ask, didn't you?"

Everyone looked at Sofia. "Something wrong?" Kato asked in concern.

"I was actually not going to tell you, but since you ask me directly, I won't lie about it."

Aya sucked in air. "Did you get fired?"

Sofia rolled her eyes. "Of course not, I'm a freaking genius at what I do."

"Then spit it out," Kato said curiously.

Sofia made a deep theatrical sigh. "Okay... so you're not going to believe this, but this Monday I started a three months' assignment with a new client and guess who my contact person is?"

No one offered any guesses. They just looked blankly at Sofia. "Who?" Kato asked.

"Oliver fucking Austin," Sofia exclaimed with a groan and buried her face in her hands.

"Who?" Sybina asked while Aya put her hand to her mouth and looked horrified. "Oh no, Sofia, you're not serious."

Kato leaned forward. "Sofia, look at me. Is this a joke?"

Sofia arched her brow. "Do I look like I find this funny?"

Aston broke into a low chuckle. "Awkward."

"Who are we talking about?" Sybina asked again.

Aya turned to explain. "You know Oliver Austin—he was Kato's best friend but then he had an affair with Kato's fiancée Diana *and* he was the one who told the press about Kato's time in Spirima."

Sybina nodded slowly. "Ahh, yes, I remember him. I just didn't remember his name," she turned back to Sofia, her eyes full of sympathy. "And he's your client now?"

"Uh-huh."

"Did he hit on you?" Aya exclaimed bluntly and color rose in Sofia cheeks.

"Oh, Oliver totally hit on you already..." Aya exclaimed.

Aston chuckled. "I don't think I've ever seen you flush red out of embarrassment Sofia... anger, yes, but never embarrassment."

Sofia shot Aston a dirty look and returned her attention to Aya. "Yes, Oliver *did* come on to me, but I told him there was no chance in hell that was happening."

Kato, who had been sitting completely still, suddenly broke into a deep belly laugh. "I'm not sure who I feel most sorry for," he finally said.

"It's not funny," Aya and Sofia said simultaneously but Kato just kept on laughing.

"It is," he insisted. "Sofia has Oliver on her shit list and then she's forced to be polite to him because he's her client. The thought of you being polite, Sofia... it's just hilarious."

"Hey, I can be polite," Sofia said, offended.

"Not to Oliver! I don't believe you. And he's going to be so provoked that you're immune to his charm that his going to try harder." Kato couldn't stop laughing and it was so infectious that Aston and Sybina joined in.

Kato was trying to talk while laughing. "It's like something from a bad movie, you know... the harder Oliver tries to charm you, the more you'll despise him, and you're one of the scariest women I know." Kato dried away a tear from laughing. "The poor guy is like a male spider trying to get close to you and you're just waiting to bite his head off."

Sofia gave him a mock smile. "Yeah, that may be entertaining on paper, but not in real life. The guy is a jerk."

"Oh, come on, Sofia, it's funny, admit it." Kato was still laughing so hard he could hardly breathe, and even Aya was starting to crack up.

Sofia crossed her arms. "Stop it, Kato... you're not helping."

Kato dried away more tears from his eyes. "Sorry, Sofia... I'm trying to take it seriously, I really am."

"Then try harder, you're starting to piss me off." Sofia was giving Kato the stink eye, but a smile lurked at the edge of her mouth.

"Why don't you just say no to the assignment? Surely someone else can take over?" Aston suggested.

Sofia shook her head. "Because I've been waiting for this kind of project. It's a great opportunity, and I want to prove to my boss I can do it."

Aya turned to Kato. "Can't you talk to Sofia's boss or something?"

"Don't worry," Kato assured her. "If anyone can handle themselves it's Sofia! Oliver has no idea what he's gotten himself into."

Sofia held up a palm. "Okay, easy now, I'm not some psycho nutcase about to kill the man. I'm going to focus on the reason I'm there and do a hell of job before I leave. Oliver is just a pestilence that I'll have to endure. I won't hurt him, if that's what you think," Sofia exclaimed.

"Oh, but you'll hurt his pride and his male ego will suffer from your rejection. To him, that's bad enough," Kato mused.

"I don't think so. I've decided to dress down to avoid his interest," Sofia said.

"Please don't," Kato pleaded. "I'll pay you to dress up and make him want you."

Sofia raised a brow. "What the hell Kato... I'm not a hooker."

"I know... I'm just saying that I'm happy to sponsor a new wardrobe if you dress to mess with Oliver's mind."

Aya looked thoughtful. "Oliver did try to put Kato in jail and ruin him, Sofia; it's hardly morally corrupted to play the player a bit," she argued, taking Kato's side.

Sofia leaned forward. "I can pay for my own damn clothes."

"Ohh come on, it'll be fun... you and I shopping like old times," Aya tempted.

"Okay, whatever, but it doesn't mean I'll let him touch me," Sofia pointed out firmly.

"That's the whole point," Aya said and Kato nodded.

"Sounds like we're going shopping." Aya clapped her hands and grinned widely.

Aston lifted his glass. "I'm so glad you moved here, Sofia, the entertainment value has just skyrocketed."

Sofia rolled her eyes. "Nothing is going to happen. I've just got to get through the company Christmas party, that's all."

"You're going to a party with Oliver?" Sybina asked.

"Yep."

"Do you think that's a good idea?" Aya asked with concern.

Sofia leaned back in her chair and crossed her arms. "No, but it's just one night and I'll keep my distance."

"Yeah, but Oliver won't," Kato murmured into his glass, fighting another grin.

"As I said." Aston raised his glass to Sofia. "We can't wait for our update next Wednesday—what will happen in the next round of Sofia versus Oliver."

Sofia narrowed her eyes. "Ha ha, very funny."

As soon as their guest left, Aston pulled Sybina into his arms.

He didn't have the patience to wait until they had cleaned up after their guests, he wanted Sybina right here and now. To his relief she returned his kisses with as much eagerness as his.

He took her on the floor and focused on her pleasure, and every time Sybina came, he felt a deep male satisfaction. When Aston finally allowed himself to come, he held himself still inside her, as deeply as he could go, and let the peace and bliss that was Sybina slide through his system and permeate his veins.

Sybina's eyes were bright and shining, her chest rising and falling in quick movements as she lay on the floor panting and smiling. Aston took in the glorious sight of his wife with her halo of dark curly hair spread around her head. She gave him a smile and laughed. "What is it?"

"I'll never get enough of seeing you like this, Ina. You are so beautiful after sex."

"Only after sex?" she asked teasingly.

"No, you are always beautiful, you know that, and tonight you were shining from within. It was hard to focus on the conversation when all I wanted to do was drag you into the bedroom and finish what we started in the kitchen."

"But you had fun, right?"

"Uh-huh." He had enjoyed himself. Sofia, Kato, and Aya were all down-to-earth people with no need to be anything but genuine, and that was a welcome change from his other, more snobbish, friends.

Sybina placed her hands around his neck, pulling at him. "Come here, handsome, let me feel those strong arms

425

around me a little longer." Aston smiled and took Sybina in his arms, impressed that she didn't get up and start cleaning after their guests. He was in no hurry; he would hold her as long as she wanted and kissed the top of her hair.

"I think this is my favorite place in the world," Sybina said and looked up at him.

"The flat?" he asked and looked around.

She laughed that crisp light signature laugh of hers and he smiled.

"No, silly, I meant here in your arms."

God, she said things that went straight to his heart, and he was starting to feel like a fucking wimp with all the emotions Sybina brought out in him. "I would do anything for you, you know that, right?" he whispered and felt their connection vibrate with love.

"Do you mean that?"

Aston nodded. He couldn't deny this woman anything. He would raise hell and heaven to fulfil her desires. She was everything to him.

"I want a child with you, Aston."

He closed his eyes. *Fuck. Not that again.* Aston covered his face with his arm but Sybina pulled it away.

"You would be a wonderful father, Aston, I know you would."

"We've been over this before, and do you even know how much work a baby is?" he asked. "Anything but that, Ina. I just don't feel like bringing more innocent children into this crazy world, I told you that before."

For a while Sybina didn't speak and Aston was worried she was going to cry. He hated it when she cried; it made him feel like a failure as a husband. He wanted his woman to be sated and happy, not miserable.

"Alright, but what about the innocent children who are already in this world and need loving parents?" Sybina asked him.

"You want to adopt a child?" he asked slowly.

"We could get more children from Spirima than Uma. Younger children."

Aston sat up with slight nausea and big eyes. "More children? How many are we talking about here?"

"I don't know. We'll take one at a time and see how it feels. Maybe one. Maybe two... who knows?"

"So you would be okay with not bearing your own child, then?" Aston asked skeptically.

"Yes. I feel so much love for Uma and she's not mine. I'm sure I could love other children as much."

Aston thought about it. Sybina would be an outstanding mother; they could skip the baby part and save a child from a hard destiny. That part appealed to him. As a soldier he was all about protecting and rescuing.

"At least think about it, Aston. You'll always be my hero for saving me and Uma, and who knows what other child might be lucky enough to have you as a protector... and father."

Aston blinked. Damn it, Sybina was doing it again, making him soft and shit. He pulled Sybina close and kissed her deeply. "I like it when you call me your hero."

Sybina smiled with sparkles in her eyes. "And I like it when you call me yours."

"*Mine.*" Aston winked. "And that's the thing... call me selfish, but I want to enjoy what we have a while longer without sharing you."

Sybina tilted her head. "How long is a while longer?"

"Until Uma gets here."

"That sounds fair." Sybina smiled.

Aston sighed. "Okay then, we can start the process of adopting a younger child when Uma gets here."

Sybina was tearing up with emotion. "Really?"

Aston kissed the tip of her nose. "Didn't you hear me when I said I'll do anything for you? I never lie, you know that."

427

Sybina couldn't stop smiling. "Thank you, Aston. I love you so much."

He chuckled and squeezed her tight. "Enough to skip the dishes for tonight and go have sex in the bed?"

Sybina shook her head, laughing. "I could never love anyone *that* much."

"Nahh, I didn't think so," Aston teased her and got up. "Okay, let's get this mess cleaned up so I can take my wife to bed."

"Is that all you think about? Sex?"

Aston pulled Sybina up and kept his arms around her waist. "Is that a complaint I hear?"

She leaned her head back and looked up at him with a beaming smile. "Absolutely not. I love being your wife, you make me the happiest woman on earth."

Aston closed his eyes and leaned his head against Sybina's forehead. When he opened his eyes to return her loving gaze his eyes were moist too. "And you make me the happiest husband on earth. I love you Sybina!"

The End!

A message from Elin Peer

If you enjoyed this book, you are going to love the next books in the Slave Series. (See descriptions below.)

You can get all my books on Amazon and please, please, please don't forget to leave reviews. It's good karma!

Now, here's a little insight into the creation of these books. From the beginning it was my plan to write a series portraying three different women experiencing slavery: Aya's story about getting kidnapped by fanatics as an infidel adult, Sybina's story of being sold into slavery as a child, and Uma's story of being born a slave.

While I was writing Aya's and Sybina's stories, a strong female character stepped forward and demanded to be heard.

Honestly, I kept pushing her aside, since she didn't fit into my theme for the series. But Sofia is not a woman to play sidekick forever; she has strong opinions and a big heart and demands to have her own story told and truth be told I really like her.

Finally I gave in and brought Sofia's story to life. To my surprise I had a lot of fun doing so, and her story turned out to be captivating, exciting, and highly entertaining. In fact one of my beta readers told me it was his favorite book in the series.

Never a slave
What if you accidently slept with the person you detest the most?

Sofia, a tornado of a woman, embraces her new life in London by living out a Saturday night of uninhibited (and partly embarrassing) sexual fantasies with a really hot stranger. She has no experience with one-night stands but figures she's playing it safe by insisting on no personal information.

Oliver Austin is used to women falling for his good looks, charm, and success. What's new is Sofia's refusing to know anything about him or to ever see him again – especially after he delivers an Olympic performance in sexual gratification.

Come Monday morning, Sofia is shocked when she realizes that her new VIP client is not only her weekend hottie, but also the a-hole who hurt her best friend in the past.

Can Sofia, who is known to be without a filter, stay professional and be polite around the man who makes her blood boil in more ways than one?

Never a Slave is the third stand-alone novel in Elin Peer's Slave series. Like the other books in the highly praised series, it offers complex characters, sharp dialogue, sexual tension, and surprising plot twists that will have you reading into the wee hours.

Buy Never a Slave and be highly entertained today!

After Sofia's story, there's Uma's story called "The Feisty Slave" where she grows up to become a young woman and moves to London. Will she ever learn to trust anyone from the opposite sex or is she too broken by the brutal men she grew up among?

The Feisty Slave
Can you be too broken for love?

Uma was born a slave and grew up in a war zone. With a good head on her shoulders and a feisty personality, she has fought off grown men more than once. Brutality, violence, and dirty tricks are her world. But when Uma is rescued from slavery a new world opens up to her, challenging her to reconsider the simplistic worldview her loving mother and the other female slaves have drilled into her brain: All men are swine!

Aidan sees Uma as a spoiled brat with an attitude problem. Still, she's new in London and he feels obligated to step up and "babysit" her until she finds her own friends. Problem is, she's the most difficult girl he has ever met. And with her constant need to provoke and challenge him she's quickly driving him insane.

Will Aidan give up on Uma and prove her right, or will he be the one guy that makes her take a chance on love?

The Feisty Slave is the fourth book in Elin Peer's Slave series. Readers call it "a must-read that will have you on needles, crying, laughing, and cheering for Uma."

If you liked the other books in the series, it's a no-brainer. Click the buy button and get to it. You won't regret it!

www.elinpeer.com

About the author

Elin is curious by nature. She likes to explore and can tell you about riding elephants through the Asian jungle, watching the sunset in the Sahara desert from the back of a camel, sailing down the Nile in Egypt, kayaking in Alaska, and flying over Greenland in helicopters.

She can also testify that the most interesting people aren't always kings, queens, presidents, and celebrities, because she has met many of them in person.

After traveling the world and living in different countries, Elin is currently residing outside Seattle in the US with her husband, daughters, and her black Labrador, Lucky, which follows her everywhere.

People who know Elin say that she's the kind of person you end up telling your darkest and deepest secrets to, even though you never intended to.
Maybe that's where she gets her inspiration for her books. One thing is for sure: Elin is not afraid to provoke, shock, touch, and excite you when she writes about unwanted desire, forbidden passion, and all those damn emotions in between.

Want to connect with Elin? Great, she loves to hear from her readers. Find her on Facebook (Author Elin Peer), connect with her on Goodreads or simply go to her website and send an email. www.elinpeer.com

www.elinpeer.com

34807923R00245

Made in the USA
Lexington, KY
28 March 2019